THE NIGHT GATE

By
JK Franks

This book is a work of fiction. The characters, incidents, and dialogues are products of the author's imagination and are not to be construed as real. Any resemblance to actual events or persons, living or dead, is entirely coincidental.

978-1-7362153-1-9 eBook
978-1-7362153-2-6 Paperback
978-1-7362153-3-3 Hard Back

Published by JK Franks Media LLC, 2021
Editor: Debra Riggle
Cover Design: Lance Burton

Email the author at author@jkfranks.com
Friend him on Facebook at facebook.com/groups/JKFranks
Visit the author's website at www.jkfranks.com

First Edition

For Mona, who always believes.

Your time is limited, so don't waste it
living someone else's life.
— **Steve Jobs**

1

Kate Cassidy moved her dive mask higher on her head and stared up at the object in open-mouthed astonishment. Rising out of the sand and driftwood was what looked like...well, a door. It wasn't a door, of course, that would be ridiculous. Still, that was her first thought. She removed a neoprene dive glove and slowly rubbed at her eyes to see if it was an apparition. She took several wobbly steps toward the object.

The last month had all been too much. First, losing her sister to what she could only feel was the most heartbreaking manner possible. Then, finding out the university where she'd been working for nearly a decade was eliminating her department. Single, depressed, and now out of a job, she'd wound up here. An isolated beach on a spec of land in the Indian Ocean. The touristy Maldives was 800 miles away. This area was frequented more by people trying to escape something than tourists looking for scenery. The marine life in the area was spectacular, though.

Kate glanced at her dive computer, wondering idly if hypoxia might have set in. She hadn't been down deep, but maybe the tanks got one of the exotic mixes of air they used for deep water dives. Sometimes those did make her a bit loopy. She breathed deeply to fill her lungs with good air, just in case. The object was still there.

It was less a door than a frame, although the frame was invisible from her viewpoint. The dimensions were easy enough to guess; it was almost nine feet high and maybe four feet wide. She shifted to her left to get a sense of dimension and realized it had none. It was two dimensional, no thickness at all that she could discern. The 'door' was not closed, it was open, and what she was looking at was a view of another place or another time. It was familiar but also off; the lighting was too dim, and the landscape and plants were off, almost as if the scale of everything was dialed up to the max.

Kate approached the thing; she mentally was beginning to think of it as a portal. It gave off no heat, no cold, no sound. The closer she moved, the scene inside seemed to shift appropriate to her movement to show her more of the view beyond. It was a forest, tropical or maybe even sub-tropical, she guessed. Definitely not a view of the arid scrubland of the nameless island she was on.

She retraced her steps; the dive boat she'd rented still bobbed in the water a few hundred yards offshore. The reef had made it too risky to bring in close, but the reef was what she had been focusing on. Then, something else had gotten her attention. What was it? A sound maybe. No, that wasn't it. More like a vibration, a stress wave moving through the water. She'd first thought it was an earthquake. It would have been almost common had it been. Just one of many that plagued this area of the globe. That might have been what led her to the beach, but why this spot? She couldn't recall. She'd just felt compelled to come here, just like she was even now moving closer and closer to the unknown object. The portal to God-knows-where.

Come on, Kate, get a grip. You have a doctorate, don't do something stupid.

She was by herself, diving alone in a remote part of an ocean renowned for mysterious disappearances and more than occasional pirates. Kate had to admit she'd passed stupid a few days back. Diving without a partner was breaking all the normal safety rules but...*well, no buts*. She had no excuse other than she was pissed off and needed to go be by herself and do something impulsive. Thinking rationally, she grabbed for her phone. She unclipped the waterproof case from her belt.

Moving closer to the door, or portal, or whatever, she absently attempted to unclip the cover on the watertight case. "I know this place," she whispered. But she didn't...she couldn't. It was not just foreign, it was alien. Yet, her sense of familiarity increased with every step she took. Forgetting the phone, she reached toward the opening before she could stop herself. Strange looking trees with fronds that were more orange than green swayed in a breeze that she could almost feel. Somehow, she knew the smell of that forest floor, the dampness, the fragrances. Not the perfume of sweet flowers, but more akin to the decay of rotting flesh. Still, her mind interpreted that not as a bad thing but just something normal.

She paused, taking in a deep breath as she forced her foot to stop and retrace its path. One step, then two. That was not her world, no matter how much it seemed to be. *I'm dead.* That was the only rationale her mind could offer up that fit. Again, remembering her phone, she reached down, freed it from the case, and glanced at the screen to select the camera feature. Even before looking back toward the portal, she knew; she could sense this place was somewhere else.

A distant hum of vehicles and vividly remembered smell of air that Kate knew beforehand would be slightly metallic. The gleaming towers of the capital city reflected the rays of a slightly brighter sun. Kamarov, she knew instinctually. That was where she should be heading. Looking at the smartphone in her hand, she had trouble understanding its purpose—why was she holding it? A shadow crossed her face, and she glanced into the portal again as a bird flew close to the opening. No, not a bird, she knew it as an Acorra, something akin to a giant, feathered butterfly. She'd had one as a pet when she was much younger. They hadn't lived in Kamarov then...

A chime sounded, and somehow, she knew she was now free to do what she wanted, what she was compelled beyond any rational explanation to do. She dropped the phone, stepped toward the door, and disappeared.

* * *

Petra looked at the display, "Yeah, she's there, her mnemonic password has just cleared." She fumbled through several papers held together with a clip. "Palio, what is the TD factor on Aragon? Can we use comms?"

"No live comms." The dark-haired boy-genius accessed some mental version of a universal almanac to spout off the answer. "Time dilation of point 172."

Petra did a few mental calculations of her own. *Kate is scheduled to be off world for eight hours. So to her, it will feel more like...um, call it fourteen back here.* "Going to be a long day, kid."

Like most of the control team, Petra had never journeyed off world. Palio had done it only once and quickly decided it was not for him. The psychological and neurological makeup of the jumpers was key to their success. Some could handle it, like Kate and Julian, and others simply couldn't.

As she finished a sandwich, Petra began to grow concerned. "Shouldn't they be in a sleep cycle by now? If so, why wouldn't she have signaled or simply returned?" Normally, whenever a jumper SideSlipped, they slipped back when the host went to bed. Not much could be learned during a sleep cycle, and other complications arose when an intelligent being's subconscious was unavailable to help clear away their mental clutter of the day.

"Days on Aragon are longer than ours, about twenty-seven point zero hours if I am correct," Palio stated. That, plus the TD of almost two, and she has plenty of time left to explore. Besides, if she found him there, you know what she is probably up to."

Petra noted the raised eyebrow Palio offered when he was faking being judgmental. The auto recall on A-class worlds was already in the jump computer. It would have all the relevant data including time dilation, season, and daylight periods. If the traveler didn't initiate a return before the mission clock hit zero, it would attempt to pull them back, against their will at times, especially if they were in some particularly enjoyable encounter.

The control room around Petra contained almost a billion dollars' worth of high-tech equipment, yet she picked up a blank yellow legal-pad and began making numerous calculations.

"Working out the gap?" Palio asked.

She nodded and continued to solve the equations. Palio could have likely done all this in his head and much faster, but Petra enjoyed doing it herself. If Kate returned now, she would have a gap of just under twenty-nine hours. Not that bad, but if she pushed it to the limit, she would be pretty useless for a day and a half.

"Should we make contact?" Palio asked.

They both knew full well the challenges of live comms on worlds with a TD of over 1.5. They used a compression algorithm to slow down the message, but often the traveler missed it entirely, or the response came back so quickly the computer couldn't interpret it. Odd, since Kate's physical body was only a few yards away. Petra could have yelled loud enough for her ears to pick up the sound waves. The issue was that the processing part of Kate's hearing was now far away on Aragon.

"No," Petra said reluctantly. As mission supervisor, it was her job to be worried, but Doctor Kate Cassidy knew the system better than anyone. She was also the one to push the limits. Theirs was one of three teams working off world today. One was in the classified section, obviously military- focused. The other was with a traveler who was only second to Kate in cumulative time off world.

"Mission Commander, we have a problem," the automated control system stated flatly.

Petra looked, not to the computer, but to Palio. "Run traces, tell me what is going on."

He nodded, already emersed in the control system furiously issuing voice commands, while simultaneously keying in command codes and sweeping away screen after screen to see what was happening. Both knew they were operating in fields which no human fully understood. While it helped to think of the mission as space exploration, in truth it was anything but. They typically learned how woefully inadequate their knowledge was when one of the teams stumbled into a problem.

"It's not us, Petra. Aragon is shifting away."

"The Fade?" she asked urgently. "Issuing the recall command," she shouted. "Bring her back now!" She shot off a message to the other mission directors as well, just as a precaution.

Palio was already unsealing the door into the launch room and heading to Kate's chair.

Petra pulled up Palio's displays and watched as the world known to them as Aragon faded from the map. An entire world lost forever to humanity. She leaned over the microphone and keyed the button. "Do we have her?" The risks were low for SideSlipping, but it wasn't zero.

Palio didn't answer but turned toward the control room camera with a relieved expression.

2

"Thad, you up?" She wondered why she even went through the motions. Being married to a career military man meant routine, structure, and a sameness. For twenty-four years she had been Mrs. Thaddeus Jackson Lewis. Her husband was more commonly known as Colonel Lewis to most people. Her spouse was a creature of habit. Even now she knew he wouldn't be lounging in the overstuffed bed but out for a run or down in the hotel's well-equipped exercise rooms. The man was a machine. His very nature seemed to be hard-wired from the manufacturer. He liked routine and consistency; that was why this day was so out of character.

The surprise trip had been his anniversary gift. Every year he tried to top what he had done the year before. Normally, the gifts were fairly routine and only slightly extravagant. She knew it was his self-imposed penance for being away so much. Still, scoring rooms at the premier resort during the swanky South Beach Wine and Food Festival, well... she could forgive a lot of sins in exchange for this level of indulgence. She heard the door open and footsteps. "How was your run?"

"Good, honey." He plucked a piece of crispy bacon from the breakfast cart. "Need to shower."

"Don't you want to eat first? It will get cold."

"I've eaten cold eggs for years, love. I'll only be a minute." He moved toward her and pulled her close.

She feebly pretended to resist his advances. "Stop, you're all sweaty."

He kissed her, then kissed her again. "Love you, Peaches!"

"Love you, too, you sweaty dork. Now go shower quickly. I want to get out to the festival before it's a hundred degrees." She loved Miami, but a Michigan girl in this heat was more than she could handle for more than a few hours.

She heard the shower start as she poured herself another glass of the delicious, fresh orange juice. Staring out at the sparkling blue ocean, "I could get used to this," she said to no one. Maybe she could convince Thad to retire down here. *I could get used to the heat, right? Besides, for a view like this and access to the best shops and restaurants, maybe...just maybe.* She let the fantasy take root. She'd always found it easy to fall in love with new places. It was hard to be a military wife if you couldn't. While some of Thad's postings had been literally 'hell holes,' Beatrice Lewis had always found something about them to love. Here, though, well, here it would take no effort on her part at all.

Thaddeus shut the valve off and watched as the massive, brass shower head slowed and ceased. A single drop of water clung to the front edge. The colonel stared at it until it grew too fat to resist the pull of gravity and fell into the drain. He stepped to the sink, not bothering to dry off, and absentmindedly went through the rest of his morning rituals. Teeth brushed and freshly shaved, he walked the few steps to the bedroom and dressed.

"That girl you like will be down on the primary stage in a few minutes," his wife called from the adjoining room. "You know, the one with the cooking show and the dogs? I hear she just broke up with that actor she was dating. They seemed like such a wonderful couple. I wonder why none of those celebrity relationships ever seem to work out."

She failed to notice the sound of her husband's bare feet as he approached her from behind until he was within arm's reach. Sensing him there, she turned, "Do you want to..." She stopped mid-sentence, taking in her husbands' appearance.

"Thad, hon, why are you wearing your service dress uniform?"

* * *

Colonel Lewis ate a leisurely breakfast and downed a second cup of coffee. An unusual luxury for a man with such a disciplined life. Pushing himself up, he surveyed the room and retrieved the two large travel cases stored in the second bedroom. Seeing his wife staring at him, he kicked the side of her head causing it to tilt sharply away. Stepping over her lifeless body, he made his way to the window and pushed the drapes as far apart as possible. The thick glass couldn't be opened, but he didn't need it to be. The panoramic view below was indeed perfect.

Dialing in the scope, he adjusted for the ocean breeze judging by the sway of the palm trees down below. Below on the beach, he saw a crowd gathering to see the next featured star. The beautiful celebrity chef and restauranteur climbed the steps and waved to the crowd. Then, the back of her head exploded in a mist of red. Chunks of bone and brain sprayed over several others behind her, including the governor of Florida. Colonel Lewis was pleased the hole in his window was almost too small to notice.

He lined up, picked out another target, and squeezed the trigger. *Squeeze gently, don't pull,* the old rifle-range instructions drifting back to him from a past he could no longer recall. Why was he doing this thing? He had no answer. Another man fell, then a young child, then a woman who was obviously pregnant. He aimed, and he squeezed another round from the rifle and another life drifted away. Another family in anguish, another town in mourning. "Thoughts and prayers, ya'll!" He laughed softly, thinking about the chaos that would result from his actions.

Laying the scoped high caliber rifle aside, he examined the window. The holes were all in the shadow along the bottom inch of the frame. He knew from hours outside that the eastern wing of the hotel would cast a shadow over these windows for another thirteen minutes. Sirens screamed from every direction outside, but he took no notice. *Slow is fast and fast is slow*, he recalled.

He released the charging handle on the second rifle, this one an automatic and slipped the muzzle of the weapon through one of the larger bullet holes in the tempered green window. Crowds had scattered and inexplicably then converged on the scene of the first victims. A line of law enforcement formed a perimeter around the VIPs. The festival guests were apparently all on their own. Vaguely, Thad recalled his son was in law enforcement and wondered how his department would respond to an incident like this.

"Incident," he chuckled. Such a polite word for such a horrific event. Thad counted rounds as he fired. He was well aware of how many the magazine held and also how many rounds it would likely take before they could identify his location. The automatic was chewing through bodies alive and dead. The glamorous, the official, and the unknown all commingled in death. A macabre tableau for the morbidly curious.

Colonel Lewis was methodical and dedicated, and he was seven minutes away from being the deadliest mass shooter in American history. Aim and squeeze, rinse, and repeat.

3

A gentle breeze nudged a few of the spartina sea grasses to exercise a brief dance before settling down once more. A dragonfly flitted near the shore where the waters of the estuary lapped softly against the reddish-brown sand. Pike Shepard breathed in the aroma, the smell of natural decay, the salt air and, from somewhere close by, the scent of honeysuckle and jasmine. Life here was peaceful, simple, and...well, pedestrian. Not that he minded that, it was he who had sentenced himself to this solitude nearly four years earlier. Cass Elliot's haunting "Dream a little Dream" drifted from the little ramshackle cabin he called home.

He lifted the ceramic mug of bourbon and sipped gently. *Maybe it was five years now.* He waved a fly off one arm only to watch it land on the other. Such was life here in the Lowcountry of South Carolina. Not the ritzy areas to the east, Kiawah, or Hilton Head. This was deeper, down the meandering backwaters of the tidal rivers. Coosaw and Seabrook were the closest things to settlements. Nearby Beaufort was the closest thing to actual civilization. He'd fixed up the old fishing camp, *sort of*. His ex-wife wouldn't have approved, but then again, what about him had she ever approved of?

How had he wound up in a wooden shack that only had running

water if the solar battery was charged? Pike drained the last of the bourbon and wished for more. That was part of why he was here. Not the biggest part, but a contributor.

One leg of the aluminum lawn chair sunk deeper into the tidal mud, and it gave a withering creak of protest. He shifted his weight to the opposite side. Distribution of mass over a fixed surface. *I'm still a math whiz,* he thought with amusement. His mind drifted back to happier times. His wife beside him, their daughter, Emma, playing down on the shaded dock. He hadn't known how happy he was then. You rarely know it until it's gone.

He heard the irritating buzzing long before he saw the little boat. That would be the one thing Pike would change about this place. Move his little fish camp farther away from the marina docks. Admittedly, his corner of Lowcountry was frequented mostly by local fishermen. The tourists and, well...most people with good sense, stopped at the newer marina on the far side of the Marine base. They carried a better selection and had far more sensible prices. Still, Pete, who ran the nearby marina, had been good to him, collected his mail, and usually let him know if anything important was going on. The small boat had been wandering from side to side in the main channel but now angled toward him. This would be her, he mused. The one Pete had told him had been trying to track him down for the better part of a week.

He could see the lone figure manning the tiller. Thin but tall, and most definitely female. *Must be dammed determined to come way out here,* he thought. Maybe she would pass on by; the channel was over a hundred yards wide here and lined with tall grasses along the marshy edges. He knew from a practical standpoint that his cabin was nearly invisible unless you knew where to look. He slouched deeper into the groaning chair and set his body language to loudly project his desire to be ignored.

"Goddammit," he muttered as the small boat adjusted course in his direction. He briefly considered walking away and ignoring the visitor, but that would mean getting up, and *well*, that was just too much effort.

The woman waved. From here, even Pike could see she was pretty, striking even. He could discern all that from a distance. He didn't wave back. She handled the boat with skill, judging the rising bottom expertly and gunning the engine briefly before tilting it up and beaching the bow solidly onshore. A gentleman would have gone to catch the bow line and help her step down from the boat. He remained seated.

"Professor Shepard?" the woman inquired, studying him as she tied her boat to the base of a particularly thick clump of spartina grass.

"Don't care what you're selling, I'm not buying."

She smiled and walked over. "I'm Kate...Kate Cassidy, and I brought you something." She reached into an oversized purse and produced a bottle filled with an amber liquid. She passed it over.

"Damn that Pete," Shepard said as he pulled the cork. "Basil Hayden too...damn good stuff. But you can still leave."

She nodded; it was the most expensive bourbon in the store. Kate noticed another of the lawn chairs lying folded nearby and proceeded to sit close, but not too close, to the irritated man. She sat gingerly on the frayed green plastic webbing. Her grandparents used to have an old set just like them probably still stored in their garage. Noting him filling his own cup, she produced a stainless-steel tumbler from her own bag and held it up.

Pike looked her over appreciably. "A splash, or a serious pour?"

"Serious, Shepard...definitely serious."

Kate nodded as he set the bottle on the sandy ground between them. She said nothing, waiting to see what the man did. She sipped the whiskey, studied the rippling waters, and enjoyed the sun beating down. As off the grid as this place was, a person could get used to it, she decided. Someone had gotten used to it. Professor Shepard was one of the more recognizable physicists in the world, or had been. His background was eclectic, but he had a reputation for solving problems. A man with tenure, prestige, and notoriety all peaking just at the time he walked away from all of it. She caught the man studying her.

"You want to know why I'm here," Shepard said, finally breaking the silence.

She shook her head. "No, I know why you're here, or at least a large part of it."

"Then what?" He took a deep slug of the amber liquid. "Miss Cassidy, I'm not interested in whatever it is you want." He saw she was watching him closely; her eyes twinkled as if she knew more of what he was thinking than he did. Time seemed to slow, then stop, the sounds of the waves lapping gently and the buzz of insects the only distraction. "What?"

Kate glanced out and asked, "Are you happy?"

Her question took him by surprise. His next emotion was anger. "I don't share my feelings, Cassidy. How I'm doing is my own goddamn business no matter how good your liquor is."

She nodded, a slight grin etching her features. She offered a half toast with the cup, "I didn't think so."

Again, this was not the response Pike expected. Not the response any normal adult would have offered. Kate Cassidy was nothing if not unpredictable. "I have a suggestion. Why don't we just cut the crap, and you tell me what you really want." His words had a sharp edge that he'd honed over a well-lived lifetime of unpleasant encounters.

Slowly, she rose and began walking toward the small cabin. He watched as she reached the far side and lifted the corner of an old canvas sailcloth he was using as a tarp. The material was stiff and noisy as she lifted it clear from what was underneath. She whistled softly. "Forty-nine?"

Still looking out over the water, Pike said, "No, but close. It's a fifty-three."

Kate walked around the vintage motorcycle admiring the details. "An original Indian Chief. Shepard, you are an anachronism. A man existing out of time."

He continued to ignore her, assuming if he did so long enough, she would give up and leave. He watched as a small mullet slipped through the spartina to snag a morsel of food. Minutes later, Kate returned to the seat and poured herself another drink. She touched the bottleneck to his own cup that was hanging loosely in his right hand. In resignation, he offered the mug for a pour and turned to look at her.

"I know who you are, Doctor Cassidy." Pike took another long pull on the drink before continuing. "I just don't know why you're here."

She smiled. "It's simple, really, Shepard." She grinned as she also took a deep drink. "I need your help."

"Doing what?" he demanded.

"We need to save the world." She took a deep swallow of the bourbon. "Actually, several."

"Go away, Miss Cassidy," Pike said in a voice that was harsh even by his standards. The woman stood and reached down for the nearly empty bottle before walking back to the boat and silently pushing it back into the water.

"She could have left that," he muttered as he watched her paddling back toward the main channel.

4

Pike stared at the snowy TV screen, the old DVD long since ending. "Why do you do this to yourself?" He walked out to the porch; a light rain had fallen during the night covering everything with a sheen like a freshly waxed car. Emma loved this place. He pushed away the darker thoughts. The ones that called for him to join them. Emma, Emily, Risson...all gone. His friend, Dewey, still kept a check on him from time to time, and then there was his mother who was battling dementia in a facility up near Charleston. That was it; that was the total number of people who might even miss him.

"We're throwing a pity-party today, huh?" He laughed, talking to himself again. "You should at least get a dog, so you don't look totally freaking nuts when you do it."

Rainy days always did this. Those were Emma's days, the time where she made the plan, what games to play, what movies to watch. Or maybe it was the unsettling visit from the woman yesterday. He wasn't sure. He stepped back inside and eyed the half-full bottle of Jack Daniels on the counter. Then his eyes shifted a degree to the right and saw the numbers on the stove. "Ten a.m." He was sure this was one of those warning signs but reached for a glass anyway.

* * *

"That's not the way you're supposed to do it, Daddy."

Emma was wearing red gym shorts and a pair of her mom's old running shoes. She was pulling her leg up behind her in a completely unnatural looking move that made Pike wince just thinking about it. "My way works just fine."

"If you don't warm up properly, you could pull a hambone or something," his daughter said enthusiastically.

"A hambone? Are you sure?" Pike asked, moving over beside her in the two-track road.

"Yeah, I mean, um...I think that's what Coach Reeves said. I just know you're supposed to loosen up your muscles."

Pike chuckled, "I don't have muscles, Sport."

"Sure, you do, Pops, you got a great big one right there." With that, she poked him in his belly and took off running, her laughter trailing along behind her like a scent chasing a flower.

Shaking his head, Pike took off after his daughter. Her interest in running had picked up some after she had given up learning the piano. He assumed it would be a passing phase, but Emma was still at it a year and a half later. As he struggled to make up the gap, he conceded she had continued to improve, too. He wasn't in terrible shape, still the same weight as when he'd come out of the Marine Corps, but Em was right. It had shifted around over the years. Still, he did what he could to stay active. She had started joining him on his early morning jogs back in the spring, and now it had become their time. They didn't talk much and rarely ran the same path twice, but he wouldn't trade these moments for anything.

"Can we go see Risse?" Emma asked as they turned out onto the main road and picked up the pace.

He knew what she meant. Risson Mack, his best friend and her godfather, was gone. He'd been killed while on duty two years earlier. They had laid him to rest on the family's land out on one of the sea islands. A community appropriately called Fort Remorse for reasons that had been lost to the winds of history.

"I don't know, Baby," Pike said, panting. The road they were on would go near it in another few miles, but there was still a half mile of the Beaufort Sound between them and his friend's gravesite. "I have a lot to do today, and we didn't tell your mom."

"Please, Dad. We haven't said hi to him in months, and he hasn't even seen my braces." She smiled at him, mouth full of wire and then those big brown eyes that could melt the hardest of fathers.

"We'll see if the boat is in the water. If so, sure."

"Cool," she said before sprinting off ahead of him, like she had any doubt at all that she wouldn't get her way.

They wound their way down one of the smaller roads to the shoreline. Mighty oaks, all dressed in their finest coats of Spanish moss, stood guard. A flat-bottomed jon boat was sitting on the bank, two paddles underneath. The once stately house it sat behind had been abandoned years earlier. Pike thought he should have known the owners, but now it was just the neighbors who kept it up, mowed the grass, and such. He guessed someone probably was paying the taxes. Whoever wanted came and picked apples or peaches from the trees in the yard or used the old fishing boat. This was just the kind of place Blackwater was. A close-knit community and a good place to raise his daughter. His own upbringing nearby had been a little rougher, but today was not the time to dwell on that.

"Give me a hand, Em." Together, they slid the aluminum boat into the water. They'd done this so often he knew just when his daughter would turn it into a contest. She would start pulling harder with her paddle strokes, and he would have to do the same to keep the awkwardly designed boat moving in a mostly straight line. Today, he was ready for her.

* * *

The late morning air had been crisp and fragrant, carrying the odors of both life and death. The saltwater marsh was one of constant regeneration, taking the season's dead to its depths and preparing to rebirth it again come spring.

He coasted up into a familiar but somewhat forgotten inlet and gently eased up onto the sandy beach. Emma was right, it was time he visited some of his own ghost. Emma faced the grave with a look of love that touched Pike deeply. His daughter was connected to this place in a way he would have never thought possible. As always, he gave her the time alone so she could commune with her Gullah Pops, as she used to call Risse. After a while, she walked away to explore the old ruins, as was her habit.

"Hey, Buddy." Pike tried an upbeat tone as he sat down on a log positioned just for this reason. The simple marker was hard to make out with the dead leaves piling at the base. With his hand, he swept the simple granite headstone clear. He was relieved to see the bronze plaque still affixed. Reading the inscription brought the conflicting feelings of pain and pride and guilt that he always felt. *Medal of Honor - We will see you on the other side, dear brother.*

Pike's gut clinched as the memories of that awful day came rushing back. He sat there staring off into space for many long minutes. His eyes finally fell on his daughter going into the ramshackle structure his friend had called home for most of his childhood. Leaning over, Pike's voice took on a near reverent tone as he spoke to his friend's grave. "Do you remember back in Miss Blackwell's class when Tommy Spars was making fun of me, and she tried to make him stop?" Pike knew it was silly to hang onto hurt from back then, but some just refused to fade, no matter how much time or distance he tried to insert. Tommy had been a friend years earlier, or maybe he'd just pretended, like so many of the kids did. Pike even admitted how hard it must have been for them. He was a weird kid. First the crazy words he would shout out, then later the fits and seizures, and finally, a mental hospital and the surgery. "He wanted to know how a retard with a lobotomy could still come to regular school."

He grimaced with the memory. By that point in his life, he had no longer bothered to respond; he'd learned that bullies didn't want to be educated, nor did they concern themselves with the facts. They were predators hunting for the weak and injured. Hunting for the ones like him. "Man, how you stood up for me that day was something. I...I'm not sure I ever actually thanked you for what you did for me back then. Not just to Tommy Spars but so very many times. But damn, man, you hit that kid so hard I think his grandmother felt it." He smiled ruefully at the memory.

"Risse, I wish you were here to talk to me," Pike said. "I'm not like you, I was never cut out to be a hero. Emma needs you; she's only getting a partial education about life in the Lowcountry. Hell, man, I'm just a pretender."

Pike rose and walked around the small cemetery. Echoes of the past rolled through his head like distant thunder. Risse's taunting laugh. He was constantly challenging Pike to try harder, always eager to see the skinny, white kid excel. No one had ever been as big of a champion for him as the Gullah kid, Risson Mack. Pike was certain that if it hadn't been for his friend, he would have probably rotted away in that damn hospital decades ago. Also, an entire village of Afghan girls and women would have been put to death by the Taliban for the simple crime of learning how to read. Risson Mack was the hero the world needed, a good man in every sense of the word, a warrior, a friend.

"Look at this, Dad." Emma was holding up something, but he couldn't tell much about it.

"Be right there." Pike rubbed the stone marker again. This man should have had a chance, he deserved a wife, kids. He deserved a life; instead, he got a piece of stone on a forgotten island in a shallow bay. Still, it was what he had wanted. Pike had retrieved the letter in Risse's personal effects, surprised to learn that he was the listed executor of his friend's estate. In the end, Risse had wanted to go home, make amends with his family, his tribe, as he called them, for leaving so many years earlier. Pike had carried out the man's wishes with a heavy heart. The Gullah were all gone now, and the state owned most of the island. Everything but this forgotten village. Eventually, it and the gravesides would all be lost to the sea, or the forest, and to history. The pain Pike still felt at losing his friend was just one of the many strings that kept him rooted here.

"What have you got, Em?"

His daughter smiled and pointed at the thing she was holding so proudly. He moved toward her, but it seemed she was moving away just as fast. "Hang on, where are you?" Confusion swept in, and he started to run after her. Panic was clutching his chest. He had to get to her, but something was wrong. His daughter was accelerating away from him now.

"You're going to need to help her, Daddy," he heard Emma say in a voice that sounded somehow older and wiser.

"Pike!"

"Professor Shepard!"

He woke up with a start, reluctant to leave the dream behind but also realizing something in the dream was off. "What? Who's there?" But he already knew. He labored to free himself from the recliner, an empty glass falling to the rug as he stood.

Kate Cassidy smiled at him as he opened the door, the late afternoon sun shining through the eaves of the porch casting her hair like a halo of fire. "You are a persistent one, aren't you?"

"Give me a few minutes and maybe let me buy you dinner," she said. "You still want to make me leave, I will."

Pike saw she had driven a new SUV out this time, no motor boat. She'd done well to even find the place by land. Most people, even the locals, couldn't. He started to shut the door then stayed his hand. It had been a long time since a beautiful woman had wanted to spend time with him. He could endure a bit more, couldn't he?

5

After a few moments of semi-awkward banter, Kate looked suddenly serious.

"Tell me, Shepard, what is your happiest memory?" she asked.

"The day my daughter was born," Pike said, trying to get a read on this confusing woman. Her expression suggested this was not the response she'd been expecting.

"How long ago was that?"

"Look, Doctor, I am not in the habit of having touchy-feely moments with total strangers nor wasting a perfectly fine afternoon."

"How long, how old is she now? Your daughter."

A look of blackness descended on his face as grief and guilt slowly replaced his anger. "Fifteen years ago." He spat the words at her like venom. "If you know who I am, then you goddamn probably know that as well."

Kate nodded solemnly. "I am sorry, Professor," she began. "I was aware of your divorce a few years earlier. I didn't have access to your full history."

Pike eyed the woman suspiciously. "Not sure I want anyone knowing my full story." That much was indeed true. Still, this woman's presence was not unpleasant; she had a relaxed easy-going nature that he was warming to even as he fought against it.

"So, your happiest memory was fifteen years ago. That would mean that every day since has been worse?"

"Sad and profound, Cassidy, but generally true, yes." He rose and began walking to the side of the cabin. Kate hurried to follow.

"I'm hungry, Doc." He was slipping a battered leather jacket on and uncovering the Indian. "Feel free to take your car, but this is what I ride."

* * *

Kate's arms encircled his waist tightly as he expertly leaned into the curves of the road winding around the western edge of the bay. The sun was casting a golden aura across the wetlands as it dipped slowly toward the far horizon. Shepard was normally comfortable and relaxed on the bike, but the presence of this woman was unsettling. A distraction he neither needed nor wanted in his life. Still, her hips pressing against his was not an altogether unpleasant sensation.

So, why had he volunteered to take her to dinner? *Just to discuss her world-saving mission?* Whatever the hell that was all about. His internal dialogue continued unabated. Truthfully, he had no idea other than one simple fact. A fact that defied all logic and was most disturbing was the sensation of rightness being with her. She was a stranger, a newcomer, but her presence was comfortable, easy. Not even friends, but there was something almost inherently *intimate* between the two of them. It was like rediscovering a childhood sweetheart who, years later, had just moved back in next door.

Pike turned off the scenic county road onto an unmarked gravel road, lined on both sides by barbed wire fence. The motorcycle slid sideways every few seconds as the tires sought purchase in the loose dirt and rocks. He would have expected his passenger to tighten her grip and fear for her safety. Instead, he realized she had moved one hand up to his chest and was gently resting her chin on his left shoulder watching the road ahead. His ex had hated motorcycles and apparently everything else about him. She'd only ridden with him a few times and never like this.

Ten minutes and two turns later, Pike pulled into the sparsely graveled parking area of a cement block structure with a rusted tin roof. A single neon beer sign in one window offered the only clue as to its purpose.

"A local find, I take it?" Kate observed.

He nodded. "The Lowcountry has tons of great places to eat, but most are overpriced clip joints designed to separate tourist dollars from wallets."

Several pickups and a Jeep were in the lot, and she could see a short dock off to the side extending into the tidal river where an equal number of old boats were moored.

They got two beers from the bar and took a seat at an empty table overlooking the water. "No menus," Pike said. "You get what they have, nothing fancy. If you don't want it, just shake your head."

The smells coming out of the kitchen and Kate's growling stomach let her know she would be sending nothing back. A server set out a small plate of raw oysters as she said, "Tide you over til the food is ready." Kate greedily took one and tossed it down, savoring the fresh, briny flavor. Pike watched her intently as she squeezed a bit of lemon on another before repeating the process. He snagged one of the local delicacies and chased it down with a swallow of beer.

"So, tell me about your mission."

They had talked briefly at his cabin before he suggested they go get something to eat. He'd admitted to attending one of her lectures years earlier at Duke University. That talk had been on the apparent contradictions of human consciousness. Not one of her more noted presentations, but solid work, which she still stood by. "First, Shepard, I'm curious. Why would you come to a workshop to hear a novice research discussion on abhorrent mental conditions? Just seems a bit random to me."

He hated to admit that one of the primary reasons was how hot she looked on the flyer he'd found stuffed into his mail slot. Beauty and brains were a killer combination he'd never been able to resist. *Who am I kidding?* Beauty alone was enough to get his attention, or at least, it had been enough. "I was in the area." He finished off his beer and signaled for another round. "Back then, I was always looking to pick up new ideas that might help me in some way."

Kate popped the last of the oysters and smiled as it went down. "Your background is quite eclectic, Professor. Instead of specializing in a single field or with a single academic pursuit, your career has been more of a shotgun blast encompassing everything from cosmology to logistics. I believe they refer to your type as polymaths."

"What can I say, Doc? I'm a Renaissance man." His smile faded. "Truth is, I get bored easily and tend to piss people off to the point they ask me to leave after a while."

She knew this was not true, not the last part, at least. "Professor, you may be a generalist, but your depth of knowledge in such a wide variety of subjects is legendary. Your teams routinely make more progress in months than most make in years. I feel sure no one ever wanted to see you go."

Pike offered a small shrug and started to speak, but the server was bringing out a bowl with shrimp and grits and something less identifiable to his dinner date.

"Frogmore's stew?" she asked uncertainly.

"No," he chuckled. "Farther south than that. Brunswick stew from Georgia. Try it, it's damn good."

Kate spooned some up and watched the orange, lumpy liquid drip from the spoon. "It looks to have already been eaten and probably previously digested." She had to admit it smelled good, though. She took a tentative bite and then another. "Wow, Pike...it's fantastic!"

He nodded. "Normally a barbecue restaurant thing, but my friend who runs the place always keeps a bit on hand for guys like me. It's a blended meat stew with a wide variety of meats but only a few vegetables, mainly onions, tomatoes, and corn. He passed a bottle of hot sauce over. "It's even better if you add some heat."

She did so enthusiastically and very much agreed with the result. "Please continue."

"Honestly," Pike went on, "I hate the silo effect so common in academia. I never saw my field as being isolated. If you're a curious sort, and most who get into scientific research are, then almost all of science is fascinating. After many years of pure research, I realized I learned far more in an evening out with my peers from other fields than I did in weeks in my labs. Broadening my specialties allowed me better understanding and kept me more open to the possibilities than others. I found that I would rather explore on my own than publish papers and wait for some other academic asshole to shoot down my theories just because I'd approached it from a unique perspective."

"Still, you made quite the name for yourself. What did they call you, 'The Fixer?' she asked.

Pike groaned. That was one of his least liked tags. "I got called in on several interesting problems. My background in engineering helped a great deal. I believe at heart I am a glorified engineer, maybe a mechanic. I tend to see things as systems. Everything fits together somehow. If you can find the connections, you can smooth out the rough spots. That different way of seeing the underlying connections often made the difference between success and failure."

"Like with Anturro?"

His eyes raised appreciably. "Your files were pretty complete, and you've done your homework, Doctor Cassidy."

"Please...just Kate."

He nodded and sighed, looking out once again at the dimming sunset and the last of the larger fishing boats moving to inland docks. "They had made some major missteps, Kate. I'm still under NDA but understand that pharmaceutical companies were not really ready to work on biologics, gene therapy, and the like. Not back then, at least."

She knew that Anturro Pharmaceuticals had been pushing the field of gene therapy for hereditary diseases before a high-profile failure stopped them in their tracks. The wife of an influential senator had been suffering from a rare disorder and was one of the first to receive the experimental treatment that involved extracting her own stem cells and manipulating them to stop making the enzyme causing the problem. "The patient died," Kate said flatly, "but that is a medical issue. Why would they have called you?"

"She never should have; she didn't die from the OTCD," Pike answered. "She didn't even die from the treatment; she died because of her body's own immune response. The research team involved was too focused on their breakthroughs and succumbed to pressure by the board of directors and probably the senator, so they rushed it."

"But you helped them recover."

"I helped..." he paused looking for the right word, "...guide them in new directions. They were on the right track, they just were using outdated protocols and assuming biologic treatments would behave the same as chemical-based ones. We had to change that mindset and, in fact, had to replace most of the key members on the team. They needed better perspective; they needed a broader view of the potential problems."

"As I recall, Anturro just narrowly avoided bankruptcy, but they did eventually recover and became one of the dominant players in genomic research," Kate added.

Pike nodded, taking a bite of fried fish from a plastic tray that appeared in front of him. "They recovered," he said modestly.

"That division probably was the reason they were purchased last year for an obscene amount of money," she acknowledged, as she, too, began digging into the main course with enthusiasm.

"Kate, let's cut to the chase. What do you need a...um...'fixer' for?"

"I am the co-director," she began, then looked embarrassed. "I am the director," she corrected, "of a research project called Cobalt. We're attempting to analyze the overlapping fields of consciousness and quantum mechanics."

Overlapping? He wanted to ask but kept his mouth shut. Her statement was giving birth to a multitude of questions in his eager mind, but none seemed to lead directly toward Pike Shepard. Best to let her get this out in her own way. Not that he was interested in helping, he was just very much enjoying listening and watching her talk.

Kate continued, "It's been long known that much of what we call consciousness is a complete mystery. We are actually diving into a specific part of consciousness and a subatomic portion of the brain's wiring."

"Ok, and quantum entanglement is a complete mystery, so why not say both are somehow connected?" Pike offered sarcastically as an absurd conclusion to her statement. Only she wasn't smiling.

"It was a leap," she conceded, "but one that many scientists have been leaning toward for a very long time."

Kate offered him some of the background data on consciousness, which he was less informed on, and then quantum entanglement, which was one of his fields of study. The linkage seemed wispy thin to him, but it did seem to stand up to initial scrutiny. "But, Doctor..."

"Kate," she corrected.

"Yes, sorry. Kate, as I recall from your speech, you're an experimental scientist, and I'm assuming this is all theoretical. So, excuse me if I fail to see what your actual involvement is or how there could be any world threatening crises looming on the horizon because of this theory."

"Professor, first, I would like to know your thoughts on a question. What is it that separates man from other animals?"

It was an unusual dinner topic but not too outlandish for two academics. He'd heard and answered similar questions in the past, but he felt strongly that this woman wanted a more specific response than his typical answers: *language, tools, intelligence, strong social norms, self-awareness.* There were lots of possible responses, but all he could think of was easily shot down. Ants may have stronger social orders than we do, but rarely we you think of them as our superiors. On some level, your dog probably knows he is a dog, but is that enough to prove he is on the same level of consciousness as his human masters? Pike did have one idea and voiced it. "Abstract thought."

Kate smiled and nodded, "That is a very good and a very unprovable possibility. There are others, but we do feel this one is key and related to much of what drives us, our imagination, enhanced sense of self, our intuition, and creativity. Now, the brain is a complex machine, and abstract thought is mostly based on uncertainty. Perhaps ability to do the unexpected would be more appropriate."

Mental light bulbs began to slowly flicker on in Pike's brain. "The Uncertainty Principle," he mumbled almost to himself. It was a mainstay of quantum mechanics developed in 1927 by one of Pike's heroes, Werner Heisenberg. He described that there is a fuzziness in nature, a fundamental limit to what we can know about the behavior of quantum particles and, therefore, the smallest scales of nature. Unlike Newtonian physics, where position and spin of particles could be easily defined at the subatomic quantum levels, neither relative position nor the spin of particles could be pinned down with any certainty. In fact, the very act of observing can affect the results. There was an odd parallel between this effect and abstract thought.

Kate smiled, realizing the pieces were finally falling into place. "Shepard, I am an experimentalist, and therein lies the issue," she began, then stopped suddenly, eyes darting wildly from side to side. Her gaze locked onto a white boat drifting slowly a few hundred feet offshore. She dove over the table and tackled Shepard out of his chair just as a sound of splintering wood was followed by a wet slap sounded.

Kate pulled on his arm to get Pike up, but he was already moving, crab walking along the low deck heading to the front of the building.

"Who in the hell is shooting?" he yelled back.

Other people were screaming and running in all directions. Another impact sounded as a round slammed into the shoulder of a large man who'd been struggling to get out of his chair. Kate glimpsed the boat moving out of range and risked rising to a crouch. Pike mirrored her and together, they ran for the parking lot.

"Do you have a phone?" he asked. "We need to call..."

"No time, they'll be on the way."

He noticed her turn away and scan up the gravel road, and for the first time, realized she had a tiny earbud in her ear. She was wearing comms gear. "What in the hell is going on, Kate, and who are you talking to?"

"Get the bike fired up, Pike, we don't have much time."

It went against both his training and instincts to turn and run. People here needed help, but he saw genuine fear in Kate's eyes and somehow knew these attackers and her presence tonight was more than mere coincidence. He spun the bike in an arc, spraying gravel and dust in all directions, hoping it would offer some cover. Kate leaped from the wall where she'd been taking cover and onto the seat as he twisted the throttle. The big motorcycle shot out of the parking lot, nearly throwing them both as they wheeled into the country road. The Indian gave a throaty roar as it topped a small rise and left the carnage far behind.

Pike let out a sigh of anxious relief. He needed to call the cops, get off the road, get Kate somewhere safe. Then he felt her tapping his right shoulder and pointing. The unmistakable sight of headlights showed a vehicle was speeding from a logging road. It would make it to the road before them, cutting off their escape route. Pike could just make out the truck in the dim light. This attack was coordinated; they were after the doctor, or him. *Why?*

Shut the hell up, Shepard, he told himself. *Not the time to be analyzing...it's time for action!* He patted one of the saddlebags hanging below Kate.

She unsnapped the leather strap and reached inside feeling nothing helpful at first. Then she touched a piece of cloth with something hard wrapped inside. Pulling it out, she realized it was a handgun. Shepard was putting his faith in her knowing how to use it. She wasn't about to disappoint. Without bothering to check the magazine she chambered a round, braced herself against Pike's shoulder and clicked the safety off.

While Pike assumed the truck had hostile intentions, he was less sure they would be legally in the right to take action. Then he saw the driver's window was down, and a long barrel was extended out and aimed directly at them. He glanced over his shoulder and nodded. "Do it!" The timing was not in their favor; the oncoming truck would be at the road at the same time they were. It was now or never. The gun Kate was holding barked twice, spitting out multiple forty-five caliber rounds. Then he saw an answering muzzle flash from the truck. He felt dread as he felt a sharp pain and noticed the bike leaning too far to one side, and he was unable to correct it.

6

"Dad?"

The sound of his daughter brought Pike up short. They had been in Spain when the first symptoms became apparent. Numbness in her arms and legs followed by a mild but persistent fever. When she stopped eating, they cut the vacation short, rushing back to Charleston where she was quickly admitted to the hospital. Days of poking and prodding had pushed all three of them to the brink. Pike held Emma's hand. "What is it, honey?" The look his baby girl gave nearly crushed his heart.

"I'm scared," said Emma.

"It will be okay, Em, I'm right here with you," her mother had said.

Not 'we're,' but 'I', Pike thought back angrily. A part of him wondered if his daughter's illness was somehow the result of the ongoing issues between him and Emily. It seemed unlikely, but he understood enough about biology to know stress could cause unexpected problems.

"I promise, you are going to be fine," he said, cutting an eye at his wife. The look hit home. He counted it as a win until he made eye contact with Emma once more. Tubes ran from her tiny arms to the steadily beeping machines. Little had he known this was to be his world for the next eighteen months.

"I don't want to know," Emma whispered. "Tell Doctor Scheidler to just tell you, ok? Whatever it is, I just don't want to know."

Pike realized his daughter had already figured out something was seriously wrong. Deep down, she already suspected her young body was trying to kill itself, and she had now decided that not knowing the exact method was better. He wasn't sure he disagreed. How could this happen to a vibrant, healthy teenager? The sense of déjà vu was hauntingly familiar. He held his daughter's hand tightly as they saw the doctor enter the room with a grim look on his face.

* * *

The beeping of the hospital monitors continued to tap out the steady beat of an uncertain future. As Pike opened his own eyes, he was greeted by an enormous daisy-shaped cluster of overhead lights. One light dimmed as the silhouette of a man's head came into view. He was holding something up to his face and bending in closer. Pike felt hot breath on his cheek as the man flashed an even brighter light into his left eye and then his right. This wasn't Emma's doctor; this was his. The memory faded away as he slowly came to the obvious realization. "You went for the spicy fish for lunch, huh?"

The doctor leaned up and backed away slightly before grinning and covering his mouth with a gloved hand. "That obvious, huh? My apologies, Mister Shepard." He picked up Pike's left arm and felt the pulse.

Pike's mind was trying to arrange the pieces he knew from the ones he did not. An attack, a woman, and they had been on his motorcycle. *Who was the woman?*

The doctor continued to check him over, making additions to the paper on a clipboard occasionally. Pike took the opportunity to look around. He was not in an exam room in the clinic, this looked more like a regular hospital room. "How long have I been here?" The doctor felt his side, and a stab of sharp pain caused him to jerk. "Shit!"

"Sorry," the man said, doing almost the same thing again and producing equally vocal results. "We thought we should keep you overnight. They moved you from ER up here around midnight. It's now late afternoon."

The doctor finished up and nodded. "Stitches look good, no internal damage, just going to be tender for a week or two. I think we can cut you loose in a few hours. Do you have someone you can call?"

Pike thought about it, he wasn't even sure where he was. "No one is with me? A young woman was with me on the bike. Was she hurt? Is she here?"

The doctor looked confused. "No one was with you. I'll get the nurse to check and see if anyone else was involved in the accident. It could be that they transported her to another hospital. Was she someone close? Would that be Emma?" He saw Pike's expression dim. "Sorry, I heard you saying that name as you were waking up."

Shepard shook his head. "No, not Emma...that was my daughter. This was someone new, we had just met." *Someone had been shooting at us, where are the police?* Surely his friend, Dewey, would have heard and probably be up here causing a scene by now. The rational side of his brain was hard at work now, trying to piece together what had happened the night before. Strangely, though, the memories appeared shrouded in clouds. The facts peeking out briefly, only to disappear again like a brook trout refusing to take the bait.

He shelved the mental challenges to ask the doctor more about his injuries, but the man was already heading into the corridor and on to his next patient. Pike ran his hand over the bandages wondering if this was how a gunshot felt. Surely there would have been more serious damage. He wasn't getting blood; the IV appeared to be just fluids. *No internal damage.* That's what the man had said, but it didn't add up. The pain he felt was real, not just his side either, but his shoulder ached, also parts of his leg and right arm felt raw and stiff. *Road rash,* he thought. *I must have laid the bike down*. "Dammit!" Wrecking the motorcycle would cause him more emotional distress than anything he did to himself.

The truth was, he always kept emotions at arm's length, not always by choice. Just another peculiarity of how his mind worked.

A heavyset nurse walked in. "Did I hear you call out? Are you in pain?"

She checked the doctor's notes as she made her way to the side of the bed. Pike saw the logo of the local hospital embroidered on her scrubs. That was one mystery cleared up. Bayside was a small regional facility, anything serious and they would have moved him somewhere better equipped, like Charleston.

"Sorry, no," he said. "I just figured out that I must have wrecked my bike."

The nurse was now looking at something on a tablet, his file he presumed. "Says vehicle accident, hon," her southern accent dripping like honey off morning flowers. "You've been asleep since I came on at seven this morning." She moved her finger to see something else on the flat display. "No family listed, and we don't have an emergency contact in our files, Mister Shepard." She glanced up. "Your phone must not of survived the accident as it wasn't in your belongings the police left."

He didn't want to tell her it was back home in his sock drawer with a dead battery. Apparently, a patient without a cell phone was far more unusual than one without family these days. Lucky him, he had neither.

"I'll be glad to call someone if you have their number. The doctor said you could leave once you can go to the toilet on your own." She pointed at a partially closed door on the other side of the room and smiled.

"Tell me, what were my injuries?"

The woman read off a list of mostly minor issues that Pike recognized, and he stopped her on 'puncture wound lower abdomen.' "I was stabbed?"

"No," she said, slightly embarrassed. "Well, I don't think so. A foreign object penetrated several inches into your abdominal cavity narrowly missing all your important parts. That's all I have in the charts. Sorry."

He again thought about the guns, the shooting at the bar. Probably best not to mention it, though, as that might cause more problems than it solved. He'd been impaled probably when he dropped the Indian. *Hopefully it fared better than I did.* But what about Kate Cassidy?

7

Pike's vision returned like a shutter sticking on an old 8mm home movie. The world came to him in stuttered flashes, with no sound and no context. "Please, God, let all of that have been just a dream," he whispered. Shapes coalesced from the flickering surroundings. Familiar smells, wet earth, and decay, not unpleasant, more like comforting. It wasn't exactly something he would have ever noticed or mentioned, but he knew with near certainty where he was. She was there, too; of that, he was positive. He felt pressure on his hand. Someone was holding it. Warm, soft, much like he had held her hand in the end.

The memory of those moments invaded his mind, the darkness seeking out every shred of light. Painfully, he forced them away. It was too much, like always. Why could he not keep his wife's or daughter's deaths from defining who he was? He solved problems for a living. He was a fixer, but he'd been unable to do anything to solve his own problem. The hand squeezed his own. Someone was there, someone was pulling him back...but why?

"Welcome back, Shepard."

The voice was calming and relaxed, the woman from the prior day, but his muddied mind could not resolve the discrepancies. "You are... Doc," he said weakly.

"It's Kate."

"Yeah," his voice croaked. "We met yesterday, maybe Tuesday," he said, his voice fading.

She offered a somewhat sad smile. "We met...yes." She looked sad. "It's okay, you will remember...in time. Just rest, for now."

Kate, yes, he thought. What is going on, was he sick? What had happened? The smells and flickers of images faded, and all became black.

* * *

The canoe was far too large for the narrow passage, but he paddled it skillfully. The dark water revealed little about itself. What horrors could it hide; how bottomless were the depths? Yet Pike knew if he stepped out, the water would barely reach his waist. He didn't want to step out; he wanted to keep going. To be more honest, a part of him wanted to keep going while another wished he was anywhere but here. Around the next bend he would see it, the old cabin, nestled so quietly back in the trees few would even notice. It wasn't an unfriendly place, just quiet, dead, and lonely. Even before it came into view, he knew precisely what it would look like. Unpainted, gray wood, Spanish moss shrouding the scene like sheets over old furniture. A single point of dim illumination coming from the kitchen window. The memory was both suffocating and liberating. A distant voice cried out... "Em."

"Shepard, time to wake up."

The fever dream fell away like a fog of cloying whiteness. The recurring dream was an all too familiar one for him. Seemed like he never reached where he was going in it, no matter how close the destination appeared to be.

"Shepard...Professor, drink this."

He felt a cup being placed in his hands; it was hot. Carefully, he raised it to his lips; he expected coffee, but instead, the welcomed gentle taste of tea met his tongue. The light was too bright for morning. "Wh..." His voice croaked like one of the cane frogs at sunset. "What time is it?" Why was that the question he needed to know first?

Slowly, the memories tentatively eased the mental door open and began to move through him like a solid breeze. The strange and beautiful doctor, them on the motorcycle, after that...what? Gunshots, someone chasing them or not, the hospital. "Oh, man." He held his head. "Just stop, Pike," he commanded himself.

The red-headed woman was back beside him, her right hand resting lightly on his arm. It calmed him measurably, although he was unsure quite why.

"You're back," she said, smiling.

"Yeah, what happened?" He sat up rubbing his head for cuts or bumps. Surely there had been an accident, injury, something.

"You're fine, Pike, just disoriented. Nothing is wrong. The docs said no concussion, remember?"

He didn't, not really. So much of the last few days seemed unhinged from the rest of his life. "You're okay? You weren't hurt in the...the accident?" Pike asked. That didn't seem like what it was, but he was unsure his memories were accurate.

He was in his bed, the angle of the sun let him know it was early afternoon. "You brought me home?"

"No, a friend of yours, I think. Gray truck with a large dog."

"Dewey," Pike said, nodding. That made sense. Someone would have called him, or he would have come looking.

She looked him over, closely examining the bandages and abrasions. "Yes, I waited out of sight, sorry. I wanted to check on you, but..."

"But it wouldn't have been safe, right?"

Kate nodded.

"What happened out there, and how are you okay? Have you been staying here?" Pike asked.

"What is the last thing you remember?"

He had to think about that. "A boat, someone shooting at us. We were running for the parking lot, then we were on the bike, and nothing more after that."

She nodded. "It's a long story, Shepard."

He looked into her face; her eyes showed something he couldn't quite identify. Loss, sadness, loneliness maybe. He moved up and slid a leg down to the floor and then the other. He felt the overwhelming desire to reach out to the beautiful stranger, to touch her cheek, to somehow help brush her obvious sadness away. His hand rubbed his face, and he felt several days' worth of beard. He'd just shaved the previous morning. "Doctor, what time is it?" he asked again.

"It's Kate, Pike." Her voice sounded on the verge of breaking. "It's about 1:00 in the afternoon." She moved toward the door. "You should eat something. Try to make it to the table, and I'll fix us some lunch."

He followed her in a stumbling, awkward gait that was something between a toddler's first steps and a zombie chasing a meal. The floor seemed to tilt downhill as his feet abruptly contacted the table leg. Pain shot through him, but it was dull and distant. He was on pain medication. That was why his head was so foggy.

"When did Dewey leave?"

Kate turned from the small stove where she was buttering one side of a cheese sandwich before dropping it in a pan. "About two in the morning. Then he was back early this morning. I hid again, but I think he knew someone was around. He acted odd. He's very protective of you."

"That he is," Pike agreed. "Kate, I have to ask, why are you still here? Isn't this dangerous for you?" He didn't know what was even going on, nor if he should be protective of this woman. After all, she seemed to be the likely cause of all his most recent problems. Still, he couldn't shake the feeling of something between them.

She placed the grilled cheese sandwiches on a plate for each of them. "Sorry, but that's about it for my domestic qualities." She took a few bites. "Your sheriff is investigating the incident at the bar. I doubt they will find much as I'm sure a cleaning crew came through immediately. Anyway, I'm fine Pike, it's not me they were after."

The words stunned him. He'd just assumed she was the target. "Why me?"

"The answer to that will take some time, and I'm afraid that's time that we really don't have. Things are moving faster than I had expected. The attacks have begun, and it's only going to get worse from here on. Simple answer is, not everyone wants you on my team."

"They shot me. How are we both not dead?"

Kate reached into a coat pocket and removed a clear tube with a metal end cap. "You were shot, but luckily, it was with something like this." She handed it to him.

It rolled side to side in his palm, and he could see it was designed to fit into a shotgun. The clear plastic casing revealed a propellant chamber at the base and a small chrome and clear ampule that tapered to a needle point near the front. A bright green piston sat at the fat end of the tube which was still partially filled with liquid.

"1.5 cc of ketamine most likely."

"They shot me with a tranq gun?" Pike asked.

She nodded. "Modified to shoot rounds of compressed air normally, but this is a new adaptation. I think one of the men I downed had it."

"Nice shooting out there, by the way." She ignored the compliment. "Did you hurt him? Was he dead?"

"We don't have time for this, Pike," Kate said, her frustration growing clearer. "You hit a metal stake when you laid the bike down. It needed more than just first-aid. Sorry, I had to call an ambulance. When I went back to the scene, I found the shell."

"So, you left me out there? You didn't talk to the cops about it, did you?"

"I haven't left you Shepard. I will not leave you, not willingly. You are too important."

. . .

"To whom?" he demanded.

"To all of us...and especially to me," Kate said, her eyes looking away briefly as the words came out.

8

During his previous forty-three years, Pike had endured more than his share of pain and loss. Still, this stranger's words pulled at him. "Why would I matter to anyone?"

She stiffened, then consciously seemed to relax before answering. "You are uniquely suited to our needs, Professor."

"Pike," he said automatically. "Just call me Pike. I haven't been an educator in years." His desire to teach had died around the same time they lost Emma.

"But you were one; an extremely good one. Why did you leave?"

Pike knew she was trying to deflect his barrage of questions. He couldn't blame her; his style was relentless at times. "I grew weary of the bullshit. I enjoy solving problems, not becoming one." He rose gingerly from his chair and placed his plate in the sink. "Honestly, I don't know, it was just time to move on," he said more truthfully.

"Is that why you never completed your doctorate?" Kate asked.

The lady has done her homework, he thought. He had graduated Georgia Tech with a degree in mechanical engineering before deciding on graduate school in a totally unrelated field. "I have a wandering spirit," he said with a note of sadness. "It was a challenging time, Kate." *One of many,* he thought.

"Still, you were tops in your class at Duke," she said. "That's a pretty impressive feat since you had transitioned from the engineering school to mathematics."

"Ancient history, Doc." Math was fun but not Pike's love. But physics had turned out to be. More accurately, the earlier work in quantum physics, so much of the field was just extraordinarily baffling. He'd found the challenge refreshing. He'd grown up obsessing over puzzles, and none was bigger than his chosen field. "Now, please tell me why I am uniquely suited to your project, and why someone would try so hard to stop me from saying yes. Please start by explaining to me what 'the project' even is."

Kate liked how quickly he moved from the mundane to the essential. She could tell he was the right man for the job. She wiped her hands with a napkin and her eyes found his. The deep brown color of his eyes was mesmerizing to her, but she had a job to do and forced herself to stay focused. "I know you are aware that one of the oddities about quantum field theory is that, in some cases, we find that for something to happen, there must be an observer. Think about that, the very act of watching is required for it to happen, whatever 'it' is. A particle, say a proton, essentially can exist in many places at once until we decide to look at it, then it behaves in a fixed and measurable place."

"Yeah, super-positioning and the probability theory," he clarified. "Your project involves quantum mechanics? So, tell me more on how this relates to your specialist as a neuroscientist."

She ignored him and continued. "You've also, then, no doubt heard the theory that all of us have a quantum connection, possibly even to other dimensions."

Pike had indeed heard the theory; it had gained popularity over the last few years. As scientists looked deeper into the subatomic realm, the interplay of the sometimes-baffling quantum fields offered explanation of everything from photosynthesis to creative thinking. "I have, but don't recall any hard science, much less practical experimentation, being done in the field."

"I began my career like a lot of others," Kate began. "I blindly followed my peers and professors into the murky depths of neuroscience. They attempt to explain the machinations of the mind in purely physical terms like chemical and electrical input and output. Eventually, I realized that explained little of what I was seeing. The brain is just an organ. While incredibly complex, much of the processes can be mapped out and measured. The intersection, though, of the physical brain and the cognitive mind is a lot less clearly understood."

"So, you got a grant to explore that connection?" Pike guessed. "I take it you found something."

"How do you know you are real?" she asked.

"Descartes?" Pike said questioningly. "I think, therefore I am."

Kate gave a nod, "Consciousness is something that scientists still can't completely agree on what it actually is. We generally refer to it as a sense of self-awareness, but is it a distinctly human trait? You yourself told me the other night that the capacity for abstract thought is a key definition."

Pike was beginning to grasp the rich complexities of applying a simple declaration on the topic. It would always unravel when inspected closely. Was a particular trait something unique to humans? Was it part of what some would call the soul? He felt sure Kate wasn't approaching this from some metaphysical standpoint; he already felt she was too pragmatic for that.

As if reading his internal debate, she continued, "Consciousness is less a part of the brain than a process of behavior adapted from the intersection of knowledge, skills, genetic biases, and something more elusive. There is an unknown quality that is likely the very spark of what it is to be human. An element that gives nuance and clarity to our world in the form of creative expression, the ability to imagine and to anticipate, intuit, or see things in the abstract. It is almost certainly the source of faith, kindness and...love." She reached for his hand almost unconsciously as she said those last words. "The simple fact is, we had no actual way of knowing how or why this elusive component of our consciousness existed."

Pike looked down at the hand holding his own. "I take it, my dear doctor, that you now know where the elusive parts come from?"

"Actually yes, we now know, maybe not the complete origins, but more than we did. What we think of as our subconsciousness provides most of it. As you may know, the subconscious actions cannot be mapped. What does it mean to be human? Surely two of the defining characteristics are that of creativity and of consciousness. We can take guesses at creativity, but there is, in fact, an extremely hard problem of explaining consciousness at all."

Kate leaned back in the chair and continued, "What we found was nothing we expected and, frankly, exposes even larger gaps in our knowledge. We discovered that at the deepest levels of the brain, where the part that we might describe as our consciousness lives, there was interaction with something unseen. We could tell the microtubules vibrated with a certain resonance and were being affected by something on the quantum level."

Pike nodded. "Quantum entanglement, Einstein's spooky interaction at a distance. Two particles whose states are linked so that they mirror what each other does no matter how far apart they are."

"Yes, that is a simple, but also very complete, description. The why and the how have eluded us as have many other aspects of the rather bizarre quantum world. What we assumed when we uncovered how quantum entanglement worked within our own subconscious, is if we could see the other end, we would find a mirror image of ourselves, or at least our consciousness.

"Like I said before," she went on, "scientists have struggled to even describe consciousness for centuries. Something in humans makes us different from other animals, but what? The Cobalt project examined the microtubules at that subatomic level, and eventually we discovered the connection that helps us explain sentient thought, creativity, morality, and more. Maybe even what we would deem a soul. Our mind is not as individual as we thought but may, in fact, be more of a hive mind."

"We are many?" Pike asked uncertainly. "What are you suggesting —that consciousness is interconnected? Like with everyone on Earth?

That hardly seems plausible. Hell, we spend too much time trying to kill each other."

Kate shook her head. "No, it's not that at all. Think of consciousness as being distributed. You share it, but not with everyone, in fact, no one in our world."

He stared at her trying to interpret the meaning behind her words.

"Look, Pike," she continued, "we knew from our experiments that all humans have these quantum connections. My assumption is this is key to what makes us—well, human."

"So, subatomic connections in our brain are essential to our consciousness?" he asked, growing even more confused.

She answered, "Does a leaf need to understand the quantum mechanics going on in photosynthesis to take advantage of the energy it provides? Quantum mechanics is at the very heart of life, maybe even the reason for life to exist."

9

"You okay?"

Pike was standing now, watching the slow-moving water push past his landing, looking back at the beautiful doctor, unsure how to respond. One part of him still wanted to tell her to leave. Whatever she was in, it was over his head and none of his concern. Still, she had sparked his curiosity. He looked again out the cabin window to the familiar bay. The waving, green, spartina grass stretching out for miles. "Are we safe?"

"For now," Kate said with measured confidence.

"I think the shrimp are still running. Let's go get some supplies. Can you stay for dinner? I would like to hear more of this, but I need some fresh air." He passed the empty spot where the Indian normally sat. The green tarp lay crumpled and lifeless on the ground. Kate clicked the remote to unlock her rental, which beeped in reply.

They stopped at Veasey's Market on Salt Marsh Road and bought several pounds of shrimp along with some fresh vegetables, sausage, and a few other items. Knowing she was in a hurry to get back to her project, he was surprised to see her relax and take a seat on his porch swing while he placed a large stockpot on the fish cooker. Soon he had a dark broth simmering away. Wordlessly, she helped him wash the potatoes and then got bowls and knives to clean the shrimp. T-Bone Walker sang "Super Black Blues" from the ancient stereo. "You know anything about Lowcountry boils?" Pike asked.

She rolled her eyes. "Not really, but doesn't seem that complicated." She moved from shrimp to chopping up a large, yellow onion while he shucked corn. He cut partially through the top part of each ear and twisted before pulling the green husk down, just like his grandmother had taught him.

"Why do you do it that way?"

He pointed the knife at the next ear. "The corn?"

He smiled. "Where are you from, Kate?"

"California, little town on the coast up near Carmel. Why?"

He expertly cut the pristine ear into equal sections and proceeded to undress the next one. "My grandmother could shuck bushels of this stuff and do it so clean there wouldn't be a silk left on it."

"Silk? Is that what you call the nasty, hairy stuff?"

Pike nodded. "There's an art to working with fresh produce, and we're lucky here. Everything grows, and we have both seafood and magnificent farms."

"Tell me about your family, your grandmother," Kate said.

He gave a cold smile and shook his head. The thoughts of his family were not one of his favorite topics. "My father was a joyless man, and my mother had dreams of living in high society. Dreams that didn't always include the infestation which she considered her only child."

She laughed and nodded, knowing the type well.

Pike continued, "My Uncle Joe was a good man...he was the one who originally built this fish-camp." He paused his work and looked around the space. "He'd originally planned for something much grander for this lot, but...well, money became an issue." The cabin wasn't much, nothing elaborate, but every beam had been hand laid by Joe and Pike's dad, and not a single nail had been used. The relationship with his grandparents, in particular, was more complicated.

"I was a problem kid, my parents divorced, moved away, and then I mostly lived with my grandparents. It was with them I spent most of my youth and all the years that really counted. My grandfather, we called him Rembert or sir, never Grandad, he showed me how to fix broken mowers and run a trotline, while Nana taught me to graft trees to create hybrids, make jelly from the abundant fruit in the Lowlands, and most importantly, to read. Lord, how that woman loved to read." Pike moved on to slicing up onions and sausage while he opened up.

"By the age of ten, I'd out-read every other member of the family and convinced the local librarian to allow me a double ration of books to check out."

"I like that," Kate said a short while later.

"What?"

"When you talk about them. You disappear into those memories, and I can see how much you miss them."

Pike was just glad she hadn't wanted to know about his ex-wife or daughter. He wasn't ready to open those wounds to anyone.

"I know you love it here, but I had no idea exactly why you do. When I pulled up on that bank out there, I thought you were playing hermit, trying to disappear from the world, but that's not it at all, is it?"

They took all the ingredients out to the porch, and in a very precise order, Pike began submerging them into the steaming heart of spicy broth. Kate entered the house and returned a minute later with two glasses, each with a large ice ball, and a half full bottle of Irish whisky.

"Tullamore Dew?" he asked, giving her a questioning look. "Will I like this?"

"Shut up and drink," she said. "If we're going to work together, you have to get some trace of civility and culture."

Pike sipped the liquor and had to admit it was some of the best. "My Dad would have hated it. If it didn't peel the lining of your throat off when you drank it, it was just dirty water."

"I take it he's gone?"

Pike nodded, "Yeah, years ago, cancer." He noticed Kate looked about to offer sympathies. He stopped her with a raised hand. "We weren't close."

"What about your mom?" she asked after several seconds of awkward silence.

"What about her?" Pike asked, wishing to avoid the subject entirely.

"Are y'all close?"

Truthfully, Pike was close to no one. It was both a blessing and a curse. "She's in an assisted living facility in Charleston. I see her occasionally." He said it as if that explained the depth of his commitment to the woman who had given him life.

They finished eating as the fading sun cast the wetlands in an amber glory. They took their drinks and walked to the water's edge, where they watched flocks of water birds settling in for the night. A distant horn signaled a shrimp boat coming in. "That was fantastic, Pike, thanks."

"Easiest meal in the world as long as you can get good, quality ingredients." They walked on. Kate sensed all that was on his mind but felt best to let him have his time to come to his decisions. They sipped the drinks until the ice rattled in the empty glasses. She liked this man and his unhurried sense of grace. There was hurt and guilt but also power over how he faced the unknown and how he processed information to get to the truth.

Pike squeezed her hand gently. "Do we need to discuss this? Are we becoming a thing?"

She looked down almost surprised to see their hands clasping together. She thought she could keep this professional, but her heart seemed to have other ideas.

Pike saw the brief flash of what he took as hurt in her eyes and immediately regretted his word choice. "I'm sorry, Kate. I'm just not used to anyone being this close. I mean, you are beautiful, way too cute for me and brilliant, but..."

"But what?" she asked.

"I don't know, I can't explain it. When I woke up today, I expected you to be there, even though I had no reason to. You have seemed somehow familiar to me even though we just met. Does that make any sense to you?"

Dragonflies hummed nervously about like attending angels waiting for a trumpet call to action. "No, Pike, it's much simpler than that but also harder to explain. But maybe in time you'll understand. Not to be crass, but have you ever wondered why your wife cheated on you?" The look on his face let her know that she'd stepped too far. That was not a subject he was okay discussing; not now, maybe not ever. "Relax, Pike," Kate said softly. "I'm just asking a question. I know you have a lot of hurt, a lot of pain. You don't let anyone close since her —right?"

Pike stared off, his jawline firm, but eventually nodded in agreement.

They continued to walk along the wooded edge of the bay. "Just perhaps she didn't get from you all the love that you thought you were giving."

"That's crazy," he said defensively. He knew he had doted on his wife. "I gave her everything. I spent time, we enjoyed doing things together. I learned to appreciate many of the things she did, cooking, good wine, travel. Kate, I put my career on hold for years. That's the real reason I never specialized or went for my doctorate." He fell silent, and they walked on letting the quiet envelop them in its asthmatic, suffocating manner.

"I tried..." Pike stopped, then continued more confidently, "No, I did the things a good husband's supposed to do. She just decided she would much rather screw someone she wasn't married to more." He knew that wasn't entirely true. Losing Emma was hard on them both. Afterward, he'd taken refuge in his work while she looked elsewhere for comfort.

Kate seemed taken aback by the rawness in his response. They walked on, the rhythm of bare feet on sand the only sound in an awkward silence. "Yes, Pike, you did all those things. I feel sure you would have." Something lay hidden in the words she didn't say. "I know you...I know your type, at least. I believe you tried your best to love her. But...did you completely love her? Was your heart yearning for her, aching for her to be happy? I'm not talking about sex, that's just a symptom. How tight was the connection between you two?"

Who is this woman speaking to me so intimately? Talking as if they had been together for years instead of just a few days. Feelings he was unwilling to examine himself, much less share with others. Still, this conversation somehow felt natural and...bizarrely safe.

Kate moved in front to face him. The slight ocean breeze made her hair glow like a fiery crown in the sunset. Then she asked something that breathed life into the silent words he was considering.

"Was it the same as how you are beginning to feel for me?"

He looked at her with an absolute vacuum of comprehension, yet also the total realization that she was not wrong. He had a sudden eagerness to take her in his arms and kiss her deeply.

Kate moved back beside him and leaned softly into him, letting her shoulder rub against his in an effortless manner. "Pike, in your mind, you just met me a few days ago. Yet, I can tell how you feel when we are close. I can tell by how you look in my eyes. Already, you know the sound air makes when I breathe it in. You know how I like my pancakes cooked. You know I love to be held and caressed after sex. You have no memory of those things, yet you know deep down our love is true."

His sharp mind seemed to be stuck in first gear trying to catch up with the quickening pace of the discussion. "So, you're saying what, we are destined to be together or something?" The words felt flat and obscene, and her response was neither confirmation nor denial.

"It doesn't matter," Kate said. She took in a deep breath before explaining. "What we were or what we have been is unimportant compared to who we *can be* to each other. There are probabilities and potential, but ultimately, it's up to us."

He waited for her to continue, but the silence grew. Finally, she stopped and faced him again, taking his broad shoulders in each of her delicate hands. "All these things you know. Just because we're connected. As soon as we met, I knew you've always loved me. And I know you could never love anyone else. We're paired. We are bonded as one. It doesn't matter when and where I came from, what I've done, what you've done. Literally, our souls are supposed to be together, they will always find each other. Innateness or tabula rasa, I think I knew that probably before I'd even found you. In fact, knowing that is what allowed me to find you."

"Wait," Pike said, coming to gasping realization of what she had just said. "So, you're saying that fate—that some predestination steers certain couples together, no matter what?"

Kate nodded, "Yes, that's exactly what I'm saying. I just want you to understand that what your wife did was inevitable. Actually, that may be the wrong word. Lots of couples do stay together because they are comfortable. Many marriages exist in a quiet, nameless, sadness simply due to the fact that once the infatuation and physical desire fade, there is nothing to sustain those chilling embers. Honey, look. I know, I know, Emily cheated on you, then left. And I'm sorry about that, but it should not rule your life."

Pike wondered how she could be so blunt and know exactly what Emily had done. Obviously, it was a sensitive subject for him. Truthfully, it was something he never discussed with anyone. Emily had left him less than a year before her own cancer diagnosis. Kate was correct. Even then, he hadn't blamed her. He'd not even been able to get mad at the man who'd stolen her away. As cliché as it was, it had been one of his close friends, a former co-worker. When that guy moved on, not wanting the entanglements of a lover with a terminal illness, she had made a desperate call and, knowing better, Pike had answered. She begged and pleaded, and he'd opened the door feeling pity and something else, obligation, but no, not love. Being with her was routine, like putting on a comfortable pair of gloves. Something he could slip on and not have to worry about.

And then the cancer began ravaging her body. Like a dutiful husband, or maybe more like just a stupid fool, he sat there and watched his ex-wife wither away and leave him all over again. It tore at him; it ate at him and pulled apart the very shreds of his reality. Not because she was gone, but because he was here. And no, he didn't love her, nor did he miss her afterward. Not the way he should have...not the way a husband should care...*right*? Something had always been missing, something far below the surface, an emptiness that he'd never been able to put his finger on.

"Kate, I don't understand any of this. My love life is a train wreck...I am haunted by loss." He moved away from her a few steps and ran a hand across his head, feeling the ridge of scars buried beneath. "Emotional connections have been a challenge for me, okay? I don't know what you think is happening between you and me. Obviously, something, but I'm not what you need. I don't think I'm the one to help you with your project, either."

"Shh. It's okay, Pike." she said, with a tone of affection. "Back when I first got my medical degree, I had a young woman come into the ER... someone had violently raped her. During the exam, I noticed some unusual lesions and drew some blood. It turned out she also had cancer. Now, she could have let either of those traumatic events define her life. Instead, she chose the opposite. The early cancer diagnosis literally saved her life."

Pike felt the topic was uncomfortably close and was searching for the point.

Kate took his hand in hers. "Never let your life be defined by the worst thing that ever happens to you. It could be your greatest gift."

Looking at this gorgeous woman standing before him, he gave in to his inner pleading. He pulled her close and kissed her deeply, running his fingers through her hair and along her perfect back. He traced the outline of the small tattoo on her arm. Some sort of mathematical formula, but the origin escaped him. Her body, her touch, her lips were so familiar, he knew this woman, this love. Quickly, he began pulling her back toward the cabin removing his shirt as he went. He would love her this night. Tomorrow they could discuss what came next, maybe.

10

Kate reluctantly moved off Pike. Her body was exhausted but ached to have him inside her once more. The fire of lovemaking was as strong now as it had been hours earlier. She ran her hands over his muscular body, loving him more with every passing second. Pike snored lightly; the evening's activities had led to another middle of the night session of lovemaking. Now, as the darkness outside was just giving way to morning, she still wanted more. Her appetite for him was insatiable.

Slipping on one of his t-shirts, she tiptoed to the bathroom and relaxed as her bladder emptied, her fingers lingering as she wiped herself clean. She could still feel him in there, the pulsing rhythm that was like a holy fire to her body...to her soul. Maybe something about the night had triggered something in him. Selfishly, though, she just wanted more.

Forcing herself to put those internal flames somewhere else, at least for the moment, she crossed silently to the front door and let herself out. The rich color of indigo was contrasted by muted gray streaked with pink in the early morning sky. She removed the phone from her purse, which was still on the porch where they had left everything the previous evening. Walking down to the waterfront, she punched a number from memory. The line connected on the second ring. She listened, then gave an appropriate response, "Buon pomeriggio."

Kate's mind shifted to the task at hand, but her body was still echoing with the delights of the past twelve hours. Unconsciously, her hand found its way inside her panties as she talked quietly. "Yes, I am still here." She glanced back at the cabin nervously. The voice on the other end rose in volume and was more expressive, as only Italians can get. "That is not an option," she whispered. "We agreed to try it my way, first." The other side of the conversation must have disagreed as Kate curtly responded with, "Stammi bene," and disconnected.

Slipping back into the bedroom, she resumed her place beside Pike. Soon her fingers edged down and encircled his manhood once more. She felt him respond as she began the soft rhythmic movements. His snores softened, and deeper, more primal sounds escaped his lips. Bending down, her lips touched his and then moved on to other parts. She maintained the foreplay until she had to have him in her. The hunger she felt was not just physical, it indeed transcended all bounds.

Never having much time or interest for real relationships, Kate had taken lovers as needed but always without the encumbrances or desire for anything more. When she told Pike she had known him before they met, that had not been a lie...it was just something hard to explain. His full erectness filled her mouth as she moved up and down his thickening manhood. She felt his fingers gently stroke her neck and back as he, too, was now awakened to the joyous pleasure.

She couldn't hide her love for him no matter how new this might be. As he began to orgasm, she knew some part of him knew her, even if he didn't know it yet. The intensity of his thrust quickened as the spasms of pleasure filled her with his very essence. Smiling and licking her lips she crawled back up and laid her head on his bare chest. His breath struggled to return to normal. "Good morning."

"Want to tell me what that was?" Pike asked, entering the kitchen a short while later.

Kate handed him a cup of coffee and smiled. "That was an 'I'm glad I met you' kind of night."

He leaned into her for a quick kiss. "The feeling is mutual, Kate, thank you. You can't imagine..." His words trailed off.

"I've been sequestered on an island full of lab rats for the past several years. I think I understand fully." She then pulled him in for a real kiss.

"So, you still need my help?"

She nodded.

"I'm sorry, but I have to ask," he began uncertainly.

The smile lit up her face, "No, last night...us, has nothing to do with it. I am not some coercive bitch willing to do anything to get what I want."

"So, if I say no?" he asked.

"I'll be disappointed. I'll need to start looking again, but it won't change how I feel about you." He was holding her close, his arms wrapped snuggly around her waist. "Tell me, how does this feel to you?" she asked.

He considered that question at length. He had a long and unpleasant history of emotions. Some resulting from childhood issues both physical and emotional. He had always been a bit socially awkward, and in truth, his relationships often comprised mimicry rather than actual feelings. He always knew the right words to say, the right time to be silent, and the right time to take action. That was not his emotions, that was his rational brain telling him how to fake it. Somehow, though, this did indeed 'feel.' It was not the result of a pre-planned strategy to win her over. He'd not even been considering her as a possibility. This just felt natural, and he told her so. She leaned into him, her head again resting on his chest, and soon he felt the hot wetness of tears.

11

The dark water of the tidal creek moved past the two like an old friend. Pike expertly moved the tiller, guiding the small sailboat into the open channel ahead. The lush, green, spartina grass was beginning to fade to its more subdued winter color. His memories of the previous night and the unexpected turn his life had taken were all closing in.

Nearly unconsciously, he hoisted the mainsail and watched as the light breeze filled it, only to spill over the starboard edge. He readjusted and tightened the rigging, watching it fill and catch. He caught site of Kate sitting near the stern. She was leaning back, the late summer sun on her pale face, red hair billowing out from beneath one of his old ball caps. The image struck him as magical and also familiar. He reached in a sea trunk, took out a light carriage blanket, and tossed it to her. The sea spray had a biting edge that foretold of cooler weather ahead. Hitting the wider main channel, he locked down the sail, pointing the boat toward St. Helena Sound in the distance. Pike relaxed and moved back to sit beside the woman.

"Why South Carolina?" she asked.

He smiled; it was a natural question. The Lowcountry was home but also filled with so much pain, so many memories that haunted him like the smell of sickness around his dying wife.

Kate continued, "No offense, I mean," she said defensively, "I know about you taking care of Emily up in Charleston. But why back here? You moved to Blackwater afterward when...well, you could have gone anywhere."

Pike caught sight of a porpoise surfacing several hundred yards to the right, and gently, he nudged the boat in that direction. A second and then a third joined in behind the first. An entire pod was soon swimming beside and in front of the boat. Kate leaned out watching them and laughing. The piloting mammals' interaction with their human cousins was always amazing and made even more fun if the person wasn't expecting it.

"I didn't realize dolphins came in, I thought this was mostly freshwater," she said.

Thankful for the interruption of her questioning, he nodded. "Saltwater marsh, the flow is all tidal, and they just come in to feed. Not that often we see them in the middle of the day, though." They watched the small pod as they darted in front of the boat and along the side.

The discussions and discoveries of the prior day and the marathon lovemaking had unsettled him in countless ways. Pike had intended to take a solo sail around the bay to clear his mind. Normally, his go-to ride would have been his motorcycle, but this was what he had, and he loved it, too. He had left the cabin alone, but Kate had joined him before he'd cast off the first of the mooring lines.

He twisted on the seat as he watched the shoreline slip past. He felt her as she moved in behind him. Her head lay on his back, her arms wrapping around him in a tender embrace.

"Where are you?" she asked with an intimacy he was not yet prepared for.

His eyes dropped, and the silence stretched out like a shadow. "Back there," he pointed.

Kate turned and saw stones crumbling down the bank under a withered oak stretching its arms out over the water.

"Fort Remorse," he said almost reverently.

"I don't recall ever seeing that on the map," she said. "I think I motored right past here on my way out to find you."

Pike adjusted the tiller and allowed some of the wind to spill from the sail. He wasn't interested in getting anywhere fast today. His mind needed time to pry out the most relevant points of what was happening and this lady's project. The sailing trip had uncovered something more he would have rather not shared. "It's not one of the better memories I have of here, but it's as much why I returned as anything."

As they rounded the tip of the small island, Kate could see more of the ruins and realized it had probably been a small rock and earthen structure but now was mostly lumps of vine-covered debris nearly reclaimed by the old growth forest. A few hundred yards down the coast, several ancient unpainted single-story houses stood in a neat line. They all looked abandoned, but tattered cloth curtains waved beckoningly at them from glassless windows. "Slave quarters?" she asked.

Pike shook his head, "Freemen, Gullah."

She searched her mind, the terms were familiar, but she couldn't access it.

"The Gullah, or Geechee, are descendants of West Africans who were brought here two centuries ago," he said. "They were slaves on many of the large plantations here in the Lowcountry. They spoke their own language, a version of Creole, but fiercely protected their true African heritage. After the Civil War, they were free to go, but many moved out here to the sea islands and set up isolated communities like this one."

He played nervously with a bit of line, tying then untying a complicated knot. "One of my friends was from here, Risson Mack, but we all just called him Risse. Risse was Emma's godfather." He nodded toward the dwellings. "From down there, third house. Mack's grandmother, Isabella Mack, was one of the last leaders of the Gullah. He said she was a Queen of the Gullah Nation, but I'm not totally sure what that would have even meant." Pike looked back at the shorelines, clearly seeing the ghost of many memories from an earlier time. "Risse used to call them a tribe of black Indians just to piss her off."

"He wasn't proud of his heritage?" asked Kate.

"It was difficult for him. The families here had very strong traditions, avoided modern life, but his mother wanted him to have a better education. Difficult for a boy who could barely speak the same language as the boys across the bay. He had one foot in the past with them and one in the future with us." Pike pointed far ahead, "The school we attended is still up on that bluff on the far side of Beaufort. Risse had to get himself there and back every day. The county school board took no responsibility in getting any of them back and forth to school. Only a few like Risse ever did it successfully."

"Were racial tensions the issue?" Kate asked.

"Not really," Pike answered. "I mean, schools were successfully desegregated long before I started. The Gullah nation had become dispersed almost completely as the young ones wanted more of what the rest of us had, instead of living in near- primitive conditions out here. The issue was how he spoke and dressed; he would never be a true Beaufort boy. Then, when he rowed that old boat home each night with his head filled with science and literature and math, he soon became more of an outcast in his own home. Risse had a brilliant mind and an equally sharp tongue. He caused friction in both of the worlds he inhabited."

"How did you two become friends?" Kate asked.

Pike swung the sail to the opposite side and pulled the tiller. Smiling, he said, "I saved his life."

"Really?"

"No, but that's how he always told it. The rumor was that none of the Gullah could swim, their bones were too dense or something. My grandparents lived in an older home off Church Street then. That was when they still had some money. One July morning, I was heading to fish over near Port Royal. I came over the bridge on my bike and saw Risson's old wooden boat overturned on the bank and then saw him shouting and splashing around about thirty yards offshore."

Pike dropped the sail and let the current push Kate and him toward a small marina ahead. "I came off the bridge as fast as I could pedal. Man, I was flying down that hill. Rode right off into the bay. I was always a strong swimmer like most everyone here, so I didn't even hesitate. Only later, when I thought about it possibly being an alligator or even a bull shark that he might be fighting, did I realize how foolish I had been."

"But you jumped in to save someone you barely knew, a Gullah boy at that," Kate said.

He shook his head, smiling at the memory. "Not that unusual, anyone passing by probably would have done the same. There's a deep fondness here for the Gullah now. One that defies our troubled history. Only thing was, he didn't need saving. When I reached him, he was grinning, and he thrust the end of a throw-net into my hand. 'Pull, man, pull. We gonna get em gud dis day,' the kid had said as he tossed his net on a massive bed of blue crabs. He was trying to pull it in as the slack tide was pulling it and him back out to sea. He was not about to let them get away."

"So, you saved the crabs but not the boy?"

"Hell, Risse could out-swim all of us. It was partially true that his body didn't naturally float the same as ours, but he'd grown up in the water even more so than we had. He was lean and strong. We got the net back onto shore, and it was the largest single haul of crabs I had or ever have seen. That kid was all smiles. Then he helped me fish my bike out of the bay and asked me to come out and eat crabs with them later. The Gullah didn't often welcome outsiders into their homes, so I politely refused, but he wasn't hearing of it. He said half those crabs were rightfully mine."

"So, you went?" Kate asked.

"I did," Pike answered, smiling. "Dewey had a small boat, and we went over and ate with the Macks that night. His mother treated us like her own. The three of us were nearly inseparable after that. Risse helped me a lot, as a kid, I mean. I had issues. Some that scared Dewey, but Risse never gave up on me. Right until Uncle Sam got involved."

Pike tied the boat off in a public space at the city marina. He took

Kate's hand as he guided her onto the dock. "Let's get a drink and maybe some proper food. I think I need to know more about what you want and why someone is pretty damn insistent on keeping me away."

Kate stepped cautiously onto the wooden dock, paused, and looked back at the expanse of water. "Did I just hear you say alligators?"

12

After a lunch of blackened fish tacos and beer at the Marina Grille, Pike and Kate walked leisurely up Bay Street past the grand antebellum homes. He still had not answered her question. "The South has its issues, Kate. Many claim the fight for secession from the union started right here on this very street. No doubt, the first shots of the Civil War were fired just up the coast. Still, there is much to love about the Lowcountry. When Sherman cut a path across Georgia, he turned his sites toward us, yet he spared this beautiful little town. Pike pointed to the Anchorage Inn and the Cuthbert House just beyond. "Right there, the best breakfast in town." The magnificent homes were ringed by moss shrouded, live oaks that looked to have been preserved under glass for the past 200 years. "Even he could not bear to see this little corner of post-war America disappear."

She looked up at him, and he knew her next question before she even asked it. "Why you, though?"

Pike shrugged his shoulders, and they moved to a wooden swing overlooking the bay and sat. "Maybe we're both out of sync with time. Me, apparently by my own hand this time, but growing up here, I think I always was...out of step, I mean, with the rest of the world."

Kate nodded, seemingly understanding. "So, you really didn't come back here to escape?"

Pike leaned back and contemplated the question. "I moved out to the cabin to escape people, yes, but I moved here to be home, to be rooted. The Lowcountry is in you from birth, and no amount of purging and denial can fully erase the silt from your veins."

"You left, you worked all over the world, lived in countless cities large and small," Kate said.

"True." He nodded. "But look around."

She saw the marina with its fishing boats waiting for the tide to turn so they could head back out. A line of sailboats bobbed in the anchorage just offshore. The street with its canopy of interlaced oaks all draped in the Spanish moss like a Grand Dame ready for her entrance. The small town was quaint, as a Norman Rockwell painting. "It's beautiful but...not much opportunity for someone in your field here, is there?" She smiled as his head nodded in agreement.

They listened to the simple sounds. The swing chains creaking on rusty mounts, joggers running by with dogs in tow, water slapping against the seawall. "I can't explain why I'm here. Not fully, at least. It's just part of me. As much a part of me as anything. I really don't know. It just seems that I'm connected to the Lowcountry. This place feeds my soul in ways I could never explain. Perhaps it's where my mind is most centered because I've always had my best ideas here." He turned to look at her and realized he was holding her hand again. "Look, I know you need me for some reason. I'm sure you need to get back to your lab, but this is home and, well...."

"And we just met, and someone nearly killed you, and then I nearly fucked you to death."

"Well...um, yes," Pike answered, his face flushed. He was intelligent, analytical. The problems occurred when he tried to apply that level of critical thinking to emotions. This woman beside him was captivating and familiar to him in ways he couldn't explain. "Should I love you, Kate?" Pike asked matter-of-factly.

She just smiled. "You know the answer to that. Your heart knows it. Maybe your brain doesn't, but your body certainly does." A brief flush of red now blossomed on her face as memories of the previous night echoed through her body.

"Is that better or worse for us?" he asked.

Kate answered, "It's inevitable for us. We're a matched set. We can go through this life...through this world...frustrated and without each other, or more contented and able to focus on other things with each other. I much prefer to choose to do things as a team. That's why I'm here instead of back at the lab looking for answers."

They purchased a bag of French pastries from a small shop and walked together around the small town. "Pike, what if every whispered thought, every inner voice, every time the devil on your shoulder whispered in your ear, it was someone else?"

He was already paranoid being out in the open only days after they had been attacked, but Kate seemed calm, and he felt sure her question was not rhetorical. "You mean literally someone else?"

"It's hard to explain, but kind of," Kate replied. "Humans are complex creatures, Pike. Far more complex than you currently realize." They passed a sports bar, the TVs all showing breaking news of a tragic mass shooting at a shopping mall in Texas.

"Shit like that is happening more and more," he said. "You're saying it's not their fault? That sounds like more bullshit excuses like people blaming their ridiculous religion, their horrible boss, or the bullies at school. Or maybe they didn't get enough hugs as a child. People have to grow the hell up and be responsible for their actions."

She took his arm and smiled sexily. "That's too simplistic, Professor. It makes a good sound bite on Fox News, but I'm sure you know it's more complicated."

"I have a stab wound in my gut that says otherwise," Pike reminded her. They walked on, nearing the boat docks. "I purposefully keep away from the twenty-four-hour news cycle. People's inhumanity to each other is depressing and exhausting. I prefer something simpler."

13

Back in the cabin, they found Pike's friend, Dewey, sitting on the porch with a fat, brown dog named Ralph. Much like his owner, Ralph acted as if simply raising his head to acknowledge them took all the effort in the world. Dewey was a large man in greasy work clothes. He had sagging cheeks, a protruding stomach, and an indeterminate hairline obscured by a ball cap that bore a logo of an auto parts store.

"You're nearly out of beer," Dewey said, holding up an almost empty bottle and grinning widely. "Who is this, Shep?"

Pike introduced his old friend to Kate who hugged the man despite the filthy overalls. Dewey winked and smiled at Pike as the beautiful woman embraced him.

"Don't make any rude comments, Dewey," Pike said, cutting his friend off even before he could think of the best line to say.

"That's hurtful, cuz."

"We aren't cousins, not really," Pike said as he looked at Kate, who was smiling. "Okay, maybe. The family lines get a little murky around here a generation or two back."

"Totally blood, Shep, you can feel it. Hell, we look like twins," Dewey said pulling Pike in close so Kate could see them together.

The two men could hardly have looked more unalike. While the age was similar, Pike was tall and appeared to be in good shape with a handsome face and dark hair. Dewey was a half-foot shorter, a hundred pounds heavier, and nearly bald. Still, she could see the two were close in other ways. "I thought Pike was a hermit. How did you two become friends?" she asked.

"Court ordered it," Dewey said with a straight face. South Carolina has an 'Adopt an Idiot' program, and he was mine."

Pike was sitting on the steps next to the dog. "Is he always like this?" she asked, indicating Dewey.

Pike nodded, "Always."

"I brought barbecue from Pop's, it's on the table," Dewey said.

"And why are you here?" Pike asked as he headed inside.

"To feed you and to meet your new friend."

Pike saw his friend had brought enough food for all of them. "You knew she was here."

"I knew someone was, after the crazy shit you were saying on the ride from the hospital. I thought I better keep an eye on you. Also, some folks were seen in town asking about you. I didn't like the way it sounded."

Pike patted his friend on the back. "Thanks, man."

The three of them bonded over craft beer and local barbecue.

Kate sat, looking at the mountain of smoked pork, chicken, and sausages.

"Did you buy out the restaurant?" Pike asked, heaping beans and ribs onto a plate.

"I was going to see if we could all go out before you leave again," Dewey said. "But I hear that y'all have a habit of getting shot at when dining out. I figured this was safer."

"Good call," Kate said as she used a fork to tickle loose a morsel of meat. Pike watched his lover in amazement; he had cleaned two ribs before she had even gotten started. Ralph was now enjoying the bones on the soft ground beneath the picnic table.

"Don't give him those, Shep," Dewey protested. "They mess with his stomach, and they're dangerous."

Pike finished another and dutifully handed it down to the dog. "See, this is why he loves me best."

"Yeah, yeah, making him fat and lazy," Dewey countered.

"You said 'before you leave again,'" Kate said between bites. "How do you know we're leaving?"

"I don't know, I just always know when Shep takes on a new job. I've known this guy all my life. I can tell you what he's going to do before he knows."

Pike retorted, "In other words, I didn't come check on the Indian yet, so he knew something was up. I always store it with him when I'm traveling. So, tell me more about these guys, the ones asking about me, what did they want?"

"Dunno. Pete, over at the Marina, said Red Jones mentioned it to him. Pete thought it was odd since a beautiful woman had just been looking for you last week. With all the shit going on, I just thought... well, you should know."

"You were worried about me, Dewey. I'm touched."

"You are indeed. Touched in the head, that is," the man responded with a deep laugh. "Look, you don't have me or Risse to look after your sorry ass no more. You're lucky being out here like this. The shit on the news keeps getting worse and worse. I really have to keep Ralph from watching the 24-hour news channel all day," Dewey stated.

"It may get worse," Kate said. "You need to be cautious."

"Ahh, I think we're fine here. These are good people, some crazies down in Savannah, but I should be fine. Thanks for worrying, though."

"No, Dewey, listen to Kate; she knows what she's talking about. This is not just media sensationalizing the most horrific story of the day. People are literally getting crazy out there," Pike said to his lifelong friend. "You know you can always come out here if needed. You know where I keep the supplies stashed. Just don't drink all my bourbon."

"Yeah, sure man. Y'all really think it's gonna get worse?" He finished the beer and reached for another. "What kind of work did you say this job was?"

"I didn't," Pike answered with finality.

"Yeah, some kind of brain study, right?" Dewey answered himself while opening another bottle of beer. "You're observing Pike to see how creatures without a brain get by," he said to Kate.

The look and wink from Pike's friend were met with a single raised finger. "Not funny, asshole."

"Kinda funny," Kate argued. She and Dewey clinked bottles.

"We do study the brain," Kate continued, trying to keep a straight face. "But we mainly focus on consciousness and how we are all connected."

"You mean like The Force?"

"Not exactly, Dewey. Just let her explain," Pike said, glad to let Kate decide what to reveal.

Twenty minutes later, their friend had a basic understanding of the concept. Kate had not mentioned what malevolent force might be driving more and more people to acts of violence.

"It does sound kinda like The Force," Dewey said. They were all sitting around a firepit now, too full to move. "Actually, it sounds like biocentrism even more."

"Bio what?" Pike asked. His unassuming friend never failed to blow him away with his varied depth of knowledge in all things obscure or conspiratorial.

"It's a bit of Boo-Hag voodoo science...or maybe it's a religion," Dewey said.

Kate laughed and picked up on it immediately. "The concept is based on the observer theory in quantum mechanics. Followers argue that consciousness is the matrix upon which reality exists. Color, sound, temperature, and the like exist only as perceptions in our head, not as absolute essences. In the broadest sense, we cannot be sure of an outside universe at all. The fact that everything in the observable universe is in precise balance for life to evolve supposedly supports this. What do they call it, Pike? Oh yeah, 'The Goldilocks Enigma.' You know, like if the Universe was a little warmer or a little colder, or if the atomic weight of hydrogen was slightly different, life couldn't have ever survived. Like the whole cosmos is just a little too perfect, you know?"

"Whoa, your cute, new friend is deep, Shepard," Dewey said, smiling. "But yeah, that's what I said, biocentrism."

"Yeah," Pike agreed. "Dewey is the only guy I know who gets smarter when he drinks."

Kate went on, "I've read through some of the stuff on the topic as well. It's an interesting approach, but I believe it was valuable more as a counterargument to Newtonian physics once we began investigating the quantum realm. The simple answer is that our Universe is right for life because if it wasn't, we would not be here to question it. This is the only type of universe in which we could have evolved."

"So, what's this about?" Dewey asked, concerned. "Doesn't sound like there's a problem for you to fix."

Kate didn't want to go into detail, so she offered a partial truth, "A set of neural tests to see if we can predict or prevent the elevation of radical behaviors."

"Test? You?" Dewey asked, looking at Pike. "Like the trick you used to do in school to impress the girls?"

"Trick?" Kate asked suspiciously.

"No, Dewey, not like that at all," Pike answered, standing up to get more firewood from his dwindling stack.

"Yeah, that was crazy, used to blow people's minds."

"Show us the trick, Pike," Kate said laughingly. "I mean, I need to know what my future boyfriend's former moves on getting dates was, right?"

"Oh, please," Pike moaned, but Dewey was gleefully gathering what he needed.

"Boyfriend, huh?" Dewey said coming back out of the house with some writing pads.

Several minutes later, Pike was staring straight ahead with Kate holding a dark towel sideways in front of his face. "Hold it tight against his nose," Dewey said. "You don't want him peeking." Dewey then wrote a word on two sheets of paper. He placed one that read 'duck' on the right side of the towel and one that said 'house' on the left side. He then put a piece of paper under each of Pike's hands and a marker in both hands and said, "Okay, Shep, draw what you see."

Pike reluctantly agreed to the parlor trick and began to draw what he saw. Both hands moved independently. One drawing a rather good version of a duck, the other drawing a simple house. Once finished, he sat the markers down. "Happy?"

Kate looked dumbfounded. "How did you do that?"

"What? I just draw what I see," Pike said innocently.

The paper on the right side showed the house and the other the duck. "You drew the opposite image of each eye. Totally different images at the same time, Pike. That's just incredible."

"He's got two brains." Dewey said triumphantly. "They can work independently. He's always seeing shit the rest of us can't. His brain is wired different from everyone else."

Pike rubbed at one of the scars self-consciously. He wasn't ready to discuss that part of his past yet with this woman; maybe never.

14

Pike wanted to order another drink but decided it was smarter to stay focused. He and Kate sat in the airport lounge in Charleston waiting on one of the few overseas flights of the day. "I think I have a grasp on what your science involves, but I'm still missing why you need me." He glanced up at the news feed where Kate's attention was focused. She had convinced him to at least come check it out. He still had more questions than answers but was willing to see where this led, especially since her organization was footing the bill and his hefty consulting fee.

"Do you see that, Pike?" She pointed to each of the flat screens mounted around the seating area. Most showed news or sports, but all the news channels were covering one horrific scene after another. He took notice but not interest.

"Like I said, people love trying to do harm to one another. Nothing new, is there?"

She turned to study him. "You really don't pay any attention to the modern world, do you?"

"Should I?" He gave up and held his glass up for another bourbon. "It just gets worse, every year, more hatred, more radicalization, more divisive rhetoric. Someone like me who relies on facts doesn't stand a chance of comprehending it all."

"It's getting worse, Pike, a lot worse. The violence, hate speech, international tensions haven't been this high in half a decade," Kate stated.

He nodded, "It's madness."

"That's exactly what it is, and that is why all this," she gestured to the broadcasts again. "All of this is related to why we need you."

"You need me to solve world peace?" Pike said with a grin. "Good luck, my own family didn't even like me."

She smiled and seemed to relax slightly. "In neuroscience, the more you study it, the more you learn, and the less you realize you know. Every breakthrough just opens up new questions. What is consciousness? What is intuition? What is the soul, what is the creative spirit? All these things point us in a certain direction, without actually letting us see much farther down the road. Infuriatingly complex and frustratingly simple at the same time. I developed a theory over the last few years that the default state of all humans is madness."

"Okay," Pike said cautiously. "Why is that?"

"Mostly through observation and anecdotal evidence," Kate admitted. "Consider the various phases of mental illness suffered by millions. The alarming increases in drug addiction to numb the pain of life. The countless junior league, soccer moms hooked on anti-depressants. You, yourself, crawling into a bottle of bourbon to numb your loss."

Pike looked like he'd been slapped, but she continued on, unabated. "Consider the claims of possessions, witchcraft, specters, and ghosts, even alien abductions. Then think of how many of our elderly must suffer through the withering away of a lifetime of memories and reduced mental capacity from dementia."

"Okay, that still makes no sense," he said, after considering it for several seconds.

"It really does," Kate continued. "If you think about it...if you remove all the social norms. There is an underlying aggression, an apex predator mindset. It's kill or be killed, eat or be eaten. Our thoughts aren't random; we are purpose-driven animals. In the last 10,000 years, we've learned how to domesticate animals and to farm crops. Life then got easier for us, and that in turn denied us our genetic mandate and helped drive us toward madness. Many of our base instincts, the need to hunt and kill and feed, has had nowhere else to go. So, we impose rules on ourselves, and we call it societal norms, moral code, laws, or constitutions. We had to legislate ourselves into behaving rationally. But that really is not who we are. We are strongly influenced by our basic instincts, which are not that far removed from primitive man.

"Take that one step further since our cognitive processes are somehow entangled to other intelligent beings. The effects are vastly different, confusing, and contradictory. Even in my own studies, I've proven, at least to myself, that some factors outside our own brain control many things. Dementia, paranoia, schizophrenia, autism, addiction. So many aspects may just be affected or even caused by bleed-over influence from that connected neural network of consciousness. This may be a disruption in that connected universe or maybe our inability to cope with it all.

"Think about this. Some of the greatest creative breakthroughs, our most brilliant artists, designers, tech giants, even Steve Jobs, claimed they did some of their best thinking while they were high on drugs. Take a hit of LSD and you're off into a psychedelic dream state. Why would that unlock an idea that would have never occurred to you otherwise?"

"Wait," Pike said, the edge of disbelief clear in his voice. "So, you're telling me that this stuff on TV is due to some mental interplay between us and the entanglement state of our brains' neural connections?"

Kate smiled. "Of course, I am, Pike. Think about it, our consciousness, at some level, is intertwined cosmically. These molecules, these particles, they're entangled with their opposites on the other side of the cosmic wall. Maybe it's with multiple versions of ourselves. While the way we do it back at the lab is artificial by means of manipulating the frequencies, certainly, some of that transference can happen naturally. Those entangled particles in our subconscious mind are there and were active long before we started looking at them. Just consider this. What if all the phantasms and ghosts, specters, vampires, and witches, what if all of those seemingly impossible coincidences are just distant echoes from our other selves coming in?"

Pike gratefully accepted the fresh drink from the server and leaned back into the overstuffed chair. After a deep draw, he licked his lips and tried to best organize his response. "I may be willing to accept your diagnosis of madness being a baseline state for human existence. We are an evolved predatory species with certain unattractive instincts hard-wired into our genome. While I am not completely sure that translates into 'madness' in the context of polite society, I'll accept it as a strong contender.

"Your hypothesis on the quantum connection, though, seems to suggest two things. One is that our brains are not somehow connected to 'The Force' or all living things, but rather to specific individuals. Further, it seems you're suggesting that the individuals at the other end of our connection might be different versions of us. That would suggest interdimensional aspects or alternate timelines. Is that what you're trying to convince me of?"

Kate's expression told him it was.

"Pike, it will just be better if we can show you. All I'm asking is to just keep an open mind, okay?"

She reached over and clasped his hand in hers. "I know I'm asking you to accept a lot on faith right now, but it's important, and yes, we desperately need your help."

Pike wanted to ask more questions, but a loud clap sounded from the concourse outside, then a soft alarm trilled. "What's going on?" Pike asked the bartender standing nearby. The man just looked perplexed. "Security breach," he heard a man say who was dressed in uniform from one of the many airlines.

A public address announcement instructed everyone that heightened security protocols were now in effect and to move into one of the designated safe areas marked by a green triangle and remain there until further notice. A second announcement let them know the airport had instituted a full ground stop on arrivals and departures. Pike gave a worried look toward Kate, but she was on her phone standing over at one of the large windows that overlooked the runways. He got the attention of the bartender again, who was frantically closing out his register and pulling the high-dollar bottles off a top shelf. "Where is the nearest green zone?"

The man pointed down, "You're in one."

New faces appeared through the doors leading to the concourse, and TSA officers manned both sides of the entrance. Pike began to relax, then felt Kate's hand on his elbow guiding him toward a far wall. "What's going on?" he asked her.

She didn't speak, but her sense of urgency was definitely elevated. He noticed she was wearing the ear bud again. They moved quickly through a dimly lit, curving corridor. They passed the restrooms and a manager's office before Kate pushed through a swinging stainless steel door into the food prep area. "Side door, far side, move!"

Pike wanted to protest but heard shouts back behind him. Not shouts of authority to stop but screams of a terror filled crowd. He pulled the door revealing a set of stairs. This would be the employee entrance, he realized. The distinctive sound of gunfire cut through the din of panicked people. They took the stairs two at a time reaching the ground level seconds later. "Now what?" he shouted.

"Outside," Kate said, motioning ahead. "Onto the tarmac, then stay close to the building and follow me." Pike was relatively familiar with the CHS airport and knew the exterior doors were all secure. Only authorized personnel got through. They found an exit door about fifty yards down. It had no handle, only a keypad and badge reader. Kate held her phone out to the badge reader, and a soft click sounded from the latch.

They hugged the outer wall, Pike certain he was violating numerous federal laws. "Why are we doing this?" he whispered loudly. "Surely security has the person in custody by now." He was afraid one of the trigger-happy agents might assume they were a threat.

"The gunman is not our concern." Kate placed the phone back to her other ear and listened intently to a separate conversation.

They rounded a corner and saw two men with automatic weapons running in their direction. The men were in blue coveralls and clearly not part of the airport's security personnel. Pike pushed Kate back behind the corner, hoping the men hadn't seen them.

He held up two fingers to Kate, who nodded but was still talking quietly on her phone. The noise of jet engines idling down finally allowed him to hear other sounds. Shouted orders behind them, someone on a radio asking questions. He estimated the men would be at the corner in seconds. He looked around the area for anything he could use. What would work against a sub-compact automatic, though? Then, before he could consider it longer, a lone man cleared the corner and pulled up short, watching a truck approaching from the opposite direction. Pike didn't know what had happened to the other terrorist, but without hesitation, he crouched low, then rushed the man, knocking both to the ground. The weapon skidded out of the guy's hands but was stopped after only a few inches by a strap still wrapped over the man's arm.

Pike's Marine Corps training kicked in. Instead of raising to his feet like the other man was doing, he launched his body on top of the attacker. He kept expecting a round from the man's partner to end the battle at any second, but none came, and Pike's total focus and fury took over. The guy he was fighting was good and moved like a snake. Every time Pike thought he had the man subdued, he leveraged himself, loosening the grip. Pike could feel the man's strength and youth, judging him to be a decade younger and probably forty pounds heavier. He groaned as he felt one of his recent stitches pop, followed by several more. Like opening a zipper to his insides, warm blood began to ooze through his clothes and hot pain flared every time he moved. He knew his opponent sensed his strength receding as he continued to fight for leverage.

"Pike, we have to go," he heard Kate shouting now.

Go? How in the hell am I going to manage that? He was barely hanging on to this beast. He felt more than heard a vehicle pull up beside them and then noticed the wheels of an airport service truck. Booted feet stepped out and one kicked out straight at the other man's head snapping it sideways and potentially ending his fighting career, and everything else. Pike unwound himself from the now limp body and braced himself for the inevitable, but instead saw an outstretched hand reaching down.

"Gotta go, Shepard, move your ass."

Kate was already heading for the opposite side of the truck, and he climbed in weakly behind her. He used a sleeve to staunch a nasty wound above his left eye. He vaguely remembered the man slamming an elbow into his face. His head was woozy, and he was unsure it was from the fight, blood loss, or sheer panic. He felt the truck lurch away from the scene and accelerate hard. They were heading to a series of large hangars ringed by a high fence and topped with multiple runs of razor wire. They passed a security checkpoint with a man in Army green camo. This was the military side of the airport, he realized.

"There's your ride ma'am," the driver said as he pulled up to a gleaming white jet.

Full ground stop apparently didn't apply to the government, Pike thought.

"Change of plans, Pike. We'll have to buy what you need at our next stop. No telling where our luggage will show up." Kate hopped out of the truck and ascended the air stairs as if this was just an everyday occurrence. "Who the hell are you?" Pike asked her weakly as he struggled to follow.

15

Emma was eleven, precocious, and not the least bit embarrassed by her new braces. The misalignment was slight, but the orthodontist recommended they go ahead and address it now. "Whoa there, kiddo."

"What, Dad?"

Pike smiled, wondering where his daughter got this much attitude from. As she looked at him, the scowl faded, replaced by a smile as she threw her arms around him. "Love you, Pops!"

"Love you too, Em."

She held the new iPhone up, taking a selfie of both of them. "I thought Mom said I couldn't have one."

He nodded. "She did."

"Won't she be mad?" Emma asked.

"Only at me, love. Only at me," he answered in a tone of resignation. "Besides, I'm going to be away a lot, and I need a way to get advice from my top social media guru."

She snorted a laugh as she covered her face to mute the giggling. "Yeah, Dad, you are all about growing those followers, aren't you?"

Pike pulled her up close, "Not so much, girl, only one person I want to stay popular with."

She hugged him again, then broke for the door yelling she was going to show her friend and would be back in an hour. Pike sat on the arm of the sofa watching through the window as his daughter cut through the neighbor's yard making her way toward her friend's house one street back.

His heart felt like it was about to come apart in his chest. Why couldn't she have stayed this age? Why couldn't he have protected her? The pain struck again but this time lower in his chest, then a mechanical clack followed by an even sharper pain.

"Oh, God!" His eyes opened to see Kate standing there with an evil-looking contraption in her hand. The feel of the jet engines brought him back to the here and now. "What is that?"

"Trauma stapler, you popped some stitches back there."

"You stapled my incision?"

She nodded. "Yeah, you were leaking, Pike. I'm a doctor, but this is about the extent of my first-aid skills."

He ran a hand up his abdomen until he felt the wound and three metal clasps holding it closed. "Thanks," he managed to say despite the feelings of pain mixed with confusion. Pike remembered the loss from the dream he'd been having as well as the absurdity back at the airport. "Kate, what is going on?"

She dropped two pills in his mouth and made him swallow them with a gulp from a bottle of water. "We're being targeted, Pike. Get some rest, and we can talk when you wake up."

"What did you give me?" He felt his eyelids growing heavy. "Did you drug me?"

Her face broke into a sideways grin. "You've been through hell. Trauma kit on this jet is light on a lot of things, but they have some world class pain meds. Get some sleep. I'll make sure you're awake before we land."

* * *

The jet bounced as it passed through an area of turbulence. "Pike, do you hear me?"

He'd been in a deep, coma-like sleep and now was struggling to swim his conscious brain back to the light. He again felt the movement beneath him and recalled where he was. His rational brain began calculating how long he'd been out and where they might be even before his eyes fluttered open. Kate was in the seat beside him, her hand firmly clutching his own.

His eyes roamed around the luxurious cabin; the craft was a larger corporate jet. The two of them appeared to be the only passengers. He knew range on most of these was around 3000 miles, insufficient for most international trips. "Where are we?"

"Nearing the coast of Portugal. We'll land in Lisbon soon." She noted his confusion. "This is a modified Dassault Falcon 8X. It has advanced navigation and extended range. We'll refuel and be swapping EAS flight crews, also time for a quick shopping trip to replace our wardrobe if you're up for it."

Pike nodded as he began flexing his arms and legs. He could feel the wound, but the hurt was not the deep penetrating kind that the original puncture had been. "EAS means government, right?" He thought he recalled them entering a secure area at the airport, but so much of his head seemed like confetti right now, he wasn't sure.

"Essential Air Services. Yes, it's an FAA designation, usually reserved for military or official government or humanitarian needs. Before you ask, no, I didn't lie to you. We are not some governmental research project. They're aware of us, though, and our role in what's happening."

Pike eased up in the reclining leather seat to a full sitting position. Her words echoed around in his head for a long minute. "Why the change from London to here?"

"The NSA feels like the ground team in London may be compromised. They were waiting for us it seems."

"Kate, who are they?"

"Fifteen minutes to touchdown," one pilot called over a nearly hidden speaker overhead.

Kate looked up and tapped at the overhead console. The speaker began emitting a soft hiss of noise. "There is more I didn't tell you, Pike." She saw his face and added, "Obviously."

"You mean all of this is not just because you found a connection between our conscious minds and quantum entanglement? I'm shocked," he quipped.

"I deserve that. Now, if you will shut up, I'll tell you as much as I can before we land." She released his hand and waited for him to agree before continuing. "How clear is your head on our discussion of quantum entanglement?"

"My head is fine, Kate. Just tell me more about the 'project' and who's after us."

"Okay." She looked absently out at the window where the pilots were descending through a cloud layer. The bright mid-day sunshine dimmed as the ride became noticeably rougher.

"You said by stimulating the brain you could observe the opposite end of the entangled quantum state," Pike said, prompting her toward full disclosure. "The way you said it made me think you discovered something else when you did that. Is that it?"

Kate smiled at how quickly he picked up on even the subtlest of clues. "What do you know of quantum tunneling, Professor?"

He had to think back. The concept was relatively recent, not even a mentioned theory when he was studying quantum mechanics. "It's when a quantum particle, or wave to be more accurate, can penetrate through what should be an impenetrable barrier."

"Yes, that's a simple but also very complete description. The why and the how have eluded us as have many other aspects of the rather bizarre quantum world. What we assumed when we uncovered how quantum entanglement worked within our own subconscious was, if we could see the other end, we would find a mirror image of ourselves, or at least our consciousness."

"I take it that didn't happen?"

Kate offered a rueful smile. "As much of our work has been, it did, and it didn't. I'm sure you're familiar with four fundamental forces in the universe: electromagnetic, strong and weak nuclear forces, and gravity. Have you ever heard the concept of why gravity is so weak in comparison to the others?"

"Doesn't seem weak," Pike said. "It's holding us firmly to the ground." He looked around and laughed. "Okay, bad analogy. It does keep the Earth in orbit around the sun, and what about super-massive black holes, they have crazy amounts of gravity. Not even light can escape."

She smiled like a teacher about to correct her pupil for missing something obvious. "You're describing large masses, huge celestial bodies. Can you imagine a magnet the size of the Earth or the sun? How strong would that be? Consider this: gravity has immense potential energy but only collectively. A gram of mass produces virtually no gravitational attraction. The gravity in a mass the size of our planet can still be easily overcome by a toddler lifting her foot off the ground or a baseball being hurled into the sky or a jet engine like this. That's with the entire planet's gravitational force pulling it down."

"I guess I see what you mean," Pike offered. "It's massive on massive scales but not so much on the lower end."

"Exactly, Pike," Kate said. "And one theory that has been kicked around for decades is that perhaps gravity is just as strong as the other fundamental forces in the universe but most of it isn't really in our dimension. What we think of as gravity is just an artifact, perhaps 'leakage' from another dimension or maybe even many other dimensions." The man's expression let her know she was losing him. He'd studied quantum physics, but some of it just didn't square with his engineering mindset.

She continued, "Let me put it in more simple terms. What if gravity only seems weak? What if, unlike electromagnetism and the nuclear forces, gravity is not confined to our everyday world of three spatial dimensions and the additional time dimension? If gravity is acting in two or three or several other dimensions and the familiar four, we may experience only part of its effects. Mathematics has no trouble describing multidimensional spaces, but our all too human brains aren't built to visualize more than three spatial dimensions."

Pike knew the math, and of course, she was right. "Kate, I can accept that as a possibility. Don't understand it...but I accept it. How does that fit with quantum tunneling?"

"If you accept there are more dimensions than we are aware of, then you need to also know that theoretically, nothing could bridge from one dimension to another."

Pike nodded, "I read a few books by the physicist Brian Green. Brilliant guy, he's suggesting that dimensions might even overlap our own, but there was likely not enough energy in a galaxy to ever open a tiny portal from one to another."

"That's true, but tunneling is not a process that has any equal in classical physics, so we don't have good models of how it works, only that it does. In studying photons, physicists found that they could even travel faster than light to pass through a barrier. Something they call superluminal speed."

Despite the pain, Pike was fully engrossed in her words. "So, quantum tunneling defies the laws of physics to work."

"Our laws yes, but maybe not everywhere," Kate answered. "Physical laws do not have to be the same from one dimension of reality to another. Gravity may indeed be stronger or weaker. Elements do not necessarily behave the same. The very laws of physics will be up to interpretation inside an alternate universe. I'm also using the terms 'alternate universe,' 'alternate reality,' and 'other dimensions' interchangeably, but that, too, is not quite accurate. It makes the explanations simpler, though."

She went on, "What we found on the other end of our inter-dimensional quantum tether was not a single entangled state of consciousness, but many. Each only observable one at a time but each just as real and just as entangled as the other. Parts of each of us are connected to each other in many, many worlds."

He leaned back in his seat, feeling a small measure of comfort in the luxuriously appointed interior. "So, through your apparatuses, you can observe these other dimensions, these other worlds?"

Kate leaned back and fastened her seat belt at the obvious sound of landing gear being lowered. "More than that, we can go there."

16

The jet touched down at Portela Airport as Pike was struggling to catch up mentally, an experience that he was unaccustomed to. Not that he was smarter than others, his mind just had abilities that even he barely understood. Still, all of this was overwhelming him. "Kate, I have to ask again, why me? What on Earth made you come to that backwater hole in the mud and pick me to get involved in all this?"

"I told you before, you're special," she said with sincere affection.

"I'm not...I am damaged goods, if we're being truthful." He gingerly made his way to the airstairs as a uniformed man stepped aboard to greet them. They were ushered down to a waiting car with a driver who looked as out of place and American as they did. "Your government connections seem keen to help," Pike whispered, not sure if the driver was read in on whatever the hell they were mixed up in.

"Name's Winfield," the young black man said. "Glad you people got out of there when you did. Sounds like things are deteriorating fast."

"Thanks," Pike said, detecting a distinctive tone to the driver's speech. "You from the South?"

"I am, sir. Mississippi."

"What part?" Kate asked, surprised by the government man's openness.

"Little town called Geneva," Winfield said. "Nobody's ever heard of it, but it was nice. Long ways from here, though."

"Were you briefed?" Kate asked.

The driver's head moved slightly up and down. "I was told to take you to the medical center for treatment, then wherever you wanted to go. Just need to have you back to the airfield by three."

The exam was less of a concern than the fact they cut away the only shirt Pike owned. It was bloodstained, dirt-streaked, and ripped, but it was his. The medic snipped it away in apparent disgust. Unlike Winfield, the medic was a local, probably under contract to the state department. She applied a local anesthetic through a large hypodermic, then began removing the staple sutures with a pair of pliers that could have come out of his toolbox back home. Despite the gruesome-looking scene, Pike only felt the tugging and pressure as he watched, fascinated by the process. His curiosity waned, however, when she later began cutting away dead tissue around the wound before sterilizing and stitching him back together again.

"Itza gowanna hurt," the medic said in broken English before handing him a bottle of pills. "You be fine, tho."

As she exited the room, Winfield stepped in carrying a duffle bag which he propped against the exam table. "Thought you might need a change of attire." He looked from Pike over to the bloody garments on the floor before nodding. "Yep."

"Thank you," Pike said, pulling out a pair of tactical cargo pants and a new t-shirt from the olive- green bag. "Got my sizes, too. Outstanding."

"The government knows everything about you, sir. Just glad to help."

Pike pulled the t-shirt on, wincing in pain. "Wait, what?"

"Just kidding, sir. She told me." Winfield pointed to Kate, who was pulling clean boxers from the bag. "I'll be just outside waiting for you."

* * *

Winfield dropped the two of them in the shopping district of Chiado, where Kate directed Pike to several shops with appropriate clothing and gear for the journey ahead. He knew that The Project, Kate had called it Cobalt, was on an isolated island in the Indian Ocean but nothing more than that. All he knew of that area was that travel was risky due to pirates.

They stopped at a bistro for a late lunch of red prawns and the Portuguese version of tapas. "For two people on the run, life isn't so bad right now," Pike said, smiling as he sipped his wine. Kate nodded, but it was obvious to him that her mind was elsewhere. He still had no idea who was after them, or why, but was willing to trust she knew what she was doing. "What are you thinking?"

"Just overthinking things," Kate said a little too casually. Her fingers snagged several of the marinated olives from a dish and popped them into her mouth. "Honestly, I asked Winfield to check out a few things for me. I'm not sure how Carapaz's men knew about our flight, and never before have they been that obvious. Something has changed."

"Carapaz?" Pike asked, putting a name at least on the otherwise faceless enemy.

She shook her head. "Can't discuss him right now. Once we're on site, we can fully brief you."

Pike reluctantly accepted her decision. "What about the feds? You ready to tell me how they're involved?"

Kate took her smartphone, thumbed a few screens, then passed it over to him. Pike saw there were numerous articles and videos in her newsfeed. As he scrolled down, he noticed they were all horrific, mass shootings, border skirmishes, domestic violence, suicides, road rage. The incident at the Charleston airport barely rated a mention in the prior twenty-four-hour news cycle. He had never listened much to the news and ignored most current events, as it served no real purpose in his life. While others seemed obsessed with the latest trending stories and minutiae of celebrity gossip, he was more concerned with the tide charts and when the shrimp were running in the sound. People in the Lowcountry were an odd mix of modern and ancient with seemingly no middle ground. He was as up to date on modern technology as almost anyone, yet personally owned virtually none of it, nor did he miss it. “The government’s involved in all of this…this…” He couldn’t find an appropriate word.

“Madness?” she offered.

“Yes, exactly, madness.”

“They’re aware of it and that it is systemic, not isolated, and they believe it tracks back to our work at The Project.”

“How could all of this be connected? I mean, other than the ones specifically targeting you and I?” Pike nervously looked up and down the avenue before adding. “How does the government know you are connected?” He wanted to hear it from her but felt pretty sure he already knew the answer. Kate ran a delicate finger around the rim of her glass before touching it to her lips. The gesture seemed both natural and seductive to Pike.

“That was a mistake, at least I considered it one until today,” she said. “We purposefully placed our labs and research out of reach of all our governments. As I’m sure you can imagine, the potential for abuse with monkeying around with people’s brains might be too tempting for them not to play with.”

“But…” he prompted.

“We made a minor breakthrough early on, something in the field of false memory syndrome. It happened to be a field that the government was highly interested in, and well, someone on our team leaked our findings. Suddenly, we found our normal funding sources drying up until we were down to just one, and then…”

“Uncle Sam came calling with an open checkbook, right?” Pike offered.

Kate nodded. “Pretty much.”

“By false memory syndrome, you’re talking about the Mandela Effect. Why would that have been of interest?” He’d read an article on the role of false memories in which groups of people firmly believed a version of the past that was inaccurate, like those who recall Nelson Mandela dying in a South African prison.

Kate bit through one of the large shrimps and savored the spicy flavor before answering. "I had studied the effect briefly, just as part of a neurological disorder. It's surprising how many people can share very specific, yet totally false, recollections of the same event. Like remembering the Challenger space shuttle disaster as being in a different year or thinking of the popular children's books being called *The Berenstein Bears.*"

"Wait," Pike said. "That's the name. I remember reading those to Emma when she was a baby."

She laughed and shook her head. "They are '*The Berenstain Bears.*' It's a minor example but surprisingly widespread. Our team amassed hundreds of examples. I have no idea why the U.S. government was so keen to know more. Maybe they wanted to see how they could better use propaganda or fake news to cover up something. But when we studied it from a more scientific standpoint, we found another likely cause."

Pike found he was leaning in to hear the answer. His curiosity at discovering new truths was the driving motivation in his life. "What's that?" he asked.

Kate explained, "Alternate realities bleed over from dimensions in which those other memories happened exactly the way they remember. I'm sure you're familiar with the many worlds theory."

He was. Many worlds theory held that every possible outcome has a version of reality out there. If you flipped a coin that landed on heads, another reality split off where it landed on tails and yet another where you lost the coin into the gutter and so on. "So, in some version of reality, Nelson Mandela did die in prison, and the shuttle exploded in 1983 instead of '86, and so on," Pike offered.

"Yes, in theory," Kate said. "The truth seems to be more complicated. We don't believe that many worlds or infinite worlds is generally the case. Not because they don't exist, they do. Or, more accurately, could. We just keep running into case after case where the conservation of energy is one of the premier constants in the Universe...or multiverse in this case. To create a new version of the Universe every time something happened seems overly wasteful and redundant. Our best guess is the multiverse, or divine power, or JK Rawling, or whoever is in charge, has some biases. While some events might trigger a timeline split, our best theories predict cosmic pressure to reintegrate the timelines will occur as soon afterward as possible."

Pike tried to make sense of that. "So, reintegration is the cause of false memory syndrome. One memory is dominant, and another subjugated and ruled as false."

"Maybe, although that memory will be just as real to those individuals as the other is to the masses. For instance, I distinctly remember a little girl who lived two doors down from us growing up. I can't remember her name, but she had blonde hair and green eyes, and it seemed like we played together every day when I was probably four or five. When I asked my mom about her years later, she said no one like that had ever lived near us. She dismissed it as being a friend I played with in daycare, and maybe that's true, but I remember being at her house and also having her come play with the toys at my house. We climbed the tree in her backyard sometimes. I've been back to that town as an adult. I went to that house, and I saw that tree. The couple who lived there have no children and say they lived in the house as long as I've been alive."

"So, we can't trust our own memories," Pike said, more as a statement than a question.

Kate replied, "Our memories are more malleable that we would like to admit."

17

Pike and Kate flew from Portugal to Doha, Qatar, where Winfield had arranged rooms for them to stay the night. In the morning, Kate had scheduled another plane to get them to her island. Pike had been to Qatar once before and marveled at how the ultra-modern mixed with the ancient in apparent harmony. Both of them were exhausted, so they ate a late dinner in the hotel's restaurant and, after a few drinks, headed off to separate rooms.

Pike lay on the bed, unable to shut his mind off. The increasing levels of 'madness,' the false memories, and interconnected consciousness. What did it all mean? And on a purely personal note, who in the hell was trying to kill them? This woman had swept in and taken over his life with effortless ease, and now he was following her like a lovesick puppy. He rolled over determined to get some sleep, but his body's internal clock was still set eight hours behind. After a half hour, he gave up and turned the TV on to an English-speaking news channel. Like on Kate's phone, the images of killing and mayhem were definitely on the rise, not just in the U.S. either. It shocked him to see footage of masked gunmen storming into a large room where they sprayed bullets into many people before being shot. The ticker said, 'Attack at the State Capital in Albany, New York.'

He heard a soft knock, followed by Kate's voice. "Are you up?" The answer to that question had several potential meanings, and he was not totally sure which was appropriate. He opened the door and simply nodded. She was not dressed for bed, he saw. "Come on in," he offered. "Or we can go out?"

Kate glanced at the TV screen and tilted her head toward the elevators. "Let's go out." Then, seeing he was standing there in his government issued boxers, she seemed to have second thoughts. She pulled him close and kissed him. It was the first real sign of affection they had shared all day. He had about decided the lovemaking of the prior week had been just to fill a physical need she'd had. Not that he was complaining, but it had saddened him. He felt something more with her, and when they were together, he assumed she did, too. They broke the kiss, and she pushed him back. "You may want to put on clothes and shoes. We can resume this when we get back."

Fifteen minutes later they were walking along the pristine La Corniche along the edge of Doha Bay. "It's getting worse, isn't it?" Pike asked. They walked on. Kate was studying the brilliant stars overhead in no apparent rush to answer. "The madness," he added, as if the question needed more explanation.

"We're under attack...and yes, it will continue to grow until it encompasses the entire globe," Kate said somberly.

"And this Carapaz, when are you going to tell me about him?"

She looped her arm in his and pointed to the distant lights. "What's over there?"

She was obviously avoiding the subject, but Pike let it go. She'd already told him this was her first time in Doha. Pike put up a hand and waved a cab over. "That is 'The Pearl,' and you haven't been to Doha until you go there." Ten minutes later, she stared in slack jawed amazement at the scene.

The Pearl is an artificial island of luxury townhome, skyscrapers and high-end stores surrounding an inner lagoon filled with the world's most luxurious yachts. Rolls Royce and Ferrari dealerships battle for attention as well as ritzy restaurants, boutiques, and hotels. "It was built layer by layer atop an old pearl diving spot," Pike said as they looked at the enormous open clamshell and pearl welcoming them into the enclave of indulgent living.

"It's spectacular," Kate said in breathless anticipation.

"Yes," Pike agreed. "A bit Monte Carlo mixed with Aladdin's Castle if Disney had been in charge of designing it." Everything here was over the top. "Helps to be the richest country in the Middle East. Qatar has the highest per capita GDP in all the world."

"But it's such a tiny country."

"True, it's not even quite the size of Connecticut. They have oil and gas reserves, though, and have been shrewd merchants since ancient times. They've taken an obscure, probably rather unpleasant, piece of dirt and turned it into an empire and tourist mecca for the jet set. Money and drive can do a lot."

Kate pulled him toward a table outside a café overlooking the protected harbor. Underwater lights illuminated the water in a radiating pattern around the circular lagoon. The server brought them their drinks and some khanfaroosh, a fried sweet bread. "Julian Carapaz was my partner. The co-director of Cobalt."

That was not what he had expected to hear.

"His technical genius is unequaled, Pike. The only reason the world has not heard of him is that's the way he wants it. When I began assembling the team, an old mentor recommended him to me, and I quickly discovered that no one was his equal for sheer brilliance and intuitive leaps. We think he has learned how to achieve near total recall via a type of eidetic memory. Every time he returned, his mind seemed to overflow from vast depths of new knowledge. Little did we know all that wisdom was also poisoning him against us...not until it was too late. Now it may be too late for all of humanity."

"When he returned?" Pike asked.

She downed her drink and signaled for another. She leaned over the rail to see a group of large fish swimming far below on the sandy bottom. "You need the full briefing, Pike. We...it's called SideSlipping. We're able to connect to the opposite end of the quantum tunnel. We get to see what's on the other side of the rabbit hole."

"You going to unpack that one for me, Kate?"

She obviously would rather not, but now that it was out there, she knew Pike wouldn't rest without knowing more. "Moving matter between dimensions is not possible, not theoretically, and as far as we can tell, not physically. Moving information is another matter, and our consciousness, for lack of a better word, is simply information. Besides, it is already entangled with the opposite on the other end. SideSlipping is a technique where we artificially excite the microtubules, the filaments really, and this way we're essentially able to sideload our consciousness into the minds of the inhabitants in the other dimensions."

Pike leaned back, speechless. He motioned for the server again, then rested his head on his hands. "Holy Mother of God." The waiter returned with two clean shot-glasses and a bottle of Blanton's special reserve bourbon. Pike cracked the seal and poured several fingers full in each. He downed his and refilled it. Kate just watched with a bemused look.

"Wish you had taken the red pill?" she asked as she picked up her glass and took a tentative sip.

He downed the second tumbler and nodded. "I have a feeling blissful ignorance would have been the much smarter choice." There was something deeply unsettling about the very act of inhabiting someone else's mind. His logical mind couldn't immediately dismiss the possibility, but this tech was light years beyond anything he'd heard of.

Half a bottle later, Pike was even more confused. They were walking along a nearly deserted section of beach facing the Indian Ocean, the high-rises backlit against the dark sky by the vibrant shopping district behind them. Kate was in a revealing summer dress, and even in the darkness, Pike couldn't ignore the curves of her body and her beautiful smile.

Kate leaned into him, and their lips met. She looked up and down the beach, then pushed him down and pulled off her panties. Straddling Pike's outstretched legs, her lips found his again as she fumbled with his belt. "Let's not waste our time in Paradise, okay?"

18

They had awoken at four a.m. in each other's arms. Pike went to fetch his still packed duffle from the least used hotel room of his life. Dressing quickly, they caught the earliest commercial flight Qatar Air had. "Your lab is in the Maldives?" Pike asked, flopping into the seat beside her.

She smiled and leaned back. "Never said that." Her hand reached over to his, she smiled, and went promptly back to sleep before they had even left the ground.

Pike had never been able to sleep on planes. Part of him loved the experience of flying too much. Other than his recent unconscious transatlantic flight, he never did more than quick catnaps, no matter the distance. He looked at Kate lying there, red hair splayed out across the leather seatback. *God, she is beautiful.* There was more, though. The lovemaking last night had stretched from the beach back to the hotel and long after they went to bed. She knew his body in ways no one else ever had. Pike seemed equally adept at pleasuring her, although he hesitated to even begin to accept that as a fact. He loved this woman, that's right, loved her. He knew that beyond doubt. A woman he had known for less than a week.

Maybe that had been her plan, the rational part of his

mind offered. *Gain your trust, cause you to fall head over heels for her. Then get you to do her bidding.* It was a fair point and could not be immediately dismissed. But then again, it was her logic that had won his cooperation—or was it? *She feels the same way about you, dummy*, the more emotive part of his brain seemed to say. He reached his hand back and felt the scar, one of two both hidden beneath his thick brown hair.

He gazed out the window to the deep blue of the Indian Ocean far below. "Transit time to Malé is just over four hours," he heard the flight attendant telling the passenger behind him. He had been to Maldives once with Emma and his late wife. They had celebrated Christmas there when Emma was nine, or maybe ten. He remembered it as a tropical paradise. While Emily had stayed up by the pool, he and his daughter spent hours diving into the crystal waters and chasing the colorful fish. She called one little school her 'island Christmas tree' as they seemed always to be nearby. Pike struggled to put the memory of her tiny face together in his mind. It had been so many years now. He could see her in her little, yellow swimsuit, but the face was indistinct. Most of his memories of her were that way now.

Tears stung his eyes as he blinked away the pain. He turned again to watch Kate sleeping beside him, her hand still holding his. Here was a new life, a new adventure...maybe even a new love. Did allowing himself to be happy somehow diminish the loss of his child? The honest truth was, Emily had already grown weary of him even before Emma was born. While she lived, though, both parents doted on her and ignored their spouse's inadequacies. Emma thought they were the perfect couple, and that illusion alone had been enough to weld them together into a unified existence. Then Em was gone, and the ugly truth came storming in like a monster held at bay until it could bear no more. The marriage crumbled and died beside the grave of their lost child.

This was a darkness Pike never shared with anyone. Emma had been the brilliant light in the Shepard family. He died every night all over again when he'd passed her empty room. He took jobs that pulled him away more and more just so he wouldn't have to go back and face the emptiness. He knew grief was what killed his marriage and his ex-wife, cancer had only been its weapon of choice. Drinking, solitude, and bitterness had been his. Moving from the city out to the cabin had been his final attempt to escape the pain. When that didn't work, there might only have been one more thing he could have done.

* * *

Pike woke up with a start as the wheels touched down and the cabin gave a sudden lurch.

"Hey, you," Kate said cheerily.

He rubbed his eyes. "I slept," he said in surprise.

"Oh, yeah. Apparently, your stamina isn't ready for that much passion followed by so little sleep."

He grinned and went to rise to join the others already waiting to deplane. Her hand pulled him back down. "Wait."

They sat and waited until all the passengers had departed. "What are we doing?" he asked, looking out at the bright, blue water beyond the high fences.

"This isn't our stop," she said.

"It's a flight from Doha to Maldives and back. We aren't going back, are we?"

She shook her head and checked her watch before glancing out the window and giving a small nod. Looking over her shoulder he saw their luggage was being removed from the cart and left under the plane's wing. "Ok, let's go."

They rushed down the stairs, grabbed the bags, and he followed her as she made a beeline for a small commuter jet parked away from the terminal. In minutes, the young pilot was completing his checks, and they were seated in a small, but comfortable, cabin. Pike was utterly confused. "Why the subterfuge? You think someone was watching for us here?"

Kate offered a small shrug. "Possibly, but not really subterfuge. This is our jet. It will take us to the island. I just didn't want to spend any more time than necessary out in the open."

The olive-skinned pilot turned around and said, "We are cleared behind the KLM heavy up ahead. Transit time should be about ninety minutes to base."

Pike did some mental arithmetic calculating flight speed of a commuter jet and the distance from anything like an actual land mass from here. That was too short for the Seychelles or anything else he was aware of. "You're flying us into the middle of the ocean?"

"Pretty much, Pike," Kate answered. "We like our distance. No one asks questions out here."

'Here' turned out to be Diego Garcia, a militarized island territory of the United Kingdom. It is an atoll just south of the equator and just over eleven miles in total landmass. Pike had to search his memory for any references to the small island. "SOSUS?"

"Very good, Professor, here is a gold star," Kate said. "The U.S. Navy does use it for underwater sonobuoy monitoring, or SOSUS, as well as a cybersecurity listing post. There's also a rather secret airbase."

"The Navy and Air Force occupying a militarized island owned by the Brits? How deep into the pocket of the government are you?"

She leaned over and kissed him; he noticed the pilot watching them in a small mirror. "Here, at Aries Site, not at all. We have nothing to do with them. The facility was just perfect for our needs, and it was available," she answered.

They touched down on an unusually wide runway that slashed through the thick jungle. "This was a backup emergency landing zone for the space shuttle," Kate said in explanation.

"I would have hated to be those guys gliding in trying to stick the landing on this tiny bit of soil," Pike said. "It seems the government has had a pretty active hand here for years. You sure there isn't more you want to tell me?"

"You have no idea," she laughed. "Lots of rumors, most of which we just hope are false."

The jet pulled up to a squat ugly building and began the shutdown procedures. Kate took his hand and pulled him toward the cabin door. She unlatched it and deployed the airstairs. He grabbed her suitcase and his duffle and followed her down. The heat hit him at once. “Wow.”

“Yeah, not far from the equator, maybe even hotter than South Carolina. The weather here is ...interesting. By interesting I mean bright and sunny or cyclonic demon from hell trying to drown you or blow you out to sea. There is no in-between.”

The pilot followed them out of the plane and locked it up, taking his flight logs. He then climbed into an awaiting SUV that was at least fifteen years old, and looked expectantly at them. “Hop in,” he said cheerily.

The man dropped them at another unremarkable building sitting closer to the ocean about a mile away. “Looks like a warehouse,” Pike said. “Can I just say, I prefer Doha or the Maldives. I’m sure this place is fine, but the amenities look a bit dated.”

Kate held the door for him, then pushed him inside as he passed. “You are here for work, not vacation.”

He leaned back and stole a quick kiss, “Nothing wrong with mixing business with pleasure is there?”

She shook her head. “I don’t know, read the NDA you’re about to sign carefully. I wouldn’t be surprised if that isn’t covered.”

19

Kate lowered his shirt; his injury was healing up well. "You'll have a scar," she said.

"One of many," Pike said in a lighter tone. Since arriving, she had shown him around a small amount of the impressive subterranean facility. What it lacked in visual appeal from up top, it made up for here. "You sure we're safe down here?"

"Much safer than most places. This island is isolated, and multiple layers of hidden defenses protect the building. Remember, most of it was built for military or top-secret purposes until our acquisition," Kate said.

"One of your people introduced herself as a quantum biologist. I've never heard that term or even that combination of sciences."

Kate grinned, "Always takes people by surprise. It won't be the only one here, I assure you. What we have come to know is that quantum mechanics plays a vital role in the evolution of life. From photosynthesis and metamorphosis to the healing in your wound. Doctor Fazula takes that principle one step further in stating that quantum mechanics is essential to life, not just some enhancement. She and Petra run the life sciences section. Back in graduate school, did you ever study the effects of light on static electricity?"

The twist in the conversation threw him briefly, but indeed he did remember the lesson. "Max Planck, yes. I remember he showed how electrical discharge happened quicker when you shined a light on the discharge apparatus. It only worked with ultraviolet light as I recall."

"Exactly," said Kate. "The more compressed bandwidth of ultraviolet light means many more photons are hitting the surface of the object making it easier for the coils to discharge. It was an amazing discovery, that particles of light could affect solid objects. What they were working on was how Thomas Edison's lightbulb produced light. They understood that a filament within would get hot and glowed with a certain radiance, but the scientific reasoning of 'how' was a mystery.

"What we learned over the intervening century was that even our sun itself wouldn't shine without quantum mechanics. Professor, you know the sun produces heat and light by fusing atoms. For example, hydrogen nuclei are slammed together so hard that they stick and produce helium atoms. The problem is that most of the hydrogen atoms in the sun's core really don't have enough energy to stick together. For that to happen, they have to overcome the repulsion of their positive charges, and they generally don't have enough energy. How they manage is through quantum mechanics, quantum tunneling, if we're being precise."

Pike nodded.

"We briefly discussed the many worlds theory," Kate said.

"Right, the infinite worlds theory in which a new timeline or reality splits off every time a choice is made. So, if there is a world in which you turn left to go get Chinese food for dinner, another reality might spring up in where you went straight and ate Italian or a third in which you picked up a sandwich in a drive-through. Are you going to explain the Mandela Effect to me again?"

Kate shook her head. "Not this time. You'll learn that quantum probabilities suggest that many worlds is highly likely. So that when you flip a coin, one reality is heads, and another is where it landed on tails. Complicate this when you consider rolling dice, or maybe the game is roulette. Imagine an outcome when every possible permutation happens. Like I said before, wWe could never rule this theory out entirely, but it seemed overly messy and a waste of resources as I said. I mean, would this apply to just humans; does it require choice made by conscious thought? Would another reality split off where the cheetah killed the gazelle, or another where the gazelle escapes, or would it apply even to bacteria and viruses, would the choices and outcomes there also create these bubble universes, these alternate realities?"

"I agree that it would become rather complex," Pike responded. "So how did you solve it?"

"Simple. We didn't." She smiled and pulled on his arm. "Follow me." The pair began walking deeper into the heart of the sprawling building. "One of the oddities about quantum field theory is, we find that for something to happen, there must be an observer. We knew from experimentation that we all have a quantum connection to these other dimensions, these hidden realms. If we couldn't see them in some way, did they actually even exist?

"This was a crucial question, maybe *the* crucial question. Through experimentation, we developed a rudimentary way to observe the opposite end of our brain's quantum connection. Or at least what we thought was the opposite end. The earliest test was done with a neuro stimulator and a modified MRI machine to generate a containment field, while our researchers electrically excited the test subject's microtubules. We call them MTs, and they are sub microscopic structures that can generate electrical charges to neurons and cells in the brain. But we also found that they vibrate in a unique pattern of oscillation. Through our continued experimentation, we found we could alter these frequencies."

"So, if I heard you right, moving a physical particle from one of these dimensions to another might take the energy equal to the mass of our solar system or Universe or something," Pike said. "But using the 'MTs,' you're still talking about quantum teleportation."

Kate nodded.

"But that's just information, essentially data. It's not like you can physically go to these alternate worlds."

"Again, Pike, you are tiptoeing into the murky waters of what is real. Many scientists believe all we are is information. Like I said, it's opening a doorway so we can mentally travel to the other end of the cosmic rabbit hole. The level at which the being on the other end of that journey is really us or not is debatable, but from a very personal standpoint, I can assure you it very much feels like us. If it is our minds inside those alien bodies, are we not really there?"

Pike paused his eating and turned to face her. "Kate, I'm having a hard time with all this. Not the theories but the reality. You say you can…what did you guys call it?"

"SideSlipping," Kate answered.

"Right…SideSlip." He said the word as if it left a bad taste in his mouth. "Jump into other people's heads and see what they are seeing. Like that crazy movie where everyone was crawling around in John Malkovich's head?"

She shook her head.

Pike continued, "It just seems fantastical, but also perversely voyeuristic, and that is if it's not just some persistent delusions that your subconscious is feeding you when you think you're making these jumps." He watched her expression to see if he was making his case or not. Instead, he saw something else. She smiled, a genuine warm smile. "You've heard all this before, haven't you?" he asked.

"Many times," Kate answered. "Nearly every time we bring in a new traveler. I said it myself. It's a good argument, very salient points, and its assumptions are quite false."

They stopped at a white metal door that Pike thought looked just like the countless others they had passed. Kate swiped a card and placed a finger in a small depression on the keypad. The tiny light turned from red to green, and the door clicked open with the sound of air pressure escaping.

The room was far larger than he'd been expecting and looked less like a research lab and more like a spa. Numerous reclining chairs lined the walls, padded mats lined one wall, and even some low platforms that may have been beds. The lighting was soft, and he could just make out the faint sounds of water, or possibly soft rain, coming from far above.

"Not what you were expecting?" Kate laughed. "This is the Project Cobalt deployment room. Currently we only have two teams off world, and they're in one of the adjacent rooms. We can talk in here and not disturb them. I thought you might like to see."

"Off world?" Pike asked, a look of confusion etched across his brow.

"Just one of our terms," she said dismissively. "Their...bodies are still here, of course. When we SideSlip, most of the conscious part of ourselves is no longer here. Everyone has trouble at first separating the consciousness from the physical bodies. The lab rats here call it, 'separating the mind from the meat.' In time, it will make more sense to you."

"But where do they go?" he asked. "To other versions of here?"

"Here as in this lab, no. Here as in other versions of Earth, yes."

Pike stared at her, his brain trying to decide which question to ask first. Then he reverted to the tried-and-true process of being 'The Fixer.' First, know what is right in front of you. He bent to examine an apparent headpiece attached to the back of the chairs. It reminded him a lot of the hooded dryer chairs in beauty shops. His great aunt had a hair salon and made him sit under one of the damn things after she cut his hair once. Kate's version was a much sleeker design, and peeking underneath, he saw an array of hookups, lights, and circuitry. "So, you moved on from the MRI machine?"

"Oh, yes. Those were unwieldy, impractical, and we found they are mostly unnecessary for our purposes. The launch chairs are only the visible aspects of the apparatus. Much of the mechanicals are behind these walls in another part of the facility," Kate answered, a note of obvious pride in her voice. "In theory, we could learn to SideSlip with none of these aids. That was what Carapaz believed, but so far, no one has made any progress on that front."

"Will you show me the science behind these?" Pike asked.

"If you feel it is essential to your job, yes."

"What is my job? So far, you've been vague. Save the world, and that this is somehow connected to the rising level of hate crimes and stuff."

Kate rubbed her temples and said, "That's just it, we don't know what's going on. It's not a problem with the science or the hardware. The senior team feels like it's bigger than that. The best way we know how to bring you up to speed is to have you experience it."

"Wait, you want me to get hooked up to one of these chairs? No way, that's not how I work. I observe, I study, I watch others make the mistakes."

"If we were talking about a systemic failure, Pike, I would agree with you. We aren't. Everything here works perfectly. I assure you, this is safe, but you will need to SideSlip to understand what we're up against."

Pike wasn't overly fond of this reality, and he had even less desire to see an alternate one. "Tell me about them. Are they somewhat like Earth, not at all like us? What am I missing if I don't do this?"

Kate looked a bit crestfallen, "You would be missing out on the greatest adventure in the entire history of mankind."

"Oh, that's all, huh?" he said.

"... and you would disappoint me," she added.

"Damn," he muttered. *You had to play that one, huh?* he thought.

20

Pike's afternoon was a rush of people, tests, and mind-numbing forms for him to sign. He was used to the NDAs and such, but some made no sense. He was already regretting his decision to accept the project when he found Kate sitting with a young man.

"This is Palio," she said. Kate watched Pike's face with a bemused expression.

"Don't let his looks fool you. He has a doctorate and could easily run his choice of labs," said Kate as she sat down beside him.

He eyed the diminutive man again. "He looks like a teenager."

"I'm nearly thirty," Palio said defensively.

"Same thing," Pike said. "I have underwear older than you," a hint of a smile echoing across his face. "What field? What's your specialty?"

"Cognitive science," Palio said proudly as he removed a dripping tea bag from a steaming cup.

Pike had to convert the mostly European discipline's name. "Neuroscience?"

The younger man nodded as he slurped loudly from his cup. "The physical side, not behavioral."

"Cellular and molecular neuroscience?"

Kate interjected, "Yes, but think smaller. His specialization is more at the nuclear level."

"Yes, yes, quantum microfilaments, microtubules, and such," Palio said.

"So, if I'm hearing you right," Pike said, picking back up the conversation they had started, "all these worlds are not like this one? How different are they? If they aren't like this dimension, how could humans have ever evolved?"

They looked at Pike, then at each other and smiled.

"It's really easier to show you than to explain it," Kate said. "The short answer is, they are not all human."

Pike began to voice his shock, but Kate cut him off. "Humanoid, or something we call pro to-humanoid, is the most common species we have found, but by no means is that all. My last jump I was in my opposite, which we would describe as a hairy version of a manatee. Some are much less identifiable than that. Back to that many worlds theory. Think about what we presume to be the evolution of life on this planet. At any point, what if something else had happened instead of what did here? What if the chemical mix in that primordial sea was just a touch more acidic? What if the chemical reaction that allowed amino acids to form the long chemical strings of life was somehow altered slightly? What if mammals never left the sea, or the meteor didn't strike the planet but glanced off the atmosphere and harmlessly back into space? The dinosaurs could still be the apex life form. Life here would have evolved in vastly different ways."

Pike could concede that point. He knew how adaptable life was. He'd always considered it somewhat of a cosmic lottery that humans had emerged from the evolutionary mire as the apex species. Even other life-forms on this planet spoke volumes to life's never-ending diversity and adaptation. "So, many worlds where different versions of our own world don't occur, but infinite other types of worlds are real?"

"You're getting there, friend," Kate said patting his arm. "Like we said, the many worlds theory would mean that every possible outcome has a version of reality out there. We find far fewer 'earths' that are similar than we would expect if mirror worlds were real. Also, we can only SideSlip into worlds where our quantum entangled species has at least as well-developed brains as our own. That could mean there are countless dimensions in which evolution never took that step. Those, as far as we know, will always be off-limits to us, but we do expect that they, too, exist."

"Because you need to have your twin on the other side to jump into," Pike said helpfully.

"Correct."

"But these other dimensions are mapped. You can predict where they are and what level the inhabiting species is?" Pike asked.

Palio took out a pad and wrote 137 on it. "That is the number of dimensions, or realities, we have observed." He then wrote the number ten to the 123rd power. That is the number of possible dimensions we now believe exist. That will be one followed by 124 zeroes, Professor. Of course, as Dr. Cassidy indicated, many of these probably don't have life, may have no version of our Earth or solar system even. In many others, our individual linked 'other' may not be currently alive."

That thought gave rise to numerous questions in Pike's mind, but he wanted to focus on the more basic first. "What I recall of quantum entanglement is that by its very definition it is a pair. So, assuming you are correct, I can see you would be able to travel...to SideSlip to a single other world where your opposite was, but not to 137 worlds. Have you somehow gamed the law of quantum physics, or am I misunderstanding something?"

Palio smiled and glanced again at Kate, who remained quiet. "We assumed that as well," he explained. "But once we began jumping, everyone came back with very different versions of the worlds they had just traveled to, so we knew the other worlds, other entanglements, were out there. In time, we discovered three especially important keys. The first and the biggest is our neural network. Our filaments in our brains contain multiple entangled connections, each potentially linking us to another reality. Second, once inside a host in an alternate dimension, we can SideSlip to other more remote dimensions that are entangled or overlapping that one. And lastly, and a much more recent development, there are dimensions that seem to be tightly interconnected, like a hub of sorts, in which the entanglement rule seems to be ignored. It is like a grand terminus. Slowly, we are learning to navigate this last one."

"So, by daisy-chaining these entanglements you can jump from dimension to dimension like stops on a subway line?" Pike asked.

"Essentially, yes," Palio answered. "We have mapping crews creating a multiverse schematic, in fact, of every discovered world."

"I'm not sure I'm seeing the intersection between your madness theory and SideSlipping," Pike said to Kate.

"It will take a leap, hon, but I'm getting there, I promise," Kate said as she rose and walked around the small room, trying to organize her thoughts in a way the man's analytical brain might accept it. "The madness, we feel, is because we are not a single entity. It connected us at the subconscious, or quantum level, to other versions of ourselves, and at times, parts of those other dimensions bleed into our own. Not physically, but it is still very real to the individual."

"So, madness is a default state if you're disconnected from this quantum bridge or whatever?" Pike asked as he rubbed his temples trying to force his mind to search for the truths in what seemed like complete nonsense.

"Our connection can be disrupted...we're not sure how, but I think Carapaz does. When that happens, entire worlds begin to fade from the local network," said Kate. "When it occurs to individuals, we aren't quite sure what the cause is. It may be that one of our others is slipping into us..."

"Holy shit!" Pike said. "So, I'm not myself?"

"Well...maybe," Palio said. "Or you may be yourself plus..."

"Not helping, friend."

"Pike," Kate said, "these connections are always on, they're a part of us as humans. We don't yet know of any species jumping into our consciousness the way our SideSlips do, but we can't rule it out. The fact is, we are more of a collective than an individual. To use the

Wizard of Oz analogy, it's not one wizard behind the curtain, it's a group."

Pike gave a slight nod, "That's not the scary part. The fact that they are all some version of me is what's frightening."

"Come with us down to the med-labs, we need to get you out on a jump," Kate said.

21

Pike watched Doctor Almira and her two technicians closely as they applied numerous wireless sensors. “These pick up my brain waves, my subconscious, neural activity?”

The doctor gave a brief nod. “Alpha, theta, and numerous others that are less familiar. Some, like REM, that you would normally need to be soundly asleep to even generate.”

“But you can trigger that with the chair?” He motioned to what was obviously one of the launch chairs placed against a nearby wall.

Kate glanced absently in the direction indicated and gave a shrug. “No need for that, our processes have advanced to the point we can do most of these with just our software and the small sensors attached to your skin.”

Doctor Almira finished examining all the placements, made a single adjustment, then nodded to the two techs who gathered their supplies and left the room. “You have questions, Professor,” she said. “My job is pretty simple. I am to make sure we have a baseline recording of your brain patterns. We check this for...” she seemed to hesitate, “for anomalies, but I will also use it for comparison when you SideSlip. Our understanding and ability to sense what is happening on the other side will get better and better. My lab has the most powerful computing on the base. We used a specialized AI to help correlate the data."

"So, Doctor, you'll train me to focus my subconscious to map out the connections?" Pike asked, then continued before she could answer, "I thought our subconscious was uncontrollable by its very nature. I mean, if I'm terrified of spiders, isn't that fear rooted in my subconscious? And even with all the facts, like I know about how beneficial spiders are to us, I can't consciously rid myself of that paranoia?"

Sandy Almira leaned back and grinned. "Professor Shepard, you have a rudimentary, quite common, and very flawed understanding of your own brain. Don't feel bad, though, we all do...or did. What we are finding is that there is not a top layer and a sub-layer to consciousness. The truth is scientists cannot even agree on what consciousness is. We say it is a sentient state of our own existence. Pretty simplistic, but I feel sure on some level a frog knows it is a frog and knows that if it lies in the hot sun all day it will at some point cease to be a frog. So, couldn't you also assume it, too, is conscious?"

She updated a screen on the computer and advanced to what appeared to be a procedural checklist. "Two main points: There are multiple layers, or states-of-being, in each of our brains, not just the conscious and subconscious nodes. It is far more interconnected and nuanced than that. Second, what we think of as our subconscious, not our conscious portion, is really the part that is in charge. Despite as you say, having no way of interfacing directly with it in any meaningful conscious way, countless research, including our own, has reached the same conclusion. More often than not, it is our subconscious brain that is deciding for us on a near constant basis. Much like the puppet master hanging out above the stage, you think you have free will, but your subconscious brain is really running the show."

She paused and let her words take root. Sandy liked that he didn't interrupt to challenge her, even though she was calling bullshit on what was likely some of his long-held core understandings.

Pike couldn't immediately find fault with what the doctor was saying. She was the expert in the field, not he but he was here to solve a problem and gathering more facts was crucial..

"So, when I SideSlip, I will occupy the subconscious brain of my... host, right?" He still couldn't wrap his head around that concept of being inside someone else's head.

"Correct."

"Okay," Pike continued slowly, "when I'm occupying the subconscious portion of it...them, um, it's not in the role of a passenger looking out the bus windows as his life goes by."

Doctor Almira answered, "All life is different, Professor, but as far as we can tell, the processes of sentient brains are not. You will be able to exert subtle but definite control over your host. That is an area in which you will get a considerable amount of training. It is a role that could obviously be abused, and therefore, excessive influence cannot be permitted. You may also find the level of control you have varies in certain species. But Doctor Cassidy would be a better advisor on that. My advice to you is to seek to know but do no harm."

"What, do you have a prime directive or something?"

She snort-laughed. "The prime directive is utter crap! Not meddling in another species' affairs, even if they were about to annihilate themselves or some other species. Being noble in your quest is great, but don't duck your head in the sand. For the most part, we borrowed most heavily from Google's mission statement."

Pike had to think on that one for a while to recall it. "Don't be evil," he said, breaking into a smile.

The doctor nodded. "Of course, that does require you to understand what may be considered normal or evil in the host's world. And that, my friend, is not as easy as it sounds."

"Why not? It seems like evil is evil, no matter what planet."

She looked up thoughtfully toward the ceiling, "There is a world, Gamma X5, in which the intelligent species has split into two distinct life forms. Both very different from each other but both occupying the same three primary land masses. Earth in that dimension never reached the same level of geothermal activity and tectonic shift, so Gondwana and Pangea supercontinents still exist. The species are remarkable in that they are symbiotic, meaning they need each other to survive. That does not mean they get along, as they have fought numerous battles."

"So where does the symbiosis occur?" Pike asked. It had shocked him the prior week to discover that not all of the Earth inhabitants were human or even humanoid.

The doctor responded, "It's very tightly integrated, much of which is still a mystery to us, but obviously, their common heritage plays a large part. They live exceptionally long lives with a short mass breeding cycle every few years. The only way we can detect that they can reproduce is through interbreeding. Our basic understanding is the original basis of the species split was gender."

"Do what?" he asked. "Will I have to go there?"

"Don't worry. If you did, it would feel completely natural to you." She stood and switched on several monitors and then tapped a number of keys to start one of the sessions. "What is odd is that only the females of species A, well, they aren't exactly females, but it is close enough to make the point. Anyway, they will choose only the most fit, the smartest, healthiest of species B, the males if you will, to breed with. It's really unusual. Not like, say, anything as close as a Nordic beauty from our world choosing to breed with a dwarf version of a Neanderthal. This more closely resembles a bear-like humanoid mating with a chimpanzee."

"Pretty freakin' weird, but okay. How does this tell me not to be evil?" Pike asked in complete bewilderment.

"Part of the post-coital bliss is that the bear mother of species A kills and eats her mate. Much like a black widow spider does." The doctor glanced at the displays on the tablet in her hands before seeing if he was thoroughly revolted. "The evil part of that is not in the consumption of her monkey baby-daddy but instead, it's if she chose not to end his life."

"So not killing and eating the little baby-daddy guys would be worse?"

"Yes, one of our early travelers made that mistake. She felt the need to do the killing and eating as normal on that world but urged the mother not to end the life of her mate. She instead kicked him from the nest they had shared for mating, and in doing so, nearly started another war. The males of species B were deeply offended. We think it's part of a culling to prevent both groups overcrowding and to encourage diversity in the gene pool, but the evidence is not back on all fronts. Several individuals wound up dead in the skirmish, and the localized community split into two smaller, and somewhat weaker groups as a result," Sandy said.

"So, evil can be a localized concept."

"Evil comes in many forms, some is universal, all is personal, and trust me, you will learn to know it when you see it."

Doctor Almira studied one of the computer screens intently. Her dark hair partially hid a face that spoke of Turkish heritage if Pike were to make a guess.

"Professor, did you happen to suffer from epilepsy as a child?"

Unconsciously, Pike rubbed again at the scar hidden by his hair. "Yes, is that relevant?" The thought of those early days filled him with dread.

"It just wasn't in my files." She flipped several pages looking for relevant data. "What else can you tell me about it?"

22

On a certain level, Pike knew all he had heard could just be some fantastical ruse. Even Palio had made an offhand comment about all life being nothing more than an elaborate virtual reality sim.

"A truth this profound should resonate through me even if I can't recall the specifics. I'm sorry to still doubt, but I must, I require proof," he said.

"You would want proof even if you helped design it, that's just who you are," Kate said as she looked uncertainly at him. "We have to show you."

"You want me to test this out?" Pike stammered.

"No, honey, we have tested it. I want you to experience it. There really is no other way for you to fully understand it."

Kate already knew he had no desire to see the other side. The very idea of his conscious brain leaving his physical body was repulsive to him, as it would be for most people.

"My body will be in that room in a vegetative state," he said. "What happens if my host gets injured or dies?"

"Pike, Doctor Almira discussed this with you. It's perfectly safe. The protocols are all in place to ensure your mind remains intact no matter what."

"What about the signs?" he asked pointing above the launch chairs in the neighboring rooms. At first, he thought it was just a cheeky bit of British humor. Signs that looked like someone had removed them from the London subway system. "'Mind the Gap.' What the hell is the gap?"

Palio leaned in to attach another series of sensors to his head, neck, and hands. "The gap is a potential memory loss, and it's usually pretty short term," the young man said. "It is a side effect of time dilation. Do you remember the Steven King book where the passengers on a plane got out of sync with their timeline?"

"Where they flew low and saw dinosaurs?" Pike asked.

"No, I think that was a Twilight Zone episode," Palio said. "The one where they go through a strange light, and everything changes. They eventually land, and the airport seems abandoned. Everything seems dull and lifeless, and food has no taste."

"I think maybe I saw a TV movie on it," Pike admitted. "They all had to wait for time to catch back up?"

Kate nodded. "It can temporarily trap your mind outside of this timeline in the same way. We can normally predict when it will occur and for how long."

Palio packed his small kit as he filled in the rest. "We believe it is most often when two dimensions are moving away from each other, or when the timeline in one dimension is running counter to our own."

"So how long does this normally last, the memory gap?"

"Not long, my friend, usually ten or fifteen minutes. Thirty hours was the longest, but that person slept through most of it as it was a very difficult Slip," Palio said, clueless to the fact that none of this was making Pike feel better.

"I...um, I think it's better if I do some more research into your process first," Pike said attempting to remove several of the sensor pads Palio had just applied.

"Pike, leave them," Kate said. "You have to do this, for me. Okay?"

Looking up into those radiant green eyes, he slowly nodded silent agreement.

"Also, we need to assign you a mnemonic key for you to use," she added.

"A key?" he asked, confused.

She ran a hand through her hair before continuing. "It's part of the protocols. So no one else can ever intercept an individual's jump. That's not possible." She quickly added, "At least not that we know of, but it just made sense to have some sort of password system. Ours is a strong memory attached to a particularly detailed neural mapping of your brainwaves. Those two items must match before you're allowed into the launch system. Even the training system will require it."

"So, what will be my mnemonic password?" he asked.

"I don't know, none of us do, we're not supposed to share them, even in general." She moved closer and in a softer tone whispered. "Mine is a very strong memory of a dream I had lying on a beach one day. A dream that wound up becoming Project Cobalt. I have no trouble vividly recalling it. I would imagine yours probably should be as well. We combine that with a numeric or verbal passcode just for an added level of authentication." Pike immediately had an idea of what he would use but stayed silent. Something had occurred to him as she was talking. If SideSlipping allowed you to only interact with another version of yourself in an alternate dimension, then why would there be a need for security? That would essentially be the same as requiring a pass phrase before you could talk to yourself. *Who else could be listening in?* He assigned that to the rational part of his brain, one more question that needed an answer. The other part of his brain was scared shitless at the moment. It was convinced all of this would lobotomize him and leave him stranded on the other side of sanity.

* * *

Early morning, the following Tuesday, Pike found himself lying on a more basic version of the launch chairs he had seen. He had numerous adhesive sensors again dotting his head and neck. "Where are the wires?" he asked.

"No wires, Boss. It uses a proprietary type of Bluetooth connection," Palio said, sliding his tablet into a cradle about the size and shape of an old-style cassette tape recorder.

"I have keyed up a very simple test connection, the most basic in fact. This will not be totally immersive, as not all of your consciousness can pass through this connection."

"Why is that? The bandwidth of your system?" Pike asked.

"No, Shepard, my system is, ugh...never mind. We think it is due to the nature of the Deltan's brains. Their microtubules are just not as complex. The dimension is literally right on top of us, so it's very easy to connect with, but yes, you could think of it as narrow bandwidth. You essentially get a ride along, but that will be pretty cool I assure you." This was to be his final step of training before doing a fully immersive SideSlip.

Pike still was not too certain about having part of his gray matter targeted by anything, but Kate assured him he wouldn't feel any discomfort. She was monitoring his vitals and comms from another room. They had both agreed it might be too distracting for her to be in here during the test. Even now, he couldn't get over what the two of them had become over the past two months. The woman was delightful in every way imaginable.

Doctor Almira gave Pike the drug cocktail of neural blockers to help him SideSlip. "Remember, Professor. When you see the doorway, you may notice multiple versions of the world beyond, you must focus on the one you want. This is superpositioning. Remember the observer rule of the quantum state."

They had been through this numerous times, but her words scared him more rather than being comforting.

"Okay, Shepard," the doctor said. "Close your eyes and steady your breathing. Try to block out all sounds and stimuli to focus on your memory. This will be something poignant you have chosen."

They had also both gone over all this earlier. "And once I have the memory in mind?"

"Let it play out fully. As soon as the system has enough to make a match, it will activate, and you will, to some degree, be on Delta Eridani."

Palio checked a few of the settings, then gave him the signal to begin.

The familiar black waters slipped by the hull of the canoe. He was nine years old and was paddling the back channels to Risse's house at Fort Remorse. The cabin was stark gray with the light of a single lantern the only color in the otherwise dreary scene. Risson's mother hugged Pike and showed him back to her son's bedside.

Risson's face was swollen, his lips bloody, and a bloody bandage hung tenuously to a wound on the boy's forehead.

"Hey, dai Shepardman, you look worsa than me, man," the boy said, a tooth missing from his lopsided grin.

Pike rubbed his shaven head, his own wound still red and obvious. The stitches ran from below his hairline across his scalp and down to his neck.

"So, you did it, you really let 'em cut your brain in two?" Risson asked.

Pike's shoulders shrugged, "I had no choice."

And then, Risse and the memory were gone. That had been his passcode; he was certain of that from the moment they had mentioned it. These were the recurring dreams; it was a scene that still haunted him. His actions, or more accurately, his condition had indirectly caused serious injury to his best friend and led to Pike, himself, being briefly institutionalized and then having brain surgery to correct his deteriorating condition. Risson Mack had stood by him for all of it.

The poignant memory faded as Pike's brain began interpreting a view he could not comprehend. He felt his arms lifting and hands reaching to make sure his eyes were still closed. They were, but he could see. Not like the memory but just like seeing with his own eyes, yet this was not a view his eyes had ever witnessed. This had to be Delta Eridani. Still Earth, if Kate and Palio could be believed, but in this dimension, Earth had evolved very differently.

The creature, Kate had suggested calling it a host or his 'other,' was running he thought as the view jostled slightly. He was looking up at an escarpment of bare, gray rock stretching up sharply from a landscape that was a deep, rust brown dotted with brilliant outcroppings of white and yellow twigs. As they got closer, these began to resemble coral more than plants. His host slowed and rose what Pike assumed was a hand or appendage. It was holding a long tubular creature that had wrapped partially around the pale, gray skin. The hand rose toward the eyes, then disappeared out of sight. When it lowered, the worm creature it had been holding was gone.

The thought made Pike want to wretch. The eyes darted up and began to track an object, several objects, which looked eerily like floating balloon versions of jellyfish. They hovered a dozen feet above the desert floor and had a shimmering light that flickered slightly. Tentacles hung like hair from beneath the bell, and occasionally, these would flare as some insect or animal flew into it and was trapped. These were thankfully off the Deltan's menu. He studied them for a short time, then began running again.

"Can I talk?" Pike asked. "I mean, to you guys?"

"Of course," Kate said via the comms bud in his ear. "Comms work great here, not so well in full off world slips."

"I have arrived," he stammered. "You were right, this is incredible," he said truthfully. "How is it I can see even though my eyes are closed?"

Palio answered, "Visual perception is actually a process of the brain more than it is of the eyes. More than fifty percent of the surface of our brains is devoted to interpreting the signals brought in via our sensors, our eyes. In this case, all of your visual cortex is functioning as normal, you are just using the Deltan's sensory input."

"So, I am actually seeing this. And he has no idea I am there, here...whatever." The semantics were baffling even to him.

"No, we don't think the Deltans are aware of us. In other species that may not be the case, but you are not even a vague thought to them. In a full jump rig, you could essentially pilot the host through exerting your conscious will."

Pike wondered how they knew he would have an 'other' on Delta Eridani, then realized he would have jumped somewhere else had that not been the case. While all of this was new to him, it was standard stuff to everyone at Project Cobalt.

He rode along with the Deltan for several hours fascinated by his first sight of another of their kind. *It's a Wookie but mostly covered in sharkskin*, he thought. The myriad landscapes were amazing as were the habits of the creatures and the impressive level of technical proficiency they had. Their homes were simple but neat and logical. They had devises with viewing screens that may have been phones or computers or newspapers, he couldn't tell from how they used them. Much was very foreign; but some things were unbelievably familiar, like a small animal the adolescents kept in the house. It looked like a guinea pig but moved with catlike grace. It was obviously a much-loved pet.

At the end of the session, Pike was exhilarated. *This was just a ride along, what must the full experience be like*? he wondered. "Ready to return," he stated as the Deltan closed its eyes and began to snore. The system smoothly terminated the connection, and he was still lying on the launch couch.

Palio was sitting beside him in a chair, grinning. "So, you want worms for dinner?"

23

"Still think The Project is just a very good VR?" Kate asked entering the briefing room later.

Pike thought about what he had just experienced. "I don't think I ever claimed that. I just raised it as a possibility."

"And now?" Palio asked, the grin spreading across his face.

"It was pretty incredible," Pike admitted. "I've seen some very good visual simulations but none that are as vivid and nuanced as real life. The Deltans are fascinating. It's a shame we can't learn more about them."

"We have teams observing them pretty much constantly. It's an easy dimension to reach, and most junior teams do a regular rotation with them. Did you happen to see the large airborne creatures?" Kate asked.

Pike thought back. "No, saw a number of smaller ones that looked like floating gas bags."

"Yeah, those are pretty common, but now and then we notice something that has to be the size of a whale or jumbo jet way up in the atmosphere. It actually undulates up and down as it moves through the clouds."

"To be honest, almost all of it reminds me of ocean life, except without the water," Pike admitted.

"Many of us felt that way, too, when we first saw it," Kate said. "It can be dangerous to see patterns of our reality on other worlds, but evolution and adaptation do often seem to find very similar solutions no matter the dimension. You'll find much that is both familiar yet very alien to you at the same time."

"So where do I need to go to really help you?" Pike asked.

"Easy there, Shepard. You just want to jump again don't you, for real this time," she responded playfully.

"We could let him go to Xylos," Palio suggested, his eyebrow raised over one eye.

"That would just be cruel." Kate walked around and sat down next to Pike. "Still...maybe..."

"What is Xylos?" Pike asked.

Kate scrunched up her face in a way that Pike could only describe as adorable, but that was probably because he was falling for her. Who was he kidding? He was already hopelessly trapped.

"We call it 'Chaos World.' It's a visual wonderland that has to be seen to be believed, but none of us have made much sense out of it."

"Is it one that is also a low bandwidth world? One that is visual only, like Delta Eridani?"

Palio answered uncertainly, "Maybe...I mean, it could be, but something is different. My personal belief is there is a barrier...a restriction. Possibly, it is something put in place by the indigenous species. It's a trip, man. We mainly just send people there to see how completely different another version of Earth can be."

"Xylos, so an X-class world," Pike said. "Opposite end of the alphabet from our version."

Kate went on to explain, "Our first traveler classed it as an X-type. The reality is, we have no idea how similar or dissimilar it is, Pike. The truth is that it's just so bizarre we have relegated it to a training mission slip only. The proximity to our reality is great, equally as good as Delta, so it's in our standard jump catalog."

"So, when can I go?" Pike said eagerly.

"You need some downtime, Tiger," she said, patting him on the leg.

"Every SideSlip comes with a mandatory interval, even on realms without a significant TD factor."

"TD means Time Dilation?" Pike asked, remembering an earlier conversation.

Palio answered, "Yes, Delta and Xylos are essentially the same TD as us, so no serious risk of memory gaps or time sync issues. Most worlds are like that, but it does change based on the specific location of the alternate dimension."

"It changes, relative to us? How is that possible? So, some dimensions are close by and easy to reach, and others are more distant and difficult to travel to? I thought quantum entanglement worked at any distance."

"He asks good questions," Palio said. "Some dimensions literally overlap our own. That may be where the dream world and the ghost Kate mentioned come into play, or autism, or any of a thousand other human conditions. Even though they are right here in front of us, it is a physical gulf that's literally impossible for us to physically breach. Think of these dimensions as bubbles in a mountain of foam. We are inside one of those bubbles. Everything we see, the planets, space, the galaxies are all within that bubble yet, it is one of many, and our bubble is touching dozens of others. Where they touch is a point of debate among our science team. Making a physical crossing is the desire, but no one knows what would happen even if we could."

"What do you mean?" Pike asked, interrupting the man.

"It...well, it gets complicated, Professor. There is no reason to assume that the laws of physics are the same or compatible with one dimension to another. Physical laws of our Universe may be unique to our reality."

Pike was familiar with this concept, and Kate had mentioned it to him as well, although it violated nearly everything he'd ever been taught about the Universe. "So, if we stepped across that membrane into another reality, we might just explode into dust and atoms or dissolve into pudding."

"Right, gravity could be much stronger there. Water could be poison to us, and oxygen highly corrosive. Or perhaps those elements never form because the atomic weights are wrong or any other number of facts. Everything on the other side is very hard to measure or observe with clarity. What does a pound weigh, especially if you are unsure of the gravity?"

Pike nodded, "Okay, I think I'm beginning to see. Please continue, Palio."

"Quantum entanglement has limits, at least for us. The farther the bubble is in the pile of foam, the more power it takes to excite the filaments to connect. At a certain point, we risk brain damage to even try. While in theory, the entangled particles' range is infinite, we do believe that the altered physical laws in some dimensions compromise the entanglement. Similarly, we believe others like the terminus worlds enhance it."

"We don't fully understand it," Kate admitted. "Sticking with the foam analogy, our bubble of reality may be constantly moving, migrating through the foam, putting distance between us and our neighbors and bringing us closer to ones that were more distant. Everything in the multiverse must move in a higher dimension of spacetime. It is possible for us to be distant in locus as well as in time. Our equipment in the lab can detect the changes, which are normally gradual, so we can make adjustments before each mission."

"So, you tend to go to the ones that are close and use them as stepping stones to go to distant ones?" Pike asked. "I have so many questions, sorry." Then, a very important one occurred to him. "You guys never told me what happens if you SideSlip into someone who is injured or...or what if they die?"

"Do you die back here?" Kate asked, a smile making dimples on her cheek that Pike found instantly magical. "It's not the Matrix, and you aren't Neo. Think of it as a broadcast. If the connection is severed, you just return here, mentally I mean, your body will have never left."

"So, there is no danger in SideSlipping?" he asked.

"We didn't say that," Palio answered. "There are many dangers, more than you can imagine," he said grimly.

* * *

Pike had been pacing but sat beside Kate as Palio finished putting away his gear and discreetly left the two to talk. "Let's take a walk," she said. He allowed himself to be led as they wandered the corridors like old lovers, becoming even more comfortable with each other every day. Eventually, they made it into the small two-room suite that he had been assigned.

"Sorry if I seem to doubt you, Kate. It's a lot to take in all at once. I still don't know how I can be of any help to you, though."

Her hand was again in his, she kissed him briefly, walked over to his work desk, and sat on the edge. "I have no choice, Pike. We, have no choice," she corrected as she stood and began to pace the small room. "We have to fix what is happening."

"Because of The Fade?" he guessed.

She nodded. "Somehow, you are the key. Right now, I have no idea how to convince you, but I know we must have your help. I need you to trust me that you are the key."

24

Rain pounded against the thin windows in thunderous sheets. Pike stared out, sipping a cup of coffee; he felt Kate coming up behind him. "Lovely morning, isn't it?"

"I like it," she said, her eyes not looking the same place his were. "You nervous about it?"

He knew she meant him taking his first real trip 'off world.' "Palio mentioned risks, what are they?"

She stroked his bare back, then moved away realizing that this was part of his process. He needed to understand, to weigh the pros with the cons. "The gap is the main one we face. The time gap, we've already discussed. To some degree we see it in about 60% of the missions."

"But that's minor, right?" he asked, turning to face her. "Just an inconvenience."

Kate nodded. "Mostly, but there have been some significant memory gaps, particularly in our first attempts. I had one that lasted about twenty hours, another had a gap of almost two days."

"Okay, temporary amnesia I can deal with. What else?"

"Well, a short-term memory issue as well. Much of the specifics you observe when you're there will fade quickly when you return. Just like a vivid dream begins to get fuzzy, then dims when you wake up. It's the same mental process. A neurochemical in our brains is, in fact, the cause of both. We have some ways of mitigating it, but it's not perfect."

That was a concern, but one of the side-effects of Pike's childhood condition was an unusual type of eidetic memory. He wasn't sure it would work at the subconscious level, but he felt like it would. "Okay, what's the biggest risk?"

Kate looked down at the floor, her tousled red locks dangling in front of her face. "Depression."

Pike wasn't sure he heard her right. "Excuse me?"

She ran a hand through her hair, flipping it back over her head as she nodded. "Yeah, it's not something many of us talk about. The biggest risk is not wanting to come back."

That puzzled him. "I don't understand, I mean, everything about my test jump felt foreign. I know I was just observing, not an actual jump but still..."

"When you SideSlip, it's fully immersive, Pike. That world will feel as much home to you as it does to your 'other.' The loves and fear your host feels, you will feel. Some places are magical compared to our reality. We have a problem recalling some people, and each of us has worlds we visit over and over again. It can become an addiction."

"What happens if someone doesn't come back, can you force them to return?"

Kate shook her head. "No, not really. Once the entanglement made is stable, you don't need the machinery to maintain it. Theoretically, we could change the resonant frequency or excite a different set of microtubules, but the consensus is that would at best cause the brain to try to occupy multiple realities at the same time, which probably would result in insanity or death."

"So, missions aren't limited to twelve hours like the doctor said?"

Kate shook her head. "We officially limit them but no, we have some that are long-duration jumps. Typically, these are the military related ones. The other groups that do those normally keep them top secret, and we only receive the briefest of information on those missions."

Pike thought he was beginning to understand. "So, you keep the body alive back here, I.V. fluids, tube feeding, and such, and they can gather as much information on the other side as they want."

"Basically, yes. It's kind of like treating a coma patient, except the patient can theoretically communicate with us, although most don't."

"Why not?"

Kate shrugged. "Because at a certain point, back here no longer feels as real. Also, depending on the connection and the distance between dimensions, real time communication just breaks down."

"Who has the longest jump on record?" Pike asked, thinking he already knew.

Kate glanced at the door before answering. Thunder boomed in the distance. "Carapaz does. He was off world for twenty-two days. Julian was a long-duration specialist."

* * *

Kate looked questioningly at Pike. Bringing him up to speed so far had been revolutionary but done in predictable, measured steps. The next bit would depend on how invested he was in the narrative she was presenting. "Shepard, if you're like Palio and believe all life is a giant VR simulation, then perhaps you would believe these other dimensions are simply an illusion. Something created and self-contained completely within our own cerebral network. Few of us have the ability to create worlds this complex or the sometimes subtle, yet sophisticated, changes between our current reality and those others."

"How do you know you are real?" Palio asked later, having sat down at the table with them for dinner.

"Descartes again?" Pike asked with a grin. "You guys have to expand your references."

Kate drew in a deep breath before diving into the most difficult part of the discussion. "My first SideSlip was into a world we now call Aragon. On it, I am a young male." She saw his expression and gave a shrug. "Yes, our physical body's gender is the least predictable aspect of our other selves. We now believe our gender on a very basic level is a mental illusion our consciousness presents as a coping mechanism. On Aragon, I live in a large settlement known as Kamarov. I don't know my name there, as labels like that don't seem important to them. I love it there, life is peaceful, the work is hard, but the place is enchanting. Not magical or fantasy-like, but just very special. In my other's body it is completely natural to me. I know the language, the history. I know and understand what he knows.

"Life on Aragon is very predictable—was very predictable," she amended. "The environment is stable and much of life is completely routine. The Aragonian dimension is kind of our cosmic constant, like the standard candle in cosmology. We can try things out. It seems to also be relatively close to our own reality, probably some overlap, although there is slight time dilation. It's been one of my favorite places, and yes, it's difficult to return from."

"The depression," Pike stated as he saw her eyes beginning to water.

She nodded.

Palio took a bite of his curry chicken and said, "It was on that world we made the big breakthroughs."

Pike looked for either of them to continue.

Kate went on, "There, on Aragon, inside this male's subconscious, I discovered something amazing. By having the techs in the lab readjust the oscillations in my neural pathways, I could sense a secondary entanglement and then a third. My...I mean, his brain is entangled with multiple dimensions, many of which are unavailable from our Universe. Aragon was the first of the terminus realms we found. Through him, I interconnect with a vast array of other dimensions."

Pike sipped the coffee and tried to accept all this as if any of it could possibly make any sense. He had parked his own preconceptions, though. It was a skill that had served him well for much of his career. While they had mentioned hub worlds during his initiation, this was the first time they offered a real explanation. "So, not all realms are connected inter-dimensionally on an equal basis," he stated, getting right to the crux of the issue. "Still," he continued, "you're connected back here, even if you do subsequent SideSlips after you go..." he searched his memory for the word they used.

"Off world," Kate said helpfully.

"Yeah, okay...off world," he said, nodding slowly.

"Sure, our physical bodies are still here," Kate said. "Much of our mental processes are still alert and sensing remotely what is happening in both realms, so depending on the TD and comms restrictions of the end dimension, we can speak or signal the control room in many cases."

Her response triggered even more practical questions, but Pike filed most of those away for later. "If you have so many more worlds to explore nearby, then I'm not sure of the relevant importance of these... um, terminus dimensions like Aragon that are pretty popular. It does sound lovely. Any chance I could go there with you?"

"Unfortunately, that is no longer possible. We do have countless adjacent dimensions to explore, though," Palio answered, a little too quickly.

"Why would Aragon be off limits for me?"

Kate's face reflected a mix of horror and loss; Pike did not understand the reason.

"It's the reason I sought you out, Pike," she said, her voice cracking as she tried to hold her emotions in check. "I was on Aragon when The Fade happened."

"The Fade," he said glumly, realizing why the subject was so tender for her.

"Carapaz actually discovered it," Kate said sadly.

"He's the one who caused it," Palio added bitterly.

"We don't know that," Kate said, giving the young man a withering look.

"We saw the slip signature, Kate." He then turned to look at Pike hoping to make his case with him instead. "Every world in our local network which failed was one that Carapaz made multiple visits to, increasing in frequency and duration right up until he dropped out of the connection."

Pike filed that away; it was circumstantial but still compelling. "Did you confront him? Is that what made him leave Cobalt?"

Kate had regained most of her composure and answered, "Yes, he believes that another species causes The Fade. We are apparently not the only ones doing this, and we are definitely not the best at it."

Palio made a dismissive sound. "He took off not long after Aragon fell."

Pike wanted to learn more about what happened during The Fade, but he was beginning to wonder if interviewing Carapaz might not be the more prudent course. "Where is he now?"

"We don't know, we lost track of him, but our assumption is he is working with the military at their jump base," Palio answered.

"The government has a base?" he asked dumbly. Of course, they would. It was a no-brainer. Who was he kidding? They wouldn't let someone else have this kind of a technological edge over them.

"I have someone looking for him," Kate said, ignoring more details about the other base. "In the meantime, we have to get you certified for a full SideSlip."

25

Pike's eyes gazed down a coastline of ragged peaks and dark, black sand. The water was a bluish gray, but the surf had a distinctive, pinkish tint.

"Where is this again?" His voice was not coming from his mouth. It was a mental voice here as he struggled to form the words brain back in the Cobalt lab. "This is Delvos?"

Kate's voice soothed him even though the sound was distant. "Yes, Pike. Welcome to Delvos, or as we commonly refer to it—Dogpatch."

The briefing had mentioned this along with a considerable amount of other info, most of which escaped him at the moment. "Why Dogpatch?"

He heard Kate chuckle. "You'll understand."

Originally, it had taken days for him to focus his subconscious brain enough to even establish his neural password. Now that very personal mental scene that no one else's engrams would be able to duplicate was very vivid to him. It had taken more weeks of training jumps for him to acclimate to the process. To be fully certified as a traveler in Project Cobalt, he had to also master the somewhat awkward communication system. They had told him it might take a week or two. He had mastered it in just a few sessions. His brain worked a bit differently than most. Sometimes better, sometimes faster, but not always.

Pike wiggled his host's toes into the sand, then felt something underfoot. Looking down, it briefly horrified him to see a body covered by sleek fur and legs that were muscular and almost like an otter. One foot, although he hesitated thinking of them as such, was mostly submerged in the dark sand.

"Can you describe what you see?" Kate asked via the comms bud in his right ear from back in the lab.

"Um, if I have to," Pike answered, suppressing a desire to vomit. "My host's foot, hand...whatever, just pulled a bug-crab kind of worm out of the sand and now is feasting on it one bite at a time."

"No," Kate said. "I mean, where are you standing? I get that you're on the beach, and only a few spots have the Lyrids you are describing. Is there a large mountain cliff ahead?"

Lyrids, Pike thought while realizing that the morsels of flesh were delicious to him now. "Yes, a giant rocky face. In profile, it looks a bit like Spencer Tracy."

"Who?"

"Never mind, Kate, you're too young. Are you anywhere close?" The two had decided to SideSlip together for this jump.

"Yes, just on the other side of the ridge. My host is getting hungry, and with a little encouragement from her subconscious. Should be there in a few minutes."

Pike knew she had picked Delvos because it was one of the worlds in which both of their opposites lived and were known to each other. It was also a species, which they called 'Delvonians,' which had little in the way of a consciousness. Although highly intelligent, they were easily manipulated through gentle persuasion of their subconscious minds. As Pike saw whom he assumed was Kate coming down the hill toward him, he took careful note of how the creature moved. He had to admit they looked very dog-like, especially in the head and upper body. The midsections still reminded him of an otter with the legs of a racing horse. *But those hands...er, feet, things.* She...or it, trotted to a stop nearby and immediately began digging in the black sand for food.

It astounded him by how much the 'here' felt natural. He'd very incorrectly assumed he would feel like a voyeur or maybe like a horse rider, directing the creature but not being a part of the animal. He instinctually knew what his opposite knew, even if much of it was beyond his human comprehension. "It's amazing, Kate. If this is just an elaborate VR sim, it's got to be the best one ever. I must ask, why here? And...maybe more importantly, why me?" Pike asked her via the comm's interface.

She seemed to want to avoid the question. "You're on the other side now. We've SideSlipped. You know I wasn't lying."

Pike considered the response. This might still be an illusion, an elaborate construct in virtual reality. By her own admission, his body and his conscious mind was still back in the lab on Diego Garcia. Still, if this wasn't reality, it was the best damn artificial environment he'd ever seen. He took a deep breath. To be accurate, his host body took a deep breath, but Pike registered the unique smells, the slightly metallic taste in the atmosphere. On Earth, his Earth, he knew it might have assaulted his senses, probably make him gag. Here it was pleasant, something akin to an ocean breeze. "You're deflecting. I would like an answer," he said. This time his host asked Kate's in its own language. "Whoa." He spoke, and his host said the equivalent in Delvonian. He'd thought about what he was going to say to Kate, and before he could radio it to her, the thought had been transferred to his host, his other.

Kate's other laughed. The creature's shoulders shook side to side while she kept digging for food.

He was having trouble getting used to being able to speak to her live like this.

"You'll have lots of questions, Professor. Let's just say, you were uniquely qualified for our requirements."

"So, you didn't just pull my name out of a hat."

She snorted, something he now instinctually knew was a laugh among Delvonians. He wasn't sure what was so funny. His hairy arm absently reached down and scratched an itch near his genitals.

"No, Shepard, we spent a considerable amount of time and resources to locate you."

"I find that hard to accept, Kate."

Her host shrugged. For vocalizations, he was hearing her voice back at the lab, but gestures and movements of her host also reflected what Kate was saying.

"Kate," Pike said, "I'm nothing special. Anything I am even marginally good at, I could give you a dozen names of people who are significantly better." The two continued to walk together, the dwellings of settlement on the distant coastline slowly coming into view.

"No one else has your unique combination of skills and intelligence, plus one other thing you seem to be ignoring," she said.

He thought about that, and the answer came to him in a clear moment of 'duh.' "You had to find someone who's entangled twin was someone close to you or at least potentially accessible here on the other side. It would do you no good to grab just anyone to jump with only for them to be on the other side of the planet." That brought up other questions in his mind. *How did she know he was a match for this one?* He still couldn't bring himself to refer to his host as a person, while seeing Kate as the creature beside him was not unusual in any way; even though they were only marginally humanoid.

"Okay, so..." Pike offered, his mental gears unspooling an idea. "I was entangled with you or someone you knew that your 'other' would be close to over here. Someone who would be...'friendly' toward you." That word seemed inadequate, but he let it go.

Kate answered, "Not just over here, on nearly every world I have visited, Pike. You and I seem to always be paired in one form or another. Still, there are other aspects of your history that were just as important."

"Like what?"

She didn't respond immediately, but slowly her words came. "Your military background...that's quite unusual for a true academic. You rose to what...lieutenant before leaving the Marines? Yet you don't seem to be a military type at all. Still, you are disciplined, have leadership skills, and can follow orders. Plus, you have a master's degree in a field that is uniquely perfect for SideSlipping to other worlds."

He considered that. He'd already assumed his military background played some part, but his degree was in engineering and quantum physics. Pike saw far ahead another figure emerging from a stand of tall, blue grass near the path. He sensed a heightened state of alert from his host body. As he eyed Kate's host, he felt an odd but totally familiar urge to mate. The sensations of the host did not exactly mirror his own. Even though he knew some part of that creature was his girlfriend, the very site of the female creature was revolting on his most human levels. Still, his host wanted her, needed her. He pushed the thought aside for now. He wanted to understand why he was the one Kate selected.

"So..."

She cut him off. "You are also overlooking one more crucial piece that makes you uniquely suited for the task at hand."

Pike's host's increasing nervousness and another thought from his overstimulated brain delayed him from following up on the subject. "So, Delvos is a D-class dimension? I mean, this is still Earth, right?" He had been briefed on the naming conventions. The first to jump to a new world had the honor of naming it. Often, it was after creatures of mythology or astronomical in nature but could, in fact, be anything. The names went from A to Z with A letter names being the most Earth-normal. So far, the teams didn't routinely visit worlds any more remote than a T-class, but that world was apparently very un-Earthlike.

"Yes," Kate answered. "One of about fifteen D-type worlds we know of, and while it essentially is our own planet, it helps to not think of it that way. We find that bias theory really interferes with our ability to see things as they actually are."

Pike was familiar with the problem and had cautioned his teams constantly to avoid it during his 'Fixer' days. If you approached an issue thinking you knew the cause, then you tended to believe everything that reinforced that belief and discounted anything that went against it. “So, the tendency is to compare things here to the more familiar back on Earth?”

“Yes, like ‘Is the ocean the Indian or Pacific?’ It’s neither. In fact, we believe it to be entirely landlocked and relatively shallow.”

They had walked up a small rise and now were on a wide trail that was leading into the village. More Delvonians could be seen in the surrounding fields and paths. “It’s much worse if you assume things about the indigenous species...the others. If you expect your opposites to act as a human would act, you will be constantly surprised.”

As if in anticipation of her statement, several Delvonian males stepped onto the path blocking their way. Pike instinctively knew from his host that these were rival males, for Kate’s other. He heard a rhythmic grunting and chanting sound from several of the individuals as they spread out and moved toward him aggressively. It did not take superior intellect to identify the potential threat these onlookers posed. Two of them were familiar, Maylok and Tor. The names came to him as easily as his own. They were his cousins, all from the same pod with a shared dislike for each other, who were now rivals for the same mate. He looked over at Kate. ‘Her.’ They were going to battle for her.

One of the Delvonian beasts, Maylok, was far larger, and he swung something like a club that just barely missed Pike’s head. His host’s head would be more accurate, but now that the fight had begun, Pike felt that he was running the show. He was suddenly piloting this massive body in a deadly fight. He leaned sideways and snapped off a powerful leg kick that connected with the massive beast in the chest. Maylok rose, yelled, and charged again in rage. Pike interpreted the words as essentially ‘It’s time for you to die.’ Despite the creatures’ stocky bodies, they moved quite fast. Still, Maylok’s, and then Tor’s, movements were rushed and inaccurate. Pike easily parried a blow from one and spun out of the way of the third who’d also charged in.

Maylok was down on one knee and crab-walked sideways to retrieve the fallen club. Tor managed to chop at the back of Pike’s knee, which left him off balance, just as Maylok made a vicious swing upward with the weapon. Fighting the natural instinct to move away from the swing, Pike leaned even closer to his opponent, inside the outer arc of Maylok's reach. As momentum took the hairy creature up, Pike came down on the soft skull plate he knew to be just above the floppy ears. He felt bone crushing as his fist drove home. Maylok's inert body hit the ground before the club did.

All three of the gang of troublemakers were down now, one of them permanently. Somehow, Pike had instinctually known this would have to be a fight to the death. Just as he now knew the others would want no more part of it since their leader had been defeated. Death here was not a crime, it was a ritual, a part of keeping the herd's bloodline strong. His host bared sharp teeth at them and unleashed a mighty roar. The two remaining scrambled back in what appeared to be shock at the unusual turn of events. He assumed they had no doubt the much larger Maylok would have been victorious.

Kate was standing away from the melee, and he could sense the look of amusement on her face. He thought he understood now why he was chosen. While there was no way to bring a weapon across the divide between universes, if you could find someone who *was* a weapon, well...

26

Kate and Pike in their two Delvonian hosts ambled into the village and settled in at a communal water fountain that emptied into a long wooden trough. Pike lapped water along with Kate while taking notice of the thick layer of algae or fungus lining the water trough. *Just like watering cows,* he thought. Yet, these were not cows, they were presumably on a similar intelligence level to humans. They could build, they had a social structure, although it seemed wildly dissimilar to humans so far. A question occurred to him. "Are the Delvonians classified as humanoid?" They were bipedal and arms and hands were marginally human-like, although covered in fur and more muscular.

"We don't consider them humanoid and even some misgivings on classifying them as proto-humanoid," Kate said. "Our biologists don't believe any of our common ancestors would have ever evolved in this fashion. Walking upright on two limbs offers a better view of the surroundings, better to spot prey animals. It's not exclusively a human trait. The Delvonian almost always settle around large bodies of water, and our belief is they most likely evolved from an aquatic or semi-aquatic ancestor. They are still quite comfortable in the water. Great swimmers, even as babies."

They moved in a common direction toward a large structure

vaguely reminiscent of a Spanish-style home, but several stories tall with a nearly flat roof. "These are the villas," Kate said. "We use them for communal eating and sleeping. There is no concept of private homes among these creatures, nor individual town names."

Pike inherently knew this already, but having the doctor state it made it more obvious. He also knew there was another village a little smaller about a day's walk to his left and multiple towns and a large marina a couple of hours north. The fact they had no name just seemed normal. The villa seemed to be made of adobe or some similar type of natural brick. He'd seen no large trees; perhaps wood or whatever the local equivalent of wood was a rarity. "Do our others, live together?"

"Sometimes," Kate answered. Then she added, "Often actually, but there are two other villas for this town. These people are surprisingly social but lack many of the norms we might associate with friendship or love. They have sex when it's a breeding cycle like now, then they do it wherever they feel like, and yes, before you ask, we have done the wild thing. But if I were to have gone and bumped uglies with Tor, or even the late Maylok, it would not have changed how we react to each other."

He considered that. "It seems very egalitarian."

"It's survival instinct, Pike," Kate said. "We have no accurate count on the population of Delvos, but it's pretty obviously not in the billions. The pods are a type of family group, and they eventually grow into a village. Sometimes pods break away to go start their own, but procreating the species with the most viable line of descendants is an imperative that supersedes anything we might think of as love or family or relationships."

"It's a herd mentality?" he asked. "At some point did they have a massive die-off, or do they just not breed in sufficient numbers to affect the population size?"

"We believe it was a die-off. They breed on a similar basis as humans. You noticed the pinkish tinge in the water?" Kate asked.

"Yeah, and a smell that seemed off," Pike said.

"There aren't anything like scientists here, so we have to gather all the evidence by observation. We believe on our Earth that a planet-wide imbalance in the oceans led to something like a massive algae bloom. In this case, though, it seemed to flood the biosphere with oxygen, which probably killed off great numbers. It's in a decline now, but this may be part of a regular cycle."

"You mean oxygen is poison to the Delvonians? Aren't we breathing oxygen now?"

"No, Pike. Thanks to some very rudimentary experimentation, we are pretty sure the O^2 level in the atmosphere is relatively low. Of course, you have to remember the laws of physics here could be dramatically different from our dimension, so our experiments may be giving false data."

Pike let that sink in; he was living inside a body that did not require oxygen to live. In fact, it might be as poison to this animal as carbon monoxide was to humans. "Wow..." Suddenly he felt very far away from South Carolina.

"Pike, are you okay?" Kate asked worriedly. He mumbled a response but very much was not. The sensation of inhabiting another life form was a brutal shock to the man. Mostly because it felt incredibly natural.

She gave him some time on his own to adjust to this new world. The strangeness blended with the familiar as he sat back and observed the hosts interacting. The language was guttural but sweet in a way that reminded him of many human cultures he'd studied. While he understood the words and the context simply by occupying the unconscious portion of the creature's brain, other aspects lacked the texture or weight they probably deserved. What we say as humans doesn't always concur with what we mean, and it was the same with his host.

At mealtime, Pike's host filled a wooden bowl with what appeared to be a stew of possibly fish with some thick, white grain, or maybe...as he looked closer, he decided it was an insect larva. Thinking about it made him gag, but the sensation the Delvonian felt was pleasure, so he, too, felt pleasure. Kate's host, and it appeared all the females, ate in a separate area of the villa. He sent a ping through the back channel to signal comms mode.

"Yes, Shepard, enjoying your dinner?" she said with a chuckle.

"As long as I don't look at it, smell it, or think about it, sure."

"So, what's on your mind?" Kate asked.

"The conversations between the males are all very literal. Most of it is focused on the meal, the weather, or an upcoming harvest. I also notice no adornment of any kind, no jewelry, no art on the walls, and I don't see much that might exist in the way of entertainment. If these guys are on a similar intelligence level as us, shouldn't there be some of that? Why is everything just so...functional and utilitarian?"

She responded with, "Hmmm. Well, consider that human intelligence hasn't changed significantly in hundreds of thousands of years. Neanderthals were probably nearly as intelligent as we are. We just have a collective wisdom of a few hundred thousand more years to draw from. Even if you just went back a few hundred years to colonial America, you would find that life was hard, focus was on the functional, and entertainment was a minor part of life at best. Still, they had faith, music, and song and other forms of art. The Delvonians may just have never developed these traits, or as we have come to believe, the very lack of self-identity robs them of the more creative aspects of life."

"So, the fact we can use them as hosts, direct them subconsciously, may also be what is stunting their development?" Pike asked.

Kate answered, "You're applying human constructs to a non-human life. I don't feel stunted here and doubt any of these others do. Would you ask a hive of bees why they have no museums? Our art and really, most of our creativity, is an extension of our self-expression. We're strongly connected to our individualistic nature and seem to enjoy finding new ways of communicating that to others, through art, books, songs, humor...you name it. And to answer your next question, no...not every species who are good hosts have this kind of functional mindset, and some have very well-developed creative pursuits. As you SideSlip into more worlds, you'll find more differences than similarities. Every culture, every dimension is unique."

Before bed, the creatures all filed out and in the direction of the beach. Bath time was also a communal event it seemed. The temperature of the bay was warm, and Pike watched in amazement as the waters lit up in glowing light around those already out beyond the surf. Kate's host, whose name he knew as Ori, came by and bumped him hard on her way to bathe. Unlike eating, bathing time was not segregated by sex. He had his creature run its arm through the water and marveled at the dripping dots of bluish light cascading off the fur.

"We believe it is bioluminescent, much like our own oceans," Kate said. "Somehow here, though, the glowing biomass also helps clean the Delvonian, probably by removing fleas or parasites or whatever the local equivalent is."

Pike could tell his own host had little interest in the beauty that was all around him. He only wanted to be clean and certainly seemed to feel more comfortable in the water. Nearly as one, all of them rolled and dove deep like a pod of seals. Pike felt the rush of water and was amazed at how good the eyesight was underwater. Small, fishlike animals and less identifiable creatures sped away from the approaching herd. "Wow."

"I know," he heard Kate say. "I wanted you to experience this. They may not have art or music, but this they very much enjoy."

Pike enjoyed it, too. In fact, it was one of the most amazing experiences of his life. Soon he found Ori was swimming beside him. Her body was circling and intertwining with his own, or his host's, he amended. *Is this Kate or the Delvonian?* The feeling was intimate and friendly. He found he didn't have to encourage any particular behavior from his own host. These two were drawn to each other.

Finally, Kate said, "We need to return, Pike. Our two others deserve some privacy."

27

"Guys, please, you must understand this is fascinating and all, but you have to admit, in theory, this could still be a massive virtual reality...a game in which we are NPCs just along for the ride," Pike insisted. "I have to still consider it just to be objective. The physical laws are different, the flora, fauna, even strata don't match our own. Despite the very rich reality I just visited, I do still need to point out the obvious. Even if it is real, we have limited access to the local science or tech, so what do SideSlips offer us in any useful way other than entertainment?"

"Shepard, if you think about it, you will get there," Doctor Xiang Win Lu stated confidently. "As a scientist, you must admit to the likely existence of other intelligent life in our Universe, yes?"

Pike nodded.

"Now, even if we, or they, are somehow capable of light-speed travel, how likely is it we will ever meet?"

Pike considered her point, already sensing where this was heading. "The travel would most likely take decades or even longer. Unless they've mastered warping space-time to shorten the distance."

Doctor Lu smiled. "Decades for our closest, more like centuries for the more promising planets, and thousands or tens of thousands for those closer into the center of our own galaxy, much, much longer to those beyond the Milky Way."

"Okay," Pike said. "I'll concede the point that finding other intelligent life is a viable reason, and this way is cheap and effective in comparison, even if it does seem more like magic than science. Still, finding others in our own Universe would offer us more tangible returns. The physics and chemistry would be the same if nothing else. Even through simple observation, we could learn more from an inhabited world in our Universe than countless ones out in the multiverse."

Kate Cassidy looked around the small conference room table waiting for one of the others to correct their new pupil. The astrophysicist, Letner, waded into the conversation with the subtlety of an elephant.

"Don't be an idiot, Shepard. We are eons from the level of technology to even begin to get close to transit times of those speeds, and even then, it would be only with automated ships or Von Neuman Probes that would have rudimentary scientific sensors and probably no way of ever getting any data back to us here on a reliable basis. That is, if light speed, much less FTL, is even remotely possible. We know that is the upper limit of our own universe. Truthfully, quantum mechanics provides the only possible way of bypassing that barrier."

Pike rubbed the side of his nose and reluctantly nodded his head in agreement.

Letner continued, "By SideSlipping to other 'Earths,' we know intelligent life does exist, and due to the great variety of biospheres we've encountered, it is likely abundant. That tells us a great deal about our own existence. For one thing, it means we are not that special. Where there is life, it will fill up every environmental niche possible."

Pike had to voice an objection to that. "But we are. You yourself said we are simply traveling to other versions of our own planet. How do we know Earth isn't the only one that is viable for life, intelligent or otherwise?"

Letner smiled and looked to Kate who nodded for him to continue. "You're a smart guy, Professor, and you already understand much about the theories of the multiverse. What is your understanding of pocket universes?"

Pike had to think for a moment; he had heard the term many times over the years but couldn't recall the context. "Essentially nothing," he admitted.

"It's all part of inflationary theory," Letner continued. "A pocket universe or dimension could be created in a bubble, possibly even one inside an existing universe. We've always considered these to be short-lived, and our Doctor Cassidy has some interesting theories of her own. The point is, these are complete universes just like our own, possibly mirroring our own, and could theoretically be embedded somewhere within our own stretch of space-time. It is even possible these would be where alternative versions of our reality exist."

"The mirror world's theory of alternate timelines," said Kate, picking up the conversation. "We've discussed it, Pike. These pocket universes could be intentionally close and temporary, if there is a high likelihood that the timelines might be reintegrated back together at some point."

Pike thought on that briefly. *What would life in a temporary world be like?* "But they would be inaccessible to us, as all the other realms, wouldn't they?" Pike challenged, remembering more of the concept now.

Letner responded, "With SideSlips, they are not inaccessible, and since they are inside our own Universe, we feel it likely they share the same physical laws. Could be our science and theirs would be... compatible, if not exactly the same." He drew the final part out in dramatic fashion.

Pike stared at the tabletop, trying to wrap his mind around what the man was saying. He'd always prided himself on being able to absorb massive amounts of information and quickly narrowing it down to the most salient points. Project Cobalt was taxing that ability to the limit. He'd once heard a noted mathematician talking about exact copies of our own world, our own reality hidden in the distant expanse of our own universe. It was all based on mathematical probabilities, though. *Hidden universes*...the thought finally spit up the obvious fact. "You've seen it! Somehow you *know* there are versions of our Universe within our own!"

Letner smiled and waggled his hands a bit. "Or vice versa, we could be in a pocket universe inside of theirs. We aren't sure, and it probably doesn't matter. A bubble within a bubble is still a bubble."

Doctor Lu pulled up an image on her tablet and pushed it over to Pike. It was one of the numerous 3D renderings of an alternate world. He had seen countless ones the artist on site created by working with jumpers when they returned. "This is Seles Prime."

He studied the image in detail. The view was an interpretation of how the planet would look from high orbit. It was Mars-like in its basic appearance; a ruddy, brownish-red ball with a thin atmosphere and just a few bodies of visible water. Seles would be very far down the alphabetical list from an Earth-like world, yet Pike could see pinpoints of light on the dark side. It would have to be inhabited for someone to have visited. He gathered this was part of what Letner was getting at and made the logical jump. "How did you determine this was within our own dimension?"

"They're very advanced, several thousand years beyond our own at the very least," Kate said. "They're particularly good at astronomical observation with some uniquely genius ways of gathering data about their universe."

"So, what, some of the star maps were the same as our own?" Pike asked.

"It's Earth, Professor Shepard. Of course, the star maps are the same...or very nearly so," Letner responded factually.

Kate continued, "No, one of our travelers was a young intern in one of their research labs. We were unbelievably lucky in that regard, but her job was to analyze the vast backlog of anomalous cosmic signals that had been detected. You know, the types our own radio telescopes listen for. Along with the rhythmic harmonics of pulsars to the burst of static from merging neutron stars, was buried something else. A signal that the local scientists on Seles had catalogued but never investigated for whatever reason."

Pike's palms began to sweat as his mind narrowed down the likely possibilities. "A transmission from us, from our Universe?"

She nodded. "A garbled transmission that was clearly from a very human sounding radio broadcast."

Questions flooded Pike's mind. That would mean radio waves could cross a dimensional barrier. How? What else? Humans had been polluting the Universe with electro-magnetic transmissions for several hundred years now. Radio came around in the late 1800s. He did some quick math on his notepad. "That would put the bubble universe within about 100 light years of here. That would practically be an interstellar neighbor, not something on the outer edge of the Universe."

"Very good, Shepard!" Letner proclaimed. "Now you see what we see. The Universe is not just much more confusing than we expect, it is more confusing than we are even capable of imagining. How is this possible? How does it affect us? Can we reach Seles, or can they reach us through traditional means? Who knows? It is what it is."

"It would seem," Kate began, "that almost anything is possible in the multiverse. Alternate dimensions may spring out of nothingness parallel to our own reality, or they may split from an existing timeline due to some seismic shift in that dimension. Something so fundamentally important as to the Universe itself allowing two realities to move forward. One for each of the possibilities to have occurred. This is consistent with what we know of quantum mechanics."

"But that implies the Universe has a process, an intelligence monitoring itself. What you are describing is God, isn't it?" Pike asked.

"Not so much, although that certainly could be one possibility," Lu responded. "The laws of the Universe are generally accepted to exist with no need for intelligent or super-intelligent interaction. Just as the observer rule in quantum mechanics, where a wave state may collapse from many to one when an intelligent being is observing. We don't understand it, but it is a fact. So, we must accept the fact that the reverse of that is also probably true. In the absence of an observer, a state can go from one to many. No God needed."

Pike stared at the planet on the screen and suddenly felt a lot more apprehensive about what came next.

Doctor Letner stood and grasped him on the shoulder. “It just got a lot more real to you, didn’t it?”

Pike nodded very slowly. *Damn sure did.*

28

"So, how does all this relate to me?" Pike asked. "I mean, I have a basic grasp of SideSlipping, I've seen other worlds. I understand Earth...our Earth," he amended, "is under threat. I know that other worlds have faded as well. Possibly only from our ability to see, but the devastation and chaos raging on them prior to the last moments points to something much more final." He leaned up on the briefing table, hands extended and clasped together. "I'm just a simple backwater college professor. What in the hell help can I be in all this?"

Letner eyed Kate, who nodded. The older man leaned back and cleared his throat before responding. "Professor Shepard, first let me say I am not convinced you can be of help to us."

Pike frowned; the man's tone seemed to live in the combative zone, no matter the topic.

"Oh, Doctor Cassidy assures me I am wrong." He held up his hands in a placating gesture that Pike felt sure was rehearsed and ungenuine. "I have learned to trust her assessments. You need to experience more of the worlds in our local network. But Kate, why don't you take some time to fill Pike in more about Aragon?"

* * *

Outside, the day was white hot with a sapphire blue sky. The ocean breeze felt refreshing and the water inviting. "We going to swim?"

Kate shook her head sadly. "We have to have security for that."

Pike glanced back out to sea; he'd shed his shoes and was already in above his knees.

"Tiger sharks," she said, as if that was all the comment needed.

Apparently, not all the security protection of the Cobalt facility was manmade. "I remember seeing a report on one of these islands. Huge spike in shark attacks in the last few years," he said.

Kate agreed. "La Reunion off Mauritius. They made it illegal to swim it was so dangerous. Not that bad here, but it's still not advised to go in without a spotter...or three."

Pike eased back toward shore and sat in the gentle surf line. "What happened on Aragon?" he asked. Her silence echoed around the sand as her expression let it be known she was still not ready to discuss it.

"What is The Fade?" Pike asked, recalling the earlier conversation. She might not be comfortable discussing it, but he was unwilling to move on to safer topics. This was why he was here after all; this was what she wanted him to help stop. May as well dig in and get the details.

Pike saw Palio walking up the beach to join them. The boy seemed to sense when his boss might need some support. He, too, seemed concerned for her state of mind. Kate's eyes were filling with tears as they took notice of Palio, and something unspoken seemed to pass between them.

"I think I told you I am a boy there. My family lives...lived in the capital. A magical place they call Kamarov," she began, her voice hitching several times as she struggled to get the words out. "Aragon is an A-type world, obviously. It is very Earth-like but more of a fantasy version of our reality. If Disney wanted to design a dimension, Kamarov would have been the star attraction." She looked out to sea as if the memories were being delivered by the trade winds. "The architecture is modern but resembles the lines of ancient castles. My town is nestled in a lush valley surrounded by mountains and a massive waterfall. The largest one on the planet is just outside the city gates. The goodness of its people matches the serenity of the place. It's hard to explain, but you know how we become that other person, er, creature when we SideSlip? With some worlds, that connection can be incredibly familiar. That was the case with me in Aragon. I love my life there, it's simple and rewarding. In fact, I was only missing one thing that would have made it complete."

Pike thought he might know what that thing was but let her continue. Their relationship was too new to him to want to make such assumptions. He subtly pointed at the ground next to them for Palio to take a seat.

Kate continued, "I had not been back in a few months. I was one of the few of us now with a host on that world, so it was like my own private treasure. Pike, I would have loved to have shared it with you. The smells of the street vendors, the festivals, and the schools and libraries. The Aragonians were obsessed with knowledge, not technology, but just gaining wisdom."

"It sounds very special," Pike said, noticing the silent tears streaming down her face.

She nodded. "Now, imagine me SideSlipping back into my other to find him standing in a scene of complete carnage. My host's family lying butchered all around him. I still don't know if he did it or someone else. The boy's mind was a jumble of anger, hatred, and thoughts of harming himself and others."

"Madness?" Pike asked.

"Yes, Pike, it's what happens before a dimension begins to fade, as it cuts the individuals off from the local network. Most calming emotions seem to dull, hostilities increase, and a person's actions seem inconsequential to them. When my host walked out of our house, I saw that the killings of his family hadn't been an isolated event. Hundreds, maybe thousands, of my neighbors lay dead, others were busy fashioning weapons out of ordinary objects or jumping from rooftops. Apparently, this had been building over several weeks or months, as many bodies were decomposing where they had fallen. The level of atrocity equals nothing we've seen on our world."

"Palio, would a sudden lack of connected consciousness cause such a moral collapse in humans?" Pike asked.

"Professor, we don't know. Humans have the built-in capacity for aggression and brutality. My thought is that it shouldn't be the case, but the murky depths of consciousness and abstract thought touch on areas of religiosity, love, loss, anger. Those are some of the strongest emotive centers we have as a species. Obviously, we are not so evolved as to be immune. In fact, we are far less civilized as a culture than Aragon." Palio eyed Kate. "You going to tell him the rest?"

Pike turned in his seat to face Kate. "The rest? What else happened before The Fade?"

The look on Kate's face was pained. "My host spent much of the last day in hiding and, at times, fighting for his life," she began. "Late in the day, I began to realize I had to leave Aragon, and since I was pretty sure by then as to what was happening, I knew I wouldn't ever be able to go back there again. It made me incredibly sad, and I wanted one more chance to see the city the way it had been.

"There was an overlook well outside the city gates that was the most beautiful view. That day it was just far enough away not to see the ugliness taking hold of Aragon. I was able to influence my 'other' to go there. Even though I could still hear the occasional screams, it was better. Then, a stranger walked up. He was carrying a weapon of some type, but he didn't threaten us. My host wanted to run, but I already knew what was coming. I urged him to stay seated and take no action. Then the stranger started speaking, not to my host and not in the local language. He was speaking to me and in English."

"What? How is that possible?" Pike asked.

"It's possible but difficult," Palio stated. "The stranger was Carapaz," he added.

"What did he say, was he the one responsible?"

Kate's tears flowed more freely now. "No...no, in fact, he said I was the one responsible. I had ended Aragon. Just like I was going to bring The Fade to Earth."

"Bring it here?" Pike whispered. "So, he was right? That's what's happening, isn't it?" he asked, not giving her time to answer before adding. "If it comes here, will the madness get everyone?"

He felt more than saw her silently nodding. "In time, we think so, yes. First, seems to be the most creative, the outliers, our artists, actors, philosophers, and such. Those individuals who are the most well connected to the creative part of their brain. Those are the most sensitive, or most receptive, we don't really know. That's just what has happened on other worlds, at least. Creativity dies, but we've already discussed my theory that it's part of our hive-mind anyway, so that may just be the result of the dimension unplugging from the network at the start of The Fade."

"What about kids? Their entire world is make-believe and creative fun."

Pike's question was loaded. Even Kate knew that his own childhood haunted him. She hesitated before answering and watched in the distance as three boys, probably from one of the military families, were laughing and weaving their way down to the water's edge. "Yes, Pike, no one is immune. The Fade is indiscriminate in that regard."

Her voice sounded tinny and far away. Still, her arms clutched him tightly as he brought his knees up and rested his chin on them. Pike knew he was missing too much vital information at the moment to see the whole problem clearly. How was it possible to cut off a planet from the multiverse? How could specific individuals be targeted before that? "You're sure it was Carapaz?"

"Yes, Pike, he's been reported on nearly all the worlds before The Fade even begins. I don't know what Julian is doing, but he is clearly involved," said Kate.

"Why would Carapaz bring The Fade here?" Pike asked, sitting back in the warm sand staring blankly out to sea. His thoughts were chaotic but he searched for strands of data that might point to a solution.

Kate slipped off her shoes and walked into the warm water. "We don't know, Pike. It makes no sense to any of us. He's just dangerous. We know he's picked up a lot more from his SideSlips than the rest of us." She had been up walking but abruptly sat beside him laying her head on his shoulder.

"What do you mean, 'picked up?'"

"It's a little hard to explain, but with some jumps, the host's mind imprints on us. When that happens, we retain a great deal of memories and knowledge from the other dimension."

Pike interrupted, "But how useful is that? Palio, you said that the physics are not even the same in many worlds, and who knows if what works there will work here?"

"That's true to a point, but many worlds are similar enough that the information does stand up, and in other cases, things are true across all worlds, just things that humans haven't figured out yet," Palio answered, still squatting beside them.

"Like what?"

"Well, just in one area—things like workable alternatives to fossil fuels for energy production. High-capacity energy storage and a recursive loop power grid in which virtually no power is lost to resistance."

Pike's mind made several intuitive leaps. Power generation was one industry he'd worked with many times. He knew that electricity was never really used up. That was the beauty of the electrical 'current.' It ran through your house powering all your devices, your A/C, your television, your phone charger and lights, then flowed back out again to your neighbors. Eventually, in theory, it would flow back to a generation plant and start over again. The heat given off by these devices from the minor heat of your phone charger or to the high temperatures of an oven were the result of resistance. That was the act of energy being converted from electricity to heat. Pike instantly recalled the equation for the rate of energy loss. This exchange, or conversion, is where electricity disappears. If that could be recaptured, or never lost, then you could get by producing far less. "You have access to that now? Some other world figured it out?"

"Lots," Palio answered cheerfully.

Kate broke in, "And the ability to broadcast electricity, although far fewer have mastered that. We don't have a good way of bringing it to market, but our board is working to license the technology."

Pike started to understand. "So, you aren't just doing this for scientific exploration...there's a tangible benefit to going to these other worlds."

"Very definitely," Kate answered. "In fact, originally, I started jumping hoping I might find a cure for my sister's illness. Sadly, I didn't, but that's the type of knowledge we want. Knowledge that can improve lives, not make them worse."

"That's why you looked for me and other scientists to become travelers? The chances of our hosts being in a similarly technical field in their world."

"Yes," Kate admitted. "That was the original plan. Even if your host is not in an area that is beneficial, you're more likely to understand the principles at work and be able to do research on it there," said Kate. "That's how we brought Julian in."

"Carapaz is a scientist on other worlds?" Pike asked.

"He is *the* scientist on most worlds," she answered. "His technical genius always seems to be recognized. He's the only traveler we've ever run into that's always in the upper echelon of scientific research. No one else equals him for sheer brilliance and access to tech. He's smart, charming, and opportunistic, and those are just some of his skills. We think he has learned how to also achieve total recall via a type of eidetic memory. Every time he returned, his mind seemed to nearly overflow from a vast depth of new knowledge. He would get frantic to make notes and start experiments. He can be a bit obsessive-compulsive on some things. Little did we know all that wisdom was also poisoning him against us...not until it was too late. Now, it may be too late for all of humanity."

"He sounds like an interesting person, shame he's the enemy." Something related occurred to Pike. "Could whatever is causing the Fade, the madness, be what happened to him? Since he jumped more and longer, it affected him faster?"

Palio shook his head. "We considered that, but I don't think so. Julian's mind seems uniquely adept at navigating the multiverse. Sandy seems convinced that he does have an eidetic memory, and that is a strong advantage for him, but no idea why he turned on us."

Pike thought for a moment, making a mental note to discuss that with Doctor Almira. If Carapaz had a photographic memory, that would allow him to capture a lot of specific information from the worlds he traveled. Pike also had a slightly eidetic memory but kept that fact to himself for now. “I’ve got an idea of how we might be able to do something similar.”

“What?” Palio asked.

“Take pictures of our SideSlips,” Pike said.

“Are you going to invent a mental iPhone, Professor?”

Not yet, he thought. *But it’s a start.*

29

Pike had a routine when it came to science; he was as methodical as a German-made timepiece. While he trusted his mind to be an accurate lens into these distant realms, the inability to precisely record what one was seeing or experiencing seemed downright anemic. He knew the comms system they used often failed because of interference with the speech centers in the host's mind. Plus, just repeating what you saw on the other side was time-consuming and slow. Imagine if you had to narrate everything you were doing during the day, as well as the actual doing. No, a better way had to be found, and he thought he had the basics of a plan.

Palio brought in everything he had asked for. Pike pulled the various pieces from the box and nodded in approval. It took the two men several days to modify a single launch chair with Pike's new equipment. The once elegant looking leather and steel chair now looked more like the poor DeLorean sports car after Doctor Emmett Brown had added the flux capacitor in the "Back to the Future" movies.

"So, you going to explain this to me, or do I just trust you?" asked Kate.

Pike smiled and invited her to sit in the contraption. "Sure, Kate.

We know that speech can sometimes be compromised, plus, it's inefficient at capturing all the detail and nuance of a host's environment. But we have imagery from that dimension hitting our visual receptors in our brain here. We also have some movement of our extremities here."

"Like our fingers?"

He smiled. "Exactly, much like when we're in a dream state, we're mostly paralyzed, but certain muscle groups are excluded. Your heart keeps beating, your lungs keep breathing, and for most of us our legs, to some degree, and our hands are free to move." He flipped up a device along the tight armrest of the chair. It was a framed, matte gray screen and reminded her of one of their tablets used for data entry, but the screen was a different texture and clearly not glass.

"It's a large touchpad, like your mouse-pad on a laptop only bigger," he said proudly.

Palio added, "We got them from security. It's the same device we use on the doors going into secure areas, those that require a palm print."

Kate nodded, recognition beginning to dawn on her. "So, we can write what we see, even if we can't speak?"

Pike nodded. "Yes, but much more. Have you ever heard of Gregg Shorthand?"

Kate and Palio both shook their heads.

"It's been around forever," Pike went on. "Invented back in the late 1800s, I believe. It uses symbols for sounds and is incredibly fast. Some journalism schools still teach it. You can write at speeds of a hundred words per minute with it."

"Is that like steno?"

"It's related, Palio. Stenography is a specialized form of shorthand used for exact transcription. It uses symbols for the chords that sounds make."

"So how does this help us, Pike? None of us know shorthand," Kate asked.

He smiled. "I do, and I can teach you."

"Why would you know it, and won't that take a long time?"

Pike glanced away, clearly emotionally connected to the answer of why. "It was an exercise I used as a kid to help retrain my mind. At first, it was just work, but over the months, I started to enjoy it. It was almost like a secret code, and I found I could take notes faster than anyone. Really screwed up my college professors that saw me making the squiggly lines. Over time, I learned some classic Chinese, which uses a single symbol for an entire word. Also, other microforms which I incorporated into my own version."

"You developed your own version of shorthand?" Kate asked, a wry smile creasing her face.

"Yep, and since I needed my assistants on project sites to be able to read it, we designed a computer program to teach it and to help decode it."

"And you have the program?"

Pike answered, "Of course. Palio downloaded it yesterday from my iCloud account. It's a pretty small executable."

She was struggling to grasp that her new friend, the Luddite, had an iCloud account, much less spoke a hidden language. "So, you'll be the only one who can use it until the rest of us learn. How long will that take?"

Pike showed her how the sensor glove slipped around your palm and wrist. "About three years normally. I do have some shortcuts, though, and you won't have to learn all of it. By incorporating some objects from computer language, I've made it even more efficient. You'll begin to see results in just a month or two and should be proficient in about nine. The training system uses a feedback algorithm that adjusts to your progress, so you're always strengthening your weaknesses."

Kate moved her finger along the grey pad, and a series of lines appeared on the display mounted above. Pike moved her hand and quickly tapped and slid multiple fingers which showed up as blips and dashes on the screen before morphing into "I miss you, Kate, when can we be alone?"

She blushed, making Palio want to lean in to see what he had written. She cleared the screen. "So, this is good for what we see but still doesn't give us an actual picture."

Pike conceded the point. "It's a step in that direction and will definitely help me. I think it will be particularly good for written information. Since our hosts can presumably read on any planet with a written language, we can read it, too. We'll just have to make sure we translate it to my shorthand and not try to write it in their native language. Mathematics, technical data, chemical formulas, physics, and more. I think this can be a big help."

"Big? Heck, Professor, this is huge," Palio said, grinning broadly.

"It's perfect, Pike," Kate said, leaning up and kissing him on the lips. "I knew you could help us. I just didn't think it would be so quick."

"I had a plan, years ago, to do a direct neural interface at some point, so I could simply think about the symbols and an app on a smartphone would register it. My version is almost 250 words per minute, and I think with the app, we could do even more. But eventually, you outpace the brain."

"Why stop with the symbols?" Palio asked, clearly racing ahead of his teammates. "If your brain is forming an image, and your neural interface can pick it up..."

Pike snapped his fingers. "That's right, man."

Kate was clearly lost and began to untangle herself from the launch chair. "I believe this part is for the two of you to figure out."

Palio was at the white board already making notes. "The images of the symbols would already be in your visual cortex, so if your interface can interpret that, with enough power, why can't it capture the entire scene your mind's eye is seeing?"

She heard Pike in enthusiastic agreement as she exited the room. With everything wrong happening in the world, she thought she might have just witnessed the breakthrough everyone on The Project had been waiting for. A way to meaningfully bring back tangible data from the other realities. That was good because they were jumping again in the morning. Pike needed to be ready to see his first X-class world.

30

Pike was again lying in the launch chair ready to see what this new world had to offer. Kate was in the control booth with Petra. Palio was getting him ready for the journey.

"So, what else can you tell me about this dimension?" Pike asked.

"Absolutely nothing, my friend."

"Nothing?" Pike said, confused.

"You'll see." Palio pulled up the interface on his tablet. "We believe the creatures there are sentient but have a complex visual system that is not binomial. The visual intake differs greatly from ours, so what we see is pretty trippy. Also, they don't share their consciousness the way other species do. Even non-visual signals seem chaotic to us. So, this works basically in view-only mode. Don't feel like you have to stay in longer than you want. Some travelers get physically ill going there."

Palio gave a short countdown, and Pike felt the slight tingling up his spine. "Ready for your passcode," the system's automated voice said.

Pike went through the process again, recalling the vivid memory with his childhood friend, Risson. Then, flickering images began to spark to life in his visual cortex. Slowly, they resolved themselves not into chaos, but into a perfect view of a very alien planet. Then the view was off, and it took him several minutes to realize he was seeing two different views at the same time. Still, it resolved itself fine, and quickly his mind adapted to the more expansive visuals. He was staring out from a ridge overlooking a wide, verdant green valley. It stretched to the horizon with virtually no deviation in width. Both sides of the valley were lined with rust-red peaks tens of thousands of feet tall. The mountain range on the right was obviously backlit by the sun as the bare peaks shown brilliantly in red and orange. The mountains to his left were shaded and dark, but their peaks were snow-capped, and he could even see what might be glaciers up in the higher valleys.

Why would they call this a chaos world or even classify it as an X-type dimension? It was different than the Earth that Pike knew but not that much so. He had the sudden realization that his host was moving; the view shifted slightly with each step, more like a human, less like the Delvonian host he had the prior week. The real shock came when the host stopped in front of a polished section of rock that was highly reflective. The creature was humanoid, with a slightly larger head and very large eyes set far apart. Its mouth moved slightly, and to his surprise, Pike heard and understood the words.

"Greeting, traveler."

Wait, Pike thought. *They aren't supposed to know I'm here. I'm simply connecting to them subconsciously, right?*

"You are called Shepard?" the creature said or thought. Pike wasn't sure which because he was no longer facing the mirror. It had moved deeper into the structure. He had not been on a ridge but in a dwelling. Apparently, the scenic balcony was just the outer section of his home. The walls were finely crafted and appeared to be hewn from natural stone. Everything he saw was of some natural material. *Yes,* he thought. *I am Shepard, and I mean you no harm. How is it you know I am here?*

His other spoke to him internally. "Our brains are wired differently than your species. We can sense when the connection between worlds is being accessed. Although none of your people have ever managed to communicate back with us."

"I'm sorry," Pike said uncertainly. "My friends said no one ever saw anything on this world."

"You must be unique in that way then, Shepard. Our brains are quite different from most other species we encounter. We believe most are unable to hear or see anything from our world. Why did your friends want you to come here if there was nothing to see?"

Pike knew the words were not in English, but he had a perfect understanding of the other's language. "They're trying to help me get used to traveling through the multiverse. They thought this was the most alien world I might encounter."

"Ahhh, not so alien after all, is it?"

Pike suddenly knew his other called himself Nianda. "I think they're just convincing me that the multiverse is real."

"Multiverse," Nianda said to himself. "Would you mind if I accessed your consciousness to better understand that word you use?"

"Um, go ahead," Pike answered uncertainly. After all, he had entered Nianda's mind without permission. He felt nothing, but several minutes later, his host spoke again.

"Thank you, most helpful. Your species' understanding of the 'multiverse' is very basic and not entirely accurate. In time, you will know how to counter the effects of variable time. For now, I have added something that may help you. A mental suggestion of sorts."

Nianda is going to help. The kindness this man was showing was encouraging. This was clearly a more advanced species than human. If he had been possessed like this, Pike would not be acting hospitably.

"Unlike your species or your reality, we are not aggressive in that way, Shepard. Our world is tidally locked to our sun, and our population all exist in a very narrow band between the night side and the day. We coexist and share openly, as that is the only way we can survive."

Pike knew that tidally locked planets did not rotate on their axis. Just like how the moon is locked to the Earth. One side of this world always faced the sun and the other the darkness of space. Scientists had always assumed such a world would be unsuitable for life, as the day side would bake in the intense heat of our local star, while the night side would stay colder than Antarctica. What event in Earth's history could have been so fundamentally different here to cause such a profound change?

"Our world, what you apparently call Xylos, does not have a single large moon," Nianda said as if answering his thoughts. "We have a ring of moonlets instead. Our world was not home to large reptile predators nor bombarded by meteors in the same way as your home world, so we had a much longer time to evolve."

"Thank you, Nianda, for sharing your mind with me. Does my being here cause you any discomfort? Should I leave?"

"No, we are very comfortable communicating this way. I believe we do not have the same need for privacy as your species. I would like it if you stayed for a few minutes longer. We should address the real problem on your world."

The ensuing conversation left Pike's mind reeling. He was unsure how much of this encounter to share with Kate or Palio. Nianda had revealed what they understood of The Fade.

"This is a truth that not everyone will accept, and few will welcome it for what it is," Nianda stated flatly.

"And that is?" Pike asked.

"A necessary step, Shepard. Something every intelligence must deal with once they reach a pivotal point."

"Can you help us?"

Nianda seemed to ponder this. "Sadly, we are unable to prevent it from happening to your version of reality. We may be able to offer some assistance, though. Let me speak with our leaders. When you return to us, I will have an answer. For now, stay safe, my friend." The lights and images in Pike's mind dimmed, and the sensation and sounds of the lab returned.

"What did I tell you, man? Crazy, huh?" Palio said, laughing. "You made it longer than I thought you would. Do you need a barf bag?"

"Is he okay?" Kate yelled from the other room.

"I'm fine, guys," Pike said, sitting up. And he was. "That was amazing."

Palio was checking his tablet again. "I think that was a record for anyone slipping to Xylos. Almost two minutes."

"Two minutes," Pike mumbled. He was certain it had been over an hour. "Xylos is not what you think."

"How's that?" Palio asked as he pulled away the sensors and began repacking his gear.

"Its very Earth-like, well, kind of. Definitely not X-class. It's a rim world, one narrow inhabitable band of life."

"You could see it, the terrain and the creatures?" Kate asked, coming into the launch room, the young woman, Petra, just behind her.

Pike couldn't think of a way to deliver the bad news Nianda had told him. For now, he would simply keep it close. Hopefully, he could still find a solution, but to do that, he desperately needed to find Carapaz.

31

The automated instructions in his ear buds were almost becoming routine.

"Fix the passcode memory in your mind and key in the numeric pin on your armrest controls."

Pike was in his modified launch chair. Kate was not going to be accompanying him on this journey, at least not initially, as he was heading to a terminus world where she had no other. From there, he would SideSlip twice more. The plan was for her to meet up with him on the last planet, Gaius.

He'd been to the terminus world, Hydron, twice before over the previous weeks. There was little to see as the population was very sparse, landscape mostly comprised, endless savannas of grass, very similar to areas of Africa. All he could tell about his host was that he was large, slow moving, and he seemed to think only about sex and food. *Pretty much a normal guy,* he'd concluded. He fixed the required passcode memory in his conscious mind and keyed in the six-digit code.

No rushing of sound or dazzling light show. The launch was essentially underwhelming by its ordinariness. Pike had learned to shut his eyes before keying the code, as the visual change could be disorienting. After all, you were slipping sideways into an alternate universe. Truthfully, though, it was the sounds and smells that let him know he'd arrived. The air felt different as well. He also knew the UV levels here were more than his Earth. He was pretty certain the atmospheric pressure was more, too. His eyes opened, and the blurry imagery that was hitting his host's visual cortex began to slowly come into focus.

"This is Shepard checking in."

That part was protocol, even though it still felt dumb to him. *I mean,* he thought, *I'm right here in the room.* Only his subconscious mind was gone, and even that was, at best, connected to this off world destination.

"Roger that," came the reply. "Secondary launch in three, two, one."

This time, Pike's eyes awoke to a world awash in color. This was his first trip to Luria. He knew it was a water world with only a couple of small land masses. This was also his first time in a completely non-humanoid host. He wanted to look down to see the body and the hands...flippers. The head didn't move with much freedom; he also felt the creature's conscious mind attempt to counterman Pike's will.

The Lurian population of hosts were known collectively as Tritons, although they were not the half man, half fish of ancient myth. The truth was more difficult to pin down, as the Tritons' bodies varied considerably among individuals. The closest approximation Pike had heard was they were porpoise-like with long appendages with winged webbing and a pair of grasping hands at the end of each front flipper. The host rocketed off into the depths, locking in on one particularly colorful animal. *Geesh, this is freaking awesome! Disney would demand big bucks to ride a simulation of this.*

"Shepard, you okay?"

Shit, he had forgotten to check in, and this was only the second jump. "Yes, Palio, sorry. Arrived, no issues, just enjoying the moment."

"No problem, man. Enjoy it for a while. Doctor Cassidy got detained on her first jump, so may be a few minutes late getting to the rendezvous."

Clouds of fishlike creatures burst apart as they swam at an impressive speed. The object was something that looked to him to be a giant Aspen leaf. It was bright orange at the front, fading to a dark brown at the rear. He could make out a few bumps which may have been eyes. Pike found himself analyzing the swimming of the creature, as the means of locomotion was a complete mystery. But the damn thing could turn on a dime. The reason for the odd shape and coloration became apparent as the leaf-fish turned yet again and darted down into a thick undergrowth of similar looking plants on the seafloor.

The Triton muttered a word that Pike knew to be a curse, although the full context of what he had described with the word was not entirely obvious. After almost a dozen trips off world, Pike was beginning to feel at ease in his host's brain, and even though he had access to the creature's sensory network, in memories and collective intelligence he still found gaps where context was obviously missing. How would someone in his own head deal with irony or satire? Kate had asked him that after one of his training sessions.

He and his host spent more time hunting and feeding. Each attack was exhilarating to Pike, and each prey animal consumed was both delicious and nauseating. The other jumpers had convinced him that, in time, he would learn how to tune down the sensory input from the less appealing nature of the hosts, but so far, he'd been unable. A few of the situations he'd already encountered had left him unable to eat for days, and one jump in particular made him constantly rise up to check down in the toilet as he was taking a shit. The idea of how that species processed its waste still unnerved him, no matter how efficient it was.

"Ready when you are, Shepard," came the voice in his ear.

"Good to go for slip."

Instead of the normal gentle shift, Pike felt a mental lurch like the clutch had popped out on his uncle's ancient pickup truck. There were multiple sensations of cold, rain, and wind, yet, still knowing he was only in his body back in the Cobalt lab at Diego Garcia. "Hey, Palio. What in the hell just happened?" No reply. He tried the comms and attempted to speak aloud but found he was unable. His body might still be in the departure lounge, but it was not responding to him. His consciousness felt untethered for nearly a full minute until the gears meshed up again and he felt a familiar sensation of jumping into a host mind.

32

Pike instantly noted the difference in the world in which he had landed. The entity of the host seemed absent, as if it was missing entirely. It obviously wasn't that his other in this dimension was gone, it was just that Pike seemed to be the one driving. The host was in the background, mentally speaking. He marveled at the distinction and wondered at the neuroscience that Palio would use to try to explain this. Turning his head, he realized that he was sensing two slightly different views. Not the way Xylos had been. This was totally different. Looking down, he saw his scaly, thin legs standing on a rocky outcropping. A dense forest extended into the distance, far below.

This is not Gaius. The briefing had included all the normal data about the target world and the host species, but that didn't seem to match this world. By focusing his eyes, he could see a shift from normal colors to something that might be ultraviolet and then on to infrared. The cliff he was on was high, but he felt no fear. Instead, he had an overwhelming desire to leap out. That, he suspected, was the host tying to exert its influence from the background, much as he had grown accustomed to doing.

Nearly unconsciously, Pike found himself extending out over the ledge, wind moving against his arms, and then the scene below changed. *Shit, we're flying!* The local species was avian! Pike knew he hadn't heard of anyone encountering an intelligent bird species. He found he could make turns simply by turning his head or dipping a leg slightly. The feeling was even more exhilarating than swimming on Luria. His view shifted as he focused on the forest floor where a meandering network of waterways cut paths through the thick canopy.

Time seemed to slow as he scanned the riverbank. Several animals seemed to sense his presence high overhead and dove for cover. The creatures stood out brightly in the IR spectrum of his host's vision. The uniqueness of this species consumed the scientist part of him. By focusing on what he was looking at, he determined the creature did indeed have two distinct forms of vision. One that was normal and seemed relatively human, despite the larger panorama and not quite binocular aspect to the world. The secondary was obviously for hunting, as it detected movement and then seemed to slow the action down and pull the target in sharp contrast to its background. Since vision is a part of the brain more than it is the eyes, he knew this was likely just an adaptation but wondered if prey birds on his Earth saw like this.

Crap, he had been mesmerized by the planet and had forgotten again to check in and let the lab guys know they had screwed up big time.

"Palio, you there?" Pike waited several seconds but heard nothing. "Doctor Lu? Kate?" He called out several more times but got no response. He jotted a shorthand note, hopeful that someone would monitor that as well. He was aware of all the things that could interrupt the communications system, even though it seemed somehow inconceivable. *I mean, my body, brain, and vocalizations are all taking place in the lab on Diego Garcia.* Still, his anxiousness was overwhelmed by the exhilaration of gliding over this beautiful world. He soared higher, wanting to see more of this planet. The lab and his home seemed so very far away at this moment.

The verdant forest was endless; higher peaks poked through irregularly like rocky islands in a sea of emerald green. He always believed the Lowcountry was the perfect wilderness, but this pristine world could be a strong contender.

Where is this place? Pike steered toward one of the peaks and soon noticed other figures flying in the distance. As he neared, he realized the silhouettes of the others didn't seem particularly birdlike. He tilted his head and engaged his prey vision to get a better look. He desperately wanted to see what the host species looked like. They were several miles away. He found he could clearly see them but for only an instant. Apparently his vision, realizing this was not food, refused to hold the magnified image in his brain for any length of time.

Within minutes, he noticed that one of the avian creatures separate itself from the flock and angled in his direction. "Maybe that's Kate," he whispered hopefully. Flying was not as simple and effortless as birds make it appear, he decided. He was at the mercy of the wind, thermal updrafts, and the sheer effort of holding a correct aerodynamic position was tiring. He knew his host's muscle memory was handling all the complicated tasks, but when he attempted to actively fly or turn in a way that used more energy, he quickly fatigued. He very much wanted to close the distance and verify the other was Kate. His path was a slow circle about five miles from the mountain, and he tried desperately to keep the other creature in his peripheral vision but lost it in the sun as he moved south of the peak.

Dejected, Pike considered heading toward the larger flock but realized the wind was taking him farther away. Soon it would be out of sight entirely. He would have to ask her once he returned if that had been her.

He found that the sun warming his 'wings' gave him additional energy, although the idea of wings didn't seem quite right. Still, it was a pleasant feeling, and he enjoyed it. Catching an uplifting thermal of warmer air, he soared higher and higher. *What on this version of Earth would have caused birds to become the dominant species?* he thought back to the sight of the others flying, and then he realized that wasn't necessarily the correct assumption. Making comparisons to his Earth simply invited errors in the analysis.

A shift in air current, or perhaps a sound, sent his host into a more alert posture. Something had changed, and seconds later, a dark shape smoothly winged in beside him and slightly above. The creature nodded its head in acknowledgment in a peculiarly human way. "Kate?" he asked, believing his voice here was only in his mind. *Is anyone even in the lab to hear me?*

The appearance of the other avian creature was not at all what Pike had been expecting. There were some similarities to a bird, but this creature was relatively humanoid. It had thin arms with webbing between the arms and torso that acted like wings. The head and face were narrow with eyes set slightly farther back, but what struck him most was how beautiful the creature was, and he inherently knew this was another male. The other smiled, an actual smile. Pike knew it couldn't be anything but. *Do species share certain traits, no matter the dimension?* His flying partner pointed down and seemed to clearly mouth the very human words of "Let's talk."

* * *

Bewildered, Pike followed. They landed on an escarpment of bare, gray rock that overlooked a picturesque lake hemmed in by towering evergreen trees. Pike watched the bird 'man,' and that was what it was, a man. Not exactly human. The wing flaps were certainly not, nor was the thin skeletal frame with an enlarged chest and muscular back, but this was what Kate would have likely called a proto-human, a species with a shared common ancestor to our own. This creature's internal passenger, though, had to be from Pike's world, his dimension.

"Welcome to Talos. You must be Shepard."

Pike was stunned. The voice was not coming to him internally but was spoken aloud. The pitch was a bit too high, and the cadence somehow off, but eerily close to normal human language. The words drifted on the air, and Pike knew they didn't belong here.

"I don't believe I know you," Pike said in an equally odd, yet familiar, voice. "This is...Talos?" he added uncertainly.

"Beautiful, isn't it? Not on the list. Not yet at least. This amazing world is just one of my little secrets—until you, of course."

The man bent down to remove what Pike had assumed was scaly leg skin, revealing a very familiar pink flesh beneath. The covering was apparel or just a sort of a legging. Glancing up, his face broke into a grin again. "Yes, they help, but they do begin to itch after a while. I was aloft for a long time waiting for you to show. Sorry to interrupt your passage, friend." He tossed one of the sock-like coverings aside. "Ingenious creatures, these avians. I believe the wing flaps were a natural adaptation. There's some large predators on the forest floor, but they were designed mainly for gliding, you know, like a flying squirrel." He pulled the other legging free and sat down on the rock, dangling his thin, bare legs over the ledge. "At some point, they began finding ways to extend the flights and added appliances to give them greater range."

"Who *are* you?" Pike asked.

"You know who I am, Shepard. You're a smart guy. Anyway, I figure the chest, arm, and back muscles evolved quickly to handle the increased load that flight demanded, but much of the rest is artificial. I assume you noticed the visual enhancements."

"Carapaz?" Pike looked at the man, the bird thing. It looked fragile and harmless, yet this may be the asshole who had tried to kill them back in Blackwater, Kate's former partner and the apparent cause of the growing mystery of disappearing worlds.

"Indeed, nice to finally meet. Sit, Shepard. These legs are not so good for standing around."

Pike was taken aback as much from the man's demeanor as he was from the fact they were speaking and interacting like normal humans. He sat down, intent to hear the man out.

"So, you brought me here?"

Carapaz nodded, the angular nose looking very beaklike in the gesture. "Don't worry, I can't affect things back at your Cobalt lab. Eventually, I knew you'd go through one of the terminus dimensions to reach the outer planets. I've been wanting to speak with you for some time now."

"Then why did you try to kill me back in South Carolina?"

"Sorry, my friend, that was not me. Let me just say there are a few things your precious Doctor Cassidy has failed to tell you," Carapaz said with an air of total authenticity.

"Like, how you can hijack the SideSlip of a traveler passing through a terminus world?"

"Yes, that was a somewhat fortuitous discovery. One that I neglected to include in my after-action reports. Sadly, though, it only works for some of us. I knew it would with you, though."

"How would you know that?" Pike demanded.

Carapaz leaned back nonchalantly, claw-tipped hands resting on the rock face, wing flaps billowing in the gentle breeze. "Kate told you she was the one who sought you out, didn't she? She was the one to find you, that you were connected?"

Pike thought back. "I assumed so, but no, I don't think she implicitly claimed that."

"Good, very good. Despite my differences with the brilliant doctor, she is not a liar, at least I have never known her to be so. Still, there are...um, omissions that can be just as damning as lies, don't you agree?"

Pike remained silent. He was also beginning to sense the nuanced rumblings that his host wanted to take back over; its need to feed was growing more earnest.

"Shepard, you have a unique brain, one that allowed you to come here like myself but also one capable of analyzing much more than would seem apparent to most. I know your history, your tragic loss, and most importantly, I know how your mind works. I know this on a very intimate basis."

Even here, the man's strong Spanish accent carried over. He talked with a polished refinement that spoke of a life gifted with the finer aspects of human life. "How do you know me?" Pike asked defiantly.

"You want proof, and you need purpose, Shepard. In a nutshell, that is all there is to you. In more subtle ways, though, there is more. I know you are consciously aware that the way you think is different, that a war rages inside your own skull."

Some of what Carapaz was implying was way too close to home for Pike's comfort. "You only think you know me," he said, feigning indifference. "Tell me why I shouldn't slip back to the lab right now? Tell me what you want."

"This is a safe place, brother," Carapaz said smoothly. "We can't really hurt each other here. I thought it would be a good place for us to get to know one another. A place for you to learn the very dark truth behind your dear Kate's project."

"Why should I trust you?"

"You should not, Pike. Always, always demand proof, you know that. Investigate everything. Take nothing at face value, believe nothing anyone tells you."

"Including you?" Pike demanded.

"Especially me," Carapaz said, his host face breaking into the same beguiling smile again.

"This was just an introduction, Professor. If I keep you much longer, you will be missed. Just do me a favor, and of course, this is totally up to you, but keep Talos between you and me for now, if you will."

"They will already know something is up, I've been here for an hour or more."

"No, my friend. That is the other beauty of Talos. It does not run on the same timeline as our lovely home world. When you leave here, you will arrive at your next destination only a few minutes after you originally should have. Talos has a time dilation that negatively coincides with our own. It will make sense to you, although you may only remember bits of this meeting initially. Trust me, though, it will come back to you within a few hours."

Carapaz stood and stretched down a hand. Pike took it and was raised gently back to his feet. The creature's claw nearly encircled the delicate wrist of Pike's host, but he felt no sense of danger from the embrace.

"We may not be friends, Shepard, but I am not necessarily your enemy."

With that, Carapaz departed the creature's body. The bird man back in charge looked down at the entwined hands and began squawking loudly.

Time to go.

33

“Repeat, Shepard, do you copy?” The voice from the lab seemed to have more than a hint of panic creeping in.

Pike looked around, taking in the surroundings, thankful that he had indeed slipped to the correct world. “On Gaius. No problem, Control,” he responded.

He still recalled bits about the unplanned jump to Talos and fragments of an encounter with someone, but much of it already seemed to have a foggy, dreamlike quality. Perhaps that was one of the possible effects of SideSlipping. He’d make a mental note to ask Palio about it later.

“There you are,” he heard Kate say. “Sorry I was late.”

He had been about to explain where he had been, but recalled she was also detained. “It’s okay, I took a bit of time on...on...” *What was it called?*

“Luria,” she offered helpfully.

“Yeah. Wow, swimming in the ocean there was incredible. Way better than Dogpatch.” He was anxious to see what the local inhabitants looked like, but it was completely dark on Gaius. “Why is it nighttime...it was early morning back at the lab.”

Kate replied, “Probably because our others are on the other side of the planet from us, genius." The comment was mock ridicule, but it still stung. The reality of what they were doing, and all the more granular details, had yet to fully settle into his way of thinking.

Gaius was an 'outer world' from Earth's perspective. Pike still wasn't totally sure how that worked since both planets' fixed place in their particular Universe should be relatively the same. Letner had explained that it was actually the dimension that was distant to our own, not the planet itself.

"The main town in this sector is up ahead," he heard Kate say in his internal mental dialogue. She was talking to him from her launch chair located a few feet away from him back in the departure room.

The air was chilly, and the night sky was lit up with dazzlingly bright constellations. The colors were vivid, and even gas nebulas could clearly be seen. "Gorgeous, isn't it?" asked Kate. "Less dense atmosphere, plus better eyesight. Still, I swear the stars are closer. Couldn't that be the case? Expansion in this reality hasn't been as rapid, or perhaps the cosmological constant is that different?"

"Possibly, but how would we prove it?" Pike asked.

"We may have a way, which was why I wanted you to come here. Your host is a scientist, and they're very good. Despite the tools and measurements being radically different from our own, there may be some evidence that you can extrapolate to help us understand those differences."

There was something he wanted to ask Kate about, but now he couldn't recall it. Still, there was so much here to take in that, quickly, his mind was absorbed into this new reality. "So, what else do I need to know about Gaius?"

"Well..." she said coyly, "you are with the most beautiful Guayan on the planet."

"It's dark out, how can I know that for sure?" Pike asked playfully. Not that he had any idea what passed for beauty to the host species.

He felt a punch on one arm. "Some things you just accept as fact when a woman says it."

He grunted and belatedly agreed. "Okay, what else?"

Kate explained, "The Guayan culture is very holistic. They live in near perfect stasis with the world. It seems to be a baseline principle within their social order."

"What, like a planet of Greenpeace nuts or something?" Pike asked.

"Greenpeace isn't nuts, but no, nothing overt or political. Here, it is implied and simply expected. They don't consider things that might harm nature. They return everything they consume back to the world in a balanced way, creating a closed loop. Even when exceptions are made, like constructing a new building, an equal amount of work goes into improving other land and transplanting removed vegetation and animals from one to the other."

"Sounds like a sixties hippy commune," Pike said as nightlights from the town began to come into view.

"Not even close. You'll be surprised."

She wasn't lying. The town ahead was magnificent. As they cleared a stand of trees, it emerged from the darkness like a new bride unveiling herself for her husband. Pike let out an audible gasp. The shimmering towers were all topped with tapered decorative spires reaching toward the stars. What he had thought were lights he could now see were simply muted illumination panels embedded in the buildings' architecture and roads.

"They're several thousand years more advanced than humans," said Kate. "That's a rough guess, but we're relatively confident."

It was unquestioningly the most beautiful city Pike had ever seen. More impressive than the futuristic scenes in movies even. "I can't wait to see it in the daylight," he commented.

Kate said, "Be prepared. Dawn shouldn't be too long now."

* * *

Sunlight didn't disappoint; the city seemed to literally grow from the Earth. Pike had never witnessed a more organic sense of architecture. The Guayans themselves were much less attractive than he'd hoped. Technically, they still fit the very broad definition of protohuman. Pike was beginning to wonder if bipedal was simply the most efficient body design for the land dwelling, tool wielding, intelligent species. While they did have two arms and two legs and a head, none were anything but vaguely humanoid. Each of the limbs seemed to have an extra joint, like multiple elbows or knees. This caused an odd style of walking. The proportions were off, too. The torso was extended significantly and had a protrusion in the front and a bit of a rounded hump on the back. Standing fully erect, a Guayan male stood about seven feet, the females slightly less. Both sexes were nearly hairless except the face, which was covered in fine, hair-like cilia that altered colors like a cuttlefish, changing with the mood. This coloration was the form of expression and also part of how the natives conversed.

Physical differences notwithstanding, the Guayans were incredibly gifted minds and unusually hospitable. Kate had told him that they believed some of the Guayans could sense when a jumper had slipped into their consciousness. One had described it as believing it was the departed spirit of her late mother who was visiting her. Pike had even heard internal queries from his host. It might have been talking to itself but seemed more like a question it was hoping to have answered. Firmly ensconced in the creature's subconscious, Pike could not manage any form of real time communication and could only offer occasional mental nudges. Still, he felt the tiniest suggestion of control there if he just took the time to unpack it. He wondered briefly if this was what Nianda, his wiser and presumably benevolent other on Xylos, had added to his mental toolkit.

He and Kate, via their hosts, walked up to a rounded building that he automatically knew was a restaurant. The nearly translucent orange glow around the roof signaled its purpose with a subtle beauty that fast-food chains on Earth would never attempt.

"Prepare to be impressed," Kate informed him via the back-channel comms.

"This place that good?"

"It has a waiting list. I nudge my other to request a table every time I come. I'm not sure she can afford it, but some things are worth going broke for."

Pike failed to understand how the act of a host eating could be that satisfying to his partner. In his previous journeys, the connection to taste, appetite, and satisfaction was more muted, somehow more disconnected than say, the sense of sight or smell. In most cases, the very act was pretty gross, so he was thankful for that layer of detachment. Still, he took her word for it as he followed her to the seating area.

"Guayan cuisine is very similar to humans' except they only have a single meal each day, and as far as we know, they do no eating or food preparation at home. There isn't the emotional connection to food like humans have," Kate said.

"So, no big super bowl parties or Thanksgiving meals?" Pike asked.

"Not even a birthday cake. At least none we have seen so far. When they eat, they want it to be the best, so they leave it to the pros. The chefs, servers, suppliers, really everyone involved in meal prep, are some of the most honored and valued in their caste in Guayan society."

Once seated, Pike began to see what she meant. Food here was art, entertainment, and music all in one. He could sense the rising anticipation in his host. The first course was a brilliant array of plants and bright pink items that might be berries. The servers placed a sculpture made of something edible in the center of the table. On first bite, Pike's Guayan host seemed to briefly enter into a state of orgasmic bliss. Even muted, the sensation of taste, which he could only superficially describe, washed over him. The salad, or whatever it was, was a combination of bright crisp flavors and a silky sauce, which had a subtle taste that was best described more as a sea breeze than a flavor. "Oh, my God!" he exclaimed.

"Told you," Kate said. "I would tell you to just wait for dessert, but the sweet course is normally in the middle of the meal, and honestly, it's all fantastic."

The meal lasted a long time, assuming time here was Earth standard. Pike guessed two-and-a-half hours, and he didn't think he had ever spent a more enjoyable time in any activity. Also fascinating was the conversation between his and Kate's hosts. They were highly intelligent and seemed genuinely happy. Still, there was a note of concern, or even fear, on one of the topics covered. "Kate, any idea what Selenas was upset about earlier?" Selenas was as close to the pronunciation of Kate's host's name as Pike could manage. Late in the meal, his host had asked her softly if she was aware of what was happening in a city that Pike knew was far to the south.

"The feeling I get is one of loss. Not personal, but when you...or your host, mentioned the name, her mental images were of violence and...rage. Something we never see from these people."

Pike decided to let it go. Later, the two Guayans were walking back along a river. His host, Alren, wanted to show affection to Kate but feared rejection. Pike understood that fear well but decided to help out his other with some encouragement. Alren moved his hand to the center of the hump of Selena's back and let it rest softly there. When she didn't reject the touch, Pike felt a sense of relief permeate the Guayan's consciousness. *Is this the local equivalent of holding hands or kissing?* He had no idea.

"Sweet," said Kate. "Was that *your* doing?"

Pike stayed silent.

34

"You still have no idea how he even made the journey."

The phone in Kate's hand trembled slightly, not at the intimidation coming from the speaker on the other end, well...not *just* because of that. The truth was, he was right. Pike hadn't mentioned it, nor had he elaborated yet on what happened on Xylos. The shorthand notes on his pad console made it clear he had not jumped straight from Luria to Gaius. Whatever the cause, he had not even bothered to double check his notes when he returned. That in itself was out of character for the man.

Kate had spent most of the day with Pike trying to uncover what he'd been doing off world. Who had he encountered and how had he even managed it? But she was no closer to finding out than when she started. Now she risked losing whatever trust they'd ever had.

"He met someone. I'm assuming Carapaz. It seems he is learning things on his own," she stated.

"Ah," the voice said with a menacing tone. "Do me a favor, Doctor Cassidy, try not to let him follow the late colonel down the rabbit hole, okay? Besides, isn't that why he is there, to learn whatever he can?"

She leaned against the table frustrated and confused. *How would they know Pike had made an unscheduled journey?* She shelved that question for the moment.

"What's going on in the U.S.? Is it getting worse?" Kate asked.

"The Fade," the voice said smoothly. "Isn't that what you guys call it? The madness, the chaos, the rage, it's all spreading. You're running out of time, Doctor. You were allowed to bring Shepard in, now we need to see results."

Allowed? The very word pushed her farther over the edge. Few people other than her knew the U.S. government had come calling early in The Project when she was desperate for funding. She knew she had been stupid and naïve. Initially, they just wanted to stay informed of the progress, no strings attached. But of course, there were strings, lots and lots of strings. What did DOD or DARPA or whomever hope to get out of this? All they had told her back then was it had something to do with global threats. They would provide interim funding through a black-budget research grant. She just needed to stay cooperative. In agency terms, that meant compliant.

The favors Kate had to request to get out of Charleston were coming back to haunt her. Now she owed them, and they wanted to collect. While at first, they just monitored for potential threats poised from the other realities, they soon came to realize the potential treasure trove of scientific and military knowledge other worlds might offer. They ran through countless algorithms to find active-duty servicemen who had strategically placed others in high-value worlds. Then they had set up their own launch facility. She knew where it was. In fact, she had been there recently. She had been under their thumb then. Maybe she could afford to finally break free. Somehow, she knew that it wasn't going to be easy.

* * *

The sudden onrush of memories was like being in a mental hurricane. Pike knew he was not fully caught up, but his being on Talos came back. This was what the gap felt like, he realized. He pulled a slightly damp rag off his forehead and eased up onto the pillows. Kate lay beside him, snoring softly. His mouth tasted sour, and he knew he must have been sick at some point in the night. He thought briefly to the horrible migraines he sometimes had as a child, the excruciating pain that persisted long after the brain surgery. So many mornings he had awoken like this, covered in his own sick.

Kate stirred softly; she must have stayed up much of the night keeping an eye on him. Pike slipped gently from the bed, quietly pulled clothes from a shelf, and eased out of the bedroom. He wanted to let her sleep, but just as much, as he needed time to think. While he didn't recall all the past days, he was aware of enough to know he'd withheld some things from Kate. The secret meeting with Carapaz, for one. Why would he have done that? Didn't he trust her? Did you keep secrets from someone you loved? The questions piled up like cord wood, but the answers stayed hidden.

What is the smart thing to do? Pike wondered. Carapaz had made the claim that The Project was part of the problem. The level of hostility all around was amping up into all-out rage, but did that require outside intervention? Humans were, after all, damn efficient at hating and killing each other all on their own. Kate was up, what would he tell her? What would he hold back? This definitely was not the basis for a long-term relationship, yet he felt that she was beginning to love him and now knew fully that he felt the same.

"Hey, Babe!" she said, walking out, looking better than any woman had a right to first thing in the morning.

"Hi, um, you're wearing my shirt?"

"Yep," she pulled it up and twirled.

"And nothing else," he said with a laugh.

Kate took a sip of coffee and sat down in the other chair. He felt sure she wanted to know what memories had returned and more about the SideSlip to Gaius, but she didn't press, just asked if he was feeling better. The return from the previous day's missions had drained him far more than usual, and now he knew why. She slipped on some running shorts, and they sat outside the small barracks quietly watching the sea birds and the occasional fish breaking the surface. He liked the fact that she didn't need conversation to fill up a space. She could be comfortable with another person just being together like this. That was pretty much the morning. Birds, *flying was awesome!*

"What ya thinking?"

Pike shrugged, "Nothing, just trying to process all you've shown me. The many worlds out there and a much more special one right here."

She leaned in and kissed his lips lightly. "So, if we're thinking deeply now, would you care to mention where else you went yesterday?" That was lousy timing, but she knew what the gap looked like, and no way he got that just going to Gaius. Director Planck had been right on that point.

"Well?" she demanded.

Pike sat and watched the birds without answering. She was beginning to realize this was not him being rude, or even stubborn, but one of the ways he worked through things.

"How much are you not telling me, Kate?"

"What are you getting at?" asked Kate. Her tone was not hostile, but not quite recalcitrant either.

"Answer me." Pike was leaving no room for negotiation.

"I'm responsible for the entire project. Yes, there are things I'm not at liberty to discuss. Nothing important, though. Nothing that will interfere with your role here."

"What about us? Are there things that will interfere with us?" he asked.

Kate knew what he wasn't saying. Was she using sex to get him to do what she needed? If she had been him, that would be her question, but he didn't ask that.

"You met with Carapaz," she stated.

Pike sipped his coffee and kept watching the gulls.

"And you chose not to mention him why? How did you escape the slip parameters?"

"I'm still gathering information, Kate. Until then, this conversation serves no productive purpose."

"Well, color me done!" she yelled, throwing her empty cup toward the breakers. Birds scattered, then glided back down to investigate.

The two sat in silence, both considering their next words carefully. Pike knew Kate was struggling to keep her emotions in check, and she was likely not going to be more forthcoming while she was vulnerable.

"You don't trust me, Kate. Now, I have reason to doubt you as well. Who's backing The Project and why do you think Carapaz is out to destroy you?"

"We have numerous investors..." she began, but he quickly cut her off.

"No bullshit." He set the empty coffee cup on the ground and stood. His physical presence loomed large over her. "Despite our secrets, I know you love me and I you. What happens in the next few minutes will determine if that is enough. Do you understand me?"

Kate rocked back in the sand drawing her knees up close. It was a reflexive action, not a deliberate one to make her seem small and vulnerable. She knew Pike wouldn't give up in his need for the truth. That was one of the main things she admired about him, and now it was the one thing she hated. "I simply can't tell you that, Pike."

"It's not just the U.S. government then, is it? There's someone else pulling the strings," Pike stated.

She didn't respond.

"You said you had made important discoveries. You had licensing agreements and research projects underway that would be very lucrative in time. Is that a lie as well?" He forced himself to relax, incrementally, at least. "I'm uncertain your investors hold humanity's future with the same importance I do."

"You met with Carapaz, didn't you? This sounds just like his line of oversimplified rationalization," said Kate angrily. "He is simply trying to divide us, Pike. He doesn't care if The Fade happens here."

"It's already happening, Kate...can't you see that? Our reality is disappearing into chaos and madness. My question to you is, are you the one, are we the ones," he corrected, "bringing it here? What if Carapaz is right, and it's this project, maybe our SideSlips to other dimensions that are causing it all?"

"It doesn't hold up, Pike. We've already investigated that. Aragon didn't have travelers, and it faded."

"You jumped to Aragon and others, maybe the indigenous species doesn't have to be the one to do the jumps. I assume some people can also do this naturally, without all your equipment. Isn't that what you said? Creative geniuses could use drugs or meditation to tap into this higher dimension of consciousness."

Kate considered it. "Theoretically, yes, someone could probably learn to jump without the launch devices, maybe some species can do it naturally. We haven't encountered any like that, though."

Pike had a thought; she could see it on his face. "What?" she asked.

"None of the species we've visited would ever say they've encountered one like us."

She looked confused, then slowly, realization dawned on her. "Others could be using us as hosts?"

35

“Good to see you again, Shepard.”

It immediately struck Pike how familiar this world looked...incredibly familiar, in fact.

"Where are we?"

Carapaz’s host body lumbered over to the edge of a wooden dock, overlooking a marshy plain with reeds, seagrass, and several patches of open water. "Looks a lot like home, doesn't it?" he asked.

Pike had to agree, "Yeah, I have to admit it does. I don't remember this on any of the charts."

“Oh, you mean it’s not any one of the other 147, or is it more than that now?” Carapaz laughed. "No, this one was a surprise discovery. A recent one. I made it. I haven't come up with a name for it yet, but I thought it looked very much like your beloved Lowcountry. As far as we can tell, the entire world is like this. Shallow bodies of water with mostly tidal marshland. A few arid fields for farming, a couple of sparse wooded tracts, but no mountains that we can tell. So, it does get quite windy at times.”

"Why am I here?"

"I thought we could pick up our conversation, Pike. We really need to get things moving. And, as you might have imagined, we desperately need your help."

Pike thought about it. Carapaz was using the same words Kate had, but for a very different reason. "I don't understand."

“Look, Shepard, you've got to see it. You've been there. You were on Gaius, right? I guess you know it’s already started there. You know what that planet is going to go through. You must know some of what’s happening back home.”

"But that's you,” Pike said. “We heard about it. Our teams have evidence that you were driving all of that conflict, all of that rage."

"You’re mistaken. And Pike, you're believing too much of what your sweetheart has told you,” Carapaz said.

Pike wanted to lash out, to let him know it wasn't like that between him and Kate, but that would have been a lie.

"Look," Carapaz continued, "our goals may not be the same. But that doesn't mean that they're mutually exclusive. I have information that neither you nor Kate has, and you have access that I don't have. We’re better off working together than against each other.”

“Carapaz, I've already heard about how ruthless you can be, how desperate your people are to achieve their goals. I admit there are parts of it I don’t get, but you are involved. That’s obvious. I’m sure it’s not smart for me to be around you. Maybe it’s time for me to leave.” The other man's host nodded awkwardly.

“What if I told you there's a way to travel into other dimensions and stay there?”

Pike considered that. Was that what he was doing? "That would defeat everything that they’ve taught us. That would mean you displace whatever the resident consciousness is in the host.”

“That's exactly right,” Carapaz went on. “And that's what's going on. What if I told you other dimensions are working against us? What if I told you everything you think you know is mostly bullshit? These realities facing The Fade are being invaded, Shepard. It isn't by us. We don't even know what the species calls themselves. But they must have been around forever. I’ve been investigating them all. You wouldn’t believe the lengths I am going through to find the truth.”

“So, that’s how you are coincidentally on all the worlds as they drop out of the local network?”

Carapaz looked away. “It’s not coincidence, no. I have a way to know it’s about to happen.”

“Right, having a seat at the planning table probably gives you a lot of advanced intel.”

“We've been trying to learn the truth,” Carapaz stated flatly. “But we're also having to battle the teams from Cobalt. It keeps expanding and keeps opening new worlds to these other travelers. Worlds that we then have to go to and protect. That's why we don't list any of the realities that we visit. Planets such as this one. Not that it matters. As far as we can tell, they still can detect the signature from the quantum slipstream. They follow it back to the sources. So, yes, Gaius is gone or soon will be. A fantastic culture lost forever.”

Julian Carapaz’s host eyed Pike with a look of disgust before continuing. “What's next, Eridani? Avalon, Sellus Prime, Dogpatch? Yeah, I know all your favorites. And how many of the terminus worlds would disappear before the entire project collapsed?”

Pike put a check on his internal emotion, stopping his frustrations just long enough to consider rationally what this man was saying. It all made sense in a crazy, ruthless sort of way. "Carapaz, there's a flaw in your story. Something in what you're saying just doesn't ring true."

"What's that?"

"You say these other beings can travel, can detect the quantum tunneling, and then somehow pass through to the other worlds. But if that's the case, it wouldn't just be a small group of our destination worlds that were targets. Not just Gaius and Aragon, it would be..."

Carapaz finished the sentence for him, "Yes Pike, it would be Earth as well."

Pike’s host sat down on the dock with a heavy thud.

“Have you not realized what's going on there? You're spending too much time off planet.”

He continued,

“The world is coming apart. Wars are breaking out in normally peaceful areas, manslaughter rates are up all over, horrific genocides are taking place in areas that have been quiet for generations. Earth is already under attack."

"And you think it's these other beings that are doing it?" Pike asked. "We don't need possessing spirits to drive us to madness. Humans are an unhappy lot. Shit, man, we excel in discovering new and inventive ways of killing each other."

"No," Carapaz answered. "We don't believe these other beings are doing it all. Certainly, they may not be the only perpetrators. You're right, Earth has always had its share of crazies, but now they've got help, help from a very determined and practically invisible species that will be intent on wiping us all out. Think about it, a species that realizes its consciousness is only information. Information they can disperse into species all over the multiverse. This may be how they breed, reproduce, evolve. Whatever the body and physics of the host is irrelevant. Just take over the host mind, drop them out of the entanglement network, and the planet is yours.

"And you're right," he continued, "it is not just a possessing spirit. You should ask Kate about the UT clock tower shooting. It was one of the first mass shootings in America. Way before Project Cobalt, hell, before either of us was born. The University of Texas clock tower shooting, in Austin, Texas. That day, Charles Whitman, a model student, bank teller, Eagle Scout, and ex-Marine, fired down from the clock tower on the campus, killing 14 people and wounding 31 others. Earlier in the day, Whitman had killed his wife and mother. Police killed him, but later, they found a letter he wrote describing a condition that seemed baffling. He believed something had changed in his brain. Something was driving him to kill. He harbored no ill will. In fact, he said he loved his wife dearly, and she had been wonderful. So, what would make him do such a horrific act?"

The story rang a warning bell deep in Pike's mind, but he let it go for now. "So, you are convinced that we, that all the planets facing The Fade, are being attacked by some unseen multidimensional force?"

Carapaz responded, "Shepard, just like you and I slip into these host bodies, other species can as well. What makes you think they all would have benign or benevolent motivations? What makes you think they would have anything resembling human intentions, whatever those can be classed as?"

Pike took notice of the body he was in at that moment. His other. The host was also humanoid, short, dark skinned, almost primitive looking. He'd really given the creature no consideration. He was there, using it like a cheap rental car.

"Yes, we come in and we push these creatures' consciousness to the back," Carapaz said. "So we can interact as people, as humans. What if we just eliminated that other intelligence...that other consciousness entirely? That's what the invaders do when they come in. Think about it. Right now, you possess all the memories, all the history, and all the legacy of this creature. The love, the loss, the laughter. Whatever has ever taken place in this host life is available to you. So, you'll lose nothing except that tiny voice in the back of your mind. Silence that forever, and this body is yours. Silence enough of them, and this world belongs to your species.

"Surely, you have been tempted," he continued. "Maybe when you swam with a fish on Luria, or when we soared high above the forest of Talos. Trust me, the intoxication of being able to move a race of people and occupy their lives could be an irresistible temptation, especially for a race needing a new place to start over. Maybe their home world or solar system was doomed. Maybe their local star was going supernova. They're not from our reality, they're not from our timeline. They're not part of our world. They are interdimensional travelers. And they are a conquering horde. They moved over planets with populations ten times what your Earth, our Earth has. They will swallow it in force. As soon as they set their sights on it."

"It sounds like they've already set their sights on it. If what you're saying is anything close to the truth," Pike said.

"No," Carapaz said, "they've just sent their scouts ahead so far. Just enough to stir up trouble to disrupt things. They like it softened up. In fact, we believe they kind of thrive on chaos. So, they come into our already volatile situation. Nobody takes any notice of them. Since they can't take over everyone at once, they have to keep the locals under control until they have the numbers."

Pike saw several holes in the man's theory. It was quite different from Kate's and didn't seem to match up with what Nianda had implied. "Why do you think they create the chaos, the rage, the murders?"

Carapaz nodded as if he'd considered the very same point. "They don't...not always. On a world like this, where the intelligent species is docile and consciousness not as dominant, they can move in nearly unnoticed. We see many of these worlds fade out. I believe it has much to do with a being's sense of self. They need to engage those worlds while the inhabitants are in a fever pitch of emotions to arrive unnoticed. Face it, Earth is in the crosshairs."

Pike mentally shook his head, and his host repeated the motion, "You're making too large of a leap. The clues are there, but your conclusion is leaving out all other possibilities in favor of the most radical. Where's the evidence? Outrageous claims need outrageous levels of facts to back them up, Carapaz."

"So, what's your theory then, Professor? We all live in a simulation?"

Pike had to admit that one stung; it was still one of the possibilities he was holding onto. "I don't know. I think there is some compelling evidence for others using humans as hosts, but I have no proof, nothing else to pursue down that track." His host animal walked several steps in a circle, as was apparently a natural gesture for the creature. "So, how do we stop them?"

"So, you believe me?" Carapaz asked, relieved.

"No, I'm relatively sure you're wrong, but even if it isn't an alien horde, I have to assume something is in our heads. How would we stop them? How do we cut our species off from the quantum connection without causing The Fade ourselves?"

Carapaz sighed inwardly. At least this man was no longer actively combative. "We aren't sure. We simply know nothing to do other than essentially lighting global backfires to help slow the spread. We're hoping you can help us figure out that part. Maybe some sort of interdimensional gateway block, a shield in the quantum tunneling, something that can prevent our humans from being controlled or even influenced. Trust me, you've never done anything more important, Pike. And unfortunately, Kate will never believe you."

Pike shrugged his shoulders. He spoke, barely above a whisper in the strong breeze. "All right. I'm not saying I believe you, but I don't disbelieve you as much as I would have expected. Tell me what you know."

"Better, I will show you something fantastic," Carapaz said with delight in his eye. "Consider this a gift of friendship."

36

Waking up in someone else's skin was disconcerting to Pike, and that was the only way he had been able to think of it. SideSlipping was more of a jolt to the system than nodding off to sleep. That moment when he realized he was seeing someone else's reality through their eyes gave him a disconnected feeling the way dreams sometimes do. That had been the way it had always felt. Every time before, until this jump, that is. *Where has Carapaz sent me?*

This time there was no separation between him and the host. There was no sense that he was either in the background subconscious or the one in charge. This just felt like him being himself. He thought about his hand and a very human-like arm raised itself into his field of vision. *Humanoid,* he thought. He was seated. Panoramic windows made up one entire wall, of the room he was in and he looked out over a scene that was eerily familiar. A rolling green meadow extending down to the shore of a large body of water. By the angle of the sun, it was late morning. Several small boats drifted about a mile offshore. In the right-hand corner of the window-wall, he saw a faint white number. The numbers were very familiar. Not exactly the Arabic style numbers we commonly use, but close enough to guess what they were. "It's a clock, or a calendar," his host said aloud. The numbers changed from 111501.0708 to 111502.0708. *Eleven fifteen,* he thought. He wasn't sure what the other numbers might be, though.

Pike rose up to go check out the scene more closely. 'He' rose up, not his host. *This is going to take some getting used to.* The hand he had noticed earlier was holding a small device. Smaller than a cell phone, but the same general size and shape. As he moved toward the window, the fingers pressed buttons on the object and the entire window changed. The outdoor scene was now one of a snowy mountain range. Steep, rocky cliffs in the distance, plunging down to thick alpine forest. The window...the entire wall, was a display. Pike's other stepped onto a darker part of the floor that faced the window display wall and in a very familiar voice, said, "Start workout." The entire section of floor started moving past like a treadmill. It picked up speed until he was running. The wall display mirrored a running trail, first through the alpine forest. The scene was incredibly realistic. Birds flew from limb to limb and called out as he passed. A cool morning mist seemed to hang on the air, and everything had the smells of damp earth and deep woods. The illusion was almost complete, except for the treadmill built into the floor and the tiny watermark in the corner, which Pike now understood was a timer, distance, and heart monitor.

After the workout, the others' fingers clicked more buttons on the small device, and then a movie came on. The actors were speaking English with a slight accent and a lot of words Pike failed to grasp. The most jarring aspect was that one of the actors was clearly a much older James Dean, the other was Harrison Ford, and the movie appeared to be a kind of sci-fi western. Both actors seemed roughly the same age. "That's impossible," Pike muttered in disbelief. James Dean had died before Pike had been born, and Harrison Ford never worked with him. He, too, was probably too young. At most, Ford would have been a child at the time of Dean's death, at least in his world. A piece of the puzzle drifted up, probably from the host's own understanding. *These are virtual actors.*

"Virtual?" Pike urged his host to the screen and moved in as close as possible. No colored dot pattern like he had seen in TVs he was familiar with. *A more advanced civilization, and one that is very Earth normal.* The display had a depth that changed as he moved closer to the screen. The quality was indistinguishable from looking through a window. This window was now showing a deep space scene with alien worlds and futuristic spaceships. He took one more look at the actors, who were exact copies of the human actors. Not close. No uncanny valley here. These were perfect replicas.

The hand then clicked the button again. The channel number briefly appeared in the upper right. A nature show, he guessed, magnificent, blue waters and a pod of whales diving deep. While the whales were familiar, they were alien as if they were variants that his world had never known, or maybe they were extinct in Pike's world. The whale songs filled the room, which Pike was also beginning to take notice of. It was simple, mostly familiar, but tasteful and polished in a Pottery Barn catalog kind of way. The host flipped through several more channels. A news report from a moon base named Armstrong, where they were battling a new strain of virus and schools had to be canceled. The reporter could have been from New York or London based on the ordinariness of it, except there was a translucent ceiling high above her head in the final shot. On a sports channel, a lively cricket match was airing live from the South Miami Islands. *Islands of South Miami?* Pike wondered.

Pike's host pressed the long button at the bottom of the remote and the window-wall scene changed again. Yes, waking in someone else's body is disorienting. An even bigger shock was waking in your own body but in a totally different world. The wall was now a mirror. Pike Shepard was staring at a near-perfect reflection of himself. "Mirror worlds do exist, Kate." This Pike appeared a bit younger, face fuller, without some of the lines and premature aging all the years of stress and booze had added to his own. He lifted his hair on one side and made a hand gesture with the remote that he knew would cause it to zoom. "No scar." This Pike had never had brain surgery.

"Did you call me, love?"

The voice came from behind, but he couldn't tear his eyes away from the image of her in the mirror. Kate Cassidy, also a few years younger, was walking into the main room, wearing a sheer green gown and nothing else. Her hair was radiant to the point of combustion, and her piercing, green eyes were noticeable even across the room. Pike turned from the screen, which automatically went back to its default pastoral scene of the waterfront. "Sorry, hon," he said hurriedly. "No, I was just watching a news broadcast."

She eased up beside him and kissed him full and long. "I love you."

"I love you, too," he said, knowing his host totally did, too. "Mrs. Shepard." The words tumbled out with no thought, but the hand he was holding was wearing a pair of rings. *Kate was...is, my wife*, Pike thought.

"Your turn, you need to hurry. We need to get going in..." Kate rotated her wrist and tapped the skin, "...thirty minutes."

Pike saw what looked like tattoo numbers on her arms start to fade as she looked again at him. "Go get ready."

Unsure as to what that meant, he stepped back and let the host mind expand to fill the gap. "Sure you don't want to join me?" he said, pulling his wife in for another kiss.

Kate pushed him back, smiling. "Doctor Shepard, that was why I had to get a second shower. We can't keep having sex. Now go. I'm going to have the car pull around front."

"Doctor?" Pike stayed in the cerebral background as his doppelganger used voice commands to start a shower that seemed to erupt from all points in the small bath. This version of Earth was so similar to his own. Here, too, he and Kate had found each other, but he instantly knew it had been much earlier in both their lives. Technology was definitely more advanced, hell, they had colonies on the moon. But nearly everything seemed familiar, so not that far ahead of his own Earth Prime, maybe fifty years, sixty on the outside. *I'm in Tomorrowland,* he thought. Not exactly, though. Some things were just different, apparently his career for one.

Pike's life here seemed to be much easier. He sensed none of the emotional scarring from his own past. He'd found true love here. What other differences would he find, and what was Carapaz' s goal in sending him here? Maybe it was just to torture him? To let him see the life he could have had. No, that wasn't it, his life had not turned out the way it had due to his choices as much as it had been fate. No, Carapaz had a bigger reveal in store, he felt sure of that. They passed a bedroom, a daughter's room, by the look of it. His host walked in, his mind full of love and guilt and maybe loss. Pike wasn't sure but understood all of those same emotions. The room was full of memories but not of recent life. This Pike picked an aged yellow book from a shelf. A children's book. *The Berenstain Bears, Finding the Truth*. *"One of her favorites,"* the man said aloud.

* * *

Stepping out the front door, Pike realized the original waterfront scene had been visually correct to where they were. One smell and he placed the home close to his cabin in Blackwater. *This is Lowcountry,* he thought. *Wonder if they call it the same here.* The water stretched out to the south with a familiar coastline, although much less wooded. The spartina grasses were different, too. These all had buds on top with tiny multi-colored flowers. When the wind blew across the marsh grass, waves of undulating colors radiated in every direction. As much as he loved his stretch of the bay, this one was breathtaking. He realized he'd stopped walking. Kate was standing patiently by a sleek silver car. Her grin was not patronizing but knowing.

"Every time."

"What?" he asked, smiling. Kates's voice was the same, but the inflections and pitch were slightly more precise. That, along with the unusual subtle accent, seemed somehow even more perfect for her. A familiar hand squeezed his as they sat looking out over the colorful marsh while the car navigated its own way back to the road. This was a version of South Carolina, and via his host, he knew they called it that. They were heading to a town called Beaufort, which was the same name as back in his world. Similarities seem to end at that. The homes were quite different, the roofs were typically low and slanted, very modern lines, muted colors, and walls which were mostly windowless. The surrounding landscapes appeared more refined but also felt natural at the same time.

"You excited?" asked Kate.

Pike had no idea about what. He was thrilled to be in this version of Earth, with her back home. He'd barely even registered the fact that his actual body was lying in a near comatose state back in the middle of the Indian Ocean, several dimensions away. He shrugged his shoulders, hoping that was the correct reaction. Too much enthusiasm might reveal what a fraud he was. "I guess." Kate squeezed his hand and smiled.

Everything he saw fascinated Pike. Gas stations were absent. The car he was in was silent, probably electric. Bait stores were still very much the same. They passed the road to where Dewey's shop was, and he wondered what he would find down that road in this version of Earth. Every time he relaxed and let the host version of Pike take over, his mind was flooded with new information. Too much new information, things he couldn't easily process. Kate had been right, you really did become the other version of you while your conscious minds were joined. He tried to relax as this Pike's memories were integrated with his own. This Kate lay her head on his shoulder and began humming a tune. The shared memory moved his host, who pulled her closer, kissing the top of her head.

Pike had called Beaufort, South Carolina, home much of his life. The charming little town was one of few spared from Sherman's torch during the Civil War. As they approached the town, it relieved him to see that the stately homes and moss-draped oaks lining the streets were almost identical to the world he knew. Some of the homes seemed to be in different places, and the town and adjacent marina were at least a half mile farther south than they should have been, but the familiarity was uncanny.

The car slowed, then stopped, as a crosswalk in the street surface began flashing. Two young men, obviously lovers, crossed arm-in-arm waving nonchalantly at them as they passed. One of the guys had breasts, Pike realized, as the car moved on down the street. This Earth had its own story to tell. Somehow, it felt amazingly familiar but still alien to him. The driverless car dropped them at the curb, and they walked in the general direction of the marina. The streets near the water were designated pedestrian only, although the signs read 'Pedonale.' The area was more crowded than he recalled from his reality, and everything had a very definite European influence.

Kate maneuvered his arm toward an outdoor dining spot beneath a canopy of twinkling lights. He tried to recall if there was a restaurant in this spot in his Beaufort but gave up and let himself just live in the moment as Kate had always suggested. Pike heard himself ordering an unfamiliar drink from the server and watched as Kate eyed him closely, then her eyes lit up at something behind him. She nodded her head for him to look. He turned as an unmistakable voice spoke. One he had not heard in over a decade.

"Hi, Daddy."

37

"Emma?"

The sensation of the entire world shifting sideways then collapsed down on Pike in one soul-shattering blow. He fought wave after wave of onrushing tears and fought futilely to maintain some sense of emotional balance as he reached out to a daughter he hadn't held since she was a child. "Oh, God, it is…" The thought became lost as he stared into the eyes of his baby girl. He wanted to reach out, but at the same time, he was mentally escaping into the shadows of his host's mind. He knew this world was different from the others he'd visited. He and this version of Pike Shepard were too close, too similar. The rivalry between host and visitor was absent. He didn't understand it, but somehow, he was him. A version of him, at least. That meant in some way this was his Emma, his daughter.

Pike could feel his host tense and fight down the onrush of panic that was undoubtedly being caused by his invading twin. He shifted his eyes away from the girl; she was a ghost, a dream. Something unreal made whole. *Damn you, Carapaz,* Pike thought.

"How is school?" the host version of Pike asked as soon as Emma sat.

"It's good, but I miss you guys. Can't wait for March."

The hidden Pike watched through eyes that he thought should be filled with tears. This was his daughter, back from the dead. More grown, more mature, but still so much like he remembered her. This was what Carapaz had wanted him to see. That our reality wasn't the only 'real' one. Other Earths existed, some obviously much closer to our own. To bring him face to face with Emma, though, what a cruelty and what a gift.

He mostly just listened to the dinner conversation. Emma was in her third and final year at the "Uni" as she put it, up in Charleston. She kept referring to it as Southern Oxford, as if it were one word. Here, too, the differences between worlds were noticeable. His problem-solving brain had been silently churning away since he'd arrived. He was certain his shorthand files back at the lab would be overflowing. Perhaps mirror worlds like this were formed when timelines and probabilities were so dramatic that multiple copies were made. One with each of the choices in play. Whatever that event was must have been significant enough that the timeline couldn't be reasonably reunited at some later point. Still, it seemed an extraordinarily close parallel. This Earth was more advanced technologically and didn't seem to be suffering the violent ills of his own reality, but other than that, the differences appeared largely superficial.

Emma mentioned that she would be heading to South America in the fall to intern on something called the Globacoms Lift Project. It shocked Pike to learn it was a trillion-dollar prototype for a space elevator. Even in his world the concept was known, but the materials and engineering required were probably centuries away. He watched Emma speak and then eyed his wife. It shocked him even more to realize they looked so much alike. He'd never thought of it before, but then again, his only memories of his daughter were as a child. Still, how could this version of Emma look like Kate? Was she their child in this reality? They certainly acted like mother and daughter. Where was Emily in this world? Did she exist, or was she dead here, too? Maybe she had never even lived. The questions and possible paradoxes were overtaxing his normally capable mind.

"Hon?"

Pike didn't know how long Kate had been trying to get his attention, but he and his host had apparently both been fixated on a shared love for a daughter. A girl raised by one but missed by both. He turned to his wife. "I'm sorry, love, what were you saying?" Pike realized with a start his double also talked in a slightly formal way, somewhat reminiscent of someone who spent their early years in Great Britain.

"I just asked if your food was okay, you've barely touched your Fra Diavolo."

Pike looked down at the dish, quite unsure of what it even was. He recognized the pasta and something a bit shrimp-like, but it had been the Pike from this world who had ordered and eaten the few bites. He was struggling not to make comparisons between this world and his own, but in his Beaufort, this was a simple seafood grille: fish tacos, fried shrimp baskets, and catch of the day. Here, it was clearly casual, but the similarities were more akin to the South of France or Amalfi Coast than South Carolina. "Sorry, Kate, just glad to see Emma. The food is great." He took a bite and indeed, it was great. The wine was also superb.

"Dad, how is your book doing?' his daughter asked.

My book? I'm a writer? Pike shrunk back, waiting on his other to pick up the questioning, but the inner voice remained silent. He decided to wing it, "It's doing okay, as well as can be expected."

Kate snort laughed. "He's being modest, girl, six-weeks at number one. Even better than his last. You know your Aunt Ava is his publicist now, right?"

"That's fantastic, and she's great, Pops. You will be on all the talk shows and eMag covers," Emma said, leaning in and giving her dad a hug. "I'm really proud of you."

"Thanks."

Pike was glad when his daughter's attention turned back to her mom. He decided to do something he'd never considered before. He mentally suggested his host clue him in on what was going on. He felt, rather than heard, the brief chuckle.

First, his host said internally, *tell me if I am going crazy. I know you're there; I know you're not just some voice in my head. I've felt you all afternoon.*

Pike was taken aback. None of the other hosts communicated like this. He spoke internally, "You aren't crazy, and I will explain all I can. You may even get another bestseller out of it. The quick answer is, I am you...we are mirrors of each other, but in my world Emma no longer exists. She's been gone a long time." Pike hoped the brief mental exchange would suffice. The internal voice of this world's Pike stayed quiet for several minutes. He needed a better way of differentiating between him and his host. Instantly, he knew his host went by Rembert professionally. Rembert was Pike's middle name, it had also been his grandfather's.

"I sensed that when you saw her. I miss my daughter, but your reaction nearly caused me to fall down sobbing. I imagine this must be hard. Tell me, other me...how long will you be staying? Should I fix up the guest room tonight?"

Staying? The thought hadn't even occurred to Pike. He was on a mission, he had work to do, but the idea of leaving this reality was nearly incomprehensible. Everything he wanted was here. Everyone he loved was here. He felt the words stumbling to form in his mind. "*No, I am, I mean, I will be gone in a few hours. I would like to spend some more time with my...our daughter, if I could. Would that be all right?*"

"Doesn't seem like I have a choice," Rembert said, then added, "*Sorry, this is just surreal. You can stay as long as you fill me in completely.*"

"*I can do that,*" Pike offered. "*Just help me to not say or do the wrong thing. I really don't know this girl, or your world.*"

"*Sure, buddy, but I think you do,*" the internal voice echoed back.

38

Hours later, the trio pulled up to the house overlooking the bay. Pike hadn't noticed when they left, but the Shepard residence was an understated masterpiece with obvious history despite the high-tech interior.

"*Originally built by a ship captain back in the early to mid 1800s,*" Rembert offered up in Pike's head.

"Surprised they didn't burn it in the war," Pike said internally, thinking this was exactly the kind of home that should have been on this site. It was two stories but not unnecessarily large.

"*What war?*"

"Civil War," Pike said.

"*Wait, America had a Civil War, seriously?*" Rembert asked.

Pike had already filled his double in the best he could about the multiverse and basic science behind SideSliping. He'd just momentarily forgotten this was not his reality. So, no war, no Sherman. He wondered if this America had used slaves. "Yeah, we had one. It was brutal and tragic, but the country survived. Wars tended to be the bloody milestones of our march to being a superpower."

"*Not sure what a superpower is, but we've had our share of wars, too. One in particular was so big we call it a world war,*" Rembert said.

"We had that, too, twice, in fact. Ended when they dropped the bomb," Pike said.

"Yeah, same for us. I heard Northern Europe was beautiful before. Guess it will be a dozen more generations before most of it is livable again."

Pike made his host stop walking, too stunned to react. "Europe was bombed? Atomic bombs?"

"Yeah, totally. America today is mostly made up of refugees from that war. Hitler dropped a nuke on Britain, and *the fallout covered most of France. Then Russia got serious and kidnapped a Nazi scientist named Oppenheimer and had help from some Jewish physicist, and well, they got the bomb, and that was it for Berlin, Poland, Norway, and Belgium. Eighteen bombs in total. The last three* were early Allied forces bombs dropped on *Moscow and Leningrad* in retaliation."

Holy shit, Pike thought. *That explains a lot. Was that the reason for the split in the timeline*? he wondered. "So, Russia got Einstein and the rocket guy. Who did America get? Did Operation PaperClip even happen in this reality? Did Russia win the space race?"

New Earth's version of Pike, the one he'd been calling Rembert, started walking up toward the house but gave a slight chuckle. *"What space race? Russia was finished as a country. The bits of that nation that were still livable went to some of the neighbor countries or the new Siberian territories, which are a province of Canada. Not much impact on getting us to space, but we did have a large influx of scientists and top minds who immigrated from Europe, so yeah, I guess it helped."*

"You're taking all this remarkably well," Pike said. "Under the circumstances, I'm not sure I would be so calm. Do you not want to tell Kate at least?"

"Do you have a Kate?"

"Yes," Pike said, almost laughing out loud. "Sort of. They're much the same from what I can tell. We aren't married, just recently met, in fact."

"Yes, I will tell her. She will know something is up, and my advice is to marry your Kate now, you will never regret it." They, or more accurately, 'he' walked on inside the main room. *"Wait, how did you have Emma if you weren't with Kate?"*

"I don't know," Pike admitted. "I was married to someone else, Emily Holland, from Mount Pleasant. Emma was our daughter in my world."

Pike realized from his thoughts that Rembert didn't know an Emily. "*Weird,*" was his only reaction. Pike came up with a list of other notables since World War Two.

"John F. Kennedy?"

"Yes, two terms, retired to Florida, died in the nineties, I believe."

"Martin Luther King?"

"*Who?*"

"Never mind. Um...Pearl Harbor?"

"*The port in Hawaii? What about it?*"

"The Japanese didn't bomb our naval fleet in the World War?"

"No, Japan was our ally. But they were overrun by China, so they didn't play much of a role."

Some findings were almost comical. "Elvis Presley?"

"Oh, yeah, the televangelist preacher. He was caught with an underage girl and sent to prison."

Also, in this reality, 9/11 never happened, although President Gore was assassinated by Saudi terrorists the following year. Bill Gates and Steve Jobs created Microsoft, but it lagged far behind another company called Apple whose founders had helped establish the modern internet. That had been nearly a decade before the world wide web had emerged back on Pike's Earth.

"What would you say was the most important technological discovery of your lifetime?" Pike asked.

The answer was there in his mind at once, "Fusion *energy production, without question."*

"Holy shit, can you show me?" Pike asked, almost pleading.

His double was the one to laugh. "*Sure, it's no big deal. We teach it in high school science classes now. I am sure I have a basic primer on it.*"

Pike was curious about so much more but asked the more personal question, "How did you know I was here?"

He could sense Rembert thinking back, subtle clues, a feeling of being off balance. *"It was a sensation that I was being followed. You know, those times you're home alone but suddenly feel like someone else is there? That was what did it. It took me hours to determine that it was in my own head."*

Pike also had a feeling of déjà vu, but then again, he was playing ride along in an alternate version of himself. "So, Emma here was never sick? And Kate's sister, I heard she's your agent or something."

"Um, no...nothing really," Rembert answered. *"Normal childhood stuff, of course. She may have had a bad scan around her early teens, but the broad-spectrum protocols would have negated anything. Ava, though, yeah, she was in pretty bad shape. An unusual cancer that almost killed her."*

"Tell me more about the broad-spectrum protocols."

"Sure, be glad to, but first let's go talk to our girls again. I know you're anxious to spend more time with Emma."

Pike did want to spend time with his daughter. He was also keenly aware that their time together was quickly disappearing. He had no idea how to find this world again. Carapaz had handled the SideSlip, so he could only guess as to anything that might help the launch team find the correct quantum slipstream. Pike realized he'd fallen into Carapaz's trap and was amazingly glad he had. Kate let them have some time together. She seemed to sense that Dad needed some much-needed daughter time.

Pike walked with Emma to the pool in the backyard. He sat beside her as she instructed the home AI to light the outdoor fireplace. The night had a slight chill, and the flames licking away at the very realistic logs was welcome.

"You seem different," said Emma.

Pike shrugged. "Just missed you." Rembert was remaining mostly in the background to give Pike this special time.

She eyed him, the reflection of fire shining on her dark hair. "I always know when you're fibbing, Pops."

Pike tried changing the subject. "What do you think the future holds?"

"For me?" She wrapped her arms in his and hugged him. "I don't know, Daddy, it's that scary time we always talked about."

"Scary?"

She nodded. "Yeah, the 'what are you going to be when you grow up,' time. Now I'm there, and I…I just don't want to disappoint you guys."

Pike loved the feeling of hugging his daughter. Several times he saw Kate watching them from a window. "You could never disappoint us, kiddo. You just being here is more than we deserve."

"Awe, you don't mean that. Remember when I punched Lisa Jackson in fifth grade?"

That was one thing he did remember, assuming it happened here, the same as in his dimension. "She deserved it. I know we got onto you but only because we were supposed to. In reality, I loved seeing that bully walking around with a split lip!"

The two talked well into the evening. It was perhaps the best few hours of his entire life. When he kissed her goodnight, it was with bittersweet tears. He knew he would likely never see her again. "*Thank you,*" he voiced internally.

Rembert quietly acknowledged it, "*I think you needed it, and I think it helped* me *to feel what it would have been like not to have her. She*'ll be *fine, Pike. You know how bright she is, how full of life.* Kate and I will protect her, love her, help her where we can. But know she is here living that life for both our worlds. *Now before you go, I need to show you something.*"

39

Upon leaving New Earth, Pike again found he had slipped back into the unnamed Lowcountry world. Carapaz's host showed up several minutes later with an armload of tubers that Pike knew to be the main food stock here. Pike was still too emotional over seeing his grown daughter to be objective but had to find out more about the mirror world

"That was not part of the normal multiverse, Julian. That was a mirror dimension. My host was me."

"Don't be so simplistic, Pike. You will find that narrow assignments such as mirror world and parallel dimensions are inadequate descriptors. Options concerning the multiverse are rarely just simply binary."

"Like good and evil?" Pike sneered.

Carapaz shook his head. "You still aren't getting it, Shepard, but you will. You're a smart guy, and I know you have to figure it out for yourself. The simple truth is, we are not one, we are many. We are the Universe; we are the face and body of God."

"I've heard it before, just more biocentric bullshit, Julian," Pike said unconvincingly.

"You saw that other world, that other you. You spoke to, felt, and loved a daughter that was somehow yours and somehow not. How can both things be true?"

Pike wasn't sure, he still could not come to terms with it. "She is what could have been, that's all," he said with more fervor than he felt.

"What do you think that she is, merely an illusion, is her life no more real than a reflection in a mirror? Come on, Professor, you know better."

"So, when did that version of Earth split from the main timeline, after the Civil War on ours? Or was it World War Two?"

"Much is wrong with that question, Pike. You're standing too close to see the obvious," Carapaz said as his host picked up more of the fleshy root and bit into it. "You saw the plants, did they look the same as our world? The animals? Was the geography the same?"

Pike thought about the rainbow colors of the marsh grass, the fact that Miami was an island, and other aspects of New Earth. "No, it was very different."

"Not so different, but subtly so, yes. It took me a while to trace back the split as well. My double there is...well, hmmm. I probably should keep that to myself for now. He is in the scientific community, though, so my access to the geographical and historical records is quite good. Plus, I'd say they are, what...at least fifty years or so ahead of us in most fields? Would you agree with that?"

Pike nodded.

"My estimates are the two realities diverged from each other around seventy to a hundred thousand years ago."

Pike couldn't contain his surprise; his host's expression must have reflected it.

Carapaz continued, "I know, so why did the two worlds continue to evolve almost in lockstep with one another? You or I could likely transition into that world and be right at home. A few differences, obviously, and fifty years of advancements to catch up on, but the realities are nearly identical. So, what was that event that separated the timelines between the dimensions...why did it not reunite at some point? I would have thought all of it would have coalesced back together into a unified reality by now. How many more of these dimensions are there? These are the truly astounding questions, Pike."

"How did my other in that dimension sense I was there so quickly?"

"Um, yeah," Carapaz said, meandering off a few steps. "It is different than other worlds, isn't it? I have assumed that it's due to the virtual symmetry, super symmetry even, of the two worlds, the two 'yous'...your history, your loves, your very neural patterns must be almost, but not quite, identical. I know my twin there seems to lock the past away from me almost as if he knows what I'm looking for. Did you find that also to be true?"

Pike realized that Carapaz had not communicated with his host the way he had. "Not really, I didn't poke around too much in the past, though. I was too blown away by the present," he lied.

"There is much to learn on that version of our home world, Shepard. Do you know they never embraced the combustion engine there? They have them for specialty uses but find the technology barbaric and a waste of resources. They never even had to worry about what they would do to the environment. My other was busy adjusting one of the induction plates beneath an old truck he has. I believe they use magnetic induction charging. They just pull over the area and the batteries charge right up. Not only that, but the roads themselves seem to have the system built right in. Amazing stuff."

It was fascinating, but Pike was sure Carapaz hadn't shown him all this to teach him about electromagnetic induction smart roadways. "So, what was the point of all that, Julian? Just to tease me with what my life could have been? Like some sort of Ghost of Christmas Future?"

Carapaz answered, laughing so hard his host body shook all over, "No, no, hardly, Shepard." His host moved toward the edge of the dock where they had been standing. "Several things, some of which you will need to figure out on your own. Mostly, it was to make you realize not everything your darling Kate tells you is completely honest. Some of it she is clueless on, but other facts she is just ignoring. There is always more to the story. Go home, Shepard."

With that, Carapaz leapt into the water and began to swim away. Pike dearly wanted to know if there was any way he could return to New Earth again, but he knew better than to give voice to that question. Carapaz already had enough leverage over him. He took one more look around, then triggered the return sequence. Minutes later, he opened his eyes. This time, his memory was firmly intact. The image of his teenage, braces-wearing daughter now was being replaced by that of the beautiful young woman she had become. Finding her had given him more comfort than he could imagine. The tears again came in waves.

40

It took several days for Pike to get over the jump to the other Earth. 'Get over' was not accurate; he knew it would stay with him forever. He still couldn't grasp where Carapaz fit into everything, but the man knew more than he let on. Still, the echoes in his head were unrelenting. He could feel the madness creeping in; how long could he keep it from consuming him?

Since his return he'd tried to keep some distance between him and Kate. There had been some awkward and uncomfortable questions on his mission and multiple request for his notes. Questions he wasn't comfortable answering just yet. He avoided Doctor Lu and Kate, and instead he threw himself into his research. New Earth was the key, he knew that, but why? There was no memory gap when he returned from there, indicating the dimension was close to this one. Why was that important? Were mirror dimensions common, unusual? Why had Kate and her teams never found one?

New Earth's dimensional split, according to Carapaz, was close to a hundred thousand years ago... what had happened? Pike spent days, then weeks researching back to a point in history that might relate. He soon discovered that the more recent prehistoric record, meaning from ten thousand to a hundred thousand years ago, is relatively barren. Not only was it incomplete, but it seemed filled with conjecture and numerous inconsistencies.

While humans had been around for the hundred thousand years, they were mostly scattered tribes. Many appeared to be nomadic and left little that survived other than a few cave paintings. Nothing seemed significant enough to warrant a break in the timeline. Of course, what would be significant in that way? Would it take a meteor strike to split the timeline, or would the premature death of an important person be enough? Frustrated, he chased the internet leads for another hour before closing his laptop and heading to the research library a half mile down the island.

Pike liked the feel of real books; he liked the smell of a bookstore or library. Something magical happened when ink met paper, something that couldn't be matched by modern electronics. The anthropology section was more robust than he had expected. He bypassed the distilled, dry textbooks and encyclopedias and instead selected *Sapiens* by Noah Yuval Harar. This one had appealed to him, as the author makes the compelling case that cognitive thinking began around 70,000 years ago. Pike made furious notes in his illegible scrawl as he read.

In another, called *Last Ape Standing*, he learned that there were likely at least twenty-seven species of humans evolving on the Earth. These alternative branches of modern humans, such as Neanderthals and Denisovans, emerged only to disappear again. Not just these three or four most of us are familiar with, but dozens. Some of these certainly came into contact with each other and battled, maybe to extinction, while others interbred and formed new lines of hominids. Could that be the reason?

Pike put his head in his hands. "There is no way," he whispered. How on Earth could he dissect a hundred thousand years of human history to figure out what was different? No, it wasn't just human history, it was the planet's history as well. He knew we had an Ice Age during that period and went to find the books to check it.

The last Ice Age ended twenty thousand years ago. That was supposedly too recent if Carapaz could be believed. Now, we are supposedly at the hottest point the planet has experienced in a hundred thousand years. That didn't seem relevant, but he made note of it just the same. It certainly could have been worse. Polar ice caps could have melted, and rising sea-levels made Miami the island city that it was on New Earth.

Pike found that the geographical record did indicate the Toba disaster during that time period. An enormous volcanic eruption that darkened the sky and possibly threw the world into an Ice Age. From reverse engineering the genetic code, scientists believe that only homo-sapiens survived this disaster and not very many of them. Estimates were as few as 3000 humans may have been all that made it. Otherwise, we would have a much greater range of human diversity by now. Was that it? Did Toba or something else like it not happen on New Earth? Would the outcome be two worlds that are that close? Pike didn't think so. A reality without Toba would have evolved much more differently.

This was the path Carapaz had pushed him toward. But why? After six hours, he gave in and called Palio to ask for help. Without telling the boy why, he gave him a very precise set of parameters to run searches on. The topics were even more broad than Pike's initial scope, not just archaeology and geology, but all the life sciences: astronomy, marine life, even ancient mythology. Palio seemed confused but glad to help. The two men set up shop in a corner of the lab's workshop, Pike surrounded by books and Palio by computer monitors.

The middle of the second day, Palio threw up his hands in defeat. "What's wrong?" Pike asked.

"I don't know what we're looking for, Boss. You said any significant events in the seventy to 100k range. What qualifies as significant, and how does this matter with what is going on with The Fade?"

Pike stared down at the large book he'd been digesting. An anthropologic record of Ancient Egyptian events as told through the hieroglyphs. He closed the book, the smell of dust and old leather drifting up. "I don't know, kid. Something, but how in the hell do we know what?"

Palio nodded. "Doctor Cassidy said you had not uploaded your last travel notes to the server yet. I'm supposed to be subtly encouraging you to do that instead of this research. It was your protocol, remember?"

Pike remembered, but he was reluctant to tell anyone here about New Earth, for reasons he was very unclear on. Who was he kidding? He knew damn well the reason. One was a daughter that he had just learned was alive and well in another dimension. If he mentioned a personal reason for jumping, much less being in contact with their rival, Carapaz, then he could be off the away teams. "Palio, do you ever go, you know, off world?"

The boy's face drew into a tightened expression of confusion. "I have, yes." He stammered, "I…I just didn't enjoy it. I believe my role is better suited to the control room."

"Kate…I mean, Doctor Cassidy, has mentioned that you thought all of this was a giant simulation. Do you still feel that way, I mean after SideSlipping?"

Palio nodded. "I believe that all life, everything around us, is a giant VR sim. Or could be. Jumping to other worlds actually makes that more likely in my mind. Like loading up a different program to play, all stimuli are basically information, with enough computing power, it could very well be. As to do I still feel that way—no. I am keeping an open mind, but what we have seen in the multiverse is rich and complex. Diversity beyond the scope of what I believe a master programmer could plan for. Why, Professor, are you starting to think it might be?"

Pike shook his head. "No…I think it might be smart to think of the problem in those terms, though. We know the multiverse has rules. Why do rules exist in simulations?"

Palio thought on the question. "Often it is to keep the players from entering areas that are not part of the simulated environment."

"Okay, good. What else?"

"If your actions would compromise another player's ability to enjoy the simulation or maybe even interfere with the core programming. Possibly even excess wasting of system resources, like energy."

Pike tapped a pencil against the closed book. "If a problem

occurred in this giant simulation, what would the master programmer do to correct it? Shut down the entire system?"

Palio frowned. "That wouldn't be practical in a large multiplayer system. More likely they would isolate the problem from the rest of the sim. Contain it and allow it to die or install corrective measures....you know, update the coding."

"Something like a pocket universe, right?"

Palio had never thought along these lines but gradually began coming around. "A universe that pops out due to a problem or significant event. Something like what we're looking for." He looked to Pike for approval, then he thought about the parameters Pike had given him. "But Boss...why are we looking here on our Earth for a specific window of time? You know something, don't you?"

"I can't tell you that, not yet, Palio. You'll just need to trust me for now." Pike stood, walked over, and leaned in close to the young man. "There's something else we need to consider, though. SideSlipping is likely not part of the simulation. I think Kate has found a pathway into the underpinnings of the multiverse. She and Carapaz are not just peeking behind the curtain, they may be monkeying in the master-programmers source code."

41

Kate pushed the thick book down from his eyes, a contemplative look on her face. Smiling, Pike marked the page and closed the cover. "I did too, I heard every word you said."

"Not possible," said Kate. "You were still reading, taking notes, and turning pages. You just muttered bits of acknowledgements when I paused to make it seem like you were listening."

"I wouldn't do that to you." Pike realized the comfortable nature of their young relationship was out of sync with reality. They talked and felt like a couple that had already weathered many years together. "You said, and I quote, 'Doctor Almira is concerned about your brain scans from one of your recent SideSlips. The journey to Luria shouldn't have had any time delay.'" Pike continued for several minutes, quoting nearly verbatim what Kate had been saying.

Kate stared dumbfounded. "How do you do that?" She threw a pillow at him. "How on Earth can you do two things at once?"

Pike shrugged his shoulders. He knew but strongly preferred not to answer. "Just a thing."

"A thing, yeah. Like the coded shorthand you taught yourself as a kid. Like the fact you have graduate degrees in two totally unrelated fields. Like the fact that you can write with both hands at once."

Pike's face darkened. But he offered no response.

Kate kept going, "Yeah, I've seen it. Palio noticed it first, you seem to do it unconsciously at times. It's almost like you have more in that head than the rest of us, Pike. Look, honey, I'm not prying, but do you ever feel like maybe...you know, you're a host? Like one of your others may have slipped into your brain?" She braced, expecting his reaction to the thought.

Pike simply smiled and reached for her hand. "Nothing like that, I assure you. This is how I am. It's how I have pretty much always been. My brain just works a bit differently than most."

Her other hand moved close and brushed the brown hair up exposing the thin scar. "Sandy says you've had brain surgery, probably in your youth." Pike lowered his eyes and stared at the book on the table. He gave a single nod.

"You don't want to discuss it, I understand."

But she didn't, Pike knew she wouldn't...couldn't. No one really could. His cousin, Dewey, and best friend, Risson, had been the only two who really knew, and even they couldn't grasp it fully. It had been too much for his mom and dad to deal with, and it had literally driven his grandparents into the poorhouse.

He walked over to his personal workspace and dug around in his laptop bag for something. He returned to the table and sat back down, holding an old picture of three boys on a beach, each holding a string of fish and grinning. She remembered it had been the only picture displayed in his fishing cabin. It was obviously very important to him, but she had no knowledge as to why.

Kate leaned in to study the photograph. "You, Dewey, and who... Risse?" she guessed.

Pike nodded.

"You looked happy. All of you," she said.

"We were. It was one of the best summers ever, in fact. That was before..." Pike trailed off. "Things just kind of went downhill after that."

"How so?" She knew he'd said his childhood was a mix of good times and very bad. She raked a finger over the photo again. "Looks idyllic until you realize it's the only picture you seem to own."

"It's not with me as a memory, more of a debt," Pike said with a grim smile. "Those boys were my best friends, and each saved me in their own way. We were closer than brothers, and I love them as much today as I did back then."

"I've met Dewey, obviously. He was not what I had expected but very sweet and very protective of you."

"They—they both protected me, often just from myself." He reached for a nearby bottle, added several fingers of the amber whiskey into an empty glass, and tossed it back.

"Kate, I'm sorry...it's not easy to talk about. In fact, I never mentioned it to my ex or Emma, but I had a monster inside of me back then." He pointed a trembling finger at the photo. "They helped me keep it under control...mostly. They gave me the chance to be a kid."

Kate felt she had walked into a mental minefield and struggled to find a safe path to retreat. "What about your mother...your parents?"

"It got bad. Dad, uh...he ran off. Just up and left one weekend and never came back. I never saw or spoke to him again. Mom tried to deal with me for a bit longer, but she was never cut out for motherhood anyway. She knew she had a son with a storm-ravaged brain, as she called it. Anyway, she gave up and sent me away."

Kate wiped a tear from the corner of one eye. "It sounds like such a difficult childhood, but you didn't let it control you."

"How do you mean?"

She shrugged, leaned over, and hugged him, kissing the top of his head. "Childhood trauma can affect some people for life. Cripple them emotionally or damage them psychologically. By and large, it seems you've managed well. You got a good education, have been top of your field, and chartered your own course through life."

"Well, my love life was not a great success," he grinned. "I mean, until recently."

"Good save there, Shepard," she said with a wink.

Pike continued, "My grandfather was very kind...he told me the struggles would all be worth it. Metal isn't strong unless it's tempered by fire. I foolishly just assumed the worse it got, the more successful I would be in time."

"He wasn't wrong," said Kate.

"No, no he wasn't, and I don't look back and see a kid that missed out on anything. I was mostly happy, despite things I couldn't control. You asked me why I lived in South Carolina, this is why: the people back there in that small town all took care of me. When I got so sick, they raised the money for an operation I desperately needed. Shrimpers, farmers, and total strangers gave their dimes and nickels. My grandfather mortgaged his house to the hilt. Doctors and nurses donated time and helped pay for bed space. The people there took care of me, and as I grew, I wanted to make them proud of their investment."

"Thanks," she said before giving him a tender kiss.

"For?"

"For letting me in a little more. You've always kept that part of your past walled off to me."

He laughed. "Hard to tell someone you loved that you were institutionalized in a mental hospital for part of your childhood."

Kate seemed to get it. He felt a slight measure of comfort in revealing all this to her. "Thankfully, it wasn't mental illness, though." He downed the rest of the drink and watched as the single ice cube swirled around in the empty tumbler.

"Rasmussen's encephalitis," he finally said.

"Wow...exceedingly rare and almost always terminal." She knew something about the disorder. "Few children live beyond ten. You were quite lucky. The seizures, though, they had to be terrible."

He nodded, reluctantly dredging up the nightmare scenes of his youth. "The seizures, violence, the uncontrolled movements, the pain. It was like being possessed by demons." Pike leaned over and placed his palms on the wooden table, his fingertips straining against it as if fighting an invisible enemy. "The shrinks up at Mansville State Hospital assumed I was epileptic and tried to keep me doped up and calm. It didn't work. They even used some mild shock therapy even though that was all but illegal by then. When they finally got the diagnosis figured out, I was nearly twelve, well beyond my expiration date. The surgery was the only option."

He pulled his hair apart in several more places revealing interconnected scars over much of his scalp. "Yeah, they call it a hemispherectomy or a corpus callosotomy as well."

Kate tried to recall the term, light slowly dawning on her face.

Seeing her comprehension, Pike nodded. "Essentially, they separated the right half of my brain from the left."

It was such a radical procedure, she'd never known anyone who had gone through it, only read of it in medical journals a few times as far as she could recall. Even then, she'd assumed the patients had all died or been institutionalized. She knew it was simply a treatment, not a cure. "Hard to imagine a person being able to live, much less have a normal life after radical brain surgery like that, but you not only lived, you also seemed to thrive," Kate said.

He splayed his fingers out on the table, then rotated his hands in an almost placating gesture. "There are some odd side effects, and it may be that my way of thinking is very unlike other people's. I have no way of knowing. I think it's part of how I figure things out. One part of my brain handles the rational reasoning and the other the intuitive and creative. They are rivals, each trying to come up with the best answer and also trying to shoot down the other side's solution. I'm not sure it would work for others, but its normal to me. So, no, I'm not a host, but in many ways, I fully understand how it might feel."

"Fascinating, Pike. You really are a very special man."

Pike didn't feel special, in fact, he had mostly felt broken for much of his life. Somehow, this project and this woman were introducing him to something new. Hope.

She leaned in close, and their lips found each other's.

42

The next morning Pike had an urgent message from Palio. Kate came out of the bedroom, again wearing one of his shirts.

"Something wrong?"

"No, I don't think so," he answered, ending the call before handing her a cup of coffee. "He left a message...said he might have what I was looking for."

"Yeah, he kind of implied you had come around to his way of thinking."

"Huh?" Pike said, confused.

"About all of us being in a giant computer simulation," she answered.

"Oh, um, no, not at all. It's just helping me think of the problem in more logical terms. Systems have to work together, or it really isn't a system. The concept of the multiverse is so large and complex, and being one of the sentient entities inside the multiverse, our view is naturally distorted. We have our beliefs and biases. Taking Palio's point of view simply draws me out of the abstract and offers perspective, maybe a glimpse into something more understandable."

Kate shook her head. "Seems like the reverse would be true, honey, but I'll take your word for it."

"Can time flow backward?" he asked.

"No," she answered a bit too quickly. "I mean, I know it's theoretically possible but..."

"But your mind can't accept it, right?" Pike said, finishing her thought.

She agreed. "So, by removing yourself from the problem, you're more open to accepting whatever answer happens to be the truth?" she guessed.

Pike expanded on the thought, "After a few months here, I realize I, and every other human, is incapable of knowing the right questions to even ask, much less understand the truth if it barged in the door and stomped the shit out of us. We aren't capable, we have not reached that point in our evolution...maybe never will." It surprised him to see Kate was frowning. "What's wrong?"

She shook her head dismissively. "It's nothing. You just..."

"What?"

"You reminded me of someone else, just then. Someone I'd much rather you not sound like."

"Julian Carapaz?" he asked, his face also wrinkling into a frown.

Kate nodded; the dour look still pasted on her face. "He never compared the multiverse to a VR... thought the concept was rubbish, but the rest of it was very much what he was working on before he..."

"Fled the reservation?" Pike offered.

"Um...yeah."

"And that scares you?"

"Of course it does, Pike. I love you."

And there it was. She had said the words he knew she was feeling. Did he tell her back...did he, in fact, feel the same way? Both sides of his brain were firing their full arsenal at each other. Neither was keeping any ammo in reserve. "I'm not Julian," he said, choosing to ignore the emotional part of his psyche for the moment. It had been an excellent answer, the safe answer, and clearly...the wrong answer.

Kate grabbed her lab coat and left the small apartment. The door swung wide, letting him hear her footsteps retreating into the distance. "Well, shit!" he muttered in bewilderment.

* * *

"So, what did you find?" Pike asked. The conversation with Kate had left him unsettled, but it was obvious that his assistant felt confident about something. Palio normally operated at a higher voltage than most others, but today he was over the top. As Pike watched him bounce around the workspace, part of a croissant hanging from his mouth, he finally had to put a hand on his shoulder to calm him down. "Might be time to switch to decaf, kid."

"Huh? Oh, yeah. Good one, Professor. Right, right," Palio responded, his head nodding in agreement.

"What's your big news? Did you find the event we've been looking for?"

"I think I finally understand what it is that you're looking for."

So far, the search for what might have caused the realities to split had been maddeningly difficult. They had been mostly relying on archaeological or geographical text for guidance. While the disasters of the ancient world were plentiful, the period they were searching predated anything resembling a civilization or written language. Pike had begun to think Carapaz might have gotten his timing wrong, or maybe finding the cause was completely irrelevant to figuring out what to do now. Still, he was obsessive when it came to uncovering the facts.

"Okay, Boss, look here," Palio said. For some reason, he liked calling almost everyone 'Boss.'

Pike started to correct him, but instead leaned in to see what the young doctor had found. He saw a printout of a standard timeline chart with numerous overlays of colored lines. "This is historically accurate?" While some events noted in the chart he understood, others seemed totally random. "Where are these data points coming from, Palio?"

"I began thinking about your analogy to a simulation," he said. "Of course, we have gone through nearly every bit of text available on this time period and found practically nothing. I mean, could a plague have wiped out a key species of humanoid? Sure, and we would have never known it. Maybe an Icelandic volcano blew and plunged the world into another Ice Age right at a critical moment as life was expanding."

"I know the challenges, Palio. So, how does the VR game theory fit in?"

"Right, right," Palio said, taking a large gulp of his double shot espresso before continuing. "If you are designing a virtual reality, you probably have to constantly make corrections. I can do basic programming, but I'm not that well versed in the complexity of building a simulation. One thing I know from coding, though, is when you have a problem, often you can do some recursive steps to identify what is missing. Look for gaps or null code to see where a correction was made."

Pike thought on that. It was actually a good approach. If you can't find what happened, maybe look for what didn't happen. "How can you do that, though?"

Palio held up a palm tablet, one that Pike instantly recognized as one of his shorthand notepads from the launch chairs.

"The mission notes?" Pike asked.

The kid grinned wide revealing perfect teeth. "Most of the jump teams now use them, all have been through the training to write the basic words."

Pike was aware more and more had been using them...some had been particularly vocal about what a help it had been. "So, you began reviewing mission data. How did that help? Seems like it would be a lot of unrelated info to sift through."

"It would be, but Petra and her team built in an index system to translate your shorthand and tag it with keywords, making a searchable database," Palio answered, clearly enjoying spoon-feeding the revelation to Pike.

"So, you found something?"

"Not at first," Palio said. "But eventually, yes. Assuming all these worlds were once Earth, events probably split most of them off. Not all the travelers get the kind of hard data we can use. I mean, who would know when a T-class world like Thera's organic chemistry switched from primarily oxygen to methane? It had to be billions of years ago. So, it's been a bit hit or miss, but I noticed the more Earthlike the world, the more events seemed in sync with one another."

Pike thought he understood, and that made sense. "So, on a D-class world, you might find similar events in the history of all those planets? And some of those might have also happened here."

"Or almost happened, Professor," Palio answered.

Pike centered in on a series of notes on the timeline. He now realized this was a multi-dimensional timeline of Earth. The amount of work the kid had put in was incredible. Indeed, a spike in trigger events was clustered around 85,000 and again at 61,000 years ago on numerous timelines but not on the baseline of this Earth. "What were these?"

43

He looked outward into a steel gray sky. Thunderheads billowed high above a rolling sea. Inside his own head a storm also raged, one that Pike Shepard knew would not pass as quickly as the one approaching from the south. Palio had indeed found something helpful. That had been a week ago. The research and his conclusions had led him to this moment.

The truth had been as soul crushing of a revelation as Pike could imagine, but somehow, he knew there was more. *Creation is at an end, and we are but echoes of a dream.* He wasn't sure where the line had come from, but he was quite sure it wasn't his own. Increasingly, he was feeling like someone else might actually be using his body as a rest stop along the highways of madness as they navigated the chaos of the multiverse.

Since visiting Xylos, and then New Earth, things had somehow become much clearer but also less certain. Carapaz had given him the clues, but even he didn't understand the full picture. Pike desperately wanted to go back to New Earth, to see Em one more time. To hold her, to tell her he loved her and wished for her a life filled with joy. Why had he lost her in this world? He hated whatever dark force dealt him the shitty hand while offering paradise to his doppelgänger on the other side.

He saw Palio waiting patiently for him on the far edge of the base runway. No flights were scheduled this afternoon, and the locals had taken to using the runway for a skateboard course. Several younger boys whizzed past, not a care in the world. He dodged the next batch and made his way over.

"Everyone there?"

Palio nodded. "Not very happy, though. Doctor Lu is the only one who schedules a full staff briefing, and that's rare."

"I don't give a damn," Pike answered. "It's time for the truth, and I want off this goddamn patch of sand and to go home."

They entered a stuffy overcrowded briefing room. Pike could feel the eyes on him, the questioning looks, the distrust. Was this how Carapaz had felt? Kate sat close to an empty chair, his chair, he assumed, but he would not be using it today. He preferred to stand to deliver the news that none of them would want to hear. The news that would likely end this project for good.

Kate lightly touched his hand and leaned in as if to ask a question. He loved her fully. He knew that with certainty now. She had been right; their souls were intertwined, but this was not a time for gentleness. He nodded to Palio, who started a short presentation. It was a curated list of the horrors going on currently in the world.

The large flatscreen displayed a war scene, civilians staggering away from bombed-out buildings, smoke drifting in front of them, and a layer of dirt or ash covering the exposed faces. Several bodies lay unmoving on the street. The scene could have been any of a half-dozen wore-torn areas around the globe, but Kate gasped, reading the banner at the bottom of the 24-hour news channel. 'Bombing in Houston.' "Oh, dear God," one of the staff said.

Palio lifted the remote, nudged the volume up, and the reporter described the incident. It was already being labeled terrorism, *domestic terror*. The date was today. A new feed in another clip showed a very different scene; a breathless reporter faced a shaky camera in a mostly failed attempt to appear professional. "Just repeating our lead story," the reporter said. "We can confirm the death toll here in Charlotte is over 700 and expected to keep climbing. Many of the city's first responders make up most of those casualties. So far, authorities are remaining silent as to the people likely responsible for the carnage." The reporter turned as the cameraman panned to a wide shot, and she continued her voiceover. "Since this is still an active emergency and crime scene, this is as close as we can get. You can just see the office building several blocks away where we are told the deadly gas released today is venting off into the atmosphere where it will hopefully dissipate. We are upwind, but if that changes, we will have to evacuate quickly. This may be second only to 9/11 for casualties among first-responders."

People in full-face gas masks ran in panicked strides, and as the camera zoomed tighter on the building in question, small groups in white or red bio-hazard suits were setting up some type of equipment. The shot cut to the news studio where the normally implacable anchors even seemed upset. "Thanks, Jill. We have other reports coming in from other events around the country. Some evidence suggests this might be a coordinated terrorist event on an international scale. Do the people there in Charlotte have any theories at this point?"

The scene cut back to the reporter who stepped back into frame as she appeared to be wiping tears from her eyes. She shook her head. "No, Bill, no real theories, but at least one of the canisters recovered from the scene appeared to indicate possible military origin." She paused dramatically and added, "I was told off the record it may have been an experimental form of VX."

The reporter signed off, and the feed reverted again to the studio. The anchor appeared to be listening to his earpiece for a moment before nodding. "We do want to reiterate that there is no hard evidence indicating our military, or any military or government, was involved at this point. Chemical weapons have been outlawed, and their development or stockpiling would be a clear violation of the Geneva protocols. That said, this was obviously not the result of an industrial accident or natural causes, and there have been other such incidents in modern history. Syria in 2018, the Sarin gas attack in the Tokyo subway in 1995, and the Iran-Iraq war in the eighties."

Kate looked up shakily as the presentation moved to a current report from Fox News where the ominous presidential podium stood empty. "Again, we are waiting on a briefing from President Henderson. We were told that was to have started several minutes ago. All we can assume is that he is still being updated on the ongoing crises unfolding across the country today." The broadcast went abruptly silent as the normally polished press secretary stepped up behind the podium. Her usual well-crafted appearance looked ragged in the harsh lights.

"Ladies and gentlemen," she began, looking out over the small gathering of reporters. "I am sorry, but the president will not be making a statement this morning."

Shouted questions cut off whatever she was planning to say next. "Has he been moved to the bunker?" one man asked. "Are we under attack?" another yelled. "When can we expect an official statement?"

The press secretary leaned into the microphone and glared at the crowd. "The president is a chickenshit. That is my statement." With that, she turned and exited out the side door leaving a room of astonished reporters scrambling to get the unbelievable soundbite out before anyone else.

Pike spoke again, "This is just today's news from the U.S. I had Palio monitoring the escalating violence, as we like to pretend we are in a bubble here that is not part of the rest of the world." He clicked 'Resume,' and the screen started again as he said, "This is more of what happened earlier this week."

"Utter devastation in Lebanon after chemical rockets slammed into a UN Peacekeeping force. Riots and armed protests in the streets of Moscow and St. Petersburg. Russian military may have seized control after a power grab between the SVR and KGB. Rumors are the Russian president has been killed or, at the very least, gravely injured."

More clips showed India and Pakistan were both gathering ground forces on their disputed borders as the two nuclear powers threatened mutual annihilation. Both Turkey and China were threatening to take action if either side took any offensive action. Ten more minutes barely scratched the surface on the rising tensions.

"Oh, my Lord," Kate said. "This is how it begins. We really are in The Fade."

Pike nodded. "While it's no surprise to this group, I think we all know it's happening. We purposefully avoid the news from out there because we know it only gets worse from here. Events like this taken over a longer period would be bad enough but maybe not totally unexpected. We live in a violent world. Pile them all into a single month or in this case, a single week, and yes, I think we can agree that we have been marked for deletion."

"How can you be so cold, so matter of fact about it?" Dr. Amira asked.

"Because he knows what is causing it. Don't you, Shepard?" Letner asked.

Pike clicked the remote, pausing the video. On screen, an armed man ran through a dusty scene toward the camera, now frozen midstep. He looked Arabic and couldn't be more than fourteen. "I do, but none of you are going to like it."

"Was Carapaz right, are we causing it?" one of the scientists asked.

Pike rubbed his eyes. They were bloodshot from the last several days of little to no sleep. "Nope, but like I said, you're not going to like the truth any better." He walked around the room and made eye contact with each of them, one at a time. "How many of you have ever SideSlipped into your exact duplicate?" His was the only hand raised.

"I slipped to a version of Earth that was so close as to nearly be its twin. I was me, but things were different. Their tech was years ahead, Russia was no longer a threat. But that version was so familiar the differences wouldn't even matter to most of us. In fact, it was better, much better."

Palio looked confused. Pike had shared none of this up until now. Petra and Amira shook their heads. "That's simply not true. We know every world you have been to. They are all mapped in the network," Palio argued.

"I did go to those worlds. They're not always where I stayed, though," Pike responded. He listened for the objections and the thinly veiled disbelief before lunging forward, ignoring their questions. "I can't get into how I breached the SideSlip protocols, but I did. I'm sure there are clues that will back that up if anyone is checking.

"We, and by 'we' I mean me and probably most of you at one time or another, have wondered if either the many worlds theory or perhaps the multiverse theory was right. While each of the dimensions has a version of Earth, none appear to be much like it. None have humans that look anything like us. That would indicate that every other dimension in the multiverse is unique. Planets and life possibly created from similar base ingredients but vastly different outcomes. But of this group of scientists and travelers, apparently I alone have been to a mirror world of this Earth. That shows that both hypotheses are true. Multiverse and many worlds theory are both true, maybe even two sides of the same coin."

He pointed to his young assistant. "Palio, what else does that suggest?"

Palio answered immediately, "If many worlds theory is true, then the branching timeline is also true."

"Branching timelines." Pike said it several times as he paced, letting the words sink in. "We've all had these discussions. If every time there is a choice or decision or opportunity for multiple outcomes, quantum theories suggest every outcome does happen. If I take you all to Las Vegas and we play roulette, every time the ball lands on black, it also lands on red in a different universe, in a parallel reality of Las Vegas. Now, according to the theory, it should also land on every other number on the wheel. So, thirty-seven more universes and maybe one where the ball falls off the wheel, maybe another where the croupier dies of a heart attack before throwing the ball. It does all get ridiculous, and my belief, both originally and now, is that's a waste of resources and overly messy. I believe Kate agrees with me that we see no reason for a many worlds version of the multiverse to work that way. Conservation of energy and such. To hell with the observer's paradox and all that bullshit. The truth is, it doesn't matter." He knew that was the way to fire up a bunch of research scientists but just couldn't resist.

"How can it not matter?" Letner asked in a voice edging quickly over to belligerence. Several others had moved back in their chairs and looked ready to stage an open rebellion.

"Okay," Pike said flatly. "Maybe it's simply better today to say…I don't care. I don't care if that's the truth because it doesn't really matter to us. What I have learned is the timeline only branches off into two realities for some really significant events. When that happens, and this is critically important, when that happens, one of those timelines is doomed to end. Many worlds theory is correct but only to a point. The multiverse seems to have a mandate of reunifying or rebalancing timelines as quickly as possible."

Kate interjected, "So, while the ball on red vs. the ball on black might be of minor significance, the other thirty-something decisions would quickly be absorbed back into the main timeline."

"See," Pike intervened, "someone was paying attention. Exactly! Except the fall of dice or roll of a roulette ball are clearly not significant events. Maybe significant for the gambler hoping the bus fare home he just placed on a bet will win, but to the rest of the Universe… not so much."

"How significant would it have to be?" Letner asked, his voice now sounding more contemplative instead of combative.

"That really is the question I have been struggling with," Pike said. "Palio and I have been looking at a range of time that I believe is when our own timeline fracture occurred. Something on the order of 70,000 years ago."

Dr. Fazula, the quantum biologist, shook her head. "Not much to go on that far back, Professor. Toba, the Ice Age, various hominids leaving Africa."

"You're right, and it took us quite some time. In fact, it took me traveling to a world as unlike ours as any you have found, Xylos. That's where I really learned the truth…it just took me some time and Palio's passionate determination for us to unravel it."

"Chaos World?" someone said.

Pike offered a tight smile. "I now have something of a friend there. My other goes by the name of Nianda. Amazing intellect. Anyway, he told me I was on the right track, but I was looking at it from a position that would never offer the right answer."

The confused expressions let Pike know he was losing them quickly. None had ever seen anything remotely like a sentient being in that world, but the very act of connecting should have let them know someone was on the other end.

"The branching of the timeline was not the result of something in our past but something in the other Earths," he stated.

He saw eyes darting around the table. Several were making notes. He wondered who would get there first. One hand stopped writing and the person looked up.

"Our timeline was the one that branched. We're the copy, not the original."

Pike gave a solemn nod. The voice belonged to the one person in here whom he hated disappointing the most. "Yes, Kate, our timeline is being ended. That's what The Fade is, and I now think it's a totally natural phenomenon. Once a world loses its connection to the rest of the multiverse, the creativity, the dreams, and even the love begins to die. The hate and violence often step in to fill up the void. I don't know why it is that way, I just know that it is. The Universe, or more correctly the multiverse, has rules, and conservation of resources is one of them. When a significant enough event triggers a split, one of those timelines is doomed, probably from the very beginning. It will either be reintegrated or terminated via The Fade. Obviously, in some cases the copy is viable enough to continue, that's why there's such a multitude of very different Earths out there. That is not the case with mirror worlds, though. I think their paths are interconnected, and one is all that can be allowed to survive."

"How do you know we aren't being reintegrated?" Doctor Letner asked.

"I believe that has already been tried several times. Now, the futures have diverged too widely. Like a bit of errant code in the software, we are TSR, as the old programmers used to say."

"Terminate and Stay Resident," Palio muttered mostly to himself.

"You're connected to the Pike on the original Earth, aren't you? I mean, more than most of your hosts?" Kate asked.

"I would say so," Pike agreed, unsure of where she was going. "New Earth, as I was calling it, but now that seems more like what we should call this one."

"Must be because of the way your brain works, but that does explain a lot."

Now he was intrigued, and he pulled out the empty chair and sat. "Like what, Kate?"

She paused briefly, as if unsure to say the rest publicly. Reaching the mental crossroad and apparently finding no easy way of avoiding it, she plunged ahead. "Several times you have mentioned the death of your daughter, Emma," she said. "I even talked to your friend, Dewey, about it. I believe you told me the day of her birth was the happiest memory you had."

Anger flashed across Pike's face, but he kept it in check. He loved this woman, but if she wanted to open old wounds, especially now, there had to be a damn good reason.

Kate moved close and placed a gentle hand on his arm before continuing. "We've checked all the records, Pike. You and your wife had no children."

44

Pike's head began to pound, a feeling instantly taking him back to his childhood. The onset of a seizure. He gritted his teeth and stumbled out of the room. Vaguely, he heard Kate calling his name. It couldn't be true. He remembered Emma clearly. The pain grew in intensity. *Shit.* He needed...he needed to be outside. And then he finally was; the overcast sky was streaked with bright sunlight. He dropped to one knee as bile rose in his stomach, and then he couldn't contain it. Vomit poured from him in a stream. He couldn't hold back the flood of tears. Then, slowly, he noticed the absence of kids on the runway ahead, and in the far distance, a convoy of vehicles heading in his direction.

"Professor, are you okay?"

"Huh?" Pike saw Palio above him and knew he was asking something. More bile rose in his stomach. *What else in my life was a lie? A false memory. Bleed over from the other side.*

The vehicles were closer; he could hear them now, and in the distance, a large plane on final approach. Something about this was wrong. Somehow, he knew instantly. Maybe this had happened on another world, but he needed to get out of here. "Pa...Palio," he stammered. He staggered to his feet. "Palio, get Kate and...run!"

The young doctor looked at his friend, then back at the

approaching Humvees, and understood. He nodded and disappeared back into the dull gray building. Pike stood and feebly attempted to put on a brave face for what he feared was coming. Dust swirled behind the lead truck as they swung into line in front of the lab. Soldiers spread out, weapons drawn, which Pike noticed were the Canadian version of the M-16/ A C8 Diemaco rifle. But why, and how did he know this? The sound of a large transport plane touched down on the far end of the runway and decelerated sharply as it rolled to a stop a hundred yards away. The smell of burnt jet fuel assaulted his nostrils. Pike took notice but was more lost inside his own head than ever. before

* * *

Forty-two minutes later, almost the entire senior staff of The Project were lining small jump seats along the inside of the Airbus A400 Atlas turboprop. Each of them had ankles and wrists zip-tied together with plasticuffs.

"Do you have any idea who this is or what they want?" someone nearby Pike asked. The interior lights were dimmed, and all he could see were shadows around him. He knew that Doctor Lu was on his right, and to his left was an empty seat, but he was pretty sure the person in the next seat was the controller named Petra. She was Palio's equal for one of the other teams.

"I demand answers," Doctor Letner shouted. Even doing so, he was barely heard over the noise of the powerful engines. "We are on sovereign soil with a charter allowing us to carry out our research on that base. You have..." The sound of something hard hitting flesh sounded before a gasp and cry of pain.

One of the guards laughed and made a comment in French. Pike knew it meant asshole. He was also quite certain that, despite no insignia on the uniforms, rifles used mainly by the British SAS, and an unmarked French transport plane, all of his captors were American. The obfuscation was clearly designed to misdirect anyone who had seen, as well as the ones who were captive. It was called rendition, the abduction and secret imprisonment and interrogation to a classified site not in the United States. If Doctor Almira would have had her brain scan running, Pike's brain activity would have been lighting it up like a Disney World fireworks finale.

His head still pounded, and that, combined with the droning of the engines and the near constant murmur of complaints from the other scientists, were pulling him down. He knew if he gave into it, if he thought about the fact his daughter had never existed, he would lose it.

Focus on things you can control, Pike, he told himself. *Your breathing, in and out. Where are they taking you? Did they turn east or west? Did Palio get away? Where is Kate?* He pondered these questions for a long time, fully considering each one before moving on to the others. When he got to 'Where is Kate?' he realized almost with a start that he couldn't feel her. Not that he couldn't see her, but ever since he met her, he seemed to know when she was close. Right up until now. He'd clearly seen her taken out of the lab, and he'd yelled insults as they savagely zipped her hands together, the grimace of pain evident on her face. Then, he'd been pushed roughly up the ramp and into the plane.

Pike's eyes had adjusted to the low light now, and he could see the shadows seated around the cavernous interior. A few were wearing black hoods, but not all. He had been close to being sick again as they took off, probably why he was not one of the one's bagged. They didn't want him to choke on his own vomit. That told him something right there. Nineteen darkened lumps with legs sat around him. That was two shy of what had been in the briefing room. He filed those fragments of information away and worked on the bigger problem. *Why would they come for us and why now?*

* * *

Pike heard the sound noticeably change and felt the plane buffeting from turbulence before settling down again. Several mechanical noises could be heard coming from somewhere up above.

"What's going on?" Petra whispered nervously.

"I think we're being refueled," Pike answered. This, too, was a guess, but somehow, he was certain of it. He stared up, sure that if he could see through the thin skin over the airframe, a large airborne tanker would be joined to the Atlas by a flexible fuel hose. He thought back to his days in the military. The range of a C-130 was a bit over 2000 miles. He assumed the Atlas would be similar. That meant Africa or Asia, maybe Australia, but Europe or America was doubtful. Too many miles and difficult fueling opportunities. Did that help? He wasn't sure, but exercising his mind was what he did. *Work the problem.* Even now, a large part of his thinking was dedicated to how long this reality had before it ended and was there any way of delaying it.

Nearly five hours later, the plane touched down. Black hoods were again lowered over everyone's heads, and Pike heard the lowering of the rear ramp. He smelled the jungle, a tropical rainforest, if he had to guess. He'd work the math out later to figure out where they were. The plane was in a darkened hangar, he could tell because of the sound echoing off several walls. The front was open. That was where the smells and other sounds were coming from.

"This way," a man with a Texas accent said. "Follow my voice people, get a move on. No lolly-gagging."

Well, they've dropped the international charade, Pike thought. Now it came down to American military or CIA...or both. He was putting good money on both, but it didn't matter. He felt sure he knew why they were here, and nothing any of them said would change the outcome.

45

The man looked at Pike through the window. He knew he would wait as long as it took. Pike no longer cared. Men from DARPA had taken over the investigation, and they had his notes, his coded shorthand. Did that mean Kate had given those to them? He hated to think that way, but it was an almost obvious conclusion.

"In the New Earth, Russia was no longer a superpower, correct? This fissionable energy source, did they mention TRISO particles?"

The voice droned on and on; Pike ignored it. The shocks to his skin no longer registering. "You ever plan on responding?" another voice asked.

This voice was different, vaguely Asian, and...and seemingly not coming from the speaker." Who is this?" Pike asked internally.

"I am called Subada, and I believe we may have a mutual friend, Nianda. He suggested perhaps I could be of assistance."

Nianda knows I'm in trouble? How is that possible? "So, you are me?" Pike subvocalized the question as opposed to just thinking it. This was very much like carrying on a conversation with someone else. This must have been what the Pike on New Earth felt.

"I am technically not you," Subada responded in a lighter tone. "My species has a unique ability to tune our quantum signature. It originally was part of how we communicated with one another. We also used it as a weapon with horrifying results. Nianda and his people helped me understand how to use it across other dimensions to connect with certain individuals when needed."

The presence was somehow comforting; this traveler imparted a feeling of strength more than fear.

"How can you help me? I'm imprisoned and being interrogated."

"I believe you are being tortured as well," Subada said.

"Level four, Professor," the overhead speaker said, and the intensity of shocks went up instantly.

"I can help with that," Pike's new internal voice said, and the pain eased off dramatically.

Pike's thinking cleared up, too. He could focus on the traveler and found he could tune out his captors completely. "Thank you. Was it you who warned me when the convoy came to get us?"

Pike wanted to know so much, but mentally suggested that Subada do the talking. "It was me, yes. I was still getting accustomed to your unique brain pattern then. Sorry I couldn't warn you better. You are correct, Pike, that this timeline is being terminated. You are wrong on the rest, though."

"I am?"

"Yes," Subada responded. "It is not imminent, and it does not mean you will disappear. It may reintegrate some of you into the original version, the one you call New Earth."

"Who makes these decisions, and how can we do anything about it? Based on what they're asking, I think these clowns feel like if they destroy Russia, then the timelines will stabilize."

"They are very wrong on that. The destabilization of Europe and that subsequent nuclear exchange was not the cause of the fracture, nor will it be the solution," Subada said.

Pike smelled burning flesh and realized the asshole in the booth must have cranked the power up again.

"He is beginning to damage your tissue; it might be best if we offer some reaction, or I could cause you to pass out. Would you like that?"

Pike very much would have liked that but didn't want to blow this opportunity to talk with someone who actually knew what was going on. "Do we have any options?"

"You have options, Pike Shepard. Your world...I am not so sure," Subada said with a mental sigh. "I can help you get out of here, or I believe I can teach you how to traverse the multiverse without the use of your quantum tunneling machines."

"I can SideSlip without the equipment at the lab?" Pike then thought of the other part of that. "How does that help this reality?"

"It can give you more answers," Subada said. "It can give you solutions that might stay the executioner's hand. Unlike most humans, your brain architecture seems uniquely suited for it."

Pike agreed, and Subada rendered Pike's body unconscious and then left him. It took the interrogator two full minutes to realize his subject was not simply unresponsive, but also unconscious.

* * *

Pike watched as a misty moon crossed a field of stars that was too bright and in the wrong configuration. He looked out over a bluish gray landscape that somehow reminded him of Scotland. The rolling, rocky hills were covered in sickly clumps of stubby grass, all surrounded by the black pitted sands he knew from his host's mind to be volcanic ash. Almost reluctantly, he glanced at the familiar ruins in the distance of what once was a glorious city. This was a place unfamiliar but also well known. Foot falls sounded behind him. The figure stopped several yards away, facing the same direction.

"You are Subada," Pike said with some assurance.

The man remained silent and simply gazed at the darkened ghost of the city. Subada's shoulders twitched. "This is my home world, Shepard. That city was known as Kava by my people, although few alive would remember that now.

"The Fade?" Pike asked, feeling sure he was correct.

"I come here often, many of my species do," the alien-man said. "It helps us keep my people's focus exactly where it should be."

The annihilation here was incomprehensible to Pike, yet he knew it was true, his host and Subada kept returning to this exact location. "You are a warrior."

It was obvious from Subada's posture, the type of outfit, and simply the understanding in his other's memory. Physically, the creature was not precisely humanoid, but he loosely fit the classification. Thick arms and massive legs with a tapered head and neck that seemed almost feminine atop the robust frame.

"So, you now understand how to slip into the quantum stream?"

"Hmm." Pike was perplexed at the question and then amazed at his answer. "Yes, I do, and thank you," Pike said. He didn't recall learning the knowledge but now understood it and marveled at it. Now, it seemed to be something he'd always known. Subada seemed to have simply left it there for him to unpack and use when he was ready.

Subada nodded unenthusiastically. "Your body is still back in that room, the prison. Do you know why?"

Pike moved forward to a rock and squatted as seemed appropriate. "I can guess. They were listening in, probably had the labs bugged, maybe even a spy in our midst. We tripped over a truth they wanted to stay buried."

"So, now they want you to disappear? Is that the correct expression?" Subada asked.

Pike's host nodded. "I'm sure they prefer that. My guess is they already knew our timeline was being terminated and just prefer the word not get out." He looked again toward the ruins of Kava and wondered what it must have been like. It dominated the skyline for tens of miles in each direction. Much larger than any Earth city Pike had ever seen.

"My people guessed wrongly," Subada said, finally turning away from the depressing view. "Much as your people face now. We started a war we could not win, in a vain attempt to reunify the timelines."

"The Kava in the original dimension was at war?"

"Yes, and our military leaders thought that was why the timelines had split. The Fade was already affecting us but not the other. As I said, our minds are more pliable. We could jump into our mirror dimensions and monitor the situation at any time."

"Things on the other world were better despite being at war," Pike said.

"Yes, they were fighting concentrated skirmishes. Like humans, we are...or were...a very aggressive species. Our leaders began to believe that one option was to accelerate the differences. They believed that a rapid termination might mean that some lives get reintegrated, that some people get to go to the better world, the better timeline."

Subada continued, "Most of our leaders seemed to think that the opposite was true. They believed that once the timeline termination happens, you're done. You're ended. You're no longer a part of anything. No past, no future, no one to even remember you ever existed. And so, they want to maintain the status quo as long as possible, which means make your timeline as similar to the original as possible, to keep them close. The hope was that at some point maybe the two realities would be close enough to reintegrate. That was what we decided. But once we started the war, it exploded on us. My people were nearly all wiped out."

"But you survived," Pike said hopefully. "I thought The Fade only ended one of two ways. You either disappear, cut off from the multiverse, or you reintegrate and forget that previous reality."

Subada gave a very slow nod, his tapered head eyeing the ruins again, the large, dark eyes blinking rapidly. "There is much we don't understand, Shep. Suffice it to say, there are more outcomes than we imagined. Perhaps Nianda could guide us, but he won't, he leaves that up to us. The ones who strive to make a difference.

"Not to be vague, but the curtain between realities is complex. In some ways, it is gauzy and flimsy as an old threadbare sheet. While at other times, it is as off limits to us as the other side of the Universe. What you see as overlap is happening all the time in millions of tiny realities popping up new dimensions and closing them out again with a similar frequency. There is an order to the multiverse. Some would call it intelligent design at work. We see it more simply as the most viable of realties becomes dominant and survives until it is knocked off by another. Most viable seems to be a hard concept to pin down. It is not based on anything simple like good or evil, or intelligence versus empathy. My theory is that the likelihood of a species thriving either through sustained population or intelligence growth seems to be the factor that keeps worlds around the longest. Those are the ones who do not 'Fade.'"

Pike wondered about Kate and Carapaz. What was their role in this? "You know which of our timelines will survive, don't you? Am I right? Is it the other one, the New Earth?"

Subada turned and faced him, then unfolded a long arm and placed it on his host's shoulder in a very human gesture. "You're now facing what all of us faced, what every world comes to at some point. The two paths are diverging. Something unusual is going on, though, Shepard. You just learned a powerful truth. Let your brain work through it for a minute."

Pike tried to dredge up what Subada was getting at. Then it hit him.

"The real question is how many fractures there are."

"Right. You now know that in this timeline, you have no daughter. But in the other one, your Emma is a healthy, young woman. Obviously, there was also a timeline in which she died as a child. That is not the one that you visited, The New Earth, so those memories are bled over from yet another."

"Is that normal to have three mirror realities?" Piked asked.

"Yes, and no," Subada said cryptically. "You see, fractures and reintegration happen all the time. We just rarely notice it because when a new future blends with the one you're in, that mixed history becomes your past. It becomes the truth they taught you in school, the memories you have always known. Consciousness is very plastic, as your people would say. Your past can mold itself to accommodate whatever happened. A third stable timeline, though, one that is paralleling two others in long duration, would be highly unusual."

Pike groaned in frustration. "So, what are we supposed to do, Subada? Try to accelerate things along the way the government wants? Or the way Carapaz seems to think, which I gather is to make us more different to go ahead and speed up the termination? I mean, The Fade is going to get us one way or the other." He knew Subada had access to all his memories, so he didn't bother explaining who he was talking about.

"Well, the fact of the matter is, Pike, neither world may survive. Everything is governed, from what we can tell, on how much each reality, each universe contributes to the whole. You've mentioned the network, or the multiverse, as being the source of your creativity. We are all the source of the creativity in the Universe. If you don't contribute, if you did not leave your world a better place, if you do not invent, develop, build, or advance your species, then you're not playing the game. You're not rendering your due unto Caesar. We're all part of this collective. And when you stop moving forward, there is no need for your game to continue as far as the multiverse is concerned. So, yes, The Fade begins when you start taking more than you're contributing. The multiverse is life, which means every world, every sentient species, must exist to support it, otherwise you are poison. You've got to be beneficial, or you will be eliminated."

"Again, Subada, what can we do? What can I do? It seems the end is inevitable."

"I would agree. But apparently, Nianda feels differently. This acceleration of The Fade here, like on our mirror world, may be due to outside interference."

"Interference, meaning someone is working against us?" Pike immediately thought of Carapaz. The man had seemed genuine, but could he be trusted? It was obvious that his wild theory of a horde of invading aliens was delusional.

"Perhaps...it would be unlikely that a single individual could manage such a feat. He would have to hold great influence over a great many key figures and manipulate events in very precise ways."

Pike's mind focused on that until a question emerged. "Subada, how many other species can travel like we do?"

The creature shrugged. "Who knows? The multiverse is very nearly infinite, but I think I know what you are asking. Who, that we are aware of, could do it if it's not someone on your Earth? Only a handful of species can slip time streams naturally, and nearly all of those are very benevolent. If I am being honest, my species is one of the few I would say can and might have hostile intent. I know of no others that have managed to use technology to enable this. Only you humans."

That made little sense to Pike. Who would benefit from speeding up The Fade? It would be a zero-sum win with a very high price tag. "What's my next step?"

"You need to escape from your imprisonment, Pike Shepard."

46

Agent Clarence Winthrop looked through the window with an amused expression. Pike Shepard was again sitting in the single chair, monitors attached to his head, chest, genitals, and even his feet. An IV line was connected to an infusion station with various chemical compounds ready to be administered as needed. The man had been a rock up until this part, but now he was going to talk. Winthrop was under clear orders from his bosses to get the answers, no matter the cost.

"We're ready when you are, sir," the technician beside him said, looking to him for permission. Agent Winthrop rubbed his temples, still fighting off a headache and the effects of jet lag. They had sent the other interrogator packing; the scientist was all his responsibility now. He scrolled the list of protocols and selected the one he always liked to start with. "Watch his heart rate," he said, almost as an afterthought.

Pike Shepard watched through half-lidded eyes as the men worked. Commander Subada was now back firmly in his subconscious brain. The alien warrior had worked on this plan for days and now was ready to execute.

"Be ready, Shep. I'll have your body reacting the way they expect up until a point."

"You are sure this is the only way?" Pike had to confess he was nervous.

"It will work. The agent's mind is weak. He offered no resistance to giving up the information I needed."

The information Agent Winthrop had unwittingly offered was incomplete, but enough. Someone had indeed sent them to a black site in New Guinea for enhanced interrogation. Winthrop himself reported to a military liaison, but Subada assumed he was working for the CIA. He'd also offered a good memory of the facility, guard rotation, and security mandates. The others being held were considered expendable. Pike Shepard apparently was not; they were not to let him die, but everything else was acceptable as long as they got the information.

"How do you SideSlip into others, Subada? That has to be handy in a case like this."

"It would do you no good, Pike. Just relax. You won't be able to do it with your own kind, anyway."

That's probably best, Pike thought as his one overriding mandate was that everybody lies. He wasn't sure he wanted to know what was going on in the heads of most people.

"Wake him up!" Winthrop ordered coldly.

Pike felt the cold liquid entering his veins, a stimulant of some kind, he guessed. The effect was nullified by Subada's near perfect control of Pike's nervous system.

"Go home, Pike," he heard the internal voice urging. "Let me handle this."

Slowly, the black water filled his mind. The sound of paddle bumping against boat hull and the smell of salt air, earth, and decay. His captors faded, and the past raced in to fill the void.

* * *

The world was not Pike's home, nor was it New Earth, although that was where he'd wanted to escape. No, he had opened his eyes to his first unaided SideSlip in the ruins of a once great empire. The last time he'd been here, it had already begun its rocky slide toward oblivion. The Fade was already firmly rooted in the topsoil of Gaius. He ambled down the once manicured lane, looking at the fallen spires of the city ahead. He knew this was preferable to whatever was going on back in that lab, but here, too, he was filled with a terrible sadness. Carapaz hadn't been lying about this world.

The streets that had been filled with vendors and shops just the month before, now they stood empty and dark. No wonderful smells of enticing food drifted from the restaurants' open doors. Probing his host's mind, Pike knew this had happened quickly. His other, Alren, shuffled through the littered street aimlessly, depressed, and acting as if he were awaiting an executioner's blade. Coming here was not the escape from reality he'd needed. Pike was about to slip out and transit to a different dimension when he saw the other Guayan, Selenas. She was obviously injured. He and his host both felt the pain of seeing a loved one suffer. Selenas was his mate, his Kate. *Now, if I could only find my actual Kate.* They had discovered from Winthrop that she was not with the prisoners.

The two moved to a communal bench that was still mostly intact. He reached out and stoked the other making soothing sounds. Even if Kate were in this Guayan, they had no way of communication. The back-channel comms they used only worked between launch chairs in the lab. He briefly tried exerting conscious control over his host, and unlike the prior time, today he found he could...it took several minutes to manipulate Alren's mouth and sound box to speak. The first time he tried to say Kate, it only sounded like wind moving through trees. Selenas was puzzled by what her boyfriend was attempting and watched him closely. She had, no doubt, seen many others acting strangely before they did something horrible to themselves or others.

After numerous attempts, Pike finally managed to shape the mouth in a way that produced a reasonable version of the word 'Kaate', and he was reasonably sure if she was in there, she would recognize it. The female just continued to look at him strangely. If she had a passenger inside her mind, she was mute. Pike turned away and looked out to a valley that was now a ruin of mud and water. He was aware a water dam had been destroyed by one of the terrorizing groups unleashing a torrent of water over a large residential area. Thousands of bodies lay buried beneath the mud. *Is this what's in store for Earth?*

Pike felt a sharp pain and knew that was feedback from some horror befalling his actual body. Subada had explained that he could block most of the pain receptors but possibly not all. It was impossibly strange to think of someone else living in his body while he was away. Like an AirBNB, he had just rented the space out for the weekend. From their time together, he was immensely impressed with Subada. He was incredibly capable; Pike was aware of the man's capacity to inflict harm, but he already felt that the man, or alien warrior, was a friend. One who was doing what he could to help, even though it might not be enough.

Pike had retreated into the background while the two Guayans talked. They were wandering through what had been an orchard of some type. Most of the pale, pink fruit lay rotting or smashed. Pike remembered having slices of this fruit in the meal he and Kate had shared. The female Guayan picked up one that was mostly intact, carefully peeled it, and using something like a dew claw on her hand, carved off a thin slice. She held it up to Alren's mouth, then shaking her head and pulling it back, made a show for him to close his eyes first. The Guayan male complied, and she dropped the slice into his mouth. It was tender and sweet, and, in the midst of all this destruction, it was eerily out of place. "Kaate?"

The female tilted her head again, then gave what could have been a nod.

Was it now her? He knew he wanted it to be but had no idea how it could. Pike's host struggled to say more words. "It izz you?"

The female went back to eating the fruit, ignoring the crazy sounds her friends was making. Pike tried speaking more, but the physical limits of sound were hard to master with the Guayans. They were still talking quietly to each other, but both were intensely watching what he was doing.

He'd been writing his symbols in the dirt with a stick but had a better idea and went back to the ruins of the restaurant. Seeking out the same table they had dined at before, he took the local equivalent of a marker from a hostess table and began to scrawl.

47

Subada's abilities to infiltrate and influence the minds of others were impressive but limited to one individual at a time. He briefly considered showing Pike the knowledge necessary to do the same. Despite what he had said, the man's unique brain was likely capable of the task, but he preferred to do this alone. It was going to be messy. Pike's body was strapped to a metal chair that was itself bolted to the floor. It had taken a brief SideSlip and gentle nudge to leave one arm just loose enough to be slipped out of the restraining harness.

Pike's respiration, brainwave activity, and heart rate would all keep registering as a semi-somnolent state. This was what the agent outside needed in order to see what he expected.

"Mister Shepard, you will now answer my questions truthfully and fully. Is that understood?"

Agent Winthrop's voice was monotone and controlled. No sense of his underlying urgency came through, although Subada had already seen into this man's particularly troubled mind. Winthrop probably deserved to be the one imprisoned far more than any criminal he'd ever questioned. Rampant paranoia fueled by an amphetamine addiction he fed only when he couldn't stand to hear the demons any longer. In Winthrop's case, the addiction was beneficial, as it kept a much darker animal at bay.

"Shepard, where is your evidence about the dimension you describe as New Earth?"

Pike, via Subada, said nothing.

"Are you sure he's awake?" the agent asked the young med tech, the agent's hand lightly covering the microphone.

Subada muttered a slurred and incomprehensible response. The question was repeated with a slight increase in tone. Pike Shepard offered nothing more.

"It's not working," Winthrop said harshly after almost thirty minutes of the barely responsive questioning.

"It's nearly double the standard cocktail," the lab tech responded, which Winthrop knew consisted of stimulants, neural blockers, and a synthetic form of scopolamine. The key to all of the cooperation drugs was to keep the signals from reaching the spinal cord, and he had to have the subject just barely awake.

Winthrop opened his briefcase and withdrew a vial. He handed the unmarked bottle to the technician, who eyed it suspiciously. "50ccs in his IV port now. Then another 25ccs in fifteen minutes."

"What is it?" the young man said.

"Don't worry about it, it won't kill him." What he didn't say was the dangerous mixture would cause excruciating pain as it attacked every nerve ending and pain receptor in Shepard's body at once.

Subada had expected this, as he knew it was what the unfortunate government man had wanted to do from the very beginning. The latent psychopath side of him loved seeing people in pain. Through Pike's half-closed lids, he watched as the assistant unwrapped a clean syringe and withdrew a half inch of clear fluid into the plastic barrel. Subada briefly left Pike's mind and entered into the young assistant who continued to pull on the plunger, drawing more of the fluid up until it was twice what the lead agent had ordered.

The lab tech held the needle up and depressed the syringe slightly to clear any air. Subada picked the moment carefully, causing the med tech to suddenly plunge it viciously into Winthrop's exposed neck.

Subada quickly returned to Shepard's mind and watched through the window as an enraged Agent Winthrop backhanded the young man so hard it sent him careening across the room. The man hit the wall with a loud thud, then slumped down hard, unconscious. Or worse.

Briefly, Winthrop glared into the interrogation room, then down at the IV controls still feeding chemicals into Pike's bloodstream. "You!" he bellowed, fully aware of what was coming. He slapped down at the computer controls before grabbing at his throat. The drug had no actual physical effects but used the body's own nervous system to bring excruciating pain.

Subada saw the display screen of the IV station blink red several times. He wasn't sure what had been triggered but began to fight to remove Pike's arm from the wide leather cuff. There was only so much he could do in countering the chemical agents, and he feared Winthrop had triggered a lethal dose of something. He had seconds before the new drug mix made its way through the clear plastic tubing and into his new friend's arm.

Agent Winthrop was no longer concerned with Pike Shepard, nor the fact that his prisoner was now clearly wide-awake and working feverishly to free himself from the restraints. Winthrop's arms and legs burned with a fire, so intense he knew they must be blistering up from some invisible flame. His ears felt like icepicks were being driven into them over and over, again and again. He could begin to feel something moving up under his fingernails on one hand. Something that was pushing its way up, forcing the nail from its bed in slow, agonizing deliberateness. Then his heart began to seize in his chest, seize and release like a hand of a giant ghost reaching into him and holding his life in his hand. "Please, God, just end it," the man cried out in agony. Winthrop had helped in the covert development of this drug, though, and knew what he was feeling was simply stage one. Now, a feeling of thousands of wasps stinging him over every inch of his body took over. His muddled mind struggled to remember how many stages the drug delivered. *Nine,* he thought. *Or was it ten?* It didn't matter...he fumbled for his service weapon, only to realize he couldn't make his hand grab it. The same with an ink pen nearby. He needed the pain to end.

Subada looked up briefly from the loosening cuff to see the other man banging his head into the concrete wall of the control room. The wall already had a bloody smear, forming a gruesome target. Pike's arm finally moved a half inch, then a little more. He twisted the hand and pulled with everything he had, the leather cuff digging into his forearm and soon offering its own bloody trail to the scene. Subada flashed one of Pike's memories. The cuff was almost the same as Pike had been strapped down with as a child during some of his episodes. Luckily, this memory wouldn't join the tormented list of others in the man's mind. It was a solid restraint. Subada knew in his own, natural form he could have simply ripped it apart. Humans were physically not as durable, though.

Subada felt the sting of the drug reaching Pike's body. At the same time, he saw the senior agent's eyes go blank as his screaming stopped. Winthrop fell hard onto the desk, freed at last from the pain of life. Pike's left arm popped out and immediately reached across and jerked the needle from his other arm. Subada wasn't sure how large of a dose Pike had received but knew there was little he could do about it now. He had been considering that if this was how one of the more stable governments of Earth treated its citizens, how would they treat an enemy? Maybe facing The Fade was the best route for them.

In minutes, Pike, back in charge of his own body, was out of the interrogation room and moving down the corridor. Subada had passed along the information necessary to free the others being held. Pike had seen the bloody remnants of the federal agent when he'd passed that room. He assumed that was where the information had come from. Subada was busy elsewhere, apparently doing more to facilitate the mad rush toward freedom.

Pike turned a corner and saw two armed men in uniform. They both instantly transformed from relaxed to full alert. "I'm going to need some help, friend," Pike said aloud. Though still fighting off the effects of the drugs, Pike knew reversing course was a waste of time. He started charging both men and reached them before sidearms cleared holsters. Without slowing, he launched himself sideways at both of the guards. His knee sunk deeply into one man's chest while his elbow throat-punched the other. Both went down hard.

Pike Shepard hadn't been in a fight since leaving the military, other than the brief recent scuffle at the airport, but he was prepared to give it everything in the next thirty seconds. Throat-punch dude was down, his windpipe was damaged, and he was choking and turning red. The one on the right, though, had more fight in him. He launched up with a withering blow of his own, hitting Pike in the abdomen and driving him up and off the floor. He saw stars and felt his insides beginning to let go. The man's fist hit again and again, and each one felt like hammer blow. Pike kicked out and caught the man's knee, which caused the man to miss on the next assault.

Pike used the opportunity to back up to the wall and try to figure out how to keep the man from drawing his weapon. His opponent had also regrouped and grinned savagely as he began to retreat and go for the pistol. The door at the end of the corridor opened, and Pike saw several other uniformed people coming through. He raced forward, totally unsure of what to do, then he was doing nothing. Subada had slipped back into control and turned Pike Shepard's body into an instrument of mayhem. He was all corners and sharp objects as he leveled the first opponent in seconds.

He darted at the others, then half-way up a wall before pivoting downward with a thrust into the back of a neck followed by a vicious kick to the face of a woman turning to point a taser at him. Pike felt two more foes behind him, but now he was the one controlling the battle space. Him, with the aid of a warrior from another dimension, that is.

Subada obviously preferred close quarters action, as he never let his quarry back away. He took the fight to them in a relentless and precise onslaught. Pike could feel the occasional blow landed by the guards, but the sensation was dulled and more an annoyance than pain. The guard farthest away removed a tactical baton and extended it fully with a flick of the wrist. Pike swore he heard Subada laugh as the object was suddenly gone from the opponent's hand, which now hung limply from a broken wrist, and was instead in Pike's.

Subada smashed another men's skulls and moved out of the way of blood spray and falling bodies. Pike marveled at the speed and grace his friend possessed, and then he was once again alone in his own body. Pike quickly disarmed and cuffed the two captors who were still breathing. He didn't think they would be a danger as neither was conscious, but he took no chances. Looking at the carnage, he knew the rules of engagement for the agents would have changed. Now he was a killer, and they would be free to end him. He raced through the door and made his way to the holding cells.

One by one, Pike opened steel doors, revealing figures in white jumpsuits identical to his. Some were asleep, others were huddled in corners, obviously expecting more abuse from their captors. All of his friends seemed relieved to see him. He exited the prison wing with a group of seventeen others from the lab. All looked in worse shape than himself. He was beginning to feel a slowly spreading paralysis on one side. He briefly wondered if he was experiencing a stroke but had to ignore it for now.

"Letner, he...um, he's gone," Sandy Almira said through a hail of tears. "I saw them dragging his body away when I was being led to questioning."

Pike put his arm around her and pulled her close. "It's okay, Sandy, we're getting out of here." He was acutely aware that at least one other team member was missing as well but decided not to mention that.

"Pike, wait by the interior door until you hear a knock, then move straight for thirty yards and get in one of the two vans," Subada said, briefly reentering his mind. The alien had also shown him the scene outside. Pike wasn't sure what he expected, a military base, maybe a hospital or research lab, but this wasn't it. The hall they were in, like the holding cells and interrogation rooms, were all starkly modern and free of anything that might identify the occupants. Outside, the building looked completely different and ordinary. They were in a ramshackle warehouse with rusted tin siding, peeling up in numerous places. Pallets of some plant material were stacked and drying, and ancient forklifts sat idle on one side. Several people, locals by the look, were loading a delivery truck. There were no guards, no fences, no cameras, or alarms that he could see in what he was shown.

The assembled group crowded along the end of the corridor. Many were moaning, more were sobbing openly. Once again, he wondered where Kate was and if Palio managed to stay free. Time passed with a slowness that was beyond belief, but finally, they heard a rustling noise outside followed by three sharp knocks on the steel door. The small panel beside the door, which had been glowing red, suddenly switched to white, and Pike pushed the door open. A wave of humid, hot air hit them as they quickly spilled out of the antiseptic corridor into the fetid warehouse, all of them thankful for the change. Pike nodded to the man who was standing by the door. It was obviously Subada.

Pike had instructed them to move as quickly and quietly as possible toward the large open doors of the building, but he felt sure most of them couldn't comprehend what he was telling them. "Petra, you lead half of them and follow this man to a van that will be just outside," he whispered to the young girl, who seemed in better shape than the rest. "I'll take the others."

"Sandy, Petra, anyone," Pike yelled, "did anyone see Doctor Cassidy?"

Most were silent. *A few are borderline shock cases,* Pike thought. "No one? What about Palio?" Again silence. A few shook their heads. Haunted, hopeless eyes stared at him, awaiting answers, awaiting punishment. *They've all given up*, he thought.

But they hadn't, not all of them. Director Lu and Petra eyed him defiantly. "Let's get out of here, Professor," Lu said with a sharp edge vehemence.

The American man spoke, "She will need to drive."

Pike nodded; he knew Subada had other tasks to handle to pull off this ridiculous plan.

"You good with that?" Pike asked Petra, who smiled and nodded enthusiastically. In under a minute, they were loaded into two transport vans and moving down the rutted muddy road. As they left the remnants of the small village, the jungle canopy began to crowd the road. Pike ignored the tingling partial paralysis and concentrated on following the path his friend had left in his mind.

An hour later, they were all seated on an ancient transport plane nestled on a grassy runway. The good-natured Australian couldn't say what had motivated him to dump his cargo and touch down here, but he was amazingly willing to give them a ride to Sydney. For the first time all day, Pike closed his eyes and let the exhaustion take him. Once again, Subada was taking care of the situation, this time through the innocent hands of an aviator named Captain Joticay.

48

The group of survivors all huddled in an abandoned corner of a freight warehouse located on the south end of Cairns Airport in Queensland. The flight had been rough but mercifully brief by international standards. As the plane had landed, the sudden realization that they were all undocumented and also dressed like escaped inmates occurred to a few. Pike was too exhausted to give this much thought, but others apparently had. Director Lu seemed to have a plan, and she was anxious to make a few phone calls.

Pike assumed Subada was still possessing Joticay, the pilot. He hated thinking of it in such evil ways, but possessing was the correct term. Subada was not riding along in the background. He was exerting his will over a potentially non-compliant host. Pike now knew in vivid detail that when needed, he could also do so with incredibly violent results. He had to also acknowledge that he had been a weapon in Subada's arsenal against his captors. That one was not so unwilling, though. He eyed the blood ringing the nails of each hand, not his blood. They had been the bullies; they had brought the fight; he had simply ended it.

"We need to move, Pike," Subada said inside his head.

Pike was in no shape. He hadn't been able to sleep on the plane and now the adrenaline, the torture, the fight, and the mix of interrogation drugs had taken their toll. “I can’t, Subada,” he said sub-vocally. “My body needs rest, I’m not like you.”

“I can fix that,” Subada said before going silent for several seconds. Slowly, Pike felt a jolt, like a cup of triple-espresso hitting his system. His eyes stopped burning, the need for sleep faded, and the aching pain in his muscles calmed.

“Damn. Nice trick, friend,” Pike said. “Can you show me how to do that?”

“You’ll know when you need to.”

Pike felt himself walking into a washroom, spinning a combination on a locker and removing clothes and shoes.

“These should fit you,” Subada said confidently.

Quickly, Pike stripped out of the jumpsuit and began dressing. “What about the others?”

“Leave them to Lu, she has it well in hand. She’s been in touch with the British Embassy, and they are not too happy about what transpired on their base. They are sending a transport, but you need to go elsewhere.”

Pike tucked the bloody prison suit in a trash bin and went to tell the others goodbye. “Where are you going?” one of the young men asked.

“I don’t know, but I have to find Kate,” he said. “Listen, when you tell them what happened, I’d prefer you not mention me, at least for as long as you can. I’d rather have as little attention as possible.”

“Have you seen what’s going on out there?” one of the Cobalt lab techs asked, pointing up to a TV playing loudly in a nearby break room. “No one is going to be that interested in you right now.”

Pike glanced up, dumbfounded to see drone footage of an aircraft carrier belching black smoke and listing heavily to one side. He wondered whose it was, then decided it didn’t matter. He turned to look at the group of people again. “Someone was interested in us, in particular, about our work on that island. This is The Fade, ladies and gentlemen. Do anything you can to slow it down and nothing that might speed it up. I haven’t got a clue how to tell you any better than that. One thing we do know is, some governments apparently are intent on stopping us."

Each of them shook his hand or embraced him like a conquering hero before he left. Pike didn't deserve their thanks but didn't have the time to explain. Sandy Almira kissed him tenderly on the forehead and whispered to him, "Go get your girl."

Then he was gone, moving around buildings with knowledge he knew he didn't possess. "Where are we going?"

"You are familiar with a man named Carapaz?" Subada asked, knowing full well the answer.

"Yes," Pike said, uncertain if this was a smart move. "What about Kate?"

Subada sighed audibly. "I'm sorry, friend, she will have to wait."

Pike hopped into a jeep behind a uniformed man. He recognized that the patches on the sleeve belonged to the Australian Defence Force. The driver didn't speak as he turned out onto the A1. Pike stared out blankly as the road hugged the coast for over an hour until they pulled into a gravel lot. The driver handed him a duffel.

"You'll need to change, sir."

Pike was beginning to get used to this, which unnerved him even more. As he zipped up the green jumpsuit, he wondered if he had just exchanged one prison color for another. Then he noticed the RAAF insignia on the shoulder. "What are you up to, Subada?" he mentally whispered.

The Jeep went straight to the flight line, and Lieutenant Bill 'Buffalo' Jennings waved for him to take his place in the F-35A Lightning combat jet. Now wearing a helmet and flight suit nearly identical to the lieutenant, Pike nodded and took his place in the cramped cockpit. He stared in disbelief at the array of instruments and controls. Subada was probably in the mind of the other pilot, or hell, who knew? Maybe Subada could fly. It seemed he could do everything else.

"I don't know how to fly," Pike said barely above a whisper. A mechanic was leaning over the opposite side, just under the open canopy. He plugged a cable into a console, and Pike could hear him and the control tower. He was freezing up in terror and also thrilled beyond words to have the chance to fly a jet like this.

"You ready?" Subada said, mentally settling back down on the conscious side of Pike's mind.

"Hell, yeah, but I want to ride up front for part of this. I mean, it is my body—I should get to drive. I assume you know how to handle this thing."

"Yeah," Subada said glibly. "Mostly."

As he heard the tower clearing them for take-off, Pike was alternately in control as he pushed the throttle lever forward and felt the power push him back deeply into the seat. Subada gratefully took over as his vision narrowed. Minutes later, as they climbed above 15,000 feet, the alien inhabitant gave a brief shout. "Now that's fun!"

Despite the epic, shit rollercoaster the last few days had been, Pike did not disagree.

49

Pike had no idea how his friend could have gotten flight clearance for the trip or cleared all the steps for a total stranger to steal a fighter jet worth millions. He assumed if the right people up the chain of command gave an order, it was all that was needed. Still, he was in a combat aircraft and sovereign countries might not take kindly to overflights, even from a country like Australia. Pike had been flying for the past hour and loved how responsive the aircraft was. He knew next to nothing about flying a plane, but this one seemed eager to please.

Subada had been darting in and out of his head, mostly leaving the piloting up to Pike, but he had inserted enough basic knowledge to ensure he did nothing suicidal. "Where are we going? Did you find Carapaz?" Pike asked internally.

"I did, yes. He is off world right now, as is your Kate."

"Are they together? How is she doing it? The lab was locked down," Pike asked, the questions rushing at him like floodwaters.

"I don't know that, sorry. I am unable to detect activity in other dimensions while I am deployed on this world," Subada said. Also, if you or I SideSlip, as you call it, to see what is going on, your body will probably die in a horrible fiery crash. If that happens, you will be just as dead in the other dimension as you are here."

"Hmmm, good point," Pike said. "How many worlds are like ours?" They apparently had some time to kill, *although we're going to get there a lot quicker in this thing*, Pike thought.

"You've seen enough worlds to know they are mostly all different. What you are really asking is about the 'people,' for lack of a better term. How are the inhabitants different? Is that correct?"

Pike thought about it for a few seconds before agreeing. That really was what it boiled down to, wasn't it? "Yes."

"They are much less easy to categorize than you might imagine. Much like humans, I might add. Could you define your species by the thoughts, beliefs, or actions of an individual?"

"No," Pike answered truthfully.

"What about a dozen, a thousand, or a million?" Subada asked. "Other cultures are very much the same. The more the level of sentience, the wider the range of ideas and beliefs. I would say your species is about average for a world as developed as yours. You have a sufficient level of advancement but still are clinging to some very ancient biases and fear. Eventually, if you survive as a people, you will realize these perceptions and tribal tendencies are holding you back."

"The aggression toward one another?" Pike suggested questioningly.

"No," Subada said ruefully. "Aggression is actually a good thing, as it can breed competition. The more aggressive societies normally are the ones who excel. It does have to be channeled, though. Much like yourself, Pike. You struggled terribly as a child. That undoubtedly made you more successful as an adult."

"We're shaped by our past," Pike said.

"Some of you are, it completely dominates others. Not just their past either, but their parents' and ancestors'. They spend so much time looking back, they are unable to move forward."

"Subada, will we survive The Fade?" There it was. That was the real question, wasn't it? "Can we?" The voice in his head stayed quiet for many minutes, then Pike saw a visual space, not with his eyes, but like a memory. He closed his eyes to the white clouds whipping by, and the room became more distinct, the shapes and feeling more defined.

It was a representation of a room on Nianda's rim world version of Earth. Subada stood opposite him near a balcony overlooking a narrow fertile plain below.

"This is a construct, a virtual meeting place for us to talk," Subada said. "I know speaking and hearing voices inside your own head can be an unsatisfactory way of communicating. My people, too, are visual creatures. It took me a while to realize your brain is unlike other humans I have slipped into. Yours is capable of vibrant visualization like this."

Pike noticed Subada looked more human in this environment. Human and vaguely familiar. "This is amazing, friend, but you're avoiding my question."

Subada nodded and turned back toward the valley. "I am, yes." He walked over and sat on the low, rock ledge lining the balcony. "I am also still flying the jet, so understand I am not totally here."

Pike thought he understood. "You went to Nianda when your world faced the end."

Subada sighed and nodded. "Yes, we were familiar with his people and their superior wisdom. I was not the first. In fact, many had sought advice from them. The answer was always the same, our world would end. Only one of those timelines could continue."

Frustration gripped Pike. This was not an answer he could accept.

Subada, who was still embedded in his subconscious, picked up on it immediately. "My people didn't agree either," the man said. "We discussed two possible solutions earlier. One was to make the two timelines more similar in hope they might gently reunify. The other was to make them more different and yours more unique and hopefully more valuable to the whole."

Pike nodded in understanding. He sensed a great reluctance in Subada to go forward.

"I am Shintu. We were warriors. I won't get into our own history, but you know the military mindset, it is much the same on any world. In our case, though, the mindset is encoded into our very being. Every one of my people serves in the military. Our school systems are branches of our military. Do you understand what that led to?"

Pike knew. "It meant your leaders looked for a military solution just like people of Earth likely will."

"Yes, it was the default belief on my home world," Subada said. "I mentioned the two options, get close to the original timeline or get further away. There is a third option."

Pike waited patiently for him to go on, fearing what the third option was.

"You can destroy the other timeline." Subada said the final words so softly Pike wasn't sure he'd heard them correctly.

"Destroy?" Pike said in disbelief. "Declare war on an entire planet, a planet of your own people?" He railed on the idea for several minutes, thinking of all the absurdities it would include. Then he considered New Earth, how advanced, how peaceful, and how much more successful it seemed to be. He now understood the military's interest in Kate's program and knew with certainty his people would do it. "Your two worlds fought to the death, didn't they?"

The alien man who Pike now thought of as Subada turned and faced him, his large, dark eyes glistened with wetness. "We did."

Pike learned it was Subada's side that launched the first sorties by inhabiting key members' minds in the other world. They initiated a catastrophic set of events on the Beta version of Kava. Within a year, the mirror dimension had detected them and began their own counteroffensive. Both sides were equally ruthless and very nearly identically matched. The end was a near certainty. The Fade still occurred to Kava, but both worlds, both timelines, were essentially ended.

"As you saw, my world is an empty husk, a burned cinder now. We have a small survivor colony on the moon. That is where I live most of my days."

"Is there no other way?" Pike asked, already resigning himself to the inevitable.

"No," Subada said. "I am sure you have figured out by now...your war has already started."

50

Several thousand miles away, Kate Cassidy's body lay in a very spartan-looking room. Her eyes stared blankly at a ceiling of acoustic tile. Much of her head and body were resting in a hard shell composed of padding, integrated with separate levels of electronic circuitry and a fine mesh of black fibers that glistened like the skin of a snake. A man watched her from a small desk a dozen feet away. He had a hawkish look with a clump of black and gray hair sprouting above a face that no one would have ever referred to as handsome. Still, this man had been on magazine covers and red carpets with many of Italy's most beautiful women over the years. Even now, his current wife, the former supermodel Lidona, was lounging outside by the palatial pool.

"Any, ah, signs of, uh, Signor Shepard?" the man asked softly.

"No," Kate said nervously. "He has been here, though."

"Ah, bene, bene," the man said. "So, the Americans are making him go off world. They must be searching as well for this mysterious dimension he found."

Kate's voice was slow to respond, distant and slurred, as was often the case when off world travelers tried to converse back in their own dimension. "Signor Albergoni, as I have told you, we have no way of knowing how he found *the* other Earth. He simply indicated he found one."

"And a how dida he do this? Do you have any idea? Are you sure it was not a programmed SideSlip?"

Kate raised a finger. "Hang on, Val, I have something." She had her host bend over, so she could see what had the others' attention. It was a papery tablecloth in the restaurant where she and Pike had dined on their last night here. The ruined eatery looked nothing like it did then, but nothing on Gaius did. The sheet was covered with strange black markings. The crayon-like marker was laying nearby. Clearly, Pike had found a way to leave a message, one only she would find. How did he make the Guayan write it, though? How could he take that level of consciousness in these beings? She was having a hard enough time getting Selenas to just stare at the paper long enough to translate it all.

"I need a pad," Kate called out.

The rotund Italian was unused to being ordered about but hurriedly fetched her a writing pad and pen. He watched as she continued to stare straight up while she blindly made line after line of strange symbols on the yellow paper. She scrawled on the page until it was filled and flipped the page and repositioned her hand so she could continue. He had no idea what was there, but there was a lot. Nearly fifteen minutes passed before Kate dropped the pen and signaled her return.

Valerius Albergoni was the sixteenth richest man in the world. His family had been in shipping for three generations before he came along. From there he'd diversified the family holdings, branching out into everything from biotechnology and alternative fuel production to fashion and entertainment. His record label was the second largest in Europe. Still, his fame and his fortune had done nothing to either insure or prevent him from being here today in the company of Doctor Kate Cassidy. It had been his money that had funded The Project for years right up to the point the U.S. government found a way to freeze the foundation's assets at a critical time. They had opened the door a crack, and the black-suited officials had stormed in like field mice escaping the cold.

Kate was rubbing her eyes and staring at the paper. Val leaned in to a speaker and said, "Espressos and merenda." She looked up slowly and nodded her thanks. "Americano, please, grazie."

"Of course, a, of course, I forget." He updated the order with his kitchen. "Now, my dear Kate, what have you found?"

What she had found was Pike's coded shorthand, something she was clearly not expecting. While she knew the basics, this would take her all day to transcribe. "You still have the files from the Cobalt lab?" she asked.

"Of course, everything was uploaded to the cloud daily," Val said.

He handed her a thin MacBook, and she was delighted to see it was a cloned OS of hers back on Diego Garcia. She'd had to leave like a thief in the night. She despised losing her team and especially Pike but knew she would have never seen daylight again if they had gotten her on that plane.

She opened up Pike's tutorial and used the computer's camera to snap pictures of the legal pad's contents. She segmented each line into files, converted them to grayscale so the system could more easily render them as symbols, and then let the computer begin the process of decoding. A steward was wheeling in a cart of the afternoon snacks, what they called merenda. Unlike the British version of high tea, this one always reminded her more of breakfast. Kate had spent several hours on Gaius looking for signs of Pike and another two hours on Luria and Delvos prior to that. She was starving and grateful for the delicious food. She sipped the coffee and ate the breads and cheeses, as well as a marvelous yogurt and fruit mixture.

"So, your Signor Pike is alive at least," her patron said as he downed most of one of the small espressos in a single gulp. "How did you know he would SideSlip to a familiar world?"

In truth, she hadn't, but it was one of the few places she could at least check. Thankfully, Val had one of the next-gen launch pod prototypes here at his magnificent home. One of his companies did the fabrication, so acquiring it was not difficult, but she appreciated it just the same.

Kate shrugged as she wrapped a date with a thin slice of imported iberico ham and savored the bite before answering. "Just a hunch." She stopped chewing as she recalled the rest. "He said his body was being tortured, and he had escaped off world to avoid the pain."

The look on the man's face was ghastly. "Ima so sorry, Kate. But how is this possible?"

She didn't know. GTR, the U.S. agency heading up their own Side-Slip had protocols that were essentially the same as hers at Cobalt: keep the traveler as comfortable as possible. They needed to stay in a semi-hypnotic state to maintain the quantum connection. She hoped the rest of the notes would be more enlightening. As she finished up the light meal with a second cup of coffee and a handful of grapes, a chime sounded from her laptop.

She walked over, almost reluctant to read the transcription. As she did so, her pulse quickened, and with every line her sense of dread and alarm grew. "He was somewhere tropical. They flew for about eight hours and were refueled once mid-air. It is the Americans...they dropped the charade once they landed."

"I knew it was those bastardi's," Val said. "Does he say what they want from him?"

"Yeah," she said, finishing the page. "They want to know everything about the other Earth, New Earth he calls it." Pike had left one additional piece of information as well, an almost oval-shaped heart with a swoop beneath. That one she had known by sight, his coded symbol for 'I love you.' Tears filled her eyes; she could no longer hold them back. She felt her friend's hand touch her shoulder lightly. This man had been more than a friend to her over the years. He was very much a father-figure to her now.

"We will find your hero, Kate Cassidy. We will find him no matter what."

51

The flight was in its final hour. Pike could see that much from the fuel readout, but they were flying over open ocean as they had been for hours at more than Mach 1.6. Subada had been comparing his people to humans. Pike learned they called themselves Shintu, or that was the closest the human language could reach. They were an ancient race, extending hundreds of generations further back than humans. On their version of Earth, a world with the same name as the capital city called Kava, dinosaurs had never arisen. Instead, a variety of mighty sea creatures, some of which were amphibious, had been the major threats.

"They were devious and intelligent creatures. Our Shintu alternated between worshiping them and fighting them with both species getting smarter every year. Several times in my people's past we very nearly went extinct."

Pike understood more of where Subada's warlike nature came from. "I can only imagine if humans and dinosaurs existed together. That would be remarkable and frightening." How differently humans might have evolved.

"There are a number of worlds where that happened. I can give you the coordinates if you want to visit," Subada said. "I think your own path was a preferred path. The other worlds still exist in a mostly feudal or tribal state. Your evolution allowed your brains to thrive and your complex social structure time to mature."

"You seem to know much of our world and humans," Pike said, more as a question. He felt Subada mentally stiffen. "You've spent time on this planet before, haven't you?"

His internal voice made a noise that Pike had learned was Subada's equivalent of a sigh. "Yes, but that was many years ago. I was still in training at the time, but I found your world bright and full of energy. I longed to return one day. Your Earth has an unusual mix of aggression and entertainment, or fun. Few species manage this balance."

"Did you have a single host back then or many?"

Subada again took his time before responding. "I had one host...he would be what you would call my 'other.' I was not mature enough to alter my quantum connection then."

Pike had many more questions, but the radio crackled in his helmet. Pike did not understand the language, so he let Subada handle the responses. Pike felt his hands pushing the yoke forward and decreasing power. The numbers on the altimeter which was displayed on his visor began to decrease. Ahead, he saw the blue waters changing to a brilliant turquoise shade and beyond that, dark green jungle with low hills in the distance.

Several nerve-wracking minutes later, they were down on a runway, one seemingly more composed of sand and weeds than concrete. A faded sign said, 'Antigua Air Station.' Pike had already concluded they were in the Caribbean but was shocked to find himself on another island.

"It's not our destination," Subada said. "Simply a stop. We will require other transportation."

Pike expertly guided the F-35 underneath an abandoned military hangar. Both ends were open to the elements, and the corrugated tin was peeled up in numerous places by frequent tropical storms. He went through the shutdown procedure and climbed out, latching the cockpit behind him. He knew the Aussies would have tracked their bird, and someone would be coming to fetch it.

"Lose the flight suit," Subada suggested as Pike turned toward the ocean, which glistened like a jewel.

Subada had left him several times in the last few hours. Pike assumed so that he could make arrangements for after they landed. Sure enough, as he neared the beach, Pike could see a decent sized boat approaching from the north.

"A boat ride to another island, an even smaller island," Subada stated with a bit of uncertainty.

"He's there? Carapaz?"

"Oh, yes, he is."

Pike waded out into the warm waters, feeling refreshed. Again, he felt Subada tense. "What's wrong, tough guy? Afraid of a little water?"

"It is not a little water. It is open ocean, and my people have a natural aversion to large open bodies of water much like humans naturally fear snakes or falling."

Pike thought on that. He supposed it made sense. "So, your host on Earth before never swam?"

Subada swore, at least Pike felt sure it was a swear word. Then he laughed. "No, the little bastard swam all the time. He loved the water, and none of my coercion techniques could make him stop."

Pike had to laugh; he found it hard to imagine anyone being able to stand up to this alien warrior, but a lowly Earth kid apparently had. The blue and white boat looked a bit rougher as it got closer. The white had been repainted so many times he was sure it was likely more paint than wood. The turquoise blue bottom faded to a deeply disturbing mix of algae green and black tar. The tar undoubtedly from many patch jobs over its long land difficult life.

"Welcome, welcome," the nearly toothless captain said, waving him aboard.

Pike immediately decided this was the darkest human being he'd ever seen.

"You go La Désirade?"

Pike nodded, assured by Subada this was correct. The man proceeded to tell him, "Many hours." It was south in the French West Indies. Beer and sandwiches were in the cooler, the captain told him in a sing-song language that was hard to understand but beautiful to hear. Pike suddenly realized he was starving. The simple food was the best he'd ever had, of that he was certain. He watched the endless miles of ocean sweep past. It was something he never tired of. Risson Mack had told him once he could tell what ocean they were in just by the feel and taste. Pike lowered his hand into the water and brought it to his lips. It was mildly salty, light, and instantly transported him to another place and time. A place of abandoned beaches, hot summer sun, and boys with too much energy and too little supervision.

"You are a most interesting human," Subada said after a short while.

Pike's eyes had been nearly closed as the motion of the boat was lulling him to sleep. He found himself in the mental construct again, only this time the scene was not Xylos. Instead, it appeared to be the observatory room on a moon. Looking down at the dark but still strangely beautiful world of Kava, he asked, "How so?"

The mental avatar of Subada sat on a long bench, looking out toward the ruined home of his youth. "In the last few months, you have been ripped away from your home, your isolation. You discovered distant worlds, the ability to travel through time and space. You found love, you were beaten and captured, and now you are in a strange place with only the clothes on your back, heading to a meeting with perhaps the most dangerous man on the planet. All that and you've not once asked to go home, nor asked for anything related to your own safety. In fact, the only thing I sense from you is curiosity and a worry about Doctor Cassidy and the boy."

Pike shrugged. "Not that special. I just like to see things through. I tend to get a bit obsessed with finding answers."

Subada smiled. "I've noticed." The alien moved around nervously.

Pike could still sense the growing unease. "What is it?"

"I fear, my friend, that our time together is coming to an end. I am unsure what else to do to help you with your mission. I can't stop The Fade," Subada said in a tone of defeat. "Nianda will not be pleased with my efforts I'm afraid."

"If there is no way to stop it...why would he have asked you to help?"

Subada looked at him queerly. "I may have misspoken earlier, Shep. It was actually I who asked him for permission to help you."

Pike mentally stepped back from the alien. "How...why would you, I mean, how do you know anything about me?"

52

The Via del Fortino was perched high on a hill above the Amalfi coastline. Kate sipped the exquisite wine and stared out at the azure blue Tyrrhenian Sea. This part of her story she had never shared with Pike. In time, she felt she would have, but now it seemed that time might never happen. Ghosted echoes rattled in her head; she couldn't face the past. A past in which she'd made so many mistakes. Now she had trouble envisioning a future that wasn't filled with even more.

"Your ambitions were pure, my dear Kate," Valerius said, coming up and leaning over the marble balustrade beside her.

His words seemed almost prescient but did little to silence her internal turmoil. "Were they?" she said.

He patted her hand before turning to the wine carafe and pouring himself a glass. He moved to one of the loungers and sat down. The view from every angle of the pool and gardens was spectacular, and there was a level of privacy that only a fortunate few could even imagine. He would never have admitted it, but they had moved an ancient ruin several kilometers because it sat on the finest view in Furore. He appreciated the past but not when it got in the way of the future. "You sought a treatment for your sister's leukemia. What could be more noble than that?"

Kate hung her head. There was shame and loss, nothing noble or pure in those memories. She loved Val like a father, but today he wasn't helping. How many years had it been since he'd approached her after a symposium with a blanket proposal to fund her research? She should have asked more questions, but she hadn't. In the end, his motives were as pure as her own. He was losing someone, just like she had lost Ava. In both cases, the search for traditional solutions had provided nothing. The search for solutions in other ways had been a last best option. Her own field was medical but so far removed from her sisters' deteriorating condition as to be useless. But it was what she had, and it pushed her to take chances, to be bold, to experiment. Now, karma was ready to balance the scales once again.

"We have a lead on your people," Val said.

She turned to him, waiting for more.

"A report from the British embassy in Brisbane. A woman claiming to be Dr. Wie Song Lu has made contact. They sanitized the report before distribution, but it implies a likely covert rendition by American intelligence."

"That's it? Where are they?"

"That's all my contact was able to discern. He said since it came from a station in Australia, that most likely the people are there. The Brits seem to be fuming mad with the U.S. right now anyway, but with everything going on in the world, it's not seen as a top priority at the momenta."

Kate thought feverishly. *What would be the smart move? Could we get to them first? Where are they? Where had they been held? Is Pike still alive?* Valerius was still talking, but she had missed some of what was said. Something about a missing military jet. "Should we go there?"

"To Australia? No, no, my child. I don't think that's wise...I have people on the ground. They are on the lookout for your people. They are checking the airports, hotels, and ports around Brisbane and up the coast toward Cairns. We know you were a high-value asset whom they wanted in that raid much more than the others, well, other than the unfortunate Signor Shepard. We must assume the Americans will have gotten word the same way we just did. No need to make it easy for them."

"What will you do if you locate them? They won't want to go with anyone else," said Kate.

He finished the wine with a satisfied smack. "I think it best not to do anything except ensure their safety. At least for now."

"What the hell, Val! Those are our people. They have been through God knows what!"

He held up his hands in a supplicating gesture. "They were not doing anything wrong, nothing illegal even. They had an international research charter, and most are not American. The U.S. overstepped its considerable bounds when they snatched them. I believe it might be beneficial to make Uncle Sam pay a bit for the transgression. Albergoni International will have a lot harder time doing that than the British government."

He saw her expression and offered a consolation first. "We will take your Mister Shepard before the Brits take custody, okay?"

Kate nodded reluctantly. It was something; it was hope, and that was more than she'd had the last several days.

"Are you ready to discuss with me what Pike found?" Valerius asked in as polite a tone as he could manage. She had once again become accustomed to his constant Italian accent, and no longer noticed it much.

Kate had been unwilling, or maybe just unable, to reveal the horrible conclusion Pike had developed. She refilled her wine and sat down on the opposite lounge chair. She proceeded to explain Pike's theory and all that it entailed. She knew Valerius could be boisterous and was prone to snap decisions, but he listened attentively and only interrupted her once for a bit more clarification.

The man sat with his head propped up in his meaty palms, staring out over the massive pool. His mouth hung open in a bewildered expression. He'd literally dropped billions into the Cobalt Project, but neither of them had ever expected a finding like this. "That would explain a lot, wouldn't it?"

Kate nodded, her eyes clouding with tears again. She dabbed at them with a napkin she'd been clutching.

Val held up a finger. "How did he go from a network world to an uncharted one on his own?" He held up a second finger. "Assuming the Americans were listening in, what could they possibly hope to gain from an interrogation? It all seems pointless. Hell, life seems pointless." Then he added a third finger. "Is there nothing that can be done to change the outcome, to delay The Fade?"

Kate didn't have the answers. "Pike was brilliant in his assessment. You were right to recommend him, and I was blind to not see he was, in fact, the one. I have to assume Julian helped him go from one world to another."

"Wait, you think my stepson did this?"

Kate knew to proceed cautiously; Val and Julian had a rocky relationship. Despite Valerius inviting Julian Carapaz into The Project to try and help find a treatment for his mom, Julian always saw much more potential. The man was indeed a genius. "Several of us have concluded that Julian developed a way of doing self-directed jumps. The ability to transition from one off world to another without a terminus world is the likely next step of that."

The Italian forced back a reply and stayed silent.

Kate added, "Yes, that might mean that Julian got to Pike. I don't know, but I think we have to assume as much."

Valerius said, "But Pike's theory sounds nothing like what we have heard from Julian in the past. He seemed to believe The Fade was caused by some mysterious race. What did he call them? The Time Lords. And that what we were doing was evil, and we had to stop."

That wasn't precisely Carapaz's message to The Project, but it wasn't too far from the mark. "I didn't answer number two or three." She held up the fingers so her friend would get back on track. "I believe the Americans' actions are connected to the 'What can we do?' It would mean that they were aware of this already, and someone higher up the food chain has come up with some ideas." She took a large swallow of wine and noticed one of Val's staff was coming up the steps.

"Dinner will be ready when you and your guest are, sir," the man said in Italian, then repeated in English for Kate's benefit.

Val dismissed him with a nod of thanks. "You don't know what the American strategy might be?"

Kate smiled. Like most Europeans she'd encountered, he tended to lump all Americans together, at least in how they thought and reacted. She shook her head. "I haven't got a clue."

Val rose to his feet while poking his bottom lip contemplatively. "But you believe Pike was correct?" He held out his arm for her to take.

She rose, allowing herself to be escorted down to the dining room. "I am sad to say that I am quite positive, yes."

53

Pike watched as Captain Jono piloted the small boat back out to sea. Despite the heat and tropical beauty, Pike sensed a chill. He suddenly felt as alone as he'd ever been. "That man is getting paid, isn't he? We didn't just steal his time and boat like we did the jet?" he asked internally.

"Of course. I Venmo'd him the money from your account," Subada said, urging him to move in a particular direction.

"You did what?"

His internal visitor laughed. "You really should catch up with the times in this world before venturing off to discover what others have to offer, Shepard."

He climbed over a berm of driftwood and grasses, scattering a collection of iguanas out of their path. "One of your bankers transferred money, so yes, the man was well paid."

"Thank you," Pike said uneasily. "So, you can just slip into anyone to take care of whatever is needed?"

"To a point, yes," Subada answered. "There are some limits for me here, but not that many."

"So, why didn't you just do that with Carapaz?"

"He's been off world."

"Oh...oh, yeah, you said that before, sorry," Pike said. "What about Kate, is she still on a jump?"

There was a delay before Subada responded. "I had to check...no, she has returned. Would you like me to slip into her?"

"Oh, my God, never use that term again...not like that," Pike said. Images of the large alien in an intimate embrace with the object of his adoration were a bit much.

Subada obviously could also see the mental pictures Pike's twisted mind had dreamed up. "You're one sick dude, Shep."

The jungle was thick on this part of the island. It took several minutes to find a game trail weaving its way through the twist of foliage, roots, and all manner of things nature had designed to impale human bodies with. Pike had been the one to suggest they land on the opposite side from Carapaz's villa, though. "I can get through this crap on my own, Subada. Check on Kate, just to make sure she's safe."

"Do you want me to make direct contact?" Subada inquired. "Should I let her know you are okay?"

Pike stopped walking. He should say yes, but the raid on the lab and some of the things Carapaz had said in the past echoed in his head. How much could he trust her? Was she being totally honest with him? Hell, maybe she was working with the Americans. How else would she have escaped? Assuming she had gotten away. All he was sure of was she wasn't on the plane, nor in any of the holding cells. Why was Kate not a prisoner? Why was she able to SideSlip off world afterwards if she wasn't working with his captors? The only conclusion he could come up with was her government connections. Maybe she had been part of it. The raid, the rendition, all of it. He hated considering that, but her reluctance to be more open about how deep the U.S. government was involved with Cobalt made it clear that he couldn't fully trust her.

"She was not a known contact to any of the men in that facility," Subada said earnestly. "Still, your caution is well advised. The stakes are too high to be assuming anything. I will check on her, determine her location and intent. If she seems overly concerned for you, I will calm her mind without revealing more."

Something about that seemed mildly troubling and manipulative to Pike, but he agreed. Before Subada SideSlipped away, he also asked him to try to locate Palio. He felt sure the kid had gotten away but felt guilty for not really thinking about him until now.

Pike walked and, at times, crawled to get through the thicket for another forty-five minutes. The sun was beginning to dip into the ocean as he finally caught sight of a lone Spanish-style house in the distance. The landscape was transitioning from jungle to more desert-like, with far fewer areas for concealment. Carefully, he made his way to the house, finding many more things in the dim light to puncture his flesh.

As he approached the final hundred yards, a series of floodlights illuminated the well-manicured grounds surrounding the home. Pike slowly moved back several steps after realizing he'd tripped an automatic sensor. He moved around the perimeter of the home looking for signs anyone was home. The lights inside all appeared to be off. He wondered what was keeping Subada. He was ready to let him know this was a wild goose chase. Then he saw a flickering blue image from one of the rooms. Someone was watching TV or using a computer.

Pike gauged the spotlights from memory. They seemed to be at each of the four corners and another set over the doors. Motion sensors had a default level of sensitivity, so random movement like wind blowing a tree limb wouldn't set them off repeatedly. He also remembered reading that motion on the edges of the range were typically less sensitive than right in front. Of course, the sensors might not be aimed in the same direction as the lights, and they might not be just motion activated. They could be infra-red or sound or who knows what. If Carapaz was that smart, he'd probably have the best tech possible. Pike took a minute to work up his nerve. He was here to meet the man, one way or another.

While he had no reference of the tech used in the sensors, he believed it was infra-red. That was useful, especially if he had a piece of styrofoam or some other inert material to hide behind. Finally, he just adopted the awkward strategy of crawling and moving as paralyzingly slow as possible. Here, too, even the grass seemed to have barbs.

Little buried landmines of sandspurs bit into Pike's hands and knees, but he kept the level of motion down to something akin to an aging tree sloth. The security lights remained off. It took him almost an hour of agonizing movement to cross thirty yards of lawn. He'd picked an area on the exterior wall that was a likely blind spot for the light sensors.

"What are we doing?" Subada yelled excitingly, causing Pike to twitch and probably also lose a little pee.

"What in the good holy hell? Why are you yelling?" Pike asked.

"I'm not yelling. I'm in your head. I can't yell, the acoustics would be all wrong. Besides, it's all dark and I can feel you are in pain."

"I'm sneaking across the lawn. I didn't want Julian to know we're coming," Pike said in frustration.

Subada's arm shot up and waved around, setting off the lights immediately.

"Yeah, wrong house, mate. Carapaz is farther down, another mile or so," Subada said, laughing. "Damn good technique, though. Bravo!"

"Are you done fucking with me?" Pike asked.

"Almost," Subada said, his sense of humor eerily perfect for an alien being. "Kate is okay, she's shacking up with a rich Italian."

Pike was now jogging down the open beach, various pin pricks of pain announcing themselves with every stride. "Do what? And can you turn down the pain from all these briars and cuts?"

"Did you fight a porcupine or something? No. I see what you did. You crawled through cactus. You need to feel this pain full throttle, just so you will remember not to do something that stupid next time."

"Ugh, I'm fighting with myself. Okay, tell me about Kate."

Subada filled him in on Kate's situation the best he could. Pike was relieved, but still confused and even more distrustful of the woman. This Italian man must have been the source of the rest of the funding, but Kate had never mentioned him. In fact, she had outright denied it.

The house was coming into view now. It was lit up like a luxury hotel. Lights blazed from every balcony and interior room. "What about Palio?" Pike asked as he approached the front door.

"Um, yeah, no to finding him."

"No?" Pike asked, surprised. He stopped his approach, waiting on the reply.

"I could not find anyone with his brain pattern," Subada said.

"What does that mean?" Pike asked, moving closer to the entryway.

"Well, he could be wearing a tinfoil hat," Subada responded seriously.

"Really? Does that work?" Pike asked.

"No, it doesn't work, you moron. I was being sarcastic. It means he's probably dead or unconscious."

"Dead?" Pike felt his heart sink.

"Gotta go," Subada said before hurriedly vacating Pike's brain.

Pike reached for the doorknob, but it opened first. He found himself staring into the barrel of a large caliber pistol held by a diminutive and extremely evil looking man.

"Mister Shepard, what a surprise," the man said in a growl.

54

She couldn't explain why, but Kate felt strangely better about Pike and the others. She was also sure of one other thing; he knew the truth about her. If the government agents questioning him hadn't confirmed his fears, Carapaz certainly had. She was a fraud, not in total, but in enough ways to matter. One thing that was true was the love she felt for the lonely man from Blackwater. Shepard had shut out the entire world, yet somehow, he'd left room for her. In turn, she had used him, used him to lure Julian out of hiding. Used him to motivate the U.S. to make its move. She needed to know where everybody stood, and now she did. Sadly, for her, all she really wanted was for Pike to be safe and for them to be together.

Kate pushed the cup around the corner of the desk and looked down at her notes. The tight, precise penmanship was a statement. It embodied the control, the rigid structure she'd held herself to since childhood. While her classmates were scrawling their names across pages, she learned to be neat and efficient in the way she thought and the way she wrote. Now in frustration with herself, she threw the pad across the room and buried her head in her hands. She thought getting to this point was all that mattered. Now, she was far less certain. Somewhere down the labyrinthian corridors, a clock chimed. Time.

That was what she was running out of, what all of them were running out of. Why hadn't she just been more honest with him from the beginning?

Pike was an innocent. He deserved to know all about Carapaz, about the GTR, about Valerius, but she had denied him anything except what was essential for him to solve the problem, The Fade. Now she knew what it was. A natural force the universe used to wipe the slate clean. Like a hurricane sweeping over an island, scrubbing humanity away in the process. How did you fight against nature?

That was what the GTR had been trying to learn all along. Her contact with them had always been careful not to reveal much, but obviously they had made more progress than Cobalt had. While she had been certain Carapaz was the cause, they had focused on the Mirror-Earth timeline. She walked over and picked up the pad again, her analytical mind still helplessly bound to unlocking the truth. Had SideSlipping led to The Fade? Were there any actions that might delay or reverse it?

Dimensional theory and alternate timelines were not Kate's specialties. She really needed Dr. Lu or Letner or her preferred pain in the ass, Pike. She laughed as she set the pen down and leaned back, thinking over the last few months. Julian had been the first to point it out to her. What world had that been on? She had to think, there had been so many. Wren, one of the bird worlds. "Okay, Avian worlds, Fazula," silently conversing with the memory of the quantum biologist from her team.

Wren was where Julian had first suggested Kate's host always seemed to have a bonded mate. Someone who was smart, loyal, and fiercely protective. She had no idea how Carapaz could know all of them were versions of Pike Shepard, but he had. Still, it was she who had ultimately found him. Kate felt a grumble of protest in her stomach. The combination of stress and rich food seemed to be increasingly disagreeing with her systems.

She made several more notes, all related to Pike's theory. One thing still bothered her, something she'd admitted to no one. She did start looking for her mate on every world, especially after Julian left The

Project. What she couldn't recall is how she had actually located him on this world. At the time, she had accepted it as fate, a very unscientific thing to do, while she recalled vividly why she had been in South Carolina. What led her to rent a boat and navigate around for days looking for a rundown cabin on the water's edge was a mystery. One that she felt strongly she needed to solve.

55

Shepard began to raise his hands as the evil-looking man's lips twisted into a grin. “Come on in.” He turned and moved down a dimly lit hall. “This is Gohr,” the man said, pointing to himself.

Pike had the odd realization that this might be the first time referring to oneself in the third person was technically correct. “Where is he?”

“Still off world,” Subada, via Gohr, said dismissively. “Man, this guy has got some twisted shit going on in his noggin.”

Pike eyed the little man cautiously as they descended a short flight of stairs and emerged into a space that seemed trapped between a medical laboratory and a smoking lounge on a country estate. Rich mahogany panels lined the walls interspersed by bookcases overflowing with ancient books. Leather club chairs sat next to white clinical beds and numerous monitors. Pike glimpsed in to see if the bed was occupied and immediately wished he hadn't.

“Is that...”

Gohr nodded. “He spends so much time off world he has to be fed via stomach tube and, well... you can smell the rest.”

“God, Carapaz, what the hell?” Shepard had now talked to this man several times in multiple forms, but seeing him now as a human was the most disturbing by far.

Subada, using the little man, was busy moving through pages of data on the computer terminal. “I know this place; the frequency is for one of the terminus worlds. You are going to have to go and get him, Shep.”

“Why don’t you? I haven’t had much luck convincing him of anything.”

“I can’t, if I leave this man’s consciousness, he will kill you,” Subada said very matter-of-factly.

“Okay, um...yeah, stay here then,” Pike said, pacing around the large room. He stopped at a window wall overlooking the darkened sea. “We could just, you know...kill him...Carapaz. You know just be done with it.”

“I cannot. He is not a direct threat,” Subada said. “Can you do it? And more importantly, is that the right thing to do?”

Pike found the act of speaking rationally to the little rat-faced man repulsive but nodded. “I...don’t know. Kate felt like he was the mortal enemy, but I found him to be very intelligent and quite persuasive.”

“We could simply force him back,” Subada said. “Although this world would create a sizeable time dilation, what you guys call ‘the gap.’”

“So, I’ll have one, too, when I come back?” Pike asked nervously. He didn’t think he had time for any amnesia.

“No, my friend. That was a result of your machine interface. Now that you can Slip without an aid, you will find that is no longer a problem.”

Pike was nervous. He had grown accustomed to his new friend and felt much better when he was close. His mouth was dry, but he nodded in agreement. Gohr handed him a bottle of water from a small refrigerator concealed behind one of the wood panels. “How will I find him? He’s always been waiting on me when we were together.”

Gohr touched his arm in a cartoonish version of tenderness. “You will simply know, Shep. Much like Kate knew to find you. It is not going to be an issue, you will see.”

* * *

"You need to go home, Shepard."

It had taken Pike hours to tune in the 'feeling' directing him to Carapaz. Or more accurately, the host body containing the man's consciousness. He hadn't bothered to get the name of the world before SideSlipping. He guessed it was a G or H class world by Cobalt's naming convention. Definitely not one he had been to before. The dominant species here were slender and graceful. The world was very populous with the sentient species seemingly everywhere. Pike had walked for hours and was still in some part of the same city.

"How did you find me?"

Pike had been concerned that Carapaz might have slipped off this world. It was a terminus dimension. How would he track him if that were the case? It had surprised him to hear Subada speaking to his physical body back on the island, telling him not to worry. The alien had been right; he had sensed Carapaz being on this planet soon after. It had just taken him longer to learn the nuances of that sensation, to zero in on his location. Another benefit of Subada's tinkering, he assumed.

"We need to talk," Pike said, refusing to answer any of the man's questions. *Let him wonder.* Carapaz's host was lounging on a large flat plaza suspended above a wide waterway. Pike's host had gone up reluctantly, apparently feeling unwelcome or more likely, unworthy. He was aware the species had a rigid caste system but much more complex than the ones on his Earth. Pike was just glad he was able to speak through them. That was still a rarity among worlds, well, except for Subada. In a fleeting thought, Pike wondered if that, too, might be one of his newfound abilities.

"Did you figure it out? And how did you get away from your new friends?"

"Was it you that set that trap?" Pike demanded. "How did they show up just as I was coming to terms with what happened?"

Carapaz was as slick as butter on a hot skillet. "You really should go home, Pike. Go back to your little corner of the Lowcountry and hide.

Wait for The Fade, you know it's coming. That seems to be what I am doing."

"Maybe I'll just wait with you, Julian. Maybe I should have Gohr pull me up a chair so we can watch the world fade out together."

The mention of the man's apprentice had the desired effect. "What are you talking about? How do you know that name?"

Getting Carapaz off base was a difficult challenge. Pike thought it best to leave him there. "Not important!" he snapped. "What is it you're doing here?"

Carapaz sighed. "I had hoped you would know that already. Why else would you come here?"

Pike shook his head. "I don't even know where here is. What do you call this world?"

"It's called Mizar."

An M class world, Pike thought, realizing it was even more alien than he'd thought. "Julian, why did you show me the other Earth, Emma, and the rest?"

The other alien body shrugged. "I wanted you to see that you can't even trust your own memories. I wanted you to understand."

"Understand what?" Pike was nearly shouting.

"I wanted you to know that there is only one outcome possible. It's us or them, and I don't think you will do anything to cause her any harm."

"So, you know our timeline is ending, that's what The Fade is?"

The creature clapped its frail looking hands together. "You figured it out, very good, Professor."

"Gohr, can you kick the shit out of Julian?" He said the words aloud but also made sure Subada heard back in the lab.

"It's an idle...ummph," Carapaz said, nearly doubling over.

Pike wasn't even sure if the sensation of pain would travel through the quantum slipstream, but apparently it did.

A flash of fire crossed the face of Carapaz's host. "You are in my house? What have you done to my assistant?"

Carapaz grimaced in pain again.

"We kicked him again," Subada said. "You know, just for good measure."

"Well, stop," Pike ordered sub-vocally.

Carapaz was enraged and rushed him. Pike nimbly side-stepped and slapped him on the back as he went by. The creature's skeletal frame felt like a cat, more cartilage than bone. Julian's power was mental. Pike had the tactical edge in a physical fight. The grayish blue skin seemed to radiate with hatred much like a squid as it readied for an attack.

"Calm down, Julian, I came to talk. Yes, I'm in your house, but you're in no danger. Gohr is being helpful against his will if that makes you feel better."

The other's face calmed slightly. "I don't care about him. Are the military guys with you? Did you bring federal agents to my island?"

Why is he so concerned about them? Pike wondered. The man's response was not what he had expected. "Aren't you working with them? Much of your equipment looks like it could have been theirs," he stated.

Carapaz remained silent.

"What are you doing here? What can you do on Mizar that is important enough to let your body waste away to nothing?"

The alien sat staring up at Pike for long moments before apparently reaching a conclusion. "Come with me, you will just have to see it for yourself."

56

"We are children pretending to be grown-ups in the home of an uncaring parent, Shepard. We pretend we know what is going on, but our minds can't even grasp it, we can't conceive of the magnitude. So, we invent myth and fable. Fairytales like Zeus and Athena, ghosts and angels, God and the devil, right and wrong. You must see by now that none of that matters."

Carapaz's voice had taken on a nearly pleading tone.

"What am I looking at?" Pike asked.

Carapaz pulled him along the boulevard toward a singular building of obvious importance. He could tell by the resistance of his host that being here was not a common occurrence.

"This race has a unique ability, Pike. Have you sensed it yet in your host?"

Pike had been so fixated on confronting Julian Carapaz that he'd been all but blind to nearly everything else. Taking a moment to feel the inner thoughts of his dimensionally entwined twin, he understood. The man was clearly terrified of the building ahead.

"Tell me, does Kate still believe that man's default condition is madness?"

Pike nodded. “She does, yes. Are you going to convince me she’s wrong?”

“Oh, she isn’t wrong, not really,” Carapaz answered coldly. “Madness is a requirement...without it we would never believe in sanity. The ying and the yang, brother, light and dark and all that rubbish, you know?”

As they neared the spherical tower, Pike felt himself forcing his host to move forward against his will more and more. This resulted in a stumbling gait that closely resembled a drunk on his way to Sunday Mass.

“You are going to have to exert more control, Shepard. Your other will never go through those doors willingly.”

Pike could see now that the building was not that large at the base, just incredibly tall. He guessed it at a hundred meters in diameter but perfectly circular at the base and extending up like a needle to an incredible height. Several hundred stories, he guessed. High above, the peak simply disappeared from sight in the bright, bluish-green sky. They were on a large plaza with the tower in the middle. He felt his host’s knees trembling, or whatever the local equivalent was. Carapaz headed for the entrance, a large arched opening ahead.

Above the arch an inscription in the native tongue read, “The future requires payment, history demands sacrifice.” The rather ominous quote added weight to the fear his host was exhibiting. Pike vanquished his consciousness to a more comatose state and took over control of the Mizari’s body.

“I discovered this nearly by accident,” Carapaz said, lowering his voice as they entered a large space at the foot of the building.

The walls were covered with glyphs and art that Pike knew were more than just symbolic. “This is a cathedral?” he asked.

“Of a sort, yes. The Mizari people are deeply religious, but we missed it originally as it is heavily entwined in their science. Unlike in our dimension, the two are not incompatible. Here, both mature and adapt with new discoveries. The faith is essentially based around a constantly developing narrative.”

“So, they don’t believe in God, or gods?” Pike asked.

"It's more nuanced than that," Carapaz explained. "They simply believe differently. They know they are not unique in the universe, and that forms a more rational basis for spiritual growth."

They were walking toward a series of risers leading up to a mezzanine level that appeared crowded. "So, they know of other species. Are they able to SideSlip, or did multidimensional UFOs visit them?"

"No...neither. They can observe other dimensions naturally and in a way that is truly unique to them."

Pike now saw the crowd of people were all dressed in a garment that reminded him of monks' robes. All were seated with something dark covering their face and mouth. He was about to ask Carapaz about it when one of the 'masks' moved on its own revealing a brighter underside below. A long tentacle uncoiled from the Mizari's head, and as it unwound, Pike noticed additional appendages going down the throat. "That thing is alive?" Smaller tendrils extended into the eyes and ears of the Mizari female. He felt an involuntary shudder run through his host.

"It is not harmful to them." Carapaz said. "The relationship is more symbiotic and serves two purposes."

"It's freaking grotesque," Pike said as the several feet of pinkish organ extracted itself fully from the Mizari who herself seemed to just be coming back to consciousness.

"To us, it is," Carapaz agreed. "The first time I did it, I nearly passed out from sheer fright."

"You..." Pike stammered, "...you did that? Why on Earth would you allow yourself to even...?" His voice trailed off as he saw others doing the same thing. Another Mizari helped the female from her seat and immediately took her place. The dutiful symbiot creature, looking more terrifying than ever began crawling up her chest to take its place on her face.

Pike forced his eyes to look away, He couldn't bear to see the personal violation that was taking place a few feet ahead. As he stared up and out, he realized this was simply one floor among hundreds where the same thing was going on.

"They call them Coticas," Carapaz said. "There is an interesting history between the two species, but I won't bore you with that just now."

"And they do this voluntarily?" Pike asked again, staring at another seated figure, this one a juvenile who was clearly anxious at what was about to happen.

"It's mostly harmless," Carapaz said. "The Coticas provide a service and keep the Mizari supplied with air and also can help cure any maladies in the body while they are attached."

"Mostly harmless?"

Carapaz nodded and began to walk, motioning for Pike to follow. "The joining and separation are unpleasant. Something akin to drowning. Also, the Coticas use the Mizari hosts for incubation of their eggs. That can be fatal for the surrogate, but they don't breed often, so that is not a tremendous risk."

Pike wanted to put his head between his knees so he didn't vomit. "What on Earth could be worth this?"

"That is the right question," Carapaz said ruefully. "There is an enormous TD with this world, but you already knew that I'm guessing."

"Yeah, I know there will be a gap," Pike said, unwilling to tell him that, according to Subada, he would not be experiencing it.

"Right. What you may not know is the timeline of Mizar runs anti to every other dimension we know of. Sorry, counter to you Americans, time here advances into our past," Carapaz said.

Pike considered that. Time being bi-directional was a concept he'd grappled with in college. He knew that didn't violate any of the Einsteinian laws of physics, but in a different dimension, those laws were obsolete anyway. Any set of physical laws could exist here.

"So what?" Pike asked after several seconds of contemplation. "When you go back to your little island, it won't be in the past. Your body will have moved forward in time, no matter that you were traveling in the opposite way over here. Do you somehow think you can move our reality back to a point before all the shit started?"

Carapaz's host stopped walking and handed him something, an interface Pike knew to be the local equivalent of a tablet computer. He poked two fingers into a slot and the imagery and text contained on the device began to display in his host's visual centers.

"The Coticas are able to organically encode and record the Side-Slips of their hosts," Carapaz said.

Pike looked at the device. This was what he and Palio had wanted to create. So far, they had only managed the digital notepad. He clicked one of the control buttons and watched a type of time-lapse record unfold on a world not so unlike Earth. "They can see the future of other dimensions...other timelines. They know what's going to happen before it occurs."

"Yes, Pike," Carapaz confirmed, "they have seen the end of all worlds. Eons ago they began recording it in living tissue of the Coticas. Here, in one of their most sacred temples, is the archive of life in the multiverse."

"So, they know how our Earth ends?"

"They have seen it, yes."

"So, you knew all along, that The Fade was not being caused by some alien horde?" Pike asked, anger in his voice. "This is how you knew which worlds were going to be next, isn't it?" Pike got the distinct impression that Carapaz's nervous energy was not just due to Pike confronting him or having people in his actual house.

"I know many things, and in time, will know it all."

57

Alex Scofield watched as the older man's thought became something more tangible. The seething anger had moved on from a slow boil to a raging inferno. Each rise of degree in his mental fever had translated his face into a mask of horror. "If you would ..." Alex began with a tone of mock supplication. In truth, Alex didn't care what the GTR director was thinking. Planck was his boss, but he knew his role with the security agency was safe despite how this current meeting was looking.

"Listen, you little shit, I don't give a good holy hell about your intentions or opinions or how you fucking felt, you goddamn millennial snowflake. You know what matters in this office, Scofield. Results, that's it! Results. Plain and simple. That is the one simple job description both you and I share. And you failed, which means I failed, and little boy...you need to understand, I don't fail!"

Alex had heard rumors of the old man's tantrums in the past. He'd even seen some of the victims sneaking out of the director's office, tails tucked between their legs like a puppy who'd just soiled the new rug. As the youngest regional director at the Center for Global Threat Response, or more often, just 'The Center,' he had no intention of cow-tailing to his raving lunatic of a boss. "Sir, Winthrop was your recommendation, not mine. ”It was a shit response, and Alex said it just to see how much more it would provoke the man.

Director Planck’s eyes focused on the assorted folders scattered across the massive desk while he slowly chewed his bottom lip. “We burned all our goodwill with the Brits. The fucking Brits, Scofield. Not the damn Pakistanis or the Sudanese...the United fucking Kingdom. For what? Not a goddamn thing. Not one shred of useable intel. We’ve now been kicked off every joint operation’s base in the world. The PM wants us added to the list of terrorist nations. Our own Joint Chiefs want someone held accountable. Give me one good reason why that shouldn’t be you.”

When things went south in New Guinea, Alex knew this meeting would be inevitable, but he hadn’t been worried, not really. GTR and The Center didn’t exist, no one would ever give him or anyone else connected to the ultra-secure task force up to investigators. The stakes were just too large. “Director, we have video.”

“I’ve seen the goddamn video. It clearly shows Winthrop losing his shit and the interrogation tech guy going nuts and injecting him with the highball,” Planck said dismissively.

The younger agent nodded. “I’m talking about what came after.”

Planck’s eyes rose to meet Scofield’s. “The escapee?”

“Yes, Director. Shepard is no fighter, certainly no killer. The file on him is very complete. Moderate combat training, still in relatively good shape, but not only did he fight like a man possessed, he was damn near supernatural. Then the buses, the plane, everything being coordinated to one of the most remote black sites on the planet. No way anyone knew where they were.”

“You are saying...”

“I’m simply pointing out the likelihood, sir.” Alex rose slowly to his feet, ready to get this over with. “Pike Shepard is being used as an agent by the other side. Whether willingly or not. Right now, he has to be considered the most dangerous man on the planet. Not only does he know what we are up against, he is an American citizen. One we just kidnapped and tortured.”

Director Planck thought on this briefly before giving a single nod.

"The short-term damage is irrelevant if the long term doesn't exist. Shit, what does it matter if...well, if we don't even exist? The man is to be considered a domestic terrorist. Put a lid on this, and I mean do it yesterday, you got me Scofield? Find him and find that damn Cassidy woman, too. We can always use her for leverage."

Alex turned to leave, then stopped and turned back. The overweight, red-faced man sitting on the other side of the desk made him sick. *This is the best patriot the U.S. government could put between us and Armageddon? Global Threat Response...what a laugh.*

"Something else, Scofield?"

"Does this speed up our timing?"

Planck rubbed a meaty hand over his uneven jaw before staring out at the Virginia hills in the distance. Slowly, he began to nod, just a little at first, but growing increasingly emphatic. "It does, yes. Time for more direct action. We can't just remain passive on this. We launch in ten days. Make sure the team is ready."

Scofield nodded and walked to the door, the briefest hint of a smile creasing his normally stoic face.

* * *

"Sir."

Scofield scowled at the junior assistant.

"We have a bank transfer from a new account connected to Shepard."

"He's not that stupid. He hasn't used credit cards, nor does he have a smart phone from what we can tell," Scofield shot back.

"It was a payment app from a new account going to a bait store in the Caribbean," the man said.

"Likelihood of fraud?" Alex asked. He knew regions of the Caribbean basin were rife with scammers of all types, skilled at extracting money from U.S. citizens.

"High," the man admitted reluctantly. "That area of the world is rife with tech bandits. They use burner phones and stolen identities to do this kind of thing all the time."

"But...?"

"Well, sir, the amount doesn't match any of our predictions...it's too low, and it's going to a known commercial business, with a fixed location. Something they normally avoid. It checks out on the surface as being a legit transfer. Stratos classifies it as a highly probable."

Stratos was GTR's native AI system that catalogued all active case files and incoming intelligence. That in itself lifted the credibility level significantly in Alex's mind. "Send me what you have and get assets moving to that location. I want to know who it was and what Shepard was paying for." He thought about tactics, not on U.S. soil. That cleared one more hurdle. "Get the info, cleanse the scene."

"You're working without a net on this one, Boss," the man said an hour later. The video call was crystal clear, using technology stolen from the Chinese running on a private network of satellites unaffiliated with the United States in any way.

Alex replied, "I know, but we had to know it was coming to this. You're sure your guys are going to be able to do the job?"

"Hell, yeah! We've been training for this for months. Everything on the other side will come crumbling down in no time. I'll guarantee it."

Alex smiled. He liked the brash young operative. "You willing to bet your life on it, Goose?"

The wiry smile cut a thin line across the man's harsh looking face. "Always do."

Goose and the rest of the highly specialized GTR GO team were not the group looking for Pike Shepard. That would be an unnecessary use of resources. The local agents could find him, then a specialized grab team could take him down. No, this team was for a very specific mission, one that Planck had just given the green light to get started. Alex gave some final instructions and signed off. The spinning globe logo of the satellite company slowly replaced the man's face. "We're coming."

58

"They know, but you don't?" Pike asked.

Carapaz's host shrugged again. A gesture that was totally unknown to the Mizaris, but Pike understood it.

"I've seen the remnants of our world in the recordings. The tomorrows are there but not the event. Not the end."

So that's what he's spending so much time here looking for. "You want to know the thing that happens to end it all," Pike said.

"If it is a single event at all. All I know for certain is we are running out of time, Shepard. I had hoped that you could help me change the outcome, but so far that hasn't happened."

"So, we can change the future?" Pike asked in bewilderment.

"I don't know. These people sure don't think so. The very fabric of their belief system would unravel if that was the case." He paused, and Pike saw for the first time how exhausted this man was. Here, trapped inside an alien body for days, or weeks even. The alien looked strung out to be honest, and Carapaz sounded nearly defeated. Not the arrogant man Pike had encountered on other worlds.

"To be honest, we can never know, not for certain. As soon as we managed to change the future, that would become our new reality. The history recorded here on these things would change as well." He tossed the tablet onto a nearby desk in frustration. "If we make the right change, chances are, we won't even be here. We might never meet even."

Pike was so far down the rabbit hole he was losing track of what reality even meant. *Examine the facts, Pike*. Problem solving had always been his gift, the rival brains, the analytical knife he could slice through the superfluous to get to the meat. How could he do that, though, when he could no longer guarantee he could tell fact from fiction?

"You found out you never had a daughter, didn't you?" Carapaz asked.

Pike nodded sadly.

"Reality, it's more nuanced than we ever thought," Carapaz began. "The Mizari faith holds that universes are like a firework display with new ones bursting into existence, blazing brightly for a time, then fading away to be replaced by another."

"None of them are supposed to fight The Fade, are they?"

"Not if you ask these guys. They believe it's all preordained, of course. A reality with a lens on the future of countless other worlds probably would feel that way."

Pike watched another Mizari separating from its Cortica, the process scaring his host and nauseating Pike. "You saw the event that caused our mirror universe to separate?" The idea occurring to him suddenly.

Carapaz made a move Pike took as a yes. Shepard picked up the tablet again and scrolled through numerous screens. There were several diagrams, and the text was in the richly descriptive language of the upper caste of Mizari. But Pike's host's mind interpreted it easily enough. He also saw a quantum frequency that didn't seem to match either version of Earth.

"I'm sure you figured out by now the event was not on our world, but theirs. Pinpointing the date, it looks to be around eighty-five million years ago. A magnetic shift of the poles was the first of the events."

Pole reversal was unusual, Pike knew, but rarely thought of as something life altering or catastrophic. "Laschamps Event?" Pike asked, using the formal name. "How could that have been the cause?"

"Laschamps was more recent on our world, not theirs, but normally it wouldn't be. In this case, though, the weakening of the geomagnetic field was more significant than any others we know of, and it appears to have occurred during a peak period for solar activity."

Pike knew the Earth's heliosphere was directly tied to the planet's magnetic field. Without it, the cosmic rays would irradiate the surface of the planet. "Life would have totally disappeared in those regions," he stated.

"Nearly so, nearly so, yes." They began to walk on. "On our Earth, the event was years later and more moderate. We had also gone through the funnel during the Toba disaster, which I don't think our twin experienced."

"So, that's what fractured the timeline?" Pike asked, mostly to himself. He was still in analytical mode, trying to get the pieces to fit. The gears in his mind were churning up ideas but no solutions yet. "How are the worlds so similar? You and I still exist on each...my family and home are not that different."

"Shouldn't there be more substantial variations?" Carapaz said smiling, knowing he'd led Pike to this point. "There were, there are."

One of the cogs in Pike's mental gearing dropped into place with a clunk. "Oh." They were about ten stories up now. He absently moved toward a window to look out as he sifted through the mental hailstorm in his mind. "My daughter didn't die on New Earth, she died in a third timeline." Subada hadn't confirmed that, but it felt right. He turned to face Carapaz, or at least the Mizari being possessed by Julian Carapaz's consciousness.

Pike continued, "Other timelines branch off during other significant events, but most don't last, they fade quickly. Only a few remain viable long enough to exist on their own." He'd started down this thought path days earlier but had been interrupted. Now it was coming back with even more texture and detail. "Dimensions that are more similar or mostly similar will typically be paired closer together, presumably so that they might be reintegrated into one, or one becomes obviously redundant or unnecessary by whatever cosmic rules the multiverse operates on."

"Survival of the fittest, Shepard," Carapaz stated flatly. "The same law that applies to bacteria and viruses also applies to sentient beings and universes. Evolution didn't start out with some grand plan to eventually build humans. It started by building multi-celled organisms, a better bacterium, which eventually became us. It did that by allowing almost every possible permutation to take place. If it worked, if it processed food better, converted sunlight more efficiently, developed a cell phone with better picture quality, well then, it flourished, while other less satisfactory versions fade away." Carapaz laughed a little and put his appendage on Pike's arm in a manner that was oddly considered the same by both species.

Pike's host appeared to be beaten down. "So, the dinosaur was doomed because they couldn't adapt to a changing world. And now we are the dinosaurs. Our entire reality is deemed less viable to the betterment of existence, so we, too, must fade out? If that's what you believe, then what are you doing here?" he asked quietly.

59

"You did find him?"

"Yes," Pike admitted, coming out of his SideSlip surprisingly alert and energetic. "You could have told me time was running in opposition there."

Subada, aka Gohr, seemed to consider it. "Time coordinates are rather relative to your own originations. I am not sure I actually realized it was reversed. Good to know, though. By the way, Pike, have you ever heard of someone, well..." Subada trailed off.

"What?"

"Nothing. This human I am inhabiting has some darkness that I find particularly disturbing. The things he enjoys, the acts committed on others of his own kind, are a peculiar kind of evil. I will be glad to be rid of him. So, what is our next move?"

Subada used a mental block that rendered Gohr unconscious and then slipped back into Pike's brain. From there, Pike could share his consciousness and access all the memories from Mizar. It was far simpler than Pike trying to relate all he had learned.

Pike closed his eyes and awaited his friend in the virtual construct they had used for meetings. Subada appeared shortly, and again, Pike felt a sudden and striking familiarity with the man. Not the same as he had upon meeting Kate. This was deeper and more detailed.

"Tertiary timelines are not uncommon, but they are so short-lived as to be irrelevant. None ever seem to last more than a few centuries," Subada said.

"But Subada, this one is out there. It's the one that's fighting us. The Fade isn't causing the madness, the violence that travelers from that third mirror dimension is behind it."

"You no longer believe your timeline is the one being ended?" his twin asked.

Pike looked down, his fingers steepled in thought under his chin as he walked. "From a viability standpoint, yes, I don't think our existence is as viable as New Earth long term. They just seem to have their shit together much better than we do. But assuming there is another, let's call it Terra. Then we may be in much better shape than them. That must be where Emma died. Who knows what else has happened there?"

"You are talking about an overlapping dimension that none of us, including Nianda or the Mizari, apparently have ever encountered. Yet you presume they can enter the quantum slipstream and travel here just as we do. They could not go undetected. Even if I was unaware, Nianda surely would have known. His people can detect such things and would have warned me."

Both of them remained silent for several minutes, each pondering over the known facts. "How could a species keep themselves hidden yet still Slip into other dimensions?" Pike asked.

"It's not just that," Subada responded. "If what you say is correct, then they are exerting full control over their hosts. When you went to New Earth, could you force your hosts to do anything?"

Pike knew what he was getting at. "No, it seems that we can only do that with certain species. Humans are not one...the best we can do is influence. A mental nudge from the subconscious and hope they do what we ask."

Subada's avatar sat on one of the low benches. "So, they are not only able to stay hidden, but they are also more capable when they

SideSlip than any species I have encountered other than my own. They must have been enhanced, much in the way I elevated your abilities."

Pike agreed, he had not wanted to say it himself, but that was the logical conclusion. "How do we find this other dimension?"

"Well, that part is rather simple, Shep. We just need to get our hands on someone being actively used as a host by the other side. Then I can tease the frequency of the quantum connection..."

Pike recalled something from the meeting with Julian, but he had stopped listening to Subada after suddenly registering what Subada had called him. Even though the alien had used the nickname often, it was one that he'd not heard from anyone but Dewey in almost a decade. So why had he not noticed it before now? Another cog slipped into place as the answer came to him like a bullet to the frontal lobe. "Risse?"

60

"In a way, yes," Subada replied simply. His normally brooding face showed a genuine warmth that struck a chord deep inside of Pike.

"You were Risson Mack, my best friend from childhood? How is that possible?"

"I told you I visited here extensively while I was in training," Subada said. "I told you I requested this assignment from Nianda. Why did you think I did that, Shep?"

Pike went through all the clues, realizing how blind he had been to what was right in front of him. Hell, worse, it had been inside his own head. "Risse was your other?"

The other man's avatar nodded slowly. "Yes, I shared Risson's friendship... his, his love for you, Pike. It may be my fault he became a warrior...a Marine. I was in combat training then, and I think some of my spirit blended with his, just like he became a part of me. Sadly, after he..." Subada stopped momentarily. "When he was gone, I no longer had any direct connection back to you, and you were so isolated, contact proved impossible."

"Why couldn't you have, you know, slipped into me like now?" Pike asked.

Subada turned away. "I tried once, but things had changed...you had changed. All I could sense was your sadness. I felt like I had let you down. I felt I had let you and Risson both down."

Pike smiled, then offered a small laugh. "You and Dewey always did feel like I needed to be protected, like I was some fragile eggshell of a kid."

Subada turned to face him. "Is that what you think, Pike?" The avatar walked right up to stand directly in front of him. "You have it all wrong. We didn't protect you because you were weak. You were the toughest kid we knew, the toughest man, too. You faced shit on a daily basis that we couldn't imagine. Your own brain fought against you surviving. Man..." Subada stepped a few feet away. "The pain you endured was unimaginable. I knew there was nothing Tommy Spars or any of those others could do to hurt you. Not really hurt you. Dude, you were our hero."

"But you're a warrior, an mf'ing intergalactic war fighter," Pike argued.

"Inter-dimensional, but yeah, kind of the same," Subada said, some of his good-natured personality asserting itself again. "I am a warrior, but you, Pike, you are a fighter. Not just that, you are the thinker. You solve problems, other people's problems. Now you need to finally solve one of your own."

Pike knew Subada meant for him to somehow go to Terra and see what was there. He had no idea why, but the very thought of it was filling him with dread. He popped out of the mental construct to stare out at the beautiful turquoise sea. If these were the end days for this planet, no one would ever know beauty like this again. He thought about Emma, a daughter who hadn't even been his, then about Kate, a woman he barely knew but felt like he'd always loved. So much in his world was in chaos, yet looking out at the ocean, the gentle waves rolling in, he was certain this could not be the end. He sighed in resignation. *Damn. A third dimension*. It was out there and it looked like he was going to be the one to verify it. This, this Terra dimension might be the key. Subada was right, he was a fighter, and it was time to get to work.

61

Her finger lightly traced the trident shaped psi symbol on the underside of her forearm. The slightly raised skin along the tattoo gave her a connection. A connection to a man she could not currently feel. The longing was there, the desire, but the man himself was missing. Kate nursed a coffee, a real cup, not the diminutive, yet potent, brew her patron favored. Her eyes took in the surroundings with an expressionless facade that reflected no warmth and invited no questions.

She sat at a corner table of Pasticceria Caffetteria Landi. An actual café with excellent coffee and some amazing baked goods. Pastries that immediately reminded her of both Pike and Palio, neither of whom she was certain she would ever see again. Val couldn't understand her desire to leave the villa. He had almost everything she could ever want right there. *Wealthy people just never get it,* she thought. The simple act of rubbing shoulders with others or reconnecting with memories from simpler times, the smell of fresh roasting coffee and heavenly scents of baking treats filled her with a brief touch of warmth that she desperately needed.

Valerius' driver was waiting a block away, and she felt sure he had others keeping an eye on her. After the brazen abduction from the lab, she had few illusions about the lengths the GTR might go to. Yes, she knew who it was. There was a history. Not one she was proud of, and in truth, she thought she had severed that connection years ago. Still the Office of Global Threat Response was the only one capable of understanding what was going on, much less taking any action. She sipped the dark coffee and broke off an edge of the chocolate-filled cornetto. A woman rose nearby. Her dark glasses and oversized purse would have been out-of-place back in America, but not here on the affluent Italian coast. Chic, gorgeous, and smelling of money, she flowed out the door on an effortless breeze that made Kate wince. "They have no idea what is coming," she whispered to herself.

She checked her watch, sighed, took one more sip, then moved to leave. She'd promised her host not to dally anywhere public. She made eye contact with an attractive man seated across the room. Clearly checking her out, he tipped his cup at her with an appreciative nod that was totally Italian. She smiled as she pushed through the doors to the sidewalk.

The jet that Shepard had apparently stolen had been located at an abandoned airfield in the Caribbean. Valerius had sent a corporate yacht with a team on the ground there now assisting the Australians in the recovery. The strangest thing of all was the military officer who'd cleared the takeoff without a flight plan or destination couldn't recall doing any of it even after being arrested outside his home in Brisbane. Pike Shepard had skills, but he also had secrets.

Kate heard a sound as she turned the corner and saw the driver falling to the ground, blood already pooling behind him. She took two quick steps toward him before registering the threat and turning. The polished woman with the oversized purse stepped in front of her with a devastating blow to the head. Kate's vision went fuzzy, and she tasted the bitter coffee coming back up in her throat. On her knees she watched helplessly as the good-looking Italian man strolled confidently up and snatched her up by one arm, half dragging her toward an awaiting gray Mercedes van.

She saw rather than felt a syringe of something going into her vein.

The GTR, Kate realized as she swam between consciousness and dark. Then, the good-looking man's head disappeared in a misty fog of gray and pink. In a trip that any heroine junky would have felt right at home in, she silently thanked Valerius. Then the pompous bitch hit her again, and Kate disappeared into twilight.

62

The smell was the first thing Pike noticed, then the noise. Even before his visual centers could interpret what he was seeing, his mind had decided it was a stockyard or perhaps an abandoned locker room. One that has been allowed to fester and mature its flavors in the hot sun. Tiny stripes of alternating gray and dark blue appeared overhead. Slowly, his mind interpreted it as bed ticking, the kind that used to be so prevalent. But outside of a military camp, he couldn't recall the last time he'd seen one. There was also another bed above him. *This is a bunkhouse?*

Confusion clouded his mind as the host version of himself slowly leaned up and slung his feet onto the bare cement floor. The room was a large space with concrete block walls. The blocks were painted in a sickly shade of green that made Pike think of an ancient school or... or...prison.

He raised a sleeve to eye level, some sort of rough muslin material. He heard a snort, and then a wet cough from the bunk above as part of a meaty arm flopped over into view. He was certain now that Pike Shepard on this world was a prisoner. *Am I still Pike, though?* He stood and moved toward a small sink and polished, metal mirror on a far wall.

Pike saw his own face staring back at him. His own but one that was far more haunted and dull than his own. This Pike...he knew he had to start referring to him as something else just to keep the identities straight in his own head. Like Rembert on New Earth, this Pike needed a better identifier. He briefly considered PR as those were his initials, then thought back to his own time in the Marines. He searched through this host's history. In the military, they'd had the same combat call sign, Marvel, after a super-intelligent character in the comics, a man named Adam Brashear. "Adam," Pike stated. "You will be Adam."

The man didn't care, he took no notice of his traveler as he moved silently through his morning rituals. He didn't speak or make eye contact with anyone. He ate a bland breakfast of pasty oatmeal and dry toast, then returned to his communal cell. He began tidying the bed, making it up with military perfection. Oddly, Pike saw he then placed pillows underneath the blankets in a way that looked like the bunk was still occupied.

Adam kept a close but discreet watch on the clock high on the wall. At ten a.m. he rose and followed a line of men toward an exterior door that Pike knew led to the recreation yard. Adam and one other man motioned to the guard. "Getting the balls, Boss." The guard nodded his consent, and the two went to a nearby supply closet where a sack full of old basketballs, volleyballs, and other gear was stuffed.

The other guy, a young black man with a ragged scar along one cheek, took the balls and nodded. "You doing this?"

"I am," Adam said. "I have to."

Pike was trying to understand the unsaid thing passing between these two but failed to grasp it until it was too late.

"They're going to kill you."

Adam gave a sad smile. "No doubt." He piled an extra ball on the stack the other man was carrying. "You got word out?"

"Yeah, man. It'll be waiting. Your money was good. Just don't let none of yo shit come back on me, okay? When they ventilate you just go quietly."

The other man hurried past the guard who was still holding the exterior door. They had missed the fact that Adam had stayed in the closet. Pike probed the man's mind but found much of it curiously blocked. Unlike SideSlipping into Rembert, which felt as natural as his own body, this was alien, he was unwelcome here. Despite the similarities between dimensions, something was clearly off on this side of the mirror.

The subterfuge became clear a few minutes later when Adam stealthily made his way back through the bunkroom, recovered a concealed bag of meager supplies, and eased toward a room labeled 'Refuse.' Pike could sense this man was as methodical as he was. He knew the guard schedules, the trash pickups, and every other relevant data point. He'd been planning this for weeks, maybe months. What transpired over the next twenty minutes, Pike would strongly prefer to never think about again.

Clearly, the Adam version of Pike was willing to subject himself to far more levels of discomfort and abuse than he would. As he slid the lid to one side, Adam rose up out of the goo. The pit full of used cooking grease and accumulated waste was everywhere including his eyes, ears, nose, and most unpleasantly, his mouth. No matter how tight he kept it shut he still had to breath, and when he did his head had slipped under the foul brew. Pike wanted to hurl as much as Adam did but both helped fight the urge. The man getting killed escaping prison would not serve Pike's needs. As far as he knew, he was the only one from Earth Prime who could travel here, and somewhere here there were answers.

This version of him was smart, clever even, and had obviously been meticulous in planning this escape. *What is he in jail for...where on Earth are we?* Only the tiniest fragments of information got through the man's mental firewall it seemed.

Pike saw angry flashes of red and orange over the mountains in the distance. Heat lightning, he guessed, just as a pair of shadows flashed by. Drawing from some untapped reservoir of his host's knowledge, he knew instantly from the outline they were the latest UV-9 Whisperjets.

The scramjet engines had been nearly silent despite their enormous thrust.

Despite the sleek aggressive look of the aircraft, this Earth had never had a space program nor ever ventured to the moon. In this timeline, the Cold War had not been very cold. The arms race was constant as was the willingness to battle over every disputed border, every ideological difference, and any opportunity to secure valuable resources. That was how Adam wound up in prison, in fact. A fact that was as confusing to Pike as it was to his demoralized twin from this reality.

The lightning storm was, in fact, a skirmish somewhere farther west, probably over land rights, immigration, or even corporate over-reach. The U.S. of A. here had no problem deploying military assets domestically or anywhere else in the world they might feel justified.

Pike probed his host's mind; this one did not talk back nor seem to notice him at all. This version of Earth was an ugly stepchild of Pike's timeline. Life was brutal here, but the country was not ruled by Nazis, nor was political infighting as prevalent as it was in his world. Something was different, though. For one thing, wealth seemed to be an unknown concept. Slowly, Pike gained more insight from his host.

This Pike's life had felt more like a hand-to-mouth existence. Survival as opposed to opportunity. Despite that, he could feel the intellect, the drive, and the hunger for more within this man. He could also feel the cold emptiness of loss. This Pike had lost a child. This Pike had lost his Emma. That, too, had set him on this desperate path.

Pike dove deeper into this man's memories. He paused to see the visions of his baby girl, her first steps, the special trips they had managed to save up for. Adam had been a good dad, a good man, despite the environment he was occupying. As he moved past the emotional valleys, Pike found himself witnessing news stories and events his world never had. A radiation leak from a midwestern reactor plant in the mid-eighties had poisoned much of the farm-belt causing massive shortages and food riots in the early to mid-nineties. Pope Thomas II was assassinated in New York City in 1994. In 2003, the U.S. lost Alaska to a joint engagement with the USSR and China who had split the territory and annexed an even larger portion of Canada.

Pike's grandfather would have called life in this dimension 'hard-scrabble.' You grew up fast, and you were tough, as there was no other way. While much of this world looked familiar, cars and cities, for instance, looked essentially the same as he knew. Aircraft were even more advanced than in his reality, and he was getting a glimpse at a version of Earth where the Wild West had never evolved. This was a dimension in which racial diversity and gay rights had yet to be heard of because of all the more demanding crises.

Locating the Terra dimension had been simpler than either he or Subada had first thought. After all his other from the third Earth's timeline had used him as a host. Subada dug deep into the mental landmines buried in his friend's subconscious. Ultimately though Pike realized Nianda had left him a way to unlock those visits and clearly saw the quantum path leading back to that dark world. Now he was here but would it make any difference?

The car was waiting, just where Pike knew it would be. He slid in... keys were over the visor. He caught a better look at his face in the mirror and nearly gasped. His host seemed to share the same reaction. The scars, deep lines, and an eyelid that drooped unnaturally over one eye were parts of the face of a man who'd walked a difficult path in life. *And now I'm an escaped prisoner, Pike thought.*

If caught, there would be no second chance, no court of appeals. Justice would be delivered by whatever lawman found him. They would read him the forfeiture act which stated that, through his actions, he voluntarily gave up all lawful chances for incarceration or rehabilitation and surrendered himself and all property he owned to the state. That would be followed by a bullet to the head or, more common these days, the compressed air charge from the tactical baton. Pike flashed on it, a scene from a movie where the cop touched the baton to the head of a man and depressed the trigger, instantly releasing a jet of super-compressed air into the man's skull. It blew the head apart with a vicious snap. The cops here preferred this as it was more gruesome, and they could upload and sell their body-cam footage for serious money. The public's appetite for violence and payback never seemed to be satisfied.

So, who had left Adam the car? Pike probed the man's mind but came away with no answers. While some of this man's world was becoming more open, he was, after all, just another version of himself. Other parts, like why he'd been put in jail, why he was escaping, and who the man was who had helped all seemed off limits to him.

"I know you are there."

Pike mentally stepped back, grasping the thought simultaneously with hearing his voice. This man's voice, Adam was talking directly to him. Not a silent, mental conversation, the man was speaking out loud while looking in the mirror.

"You're me — right?"

Pike was too shocked to respond, and when he tried, he found he was unable. His actions were very limited in this dimension.

"I can feel you. I'm sure you know what I mean. We've known about the other sides for a century or more."

Adam continued to talk aloud although it was unnecessary. Pike could clearly hear the man's thoughts, at least the ones he wanted to share.

"I resisted...we resisted, I should say. I suppose you know by now; it is us who are trying to cause your timeline to collapse, instead of ours. Sorry, pal, no hard feelings and all." The man rolled down the window, an actual hand crank window on this new car. He tilted his head out and spat, the thick mucus globule sailing away into the desert air. He leaned in and looked up at the mirror and tapped at his weather-beaten skull. "You in there?"

"I'm here," Pike mentally said with an intensity blazing white hot with the truth this man had just confirmed.

"Oh, ok, I guess that's you," the host said, his mouth hanging in a lopsided grin. He raked more of the greasy residue from his hair.

"They will be coming after me. Not sure how long I have. Took everything we owned to put this plan together but....well, it won't work."

Pike realized this version of him was mainly talking to himself, talking to hear his own thoughts. He was a tormented soul in ways Pike couldn't quite understand.

"She knew. She was always right, you know?"

Pike had lost track of the man's words but understood clearly who he was talking about. The 'she' who tormented this Pike was Emma Shepard, a daughter whom he'd lost years earlier. Pike could sense the black, cold depths of loss but no mental images; no memories escaped so he could examine them. This was the father's pain which he'd shared for so long. This was the man whose life had infected his own. And then he knew with certainty.

"You were the one who traveled to my world!" Pike felt his rage unleashed and knew he was all but shouting at the man, at himself. "You ran The Project here. It was your technology, your science!" Pike yelled, understanding more of the truth now. If his other heard the internal voice or cared, he showed no reaction. The drooping eye looked in the mirror for a long moment as the car kept speeding away from the now setting sun.

"Here they come," the driver said, looking back.

Pike could see flashing green and yellow lights in the distance. He knew that was the local equivalent of law enforcement here. "This is going to suuuuck," the man said, drawing the word out.

Pike could see the lights each time his twin looked for them in the car's mirror. They seemed too high, not from another car chasing them. Then he knew it was not a police car, it would instead be a small enforcement drone. An autonomous flying copter with non-lethal measures designed to incapacitate a subject long enough for the actual law to show up and pass judgement and then offer a swift execution.

"Shit...tracker," Adam said bitterly. He searched up his arms and quickly ran a hand over his face and neck.

Pike knew the man had feared this. The rumor was all prisoners were tagged with a freckle sized tracking device under the skin upon arrival. His other recalled the shots and test for various diseases. *Yeah, they could have tagged me.* Then all they had to do was activate it once a prisoner fled, and they could zoom right in on him. Strangely, Adam didn't seem that concerned.

Reaching in a storage compartment, Pike's other retrieved a black cylinder with a silver tip. He flipped a lever, and the little unit began to hum. *Someone had planned well for this,* Pike thought just before his other brought the device to his neck and depressed the trigger. The sound of a loud snap of high-voltage electricity and the acrid smell of ozone and burning skin were the last things Pike witnessed before his other passed out.

63

The two men sat facing each other. Pike felt the man's goodness despite Gohr's appearance, which he still found disturbing on a nearly primal level. "I did it, Subada. Not me, but the other me." He took a long pull emptying the glass tumbler before continuing. "That dimension is mired in violence and darkness." The return from what he had been calling the Terra dimension was the most jarring SideSlip he'd done to date. This one had roiled his insides and twisted his view of everything he held onto.

"Reality," the crooked mouth started to say, "is less real than most people believe. Few species can see their mirror world selves. For centuries we thought we were the only ones until the people of Xylos showed us others. I have never heard of any species that had more than one mirror world, Shep."

Pike still couldn't fully come to terms with Subada also being his childhood friend Risson, or an alternate version of him at least. It did help explain the familiarity, the bond the two had already shared.

"This other Pike, his world, they simply want to survive," Subada said, Gohr's voice sounding strained, possibly from disuse.

Pike doubted the little troll of a man ever said much. "They are very determined people. From what I gathered they have fought for eons. War seems to be the first course of action in any dispute. Fights are common even among loved ones.

It's a brutal existence, but still, it's one they don't want to give up, one they are very willing to fight for. It may be that they are unaware of the New Earth and assume if our timeline is terminated, they will live on."

"They have obviously been here...they know how to SideSlip," Pike said in agreement. "To them this world must look like a paradise."

"Much like New Earth does to you," Subada said, pointing a gnarled hand at him.

Pike laughed and told him not to do that again. "It's too creepy."

"This man is a walking horror movie, Shep. I still can't understand how Carapaz trusts him to be his caretaker when he's away."

Pike glanced through the patio doors to the lab where even now Julian Carapaz's body lay, machines monitoring his every breath. Every heartbeat came and went at the appropriate second, but the man was not here. "Julian is an addict," Pike stated flatly. "He will do whatever it takes to keep the high going." Pike was not sure when he realized that what the Coticas offered came with a price. "But he will never return, not in any meaningful way. Living back inside his body here would be a prison, it would be death."

Pike had pieced together the facts until the truth was inescapable. The Coticas allowed the Mizari to not only witness the other worlds but to record the memories. The hunger for knowledge was accompanied by a euphoric thirst that refused to be sated. The Coticas enticed the Mizari via a narcotic effect which increased the pleasure centers to a point that the need for information was a desperate addiction that had to be fed regularly. This symbiosis was not as one sided as it had originally appeared. It was, in fact, the Coticas that were using the Mizari, not the other way around. "Carapaz's own curiosity is literally killing him."

Pike helped himself to the man's very good liquor and offered a silent toast before bringing it to his lips. He was incredibly thankful he had not taken up the man's offer to see Earth's future.

"We need to leave, Pike," Subada said quietly.

Pike knew there was not much more they could learn from here, but the place was isolated and safe, at least presumably so. Carapaz had been extraordinarily paranoid if nothing else. "What's the rush?"

"While you were away, I disabled our evil little friend here and did some snooping," Subada answered.

Fear instantly raced up from the small of Pike's back. "What's wrong?"

Subada was clearly reluctant to say but forced the words out, "It's Kate."

64

Doctor Kate Cassidy tilted her head up. The action brought on waves of nausea. *What did they use on me?* Her sense of time was off. This was the third time she regained consciousness, but she had no idea how many hours...or days, had passed since she had been taken. A fuzzy shape began to form in front of her, a dark silhouette against a light background. It was formless, indistinct, but slowly solidifying into a more recognizable entity. It was a man. As his face swam slowly into focus, her brain finally interpreted that the random sound she had been hearing was the man speaking.

"Doctor?"

Kate managed to fix a single eye on the man. He was relatively young, early thirties, she guessed. Nice looking except for the eyes. They were cold and dark. "What do you want?" Her voice sounded like sandpaper on a rusted pipe.

He smiled. Not an actual smile, just a slight change in the shape of his lips. *A predator's smile,* she thought. "I want to know what you know."

"Who are you with?" Kate demanded, her head still pounding from whatever they had done to her. She was restrained, her feet to a chair, and from both forearms, a thin cable ran through a metal loop mounted into the tabletop. Across from her, the man was staring blankly, the same fake smile barely creasing his face.

"You know who I am with." He pulled out the chair he'd been leaning over and sat down, clasping both hands together on the table. "I am with the same group you are with."

"GTR," she said in sad resignation. The man's smile became slightly more pronounced.

"I'm Alex, by the way. I mean, there is no reason we can't be civilized, right? Would you like something, tea, coffee?"

She'd just had coffee when the bastards kidnapped her. "You killed people to take me. You were on Italian soil. Do you know how many laws you broke?"

Scofield was impressed with the woman; she had not demanded her release. She had not asked where she was or even how long it had been. "We had hoped to do the pick-up on the island, your disappearance forced our hand."

Kate reached a hand up to rub her eyes. The cable stopped her just short of her face, so she lowered her head to clear her eyes and give her time to think. Valerius would be bringing all his assets to bear on finding her and making her assailants pay, but even with his billions, that was small change compared to the U.S. government. "It wasn't me you wanted; you took Shepard. He was the real prize, right? He figured it out, didn't he? Everything..." She raised back up stiffly, a pain in her stomach she recognized as hunger stabbed at her. She must have been unconscious for a while. "How did you do it, have a mole, bug our computers, or was it listening devices? You knew what was said in that conference." Doctor Lu was an admitted paranoid and had the entire facility swept for listening devices weekly. Their computer security was some of the best in the world.

Scofield nodded and pointed up toward the ceiling. Kate's eyes followed the path up. She stared for several seconds before understanding dawned on her. "The lights."

"You were supposed to inform us of any breakthroughs. That was our deal, Kate. Yes, the lights were designed to pick up sounds. Fluorescents flicker at a rate that is nearly imperceptible to the human eye, but we can train a camera on a room with the new bulbs and decode everything that is being said. Passive audio detection that will never show up on any sweep." Scofield then leaned over, maybe to assert his dominance, maybe just to make a point. "Now tell me why, Kate Cassidy, did you not send us the intel before that meeting? Do you not understand what is happening out there?" He pointed back over his shoulder as if 'out there' was just on the other side of the solid metal door behind him.

Kate thought of all the news reports Pike had shown. She had chosen not to watch any TV in Italy. Her little corner of Salermo seemed insulated from the violence and horror going on elsewhere in the world. Now she knew she had been simply hiding from the truth. "Pike didn't share his breakthrough with me." She paused, forcing herself to hold eye contact with the cold man. "My agreement was to share anything relevant to The Fade. Until that meeting I had nothing new to offer."

She hated herself for that. The agreement she had made so long ago seemed like ancient history. Yes, several times the GTR had made a request of her, such as training a new traveler, but mostly they had left her alone, or at least that's what she had let herself believe. "Where is Pike now?"

There it was, Alex thought. The first real answer from the woman. Now he knew her weakness, she had feelings for the man; she hadn't just been using him for sex. "It was a mistake to involve him."

Kate considered this. Why would the Center think that? Didn't they want to get to the heart of what was happening, too? Then a sudden realization struck her. "It was your people at the café in Blackwater and again at the airport?"

"You've been under surveillance since the beginning, Kate," Alex offered as a defense.

"You didn't answer the question."

The agent held up both hands as if to show that they weren't shackled to the table. "I'm not the one being interrogated, good doctor. But yes, we were caught a little off guard by your boat trip into the marshland. We had to make some moves, rash moves as it turns out, but we had no idea then who you were meeting with. Once we learned it was Professor Shepard, someone higher up the food chain decided he should not be involved. "

"Why?" Kate asked.

Scofield shrugged. "Who knows? My guess is that he had no relevant skills to offer, at least on the surface. Bringing him into a highly secure environment was too high of a security risk?"

Secure environment, she thought. *Ha!* She'd almost convinced herself that no one cared what she was doing with Project Cobalt. But the entire time, the GTR had been the ones in control. "But he did have the skills we needed, didn't he?"

Alex was beginning to realize his prisoner was getting more information out of him than he was from her. "Kate, look, you have no family, few friends, and have been working in isolation overseas for years. Who do you think will miss you?"

Kate sadly considered that. Val and Pike, she guessed. She wasn't close to her co-workers, other than Palio. It wasn't a long list. The man was right, he could hold her here indefinitely...he could torture her. Hell, he could kill her with no real repercussions, and she knew the GTR typically didn't care about consequences anyway. "So, what do you want, Alex? You heard the same thing I did. I know nothing more than you."

Alex patted the table, then stood up abruptly. "For your sake, doctor, I hope that isn't true." The door slammed hard behind him with a heavy metal clang as he left.

65

"So, where are they?"

"I don't know, Shep, I'm working on it."

Pike had been infuriated to learn Kate had been taken. Subada had told him he had slipped into Kate, but she was unconscious. Or yes... maybe worse. Then he'd jumped into her Italian patron, who was besieged with grief and rage. Valerius Albergoni had been in conversations with the head of the regional carabiniere commander, whom he was in the process of verbally dismantling.

"There are few facts," Subada said. "Valerius is convinced it is the Americans, but no one seems to be buying it. So much violence in the world right now he might as well be shouting into the wind."

"So, if it is the Americans, then you can find out who?" Pike asked.

"It's not like I know what every member of your species is thinking or doing. I must have a trail to follow. There is an organization, one that Valerius thought of but did not mention when he talked to the police."

"Who?" Pike almost yelled.

"The GTR, something he thought was called the Office of Global Threat Response," Subada said.

Pike scratched his chin, trying to recall if he'd ever heard of that agency. "Nope, never heard of 'em."

"Pretty sure it is the same group that took you prisoner. I am slipping back upstream now. It's complicated in that..."

"We didn't leave many alive at the black site, right?" Pike said, beginning to understand the challenge.

"Right, and no one I have slipped into in Washington seems to know anything about it. I even had one of the people run a search on Stratos and came up blank."

Pike had heard rumors about the super advanced computer system that was supposed to link all the agencies involved in national intelligence together. Apparently, it wasn't just a rumor. Frustration and anger were raging war inside his head, so he faded from the virtual meeting place back to the real world. He stared at the still unconscious Gohr and listened to the telltale monitor beeps coming from Carapaz's lab.

He spoke into the air, knowing Subada was still listening there inside his head. "If this is the same group that hit us on Diego Garcia, then they know about SideSlipping, they know about the other Earth. It has to be them who want to take the battle to the other dimension."

"A fair assumption," Subada stated. "It will also be them who are coming here now."

Subada had admitted to leaving a money trail to this island, a thin one, but enough that if someone really wanted to find Pike Shepard, they could. Now, Pike wondered why the alien had done this on purpose. It seemed reckless, but the warrior had wanted to flush these people out of hiding. Few agencies of the U.S. government coup operate on foreign soil with complete impunity, even in chaotic times like these. "So, you're going to draw them out, and what? Do I just let them take me again? Is that how we find Kate?"

"No...no, Shep, not freaking hardly," Subada responded.

The line sounded so much like his old friend, Risse, Pike had to take a moment before replying. "So, what are we going to do?" In the distance, Pike heard the distinct sound of a small plane.

"Get a travel bag ready, one for both you and Julian," Subada said. "While you do that, I am going to leave a nasty little surprise for our new friends.

* * *

Two hours later, Pike sat in the second seat of the old King Air turboprop plane. Behind him, the seats had been removed so the gurney holding Carapaz could be secured. The ten-year-old plane had been regularly used by Julian and Gohr over the years. The pilot, a Venezuelan, was skilled at low-ocean flying and looking the other way on anything questionable, as long as the price was right. Subada took care this time to pay via one of Carapaz's hidden accounts for the services needed. If the man seemed surprised at the request and then seeing his customer wheeled out to the dirt runway on a hospital bed, his expression did not change.

Pike hadn't spoken to the man other than to exchange a hello, which turned out to not be a universal greeting. Not on this flight, at least. Subada had handled the transaction via Gohr, who he was now inhabiting back at Julian's beachside compound. Pike was on his own, and instead of racing to find Kate, he was playing nursemaid to a man thought to be her worst enemy. At least until today. Subada had somehow forced Carapaz to return home, home in this reality. How, Pike didn't understand. He knew Julian would be facing a long recovery period while his memories caught back up to this timeline. The gap was never fun, but this one could take months. He wasn't sure Carapaz would even survive. His body was in a severely weakened state.

As the aircraft buzzed a few dozen feet above the turquoise green water, Julian Carapaz drifted somewhere between sleep and the afterlife. His body had a gray pallor and was rail thin. The once vibrant man and brilliant mind seemed a shadow of his former self. While Pike had never met him in this dimension, he'd seen pictures. He knew his reputation and his energy. "I hope you found what you needed, Julian." He wasn't sure if the multidimensional addiction to the alien symbiote would even be something one could recover from.

The pilot nudged the nose up to dodge a flock of pelicans, then dropped it again suddenly. The jolt shot fear through Pike like electricity. Dangers were going to be everywhere today it seemed.

66

The little man watched the dark specks falling from the clouds. Gohr had been awoken by Subada, who had also calmed him slightly by embedding a false memory of him secreting Julian away to safety earlier in the day. Subada then suggested that an enemy was coming, one that would have to be dealt with. While Subada expected to feel tension and fear, he felt the opposite from the man. The scarred and ugly man seemed to calm visibly and looked to the skies in anticipation of what was to come. This troubled little human was unlike any other Subada had ever possessed. He was a weapon. This man had a ball of pain inside for so long, he may well have been born with it.

Gohr lowered the binoculars as he saw parachutes open just a few hundred feet above the island. *They will be here soon.* "Time to get the party favors ready," he said in a voice that reeked of pure evil and a sense of delight. Subada had already decided to cause the visitors as much damage as possible. This was the group that had kidnapped Shep and, undoubtedly, had also taken the woman he loved. They needed to be dealt with, and he was beginning to think Gohr might just be the perfect tool to fix the problem.

Subada had made note of the man's fighting skills. He was sneaky and a brawler. He'd grown up in a rough part of Armenia before moving to Tbilisi after his parents were murdered. Even Gohr had no idea how old he'd been then. He'd gone into what passed as an orphanage, a faceless gray human warehouse dating back to the Soviet era. The hunger and sickness were only interrupted by the beatings, fights, and murders among the orphans. They kicked Gohr out into the streets a few years later, deemed unfit for rehabilitation by the government bureau that oversaw the facility.

Subada had encountered many horrors during his travels, and as he nudged into the dark recesses of the bodyguard's mind, even he was appalled at some of what this man had experienced. Part of him assumed if he dug deep enough, he would find a small measure of compassion or kindness. But that drawer was empty. This man was devoid of humanity. He was a weaponized version of hate. Subada questioned the wisdom in making him a better version of that weapon but in the end, offered the knowledge that would improve the lethality of Gohr's abilities even more. There was little chance the man would survive the team of elite agents closing in, but hopefully, Subada could help him make it painful for them. He simply wanted access to whichever one might know who was next in the chain of command.

* * *

"Pike, this man is a one-man war machine," Subada told him, meeting up in the virtual space they had gotten so used to using.

Pike leaned back and closed his eyes, trying to block out the vomit-inducing flying style the pilot had. "Good to hear from you. I take it the agents are on the way?"

"Yes, they are on the island already. Gohr is launching small drones now to give better coverage. He has an arsenal of weapons and a control room in a sub-basement that looks like a perimeter defense system. The little monster has a battle plan, but I must confess, the specifics are escaping me for now."

"You don't know for sure? I thought you know what your host knows."

Subada's avatar smiled in the strange little way he had. "Normally, yes, but this individual's mind doesn't seem to focus on details like that long enough for me to dissect them. His mind is a cyclone of tactics and weapons. You should see what he had under his bed."

"You still think this is the..." Pike tried to remember the group, ..."the GTR?"

"My guess is yeah, or maybe contractors for them. It seems to fit with their operating style."

Pike had wanted to stay and help, but he knew that would have been unwise. "So, what am I supposed to do with Carapaz...why did I bring him?"

"You would have just left him to be taken or killed by them?" Subada asked. "He's a scientist like you."

"We're not friends, Subada. I still don't know whose side he's on. He could be working with Washington for all I know. The commandos show up, he prepares them a lovely lunch, and Gohr serves canapes."

"Pffttt," Subada said with a snort. "Doubt that."

"I'm just saying he's not our friend, he's not our responsibility," Pike added.

"That doesn't make him your enemy, and he could have learned more from the Mizari. Information that we need to know. This battlefield is about information, Shep. The ones who know the most are in charge...that is why you scare them."

Pike considered that it was possible, and he knew national security agencies didn't typically like being at a disadvantage. Still, they had Kate. She was his only real concern now.

"You will be landing in twenty minutes, Shep," Subada said. "By the way, the pilot thinks you're an easy mark. He's going to try to extort more money from you to get Julian to a medical aid ship that will be coming in a few days."

"I am an easy mark," Pike agreed. "I don't speak the language, have no idea where I am, and not sure what I should do next."

"You'll be fine. Just get Carapaz settled in. Hopefully, by then, I'll have the location where they are holding Doctor Cassidy. I'll likely be out of touch the rest of the day, so you will need to handle this, okay?"

Pike nodded reluctantly; he knew his friend was going to be doing a lot of head hopping in the coming hours to get the information he needed. “I know, friend, and thank you.’

Subada’s avatar smiled, then flickered before briefly appearing as Risson Mack. “You got this, Shep.”

67

Gohr watched the monitors displaying both aerial feeds from the drones and a perimeter view from the main house. It was a six-man team, although one appeared to be a woman. He didn't care; he was an equal opportunity killer. "They should have brought more."

Truth was, these odds were very much to his liking. He had fought all his life, always against bigger opponents, bullies, aggressors. He hated his life, knew how he looked to others. Somehow, he'd managed to turn at least some of that self-loathing into a skill, a craft that had made him a desired asset to certain parties. That was how he'd eventually come to know Julian Carapaz. He raised a hand and twisted a knob on one of the display panels, his stubby fingers clumsily twisting at the controls. Technology wasn't his strength, weapons were...any weapon. And, for some reason, today he felt even more confident in his abilities.

Two of the soldiers approached the compound, one from the south and one from the east. They had waited until the sun dropped below the ocean, casting the island in twilight. They were well trained, disciplined and, Gohr had no doubt, very capable. His assumption was that they were American simply due to the M16s they carried, although two had HK-416s. American SpecOps tended to carry a variety of weapons, whatever they felt most comfortable with for a particular mission. Other nationalities tended to all carry the same types.

It seemed ridiculous that the U.S. would risk invading a tiny island belonging to another country, but it had happened before. Back in the early eighties, they had literally gone to war on Grenada, a speck of land only a few hundred miles farther south in the Caribbean. This would not be that type of engagement, though. This one was covert, off the record. Gohr felt sure cell phone signals were already being blocked, and power would likely go out soon. That was fine. The bunker had its own power source, and he had satellite phones, but there was no one he needed to call. It did still trouble him that he couldn't remember where he had sent his boss. The man wasn't in good shape, so maybe he'd flown him by air ambulance to a private clinic on the mainland...*why can't I remember?* Briefly, he wondered if Julian's problems were contagious. Many times, when his boss awoke from his mental trips, he couldn't remember shit for days.

Gohr marked each of the soldier's positions in his mind, then stood. He made one more check of his gear before turning out the lights. He traveled lightly and preferred edge weapons to firearms. He slipped out of the safety of the control room and sealed it behind him. He gave his eyes several precious minutes to adjust to the dim light, then exited through a small drainage tunnel that would emerge on the eastern side of the property. He felt his heart begin to accelerate in anticipation. Several steady breaths controlled it, and he moved silently down the corrugated metal tube.

Minutes later, he had silently moved to within a meter of one of the men. He'd quietly wormed his way beneath the low shrubs until he could make out the man's whispered communications. Gohr pulled a fixed blade karambit from the sheath built into his tactical vest. He'd had the wicked, curved blade custom made to fit his small hand and fingers. Such a tiny thing, but oh, how it loved to sing. He felt the weight, took comfort in its razor edge, and once again felt a surge of confidence that was nearly overwhelming.

The soldier was shifting, probably to get a better view. Gohr could smell the man's sweat. Like a predator, he could nearly feel the other man's anticipation, excitement, and maybe just a touch of fear. Gohr mentally reviewed the other positions, then waited for the man to mic click. That was the check-in signal, he was sure of it. He would likely have a few minutes before the man was to check in again. He moved in speed that surprised even him, propelling his child-like body up and past the man in an instant. His enemy fell forward onto his face, the life draining from a large gash in his throat. Gohr was already moving to the next target. The clock was ticking, and surprise was always his best weapon.

* * *

Subada silently watched the little assassin operate. He had to admit, Gohr probably did not need his help. One pint-sized man up against a solid team of tier-1 killers. Gohr hit the woman next as she was targeting a window on the house. He drove a dagger under her combat helmet as he raced by in the darkness. The blade severed the spinal cord where it met the brain stem, paralyzing her before she died. *Keep one alive,* Subada kept praying. *I need to know who they work for.*

He watched through Gohr's eyes as he killed and felt the exhilaration, not in the taking of the life, but of a job well done. As a warrior, Subada also remembered very similar emotions. That was where his bonding with this little monster ended. The storm of rage and desire to bring terror to others was a maelstrom of hatred in the little man's head. As another of the soldiers went down, Gohr snatched the earpiece and, almost as an afterthought, slashed his knife across both eyes of the fallen man. Subada felt himself going numb to the bloodshed and sealed himself off from as much of the carnage as possible. He was no longer in control of Gohr...the mans' own demons were.

Gohr moved to the next man, but the element of surprise had been lost. This soldier had heard something. He swept his rifle, looking for a target to light up the night vision optics. Gohr threw himself flat on the ground with barely a sound. The clothing he wore blocked much of his body heat, and at this angle, he would blend into the heat signature coming off the still warm ground that had baked all day in the tropical heat. The clock in Gohr's head clicked down to fifty-two. That was when the rest of the team would know something was up. *Well,* surprise was only one of his weapons.

He slipped in the enemy's whispermic earpiece and made his way directly between the next two. He looked away as he tapped a small remote in his pocket, flooding the back yard with light from security lights high above. He hurled a heavy tactical knife at the one on his right, then turned and charged the other.

These two were both close to the house and were disoriented by the blinding light suddenly in their night vision goggles. Gohr heard the sound of the knife driving home just as he leapt up, somersaulting in mid-air as he looped a garrote over the other soldier's neck, his momentum pulling the cable deep into the man's throat. The soldier who'd been reaching to shield his eyes now grasped feebly at his neck.

The earpiece cracked in Gohr's ear. In the chaos, he'd lost track of the sixth man, the leader. He was the one he needed to question... although he couldn't remember why.

"Ox-2, I thought you killed the juice. Why are those lights on?" he heard through the mic.

The man was practically shouting. All pretense of this being just another routine covert 'snatch and grab' op was out the window. *As soon as he realizes Ox-2 through 5 are all down, he'll be going on the defensive,* Gohr thought. The clock in his head clicked to nineteen.

"Don't kill him, don't kill him," Subada said in the diminutive man's head. I just need a name. He needed to get close enough, then usually he could sense who the person was and SideSlip into their brain. He could do it now, but he knew Gohr would simply kill the man, and that would be a waste of time and energy. Subada hadn't managed to find out who the people were that ran the Office of Global Threats, and that was key to helping Pike stop the madness and getting Kate back.

The buzzing of an angry bee sounded as a round whizzed by Gohr's head. The clock in his head immediately reset to zero. The little man knew the one he wasn't supposed to kill was now hunting him. The assassin's training took over, and he attenuated his ears to detect the full path of the round, immediately tracing its flight path back to a small sand dune a dozen yards off the north side of the beach house. The location was out in the open but concealed the shooter well. It also left Gohr nothing but open ground between him and any cover or…the shooter. *Finally, a real challenge*, he thought.

He felt on his back for the kid's backpack he used for his gear. Using his stubby fingers and the muted sense of touch, he extracted several items, knowing the man was out there also trying to center in on him. Already flat against the ground, Gohr crab-walked several meters farther into the open, hoping that would be opposite of where the man expected. Taking advantage of a large tropical flower, he looked at the device he had removed and quickly punched several keys. Almost at once he became aware of another buzzing sound, only this one was not from a passing 5.56 round.

The sound came from high overhead but was obviously descending rapidly. Gohr timed it carefully, jumping up and running stooped over and low to the ground, circling farther to the north to come in on the opposite side of the diving drone. He would have loved to be looking at the camera view from the drone to see the man's shocked expression…maybe he could do that later.

"Don't kill him, don't kill him…" Subada felt helpless watching the little man attack. Gohr was a ball of fury, and despite being outgunned and outmanned, he had been on the offensive from the first moment of contact. Subada kept mentally yelling, then physically doing his best to intervene, but Gohr now held matching knives in both hands. He topped the dune in a diving motion that caught the other man completely off-guard. The heavy drone buried itself into the nearby ground with a thud. Gohr slashed twice, then dropped the knives and climbed out of the shallow depression, watching the man.

The soldier appeared to be completely at a loss. He still had his weapon. The little man had not even bothered to disarm him, yet the gun felt like it weighed a thousand pounds. He couldn't lift it to fire. Captain Rupert Gillam, Jr. of Beaumont, Texas. A former Eagle Scout and seasoned Army Ranger, now on semi-permanent reassignment to the Center, watched helplessly as the gun softly fell from his fingers into the sand. Blood dripped from his empty hand. He realized the underside of his gun arm was sliced open just above the elbow. Likewise, he felt a spreading stain of warmth in his inner thigh.

"You're going to bleed out," Gohr said as he sat down on the sand and drew in a deep breath. He tried to remember if he had even breathed since the first attack. He decided he hadn't. "Sorry, I was supposed to keep you alive."

Captain Gillam sat stunned. This one little man had taken out his entire team and apparently killed him as well. He tried helplessly to call command, but no sounds made it past his lips. He heard the radio calls in his earpiece, but they were becoming fuzzy and indistinct. He watched as the evil-looking gnome sitting a few feet away suddenly toppled over unconscious. Then he felt hands attempting to staunch the blood flow from his femoral artery. Hands...his hands. He also felt strangely calm and certain that things were going to be okay.

68

It was late the next afternoon before Pike had the feeling of the presence of Subada again. He looked out over the isolated bit of beach, thinking again about Kate and how much his world had changed since she came into his life.

"I'm working on a location, Shep, but there is a problem."

"Risse...shit, I mean, Subada, why is there always a problem? You slip into humans at will. You can exert control over them to do — well, almost anything. How can the location of a prominent scientist be a challenge?"

"It shouldn't, Pike, and that is the problem."

Subada told him about the battle on the island and Gohr killing everyone, but not before he learned who the commander's contact was. He'd spent the intervening hours getting Gohr away from the island and head-hopping his way up the chain of command at GTR. "None of these people work for the U.S. government. Not according to anything official. Stratos has only routine civilian files on each of them. The highest-ranking official, the one who handled logistics for the op on La Désirade, is employed as a Senior Commercial Architect for a prestigious firm in Virginia."

"An architect?" Pike asked in disbelief.

"Yes, and that is what his degree is in. He's posted articles in trade magazines. His social media, everything, has this perfectly crafted cover. His office is literally in the design firm."

"But you got into his head...he's not designing buildings, is he?" Pike asked.

"No, of course not. I am just trying to let you know how deep this cover goes. This agency literally does not exist, at least not in any centralized way I can discover. They seem to have taken a cue from the terrorist cells who never meet but operate independently with only a few occasional contacts of no more than one or two people. From the architect, I have a name, a senior man apparently."

"So, go. You know who it is, can't you find him?"

"I have found him...that is to say, I know how to connect to him. His name is Alex Scofield, but I am unable to SideSlip into his consciousness and discover anything."

Pike thought about that. He only knew of one reason that limited Subada's abilities like that. "He's off world?"

"That would be my assumption, Pike, but there is one other possibility to consider," Subada answered in a less certain tone. "I may not be able to SideSlip into him because someone else is already using him as a host."

Pike suddenly stopped his pacing down the beach. "What, you mean our government agents may be..."

"Inadvertently working for the other side?" Subada finished the thought. "Yeah, Shep, that's exactly what I mean. Think on it, as it makes a weird kind of sense. Look, I have to go. I'll meet you tomorrow, and hopefully, I'll know where they're holding her by then. Look, dude, keep in mind breaking her out may not be our most pressing problem."

Pike had already seen far enough down this path to know that. "The Fade. These guys are ready to take us over the brink, and apparently they have the right people in position." He felt Subada's mental head nod before the alien presence disappeared, and he was again all alone, staring out at the water.

* * *

The luxury yacht dropped anchor several hundred yards offshore. Pike had already made all the arrangements using the contacts Subada had supplied. The mobile gurney with Julian Carapaz was carefully deposited into the smaller transport to take them to the anchorage. He had to admit Subada had found them a damn nice boat. The cobalt blue and white vessel had to be well over a hundred feet long. Supposedly, it was outfitted with a full medical ward as well. Julian had still not regained consciousness, but Pike and the local village doctor had kept a check on him since arriving. Here on this nearly uninhabited corner of Honduras was about as off the grid as they'd imagined. Now, though, they had to move.

The GTR had feet on the ground on Carapaz's island. They would find the pilot that had flown Pike to the mainland, and from there they could eventually trace his path through numerous towns as he wove a winding course northward. Pike might have slipped through mostly unnoticed, but he'd initially needed an ambulance for Julian, then a van, and eventually, just a battered old truck. Handling all that in an increasingly dangerous part of the world had drawn more attention than he needed. Once they found the last spot, Subada was sure the GTR would use satellite images to identify everything going in or coming out.

For that reason, Pike had done all he could to be invisible since crossing into Honduras illegally several days earlier. He'd done his best to cover his tracks getting to this isolated stretch of coastline Subada had selected. Now they would have to see if the subterfuge had really bought them any time. The sailors on the massive yacht gingerly lifted Carapaz's limp body onto a gurney and wheeled him toward a door on the main deck. As Pike stepped aboard, he heard the anchor being raised and the muffled sound of the big diesel engines firing up. The entire process had taken less than twenty minutes, and Subada seemed sure the time was within a window where satellite coverage was poor.

The crew welcomed him aboard, and an attractive woman with long, dark hair showed him to a lavishly appointed stateroom. The woman, whose name he learned was Leah, politely suggested he could use the washroom and would find a selection of clothes in his size in the armoire. "I'd like to go check on my...um, friend," he said, before stepping into the luxurious room. While he had no real bond with Carapaz, he did now feel responsible for him.

"The doctors are checking him now," Leah said with a cheery smile. Her long, dark hair and slightly Asian features made him think of the Philippines or South Pacific, but the accent was clearly more European. "Shower and change and I will take you down."

Pike nodded his assent; he couldn't even recall when his last actual shower had been. He felt sure he probably reeked.

Twenty minutes later, Leah led him down the corridor to the medical suite. The lone bed was occupied by Julian, who was hooked to an IV and various monitors. A round-faced man stood at the foot of the bed, his hand lightly patting the patient's foot. He looked up as Pike walked in, and his face lit up.

"Signor Shepard," the man said with a smile as he briskly made his way over. "Grazie, grazie...thank you so much for taking such good care of my child." The older man hugged Pike and pulled him in close, kissing both cheeks. His own face was wet with tears.

"Julian is your son?" Pike asked in confusion.

"Si, yes, I mean," the man said.

"Signor Carapaz, is this your vessel?"

The man looked briefly confused, then bellowed laughter. "No, Pike, Julian is my son by marriage only. He uses his mother's surname. Mine was apparently too much of a burden. Apologies, my name is Valerius Albergoni and yes, this is one of my fleet. When I got the call yesterday, I flew into Caracas. "Julian is my stepson, but..."

Pike saw the pain behind that statement. "He's a brilliant mind, Signor Albergoni."

The other man smiled, and his eyes twinkled. "Please call me Val and thank you for saving his life. I have no doubt what would have happened if you hadn't. I am totally in your debt." He looked back at Julian and moved Pike toward a private seating area in an adjacent room. Both men sat, and a steward placed a coffee service tray on the table between them.

"Oh, man, coffee." Pike smiled as the young man poured both of them a steaming cup before disappearing silently through a nearly unseen door.

"You bring me my son while I failed you, Pike," the man said, sadness clear in his expression. "I am so very sorry about your Kate."

The name slammed into him with sudden realization. This was the Italian man Subada had mentioned. The one who had been protecting Kate before she was taken. *He was Carapaz's stepfather?* Why had he not known that? "Kate was staying with you?"

"Si, she was my guest, and I failed to protect her. She was desperate to find you, Professor Shepard, just as you undoubtedly are now needing to find her."

"And it seems the same people are responsible for taking us both."

Valerius nodded. "We live in interesting times, my friend. I am curious...the caller said you might also know where to find your Kate."

"Working on it," Pike answered before sipping more of the exquisite coffee.

"Tell me, Pike, how were you able to fly a military jet from Australia to here? That was a most impressive feat, and Kate said she was unaware of that skill."

Pike smiled. "Just beginner's luck." No way he was going to mention Subada to anyone. They really would think he was crazy.

"I think this is no true, my friend. You are a most capable man, of that I am quite certain. My Kate would not fall in love with anyone ordinary."

She had talked to Val about me? Pike was filled with love and sadness. Despite his girlfriend's secrets, apparently the bond they shared was not false. "How did you and Kate meet?"

The Italian's face dimmed noticeably. Pike could sense the reluctantly surfacing, buried memories. "It was difficult time. Her sister's illness was in the final stages, as was my wife's, Julian's mother. We both were in pain, feeling helpless, which as you no doubt know is an unnatural place for our dear Kate. I think we both wanted answers and to feel like we were helping in some small way. Eventually, Kate told me about her research project and how she thought it could one day offer hope to sufferers of many of our diseases. After the death of my wife, I invited her to my villa in Italy. We had her dear sister transferred there as well. There was nothing more medically that could be done for her, but we did our best to make her final days a happy time."

"That was very kind," Pike said honestly.

"I saw through her pain, I saw the great intellect, the drive lurking there in that beautiful woman. Julian is very smart, too, but Kate has something more."

Pike nodded, "She does, she has heart."

Val snapped his fingers. "Exactly, my friend. She loves with all her heart. She tackles everything with passion. Very much like an Italian. Can you imagine being loved by a woman like that and then having her stop? It would be like the sun stopped shining."

A thought occurred to Pike. "Were she and Julian, you know..."

Valerius laughed deeply and shook his head. "They were very close. I think Julian wanted more than friendship, but Kate had adopted him as her little brother by then. She loved his mind, but that was all. As you probably know, my Julian can be as cold as Kate is fiery."

Pike nodded. Valerius leaned in close. "I would love to know more about your trip to the mirror world, Professor. The businessman in me is always eager for new ideas. Kate said you had seen other wonders."

"I saw many wonders, Val, yes" Pike offered. "Would any of your companies be interested in a cheap and stable way of producing fusion energy?"

The Italian billionaire's eyes lit up. "Si, si, indeed, that would be incredible. It would be worth trillions."

Pike knew the patents would have an incalculable value, but more importantly, it could offer cheap, reliable electricity to parts of the world where it was now a luxury. Val's company had a history of balancing the profitable business with a large percentage devoted to non-profit or humanitarian endeavors. A partnership with them seemed like the smart move.

Leah glided in and whispered something to Valerius, who stood and motioned for Pike to follow. On the main deck, Pike heard a faint thumping from the distance. "Our mutual friend," Val said, pointing to a dark speck just coming into view.

69

Gohr looked like a child climbing down the steps from the helicopter. Pike was unsure if he was acting as Subada's host at the moment. The alien had been doing a lot of work trying to chase down the GTR leadership and the location where Kate was being held. Thinking of Kate still left Pike with mixed feelings, seeing how much Valerius cared for her, and he was Julian's stepfather. So many secrets, but it did seem clear that Kate wasn't willingly working for the GTR. Hearing Val describe the kidnapping, it seemed anything but willing.

Gohr hugged Leah and then Valerius with a tender affection that seemed out of sync with the man. Then he walked quickly toward Pike, who visibly stiffened. "You help," Gohr said in heavily accented English. Pike knew instantly this was not Subada.

"I not remember much, but I know you help my friend. I am indebted to you." He held out a hand, which Pike shook. Remembering all the things Subada had told him about this man, he was glad to count him as a friend instead of an enemy.

Leah then took the new arrival down to the medical suite to see Julian, who was still in a comatose state but showing signs of improvement. As they left, Valerius walked over close. "That is a good friend to have, Signor Shepard. I told him how you cared for Julian and moved him across hundreds of miles in the jungle to get him to us safely. They have a bond that is unshakable." The man leaned over the rail and studied the water passing by. "Have you ever had a friend like that, Pike?"

Pike smiled, realizing the powerful honesty in that question. "I have, yes. Good friends are a rare find."

"So, what is next?" Valerius asked. "Once we find Kate's location, I mean."

Val appeared confident they eventually would. He had an army of researchers looking everywhere. So far, all he seemed certain of was that she was in America, so they were heading in that general direction. Due to the rising tensions, there was a good chance that American waters might be closed soon. Pike figured it was better to be inside the borders than out.

"Have you ever heard of the GTR?" Pike asked Val.

The older man rubbed his short beard and nodded. "More accurate to say I have heard a rumor of it. Something called the Center. Very clandestine, even by American standards. You think this is the group that took her?"

"I have reason to believe so, yes. We...I traced them to an office park in Virginia. It seems the leadership is mostly embedded deep in other offices. Non-government, unrelated business that would never be on anyone's radar."

"A covert distributed shadow agency," Val said, catching on quickly. "Ingenious, like they took a page from our Cosa Nostra, er...Mafia."

Pike agreed. "I have a name, but it could just be a cover. Alex Scofield. You think your people could find him?"

"If this Scofield has our Kate, then we will find, si. Let me make some calls." Valerius walked away, pulling a smartphone from his vest pocket. Pike looked out to sea; a distant coast sat low on the horizon. It was a perfect day in an increasingly imperfect world.

Meeting his others on Terra and New Earth was a jolt to Pike's psyche. Unlike the other worlds of the multiverse, meeting his mirror twins made him acutely aware that he was not a single entity. His two doppelgängers on the other side, the Pikes he'd begun calling Rembert and Adam, were possibilities, versions of him that could have been. He'd been developing a working theory that one's body is a machine; one's mind is the computer controls. What was not known was that the computer is not a stand-alone node, it is simply one node on part of a much larger network. One that extends across the multiverse.

He needed to speak with Nianda. The path forward was too challenging to navigate without help from someone with a better perspective. He went to his stateroom to attempt the SideSlip to Xylos.

* * *

Pike found it odd that he still used the same mnemonic memory to enter into the quantum slipstream. He wasn't sure it was necessary. He no longer required anything as elaborate as a launch chair, but it was a habit. Now, the memory had a twist—instead of visiting Risse's grave, Risson Mack was standing there. Oh, he knew Subada wasn't Risson, not really, but he was his other, his familiar. He was as much Risson as those other Pikes were him. There seemed to be a fundamental truth in that thought, one he needed to hang onto before he filed it in his mental desk drawer. He was looking out over the rim-world version of Earth.

"Welcome back, Pike Shepard."

"Thanks, Nianda, it's good to be here. Much has happened."

Nianda began to turn, offering Pike a striking panoramic view of the scene and then the living space. "So, I hear."

Seated on a stone bench was another Xylosian, if that was the right word. This one he instantly knew had to be Subada. The two took a moment to catch up while Nianda waited patiently.

"You have discovered a dark Earth, a third timeline? Most unusual," Nianda offered.

"Yes, but I thought your people could sense everything in the multiverse," Pike stated.

Nianda was clasping his long arms behind him as he paced. "We see further than most, but not everything. When worlds drop out of what you call the local network, even we lose track of them. The quantum signatures get a bit too unpredictable to easily follow."

"Is that why Subada has been unable to SideSlip to it?"

"It is part of the reason, but not the only one," Nianda stated cryptically.

The other Xylothian, *maybe that was more accurate*, stood up. "I need to travel to Terra, to help Pike," Subada stated.

"You can help him best right where you are, warrior. He will need your strength."

The response seemed to physically push Subada backward. Clearly frustrated, he

raised his hands questioningly toward Pike.

"Shepard, will you allow me to probe your mind? It will help me if I can see what is driving them to attack you."

Pike had no objections and gave his consent. For a man obsessed with privacy, so paranoid about people knowing personal stuff about him, he was now allowing total strangers, aliens even, to routinely romp through his subdivided gray matter. The truth was, he was willing to do anything to save Kate. Yes...and possibly save the world—but mostly to save her.

"The world you called Terra has the Porta Noctis," Nianda stated.

"Porta what? What the hell is that?"

The Xylothian that was Subada said simply, "The Night Gate."

Nianda was back on the balcony, clearly irritated. "I'm sorry, Pike Shepard, helping your world may not be as straightforward as I originally thought."

"Why not, what's changed.?"

Nianda's hands pulsed a purple color, clearly an expression of strong emotion, but he repressed it before Pike could know more. When he spoke again, it was measured and controlled. "Your kind like to think of life as a journey, a roadmap with a starting point, several destinations, and a clear endpoint to the journey. In truth, life is more like a labyrinth, with blind alleys, pitfalls, and traps. When a species enters the multiverse, we take note, it means they have evolved and adapted to a point of greater understanding.

"Most species that travel do so with aid of an enhancement apparatus much like you did originally. This offers numerous safeguards. Normally, they are passengers in their familiars on other worlds. However, a few like your Terran neighbor, skip that step and develop a very different technology. Something that taps directly into the latent energy of the multiverse. We know it as the Night Gate. Using it to jump can allow total control over the individual on the other side. Also, in time, they will learn how to possess others, not just their familiars."

"Holy shit," Pike said. "It's a good thing we didn't discover it. We probably would have gone down that same path. "

"Oh, you did." Nianda said.

"No, we didn't. I went through all of Cobalt's science. Nothing like that exists."

"No, not *your* project. It was many years earlier, a different culture." Nianda began looking for something in a stack of parchment.

The other alien spoke up. Pike wasn't sure if it was Subada or the native. "Egyptians."

"Yes, yes, that's it. Does that name ring a bell, are they..." Nianda stopped talking. He already sensed the realization coming from Pike's own consciousness. "Yes, your ancient Egyptians discovered the process. It was an unusual time, one of those blind alleys in the labyrinth I mentioned. Numerous dimensions overlapped your own. The most sensitive of your people gained insights. You've no doubt noticed similarities in the very dissimilar cultures of ancient Egypt, Mayans, Chinese, and countless others that were lost to history. They built a crude version of a Night Gate. Only the high priests were allowed to use it, but when they did, they discovered marvelous new lands and strange people. They built artificial mountains to mimic what they saw on other worlds. Read their language and you will see references to many futuristic objects they saw but clearly didn't understand."

Pike was already familiar with some of what Nianda was sharing. He'd seen hieroglyphics that seemed to clearly indicate things like lightbulbs, spaceships, and astronauts. "So, they traveled through and took control of people in other dimensions?"

"No, no...well, maybe," Nianda said. "We don't know, as it suddenly stopped even before my people decided to take action."

"Why would you have taken action? I thought your preference was to simply let things play out naturally."

Nianda's torso rose up and down quickly, what Pike now knew was the equivalent of a head nod. "That is our way now, but many thousands of years ago we were a bit more nurturing. None of us want to see a promising young species destroy itself by acquitting too much, too soon. We feared your Egyptians could doom your entire civilization to The Fade."

"Like what is happening on Terra?"

"That timeline is finished, Pike. They cannot escape it. The end will come. Already, they are cut off from the rest of the multiverse. You're their closest dimensional neighbor, so they are going to turn every resource possible to either destroy your world or to inhabit it."

Pike flashed on Carapaz's analogy of the horde that would infest the inhabitants in a new world, pushing the original consciousness out until it was completely gone. "With the Night Gate, can they occupy the minds of my people for...for longer duration?"

"Yes, Pike, they never have to leave. They can invade your world entirely. While your Carapaz was wrong on many things, he was not incorrect on all of them."

Pike looked to Subada. They both knew where he was heading.

Nianda sat heavily, his hand on the shoulder of Subada's host. "If he is going in alone, Subada, he will need some additional tools."

70

The awakening was as abrupt as a punch to the face. Pike was beginning to feel like every visit to this dark and tangled reality would be this way. Calming himself, he focused on the techniques Subada had helped him with. He shielded his consciousness so this Pike, the one he now referred to as Adam, would be less aware of him. Would it work, would he be able to stay hidden long enough to discover who was behind the intrusions and attacks on his world?

One thing that was quickly obvious: they were no longer in the arid lands of New Mexico. Either Adam's prison break had been successful, or he'd been sent somewhere different to serve out his sentence. Then Pike remembered they would not have put him back in prison, not here in this brutal reality. Escaping from prison was to live forever under a death sentence. Pike's host was trudging through a mud-soaked forest. With each step, his boots sank deeper into the thick clay soil. The humid air and smell of leaf rot permeated the air.

Subada had told him that shielding himself from his host would also make it more difficult to hear and feel the man's thoughts. Some of what he was able to feel was disquieting. Not fear, more like anger or hatred and loss...always the loss. The images passing through his other's mind were a mélange of strange yet perversely logical flashes. One was of his daughter, his Emma, that was so tender and mournful that Pike felt he, too, was once again mourning the loss of a child. Kate slamming the door as she left Adam so many years ago. Not the red-haired beauty that he knew, a dark-haired Kate with deep mournful eyes, but still definitely Kate. They had loved each other... maybe still did. But that had not been enough after losing Emma.

Then, snatches of what might have been the crime that landed the man in prison. A man that was somehow familiar to Pike, yet also unknown. A man that pushed for him to do something... something. He just wouldn't focus on what. Pike knew he could probably urge his dark twin to dredge up the memory more fully, but that also risked revealing himself, which he was reluctant to do. This Pike was not a friend, not an ally. He would fight to save his world, no matter how far off-track it might be. *Who was he to assume that, though?* Pike wondered. Perhaps this world was safe, and it was indeed *his* reality that was facing The Fade. *Would I be any different as a citizen of this world?*

The trees began to thin. Pike saw dark shapes overhead in the fading sunlight. Red-tinged shadows that flickered between tree branches. Flapping wings and inconsolable cries. Then he saw what the murderous crows were feasting on. Adam's eyes glanced back down quickly, but Pike had seen. The first few haunting refrains of a Billy Holiday song rang through his head, "Southern trees bear a strange fruit. Blood on the leaves and blood at the root."

The visiting Pike had complicated and often conflicting views on racism. He had to acknowledge his own heritage and presumed biases as a white man in the South. To him, though, segmenting one group for increasing preference inevitably would lead back to increased prejudice. While Rembert on New Earth had escaped America's racist turmoil, Terra, like his own world, clearly had not. The black bodies hanging far above were just one more offering to the gods of hatred in this nation's blind pursuit to escape an end that seemed inevitable. This world fading out of existence seemed a beneficial pruning in his mind.

Pike could tell his dark twin took no joy in the sacrifice, but as the horrific scenes fell farther behind them, it did not evoke any other emotions either. Adam was too wrapped up in his own hurt, his own loss, to feel anything for other people. From a buried memory, Pike knew the people of this world had mounted a push a decade earlier for gender and racial equality, which had backfired badly. It had polarized families and nations alike pushing many countries to civil war and the U.S. to turn a blind eye to blatant acts of racial terrorism. Inadvertently, this was what had pushed Adam to commit the crime for which he'd been imprisoned.

He crouched in some low shrubs and eyed the unpainted wooden structure for at least twenty minutes before rising and cautiously approaching the backside. A rusted pickup sat off to one side, only three tires inflated. Far off a dog barked, the baying sound of a bloodhound. He froze, listening intently, then heard the chiming of other dogs as they pursued something in the opposite direction. The clapboard siding on the structure was uneven and warped, as if hanging onto the wall studs out of spite. Pike's other pushed an ear to one of the wider cracks and listened intently but heard no sound. Carefully easing to the only door under a rusted tin overhang, Adam pushed the door open as silently as possible and quickly stepped inside, his eyes instantly falling on the twin barrels of a shotgun leveled at his chest. The view narrowed even closer to the dark-skinned finger already pulling the hammer back readying the weapon to deliver its killing blow of buckshot.

"Hello, Risson."

* * *

The wooden chair squeaked loudly as Risse sat down heavily, extending his right leg out straight and rubbing at his knee.

"Still giving you fits?"

"Ugh, damn thing, every time it starts to cloud up. Seems like the goddamn VA would offer some treatment but oh, hell no," Risse said.

Pike knew that the Marine Defense Force had drummed Risse out on a dishonorable discharge after the chopper crash where he'd been injured. His only sin was surviving and being black. In this world, that was unusual only in its ordinariness.

"I guess you saw my neighbors on your way in?"

Adam, nodded, "I did. The crews are getting bolder. Dogs are still on someone's trail out there."

"Shit, fool," Risse said. "We all know the score. Ain't none of us getting out of this alive." He slid the coffee cup on the table closer and lowered his eyes. "They don't hate blacks, I mean, no more than usual. Everybody's just scared, Shep." He raised the cup and took a swallow, grimacing slightly as he did.

"You still making your own?" Adam asked, knowing his friend had never drunk coffee.

"Smooth, brother. Best around. Sides, old cripple like me gotta' do sumpin' to make a living, ya know?" He took another deep swallow of the home brew, frowning less this time. "You still going back up there?"

"I have to," Adam said.

"They gonna be looking for you. Nobody down here gives a shit about a federal escapee from out west, but you made some enemies, Shep. Powerful enemies, ones that going to be on the lookout for you starting up some more shit. You gonna to be hanging in a tree, too, if you get caught."

Adam shook his head. "They wouldn't waste their time, friend. Air charge round to the back of the skull and then toss me in the ditch. 'Death by ventilation' they call it."

Risson Mack pursed his lips and gave a solemn nod of agreement. "She still up there, up there with 'em?"

Adam shrugged, "I guess." He leaned over and pulled the quart jar of clear liquid closer. He unscrewed the brass lid and took a heavy pull. "She would have taken over after..."

"Yeah, I know...after you lost yo damn mind and tried to undo the whole thing," Risse said flatly. "I never understood any of that stuff, other dimensions and alternate timelines and shit. I do know that things just keep on getting worse and worse in tha here and tha now."

The conversation's twists and turns had been challenging for the connected Pike to keep up with. But one thing was evident to him. The 'she' was Kate Cassidy, and that she was one of those in charge of Terra's SideSlip project, the Night Gate. Kate was key to stopping what they were attempting to do. The other realization nearly made him sick. He, Adam, had helped her. Hell, he had been in charge of putting the project together, but apparently, he'd had a change of heart. Pike couldn't get more info from his host without letting his own defenses down, and he still wasn't ready to do that just yet.

Adam was as desperate to get to Kate as Pike was back in his own world. The difference was, Adam was willing to stop her, no matter the cost.

"She still loves you, ya know," Risse said, a grin etched crookedly across his weathered face. "She can't be all that smart."

Adam just shook his head, but inside, he did still harbor some hope, hope that might defeat his goal of stopping the project before it was too late. "I can't think about that, Risse. This is bigger than us. I made that choice years ago."

"You lost your Emma, man; she was my godchild, too. I loved that precious girl. That was why you guys started the Porta Noctis...you knew she was still alive somewhere out there."

"But she wasn't," Adam interrupted. "It was all just bullshit, mind games, and paradoxes. The Night Gate did nothing to bring her back."

"Maybe so, but Kate found something. She found an answer, didn't she? One powerful enough for her to sell her soul to the government."

Silent tears streamed down Adam's face now. Acknowledging the loss of both of the great loves in his life was more than he could bear. He had been the one to start the project, Kate had come in reluctantly later on. When she found out his actual goal, which was finding Emma in some other timeline, she rejected it and him. She said it was morbid and perverse. She had hated him for it, but that hadn't stopped her from eventually seeing the other possibilities of the Gate. That other version of Earth had far fewer issues than this one did. It wasn't perfect, but it was better. The reunification project had been her idea, hers and that damn Alex.

Alex, Adam thought. *Alex Scofield.* The name sent Pike reeling. That was why Subada hadn't been able to infiltrate any further in the GTR. Alex was from this side; he was the one pulling the strings, and if he succeeded, then the two dimensions could rejoin, or more likely, one or the other would fade out entirely. Adam suddenly had a destination, a purpose, and it was not where Pike would have ever guessed.

71

Doctor Kate Cassidy was many things, but weak or helpless were not included in them. She'd been underestimated by her parents, professors, and peers. They all reasoned her radiant good looks and outgoing personality just couldn't be matched to a mind that sharp. That seemed to be the common point of view, and she could tell these government clowns were dismissing her the same way. She was bait for trapping Pike at best, or just a nuisance they wanted out of the way at worst. In either case, she could use it to her advantage. She wasn't sure how just yet but would be ready when the time came.

Increasingly, she found herself alone in the tiny room Scofield called her 'apartment.' It wasn't a cell, but still very much a prison. She worried about Pike. He'd been held by these same people; she was certain of that now. Yet, he'd escaped and freed nearly everyone—how? Clearly, there was more to the man she loved than she realized.

Kate heard someone outside, then the door opened as a dark-haired woman walked in. For the last several days, this had been her jailer. She never spoke, never responded to questions. Simply stood there, motioning for Kate to come with her. The process had become routine. She would be led to the cold, gray interrogation room. A tray of food and a glass of water awaited her if she cooperated. If she resisted, the food was thrown away while she watched. She had not eaten in five days, and weakness was beginning to wreck her system. She'd been dealing with sporadic nausea for much of the past few days. She needed to eat; she wanted to eat, but to her, it was more important to disallow these people any leverage over her.

Her guard forced her into the metal chair and looped her restraints through a loop welded to the table. "They're stepping up their game," Kate said in a pleasant voice that echoed hollowly. The prior days the meals had looked like something from a summer camp cafeteria or even MREs. Today, though, the steel tray was replaced by actual dinnerware, two pieces of French toast, bacon, and fresh fruit, including her favorite, raspberries. They were doing their homework; this would have been her go-to Sunday morning breakfast. It made her wonder how much about her life they knew. Kate stared at the food, her stomach twisting into knots as she fought the urge to shove it all into her mouth.

Out of the corner of her eye, she saw a shadow separate itself from the far wall and approach the table. Alex Scofield's grin was more than she could deal with right now. He pulled the opposite chair out, propped a single foot on it, and leaned over, clearly leering at her. "You really should eat, Kate. You know you want to. Besides, your little protest is pointless. We can always strap you down and put a feeding tube in."

She knew that, but she had no intention of making anything easy for them, especially not this snake. Strange, but she had realized she had met him once before, years ago. He hadn't seemed capable of behaving like this. Whatever was happening in the world now must have unlocked the man's darker side. Kate picked up the plastic cup and drank most of the water. Food she would forego, but she knew better than to get dehydrated. The man across from her just smiled.

"Tell me, Doctor, what was your plan going to be?"

She looked up at Scofield quizzically.

"To stop it?" he continued. "What do you call it, 'The Fade?' What's the plan? Supposedly you know another dimension is the cause. What could you do to alter that?"

That was a question she'd been trying to discover since Pike had spoken it into the world less than two weeks earlier. She shrugged. "I have no idea, Alex."

"No idea?" the man said in a tone that clearly indicated he was unconvinced. "You have the greatest collection of brains devoted to the study of parallel universes on the planet, and you have no contingency plans for this? How much money did the U.S. government spend to fund your studies?"

It was a lot; she did know that. More than even Val had put in. Uncle Sam could manufacture money as it needed. The amount had never seemed consequential…until now. The question had to be rhetorical. The man didn't need an answer. She decided to clarify one point, though. "We didn't study parallel worlds; we studied the multiverse. Not the many worlds theory. The truth is, we have never found a dimension that is even remotely close to this one." She was engaging more than she wanted, but she was curious to know what Alex knew. Nothing she'd revealed would be new information to him.

"Oh, but that isn't true now, is it?" Scofield pulled a small remote and hit a button. Instantly, Pike's words filled the space. The audio was distorted, but still clearly his last morning briefing.

"I slipped to a version of Earth that was so close as to nearly be its twin," Pike said. "We, and by 'we' I mean me and probably most of you at one time or another, have wondered if the many worlds theory or the multiverse theory was right. While each of the dimensions has a version of Earth, none appear to be much like it. None have humans that look like us at all. That would indicate that every other dimension in the multiverse is unique. Planets and life possibly created from similar base ingredients but with vastly different outcomes. But of this group of scientists and travelers, apparently I alone have been to a mirror world of this Earth. That shows that both hypotheses are true."

Scofield clicked the button on the remote, and the room again fell silent. The eeriness of hearing Pike's voice in this awful place made Kate feel just that much more disconnected. She felt the bile rising in her stomach. She fought down the sickness that would give the asshole across from her too much satisfaction.

"He said that both hypotheses are true. Would that mean over there you and I are both in this identical room? Maybe over there you are in charge, and I am being questioned. Have you thought of all the possibilities, Doctor? Of course you have, thought experiments are your specialty as I recall. I feel sure you have played this out a hundred ways by now, a thousand. All I want to know is what would be your best guess on how to stop the other side from whatever it is they are doing?"

"Can't help you," Kate said honestly. "None of us ever saw a mirror world. None of the dimensions were remotely close to this one. If you were listening the entire time, then you know that, and this is simply... theatre." She waved one of her arms around the room until the restraining cable abruptly ended the gesture.

Alex Scofield took his foot off the chair and sat down. He stared at her for a long time, as if he was trying to decide something. Maybe he just wanted her to remain uncomfortable, but she sensed it was more.

"It must be hard..."

Kate knew he was baiting her and clamped her mouth tight. This man across from her was evil, evil in ways she'd never even dreamt possible.

He continued, "The Project was your baby. You knew everything about it. Oversaw every single detail. Then Shepard waltzes in and somehow manages to pull the curtain back revealing all this stuff that was hidden from you. He could even go to worlds no one else could. No, that had to sting, didn't it? Just a little. Maybe a lot."

"Scofield, are you the AIC, or is there any way I could be questioned by someone with a bit more intelligence?"

Anger briefly flashed in the man's eyes. She had scored, but he recovered quickly.

"I am the agent in charge, and you will answer my questions. You and Pike Shepard were close. Intimate even," he began slowly. He could see the rage rising in the woman. "Just hear me out." He patted the air with one palm in a placating gesture. "I am simply saying he may have told you more than he told the rest of the scientists."

"Like what?" asked Kate, unable to keep the harshness out of her voice.

"Like how he managed to go somewhere in a few months that no one else has gone to at all."

"You listened in to everything else. You didn't bug our bedroom?"

"Oh, yeah," he said. A lewd grin on his face. "We very much did, but y'all didn't just screw there."

Kate was steaming now. No way she could allow herself to be dragged down emotionally by this asshole. She had messed up once taking the government's money. She would not screw up with them again. With everything she had, she calmed herself, forcing the rage back into its holding cell. She stared up into the darkened corner of the room where a small red light had been blinking. "What I know stays with me unless whomever is in charge of all you dickless pansies wants to talk to me."

She didn't see the slap coming, but she felt it. Her eyes tunneled into narrow pinpoints as she fought off the tears. *Don't do it, don't cry, Kate.* This man did have a simmering rage, a temper, and he'd just lost it during an interrogation. In most agencies that would not go unnoticed. The GTR wasn't like any other government office, though. Hell, it didn't even exist. Still, Alex Scofield answered to someone.

The agent was leaning over directly in Kate's face now. His own anger had tipped over the boiling point. When he spoke, droplets of spittle peppered her face. "You goddamn bitch...you've always been a bitch. What is Shepard planning?"

"Is that the way you talk to your boyfriend?" This time she was ready when the hand swung. She lifted her arm, trapping his in the cable restraint, which she then snatched down as fast as she could. His wrist smashed into the side of the table. The sound it made was sickening. It might not be broken, but she'd scored a hit. Undoubtedly, it would be a pyrrhic victory, but damn, it still felt good. He screamed at her again, bent over, and holding his wrist, backed away from the table. Briefly, Kate wondered if he might have a gun. Then the door opened, and the brunette woman came in and pulled him away. Again, the door slammed closed.

Kate lifted the tiny cup and poured syrup over the French toast and began to eat her first meal in days. She smiled at the camera as she bit into a plump red berry. No, she would not cooperate, nor would she play their games, but damn...raspberries.

72

Pike opened his eyes to find himself staring into the face of a nightmare. Slipping back to his own reality was less of a shock now, but it still often left him unsettled. Seeing this hideous man so close nearly sent him over the edge. "Hello, Gohr."

"It's Subada, just wanted to screw with you, man."

Pike found himself embracing the man, who was his friend despite his current appearance. "Jerk! Listen, Subada, I may have a possible location." Pike began to tell him some of what he'd learned from the other dimension.

"So, why do you think that is where they are holding Kate?"

Pike admitted he wasn't sure. "I think fate, or the Universe, or whatever just has a wicked sense of irony."

"But if what you say is true, Kate may be the real enemy over there. She could be the one pushing your world into The Fade."

Pike was sitting on the side of the lounger. "I know, I know. I'm still working on that, but I suggest we get moving in that direction. We should talk to Valerius." A steward approached with a tall glass of lemonade. As tense as things were, Pike couldn't complain about the accommodations.

Gohr's head nodded. The familiar ragged scars lining his face had a new collection of battle wounds Pike had not noticed the prior day. "He's still down with Julian." Gohr looked away briefly. "Say this for the man. He is loyal. Even after all Julian put him through, he still cares deeply for him."

"And Valerius is okay with you…I mean, Gohr being aboard? I know he welcomed him earlier but I assumed that was just because he worked for his stepson."

The look of confusion on Gohr's face took a moment to register. "Ah…yeah, well, Val was the one who hired him…to look after Julian. Gohr worked for some questionable families in Italy for a while. Valerius has an eye for talent and managed to acquire his services."

"Gohr survived the assault on the island," Pike said with obvious respect. He'd known that already, but still seeing the wounds brought it home. They were fighting a real enemy.

"You should see the little monster in action. He is methodical, precise, and absolutely ruthless."

"So, how is Julian doing? Any change?" Pike asked, rising to his feet unsteadily. Gohr reached an arm up to support him with a surprising amount of strength.

The little man gave a shrug. "Still the same. Val's doctors know very little about the problems of time dilation. No one knows how drug addiction in a parallel world might affect our physical bodies back home." He turned away. "All they can really do is keep a check on his vitals and let him rest."

Pike looked out the open door at the turquoise waters.

"What's wrong?" Subada asked.

Pike remained silent for a moment and just leaned against the door, looking wistfully out. He could taste the salt, and it made him long for home. "It's Kate," he said, finally. "Not my Kate, but the one from the Terra dimension. "She's bad, Subada, like the cause of all this."

"And you wonder if your Kate could be that person." Gohr walked up beside Pike and glanced out. "That kind of person," he amended.

Pike gave a nod.

"Shep, we are all a product of the choices we make. Our lives are built layer upon layer by choices, actions, and consequences. I imagine, despite the differences between you and your other in that realm, you probably noticed more similarities than differences."

"He was me," Pike conceded. "Different, darker...riddled with pain and guilt, but yes, he and I are much alike."

Subada laughed. "And if the version of you from New Earth were to visit you here, then he would likely use the exact same description of you."

Pike thought on that for a long moment. He watched a seagull swoop down and steal something off a dining table where Leah was sitting. "We all have the capacity for good or evil?"

"It's less easily defined but, in essence, yes. Is Kate or Pike in that dark world fighting for Terra to survive all that wrong? They might be heroes, not villains. Asking one man to give up his life to save a loved one is one thing. Asking one man to give up his world to save someone else's would be inconceivable to most species."

"I just don't know what to think anymore," Pike admitted. "I've spent my life trusting my mind to solve increasingly complex problems. Now I can't even know if my memories are my own, much less right from wrong."

Subada reached Gohr's arm out to place on Pike's. "You are a good man, and you are my friend. We will get through this. Nianda would not have allowed me to stay if it were impossible."

* * *

The yacht had been sailing north at top speed for over twenty-four hours. As they neared the coast of the United States, they became aware of heightened security. The yacht's captain reported the coast guard's demands to enable the DTPOs transponders as soon as ,they were within range. Patrol boats and several Navy ships littered the horizon. The yacht was under U.S. registry, so they would not normally be required to report to the customs dock. Odd, since few of the guests aboard were from the United States and in one case, not even from this same world.

Pike watched the familiar coastline slipping by. *Why here?* He heard a moan from the medical bay. Julian Carapaz had been semi-conscious for the last few hours, but totally incoherent. His mind was a mess, and his body still hovered near death's door. Pike had sat with him for several hours earlier, so Valerius could reluctantly get some much-needed sleep. "We could use your help, Julian," Pike had said to the husk of a man lying under the sheet. For some reason, he felt sure Julian knew what was about to happen.

The massive boat eased into a space at the Port Royal Marina that just barely accommodated her. Pike had known she would be too big for the city docks he often used in Beaufort. After everything of the past few months, fate had brought him home again. Home to Kate, he hoped.

On Terra it had been obvious to his double where Kate and Alex would be. A remote section of the Parris Island military base in South Carolina. Pike nearly screamed inside the man's head when the thought flashed by. According to Subada and Valerius, the GTR operated without fixed offices. They 'borrow' space, facilities, and equipment as the need arises. Apparently, an old lab and holding facility on what was the Marine base a few miles from Blackwater was what they had chosen. Pike had dwelled on that ever since. He and Risse had been around that base all their lives, then both had gone to basic training there. Risse had even been stationed there later in his career. *Was that just coincidence or some form of cosmic fate?* It also made him question his Kate's arrival at his doorstep. Maybe she had already been in the area. After all, if this was the government's test site for off world activity, wouldn't that have been of interest to her?

The small group had discussed numerous scenarios on how to get onto the base. The doctor onboard had assured Valerius that they could provide for Julian as well as any hospital and to simply allow the patient to stay aboard. Valerius seemed eager to see the town of Beaufort and reserved all the rooms in The Cuthbert House B&B for him and his staff. Gohr, Leah, and Pike were tasked with finding Kate.

"Can you find her?" Pike mentally asked Subada.

73

After a scenic drive on mostly back roads, Pike pulled to a stop in front of a building that must have looked old when Lincoln was a child. He hated to involve anyone else, but there was one person who knew everything about the Parris Island facility. He ignored the front door and instead took a side porch, stopping by an old gray drink box to retrieve an icy cold soft drink. He popped the tab as he turned the corner to the back of the ramshackle structure.

"You owe me a quarter for that, Shep," a gruff voice said.

"You know you're losing money on those. Drinks haven't been that cheap in a long time." Pike knelt down to scratch the ears of a brown dog who barely registered his presence. A man in overalls, that at one point may have been blue, was mostly underneath a motorcycle frame suspended by chains from an overhead beam.

"It's okay, I've been covering for your broke ass since we were kids, anyway. I know you're retired and on a fixed income now. Stop coddling Ralph, too. He's already so damn fat and lazy the rabbits don't even run when they see him."

Dewey moved toward him, then muttered, "Just love how you show up out of the blue like this, Pike." The big man ambled by on his way to get another beer. A raucous sound erupted from his backside as he passed. "And before you say anything, I didn't fart, that was just my ass blowing you a welcome home kiss."

Pike looked down at Ralph, who had raised his head slightly at the noise, then nestled it back down on his paws to continue his nap. "And don't bother my dog, he's had a busy day of battling monsters and mailmen."

Ralph gave a half snort before rolling over and facing away from the two humans. Pike squatted and scratched the dog behind the ears again. His back leg twitched, but otherwise, he gave no acknowledgement of the attention.

Pike stepped off the low porch to the ground. "Ralph still loves me more than you, that's what you can't stand."

The large man put a wrench down, grinned through a smear of grease, and popped the cap off the beer. "Everybody loves your dumb ass better, Shep, but you're too stupid to know it. What happened to the redhead? You run her off, too?" The mechanic put his beer down and moved toward him again with a single step as he wrapped Pike in his giant arms. "Good to see you, man. Been worried about you."

"Good to see you, too," Pike said. "Why the worry?"

"Shit, man, all the crap going on. You guys left so quick, then that shit up at the airport and you know, just everything. I came out to that toolshed you insist on calling a house a few times just to see if you came back. But of course, you were AWOL or too drunk to open the door."

"Yeah, look, Dewey, I um..." Pike was unsure how to ask what he wanted. Dewey was the third part of the gang, best friends since before first grade. He and Risson Mack had formed the committee that kept the weird kid with the seizures from diving off the city bridge. "I'm not sure where to begin, but it's damn good to see you."

"The same, brother. You need to stick around more. You must let the Lowcountry creep back into your soul." Dewey sat down heavily on the edge of the raised, wooden porch.

Pike looked around, thinking how remarkably Dewey's place resembled Risson's cabin back on Terra.

"So, why are you here, Shep? You didn't come down just to check out your other pretty lady over there." Pike saw a corner of his motorcycle peeking out from under a gray tarp.

He sat down heavily beside his friend. Ralph walked slowly up rearranged his seemingly dissociated parts to wedge between them. "I need some help...Kate's in trouble."

Dewey shook his head, removed his ball cap, and wiped his nearly bald head with a mechanic's rag, leaving more grease streaks. "Well, shit, why didn't you say so! I like her, and Ralph approves, and you know how big of an ass he can be." They both looked down at the dog that looked like he wouldn't voluntarily move anymore in this lifetime, and possibly the next. "Pretty obvious that something had kindled with you two. I'm not a real trusting sort—you know that, but I didn't get any red flags with this one."

"Unlike the last one?" Pike replied, already knowing the answer. Dewey and Pike's ex-wife had never hit it off. Emily was beautiful and talented, but Dewey had always been fiercely protective of his slightly smaller cousin. 'That girl is trouble, Shep.' That had been his first and permanent pronouncement shortly after meeting Emily.

"You've always had shit-luck picking the right girl, man, but I ain't gonna speak ill of the dead. I don't need no bad karma raining down on my ass for that. Let's just say this one got the right juju for you." Dewey stood up and fetched another cold drink from the cooler. "Here, too late in the day to drink alone." He swapped Pike's half-finished Coke with a beer. "So, what kind of trouble and how can I help?"

Pike downed several deep pulls from the can. "Couple of things. You still have access or friends over at the base?"

"The Marine base or the air station?"

"Marine," Pike said. The air station was on the other side of Beaufort.

Dewy thought for a minute, clearly uncomfortable with committing to doing anything as risky as Pike might be suggesting. "I may have some friends," he finally said.

Pike nodded. "I don't want to get you in any trouble, Dewey. I've known you all my life. You beat up Charlie Stimson in first grade because he was picking on me."

"Actually, Risse did the deed on Charlie...I just had to threaten." Dewey burped and laughed at the same time, making a sound that was both gross and somewhat inhuman. "I remember that day. Charlie was making fun of your damn highwater pants. They must have been two sizes too small for your skinny ass."

"Hey, I grew fast as a kid."

Dewey eyed the tall, solidly built man beside him. "You did, Shep, you did, but your momma did dress you funny. I have to side with Charlie on that one."

Pike wished there was a way to introduce Subada to Dewey. He felt sure both of his friends would pick right back up where things had ended so many years ago.

"You want to know if you can trust her?" Dewey said, finishing a thought that had been plaguing Pike for the past several days.

"Yeah, buddy, I guess so." Pike stood and eased over, peeking under the tarp at the Indian. "I'm pretty sure she is over on Parris, just not totally sure it is against her will. Have there been other incidents, anything else you know of? There seems to be a lot more going on than I can get into right now."

Dewey played the redneck mechanic to perfection, but Pike knew his cousin just used that as a cover. He was as sharp as anyone. While his career had been as colorful and eclectic as the pile of junk rusting in the edge of the nearby woods, Dewey was a bit of an unexpected prodigy who could discuss topics from quantum field theory to the decimation of coral reefs in Australia.

"Lots of craziness around, Pike. You heard about that shit over in Charlotte. We think someone tried to bomb the Marine base, too, but you know, we're a small town. Off the radar, not much happens here. Hell, not even General Sherman thought it was worth his time to burn the town when he marched through."

That was not entirely the way the story went, but Pike got the point.

"Getting onto the base, though—that's going to be a big ask. Just tell me what you need. I'll do whatever I can to help you get your girl. You know that."

"That's just it, man, I don't know yet. But yeah, I think we're going to need to get onto Parris Island."

Dewey tilted his bottle up high and let it drain down his throat with a satisfying sound. "Do you have any idea how tight security is right now? Do you remember how tight the Capitol security got after that mob stormed it after the election? Imagine that several times over, friend."

"Well, shit." Pike knew he should have assumed that. Tensions were high, the nation was on high alert. Of course, the GTR would be embedded some place secure. He had Gohr and a disembodied alien warrior. What could they possibly do?

"Something else you ought to know," Dewey added slowly

74

"You don't know who it is?" Dewey had just told Pike he thought someone had been staying at his cabin. While he'd already decided going there wouldn't be a smart move, he didn't like the idea of someone else setting up residence there. Despite his bulk, his cousin Dewey was a hell of a hunter and could track nearly anything. If he said someone had been there, it was true. Now Pike needed to know who it was.

"Screw the cabin, dude. If you're planning on storming Parris Island, you need an army...and the Navy," Dewey said.

Pike was still trying to work the problem, and this new distraction was just one more piece that didn't fit. He fished a new phone out of his pocket and thumbed one of the few numbers stored. Valerius had assured him the devices could not be tracked. They were custom made in small numbers by his own factory outside Milan.

"Speak," Gohr's gruff voice answered.

Pike told him what he needed and hung up.

"You sure that's a good idea?" Dewey asked.

"Nope," Pike answered. "We need to catch a break, and this is the only way I can think of." In very general terms, Pike had shared with

Dewey what he could of the events of the past few months. He left out everything to do with Subada, though.

An hour later, Dewey, Pike, and Gohr were all in position, staking out Pike's cabin. While there was no obvious sign of recent activity, the place definitely was giving off a 'lived-in' vibe. Tiny sounds of possible movement inside, a smell of cooking food. None of this made sense to Pike. Very few people knew of this place. Also, it seemed certain the government would know the location by now and be staking it out just in case Pike stupidly showed up. Which, of course, he just had.

Pike eased over to a large trash can he kept near the side of the house. As quietly as possible, he raised the lid and peered inside. The others saw him lifting several items up to inspect, then closing the lid again with a smile on his face. He seemed to mentally check off several facts before moving on. He now was pretty sure he knew who was inside.

Easing up onto the porch, he made his way to the door and knocked softly before trying the handle. The door was locked, but he soon heard footsteps, and the door opened a crack, then swung wide.

"Hello, Palio, making yourself at home?"

The young scientist rushed onto the porch and embraced the older man. "Oh, my God, I...I thought I would never see you again," he said. "Are you injured? Did they hurt you? How are the others?"

Pike motioned with his head for them to go inside.

"Yes, yes, of course, how stupid." Palio turned around and entered the dimly lit interior.

Pike could see the remnants of a takeout container from an expensive restaurant in downtown Beaufort. Looking around the familiar space, he saw Palio had done some things right, like hanging dark sheets over the windows to black out light. A bedroll and toiletry kit were perched on the sofa. "You could have used my bedroom."

Palio blushed and nodded. "It didn't feel right." He looked around at the mess he'd made. "I didn't know where else to go." Then he got a puzzled look. "You didn't seem surprised to see me."

"No one else I know would break into my house and eat gourmet pastries. I saw the bakery wrappers in the trash."

Palio nodded. "Are you alone?"

Pike almost said no, but then considered the question with more scrutiny. How was Palio here? How had he made it off Diego Garcia? "Yes." Gohr and the others were undoubtedly listening in via the open comms channel on the phone. All of this seemed a little off, a bit phony. And after all, where were the GTR agents?

"Look, Palio, they have Kate."

The young man put on an expression of surprise, but he failed in the attempt.

Subada popped into Pike's head. "Just wanted to see who it was and, Pike, I might be able to SideSlip into him now." Seeing who it was, Subada could obviously sense Pike's growing assumptions.

"You know who they are, don't you?" Pike said to his former assistant.

The look on the young scientist's face spoke volumes.

Dewey's voice was in his ear, whispering, "We have movement in the woods. Should we engage?"

"Tell me what you know, Palio. Where have you been and how involved are you?"

Palio looked at the floor. He swallowed hard, and glancing back up, tears filled his eyes. "I am so sorry, Professor. I never thought it would come to this."

"Shep, do we engage?" Subada, back in Gohr, asked him more urgently.

Pike was trying to pay attention to both conversations and work the problem, come up with options. What got him closer to Kate? Then he knew. Mentally, he sent word for the others to stand down and take cover. He covertly fished the earbud out and tucked it into the cushions of the recliner he was sitting on.

"You were feeding them intel the entire time, weren't you?"

Palio was visibly shaking now. "No, it wasn't like that. I thought they were trying to help us."

"You were the one framing Carapaz. Making it seem like he was the cause of all this." Pike's voice had deteriorated to a low growl. He could now sense a very agitated Subada back in his head and clearly heard sounds of movement just outside.

"Ten agents in full tactical gear," Subada said internally, then added, "We could take them."

Pike smiled slightly at the man's, or alien's, confidence, but he was pretty sure he was correct. Gohr was probably straining at the leash to be let loose on the bastards. The door splintered as something hit it hard. "Let them take me, but be ready," he said internally.

"Ok, friend, but I'm with you if you need," Subada stated.

Pike saw the twin taser barbs flying toward him even before he registered the man standing there. Deciding quickly not to be too obvious, he moved sideways enough to dodge one of the barbs. The other pierced his side, just under the ribs. The numbing electrical charge never came. Pike felt himself moving again like a warrior, a superhero. He was unsure if this was Subada or just the instinctual knowledge the aliens had given, but he was thankful. The attackers using a taser instead of a bullet let him know they wanted him alive. That was useful information and meant he could likely get away with a lot more.

He launched himself at the second guard, smashing an elbow into the man's nose. The first agent was busy trying to decide what to do with the useless taser. Pike spun around and connected a boot to the back of the man's head, sending him headfirst into a nearby wall.

Shadows and smoke filled the old cabin as more men rushed in, and someone stupidly tossed a stun grenade in past the breeching team. Pike instinctually closed his eyes, opened his mouth, and plugged his ears. The blast affected Palio and two of the other agents much more than their intended target. Pike had removed a large walking stick from a rack and proceeded to crack open the skull of one man and subsequently jam the other end into the throat of one more. He was only trying to make it look good, but soon five of the agents were down, and they hadn't touched him. He turned for the door just as something else punched into his chest. Looking down, he saw the feathered dart. The world went black as he fell.

75

"Mister Shepard, welcome back."

Pike came back to reality with a splitting headache and a room that was too bright from overhead fluorescents.

"You should take these. The after effect from the ketamine can be nasty," the faceless voice offered.

Pike's eyes focused on a hand, pushing a clear plastic cup in his direction. Two small capsules lay next to the cup on the gray painted table that looked to be a holdover from the last world war.

Pike reached out an arm to the table, realizing he was shackled. His handcuffs were connected by long chains that went down to somewhere below him. He could free up one arm only by lowering the other the same amount. He took the pain relievers and sat back. He was where he wanted to be. All day he and Dewey had worked on potential plans to get him on the base, and in the end, it was simple, just get caught.

"I am Agent Scofield, and you are going to help me, Shepard. Do I make myself clear?"

Pike shrugged. "Sure, whatever."

The agent moved closer, blocking out some of the light. His face slowly came into focus. It was a familiar face, but only from his twin's memory on Terra.

"You need to take this seriously, Professor. You escaped from a federal security camp; agents were injured. Some died. That's on you." He clicked a button on a remote and the scene of Pike fighting his way out of the black site prison in New Guinea played in high-def on a massive TV mounted high above.

Pike watched the scene, somehow both fascinated, and detached. His memories were of fighting beside his friend Subada, but in the video clip, it was he alone doing it all, inflicting all the damage.

Agent Scofield fast forwarded to another clip, this one outside. A jet airliner landing in the distance. Then Pike saw himself and Kate. This was the airport in Charleston. Pike watched that fight with the gunman unfold. He knew what the agent was going to say.

"You were a Marine, a good one by all indication, but you never saw action. You had self-defense training, passed with marginal scores on your PT. Your FFI called you quite mediocre. So, you see my confusion."

Pike did but remained silent.

"How does a man go from an average fighter to a killing machine in a few months working in an isolated laboratory?"

"They had a great fitness center and lots of pilate's videos," Pike offered with a faint smile.

Rage flared in the agent's eye. *This man wants to be just as infuriating as his girlfriend*. "Funny, really damn funny, Shepard. Okay, tell me this, since you are so clever, how did you figure out your many worlds theory about The Fade?"

"I'm just a really smart guy, ask anyone," Pike said smugly. The blow knocked him out of the chair as stars exploded behind his eyes. Unseen arms lifted him, and the chair was placed beneath him again. This was turning into the black site all over again. Before he was too injured or drugged into oblivion, he had to get close to Kate. Subada couldn't use him if his body wasn't functional.

"Look, Scofield, I'll make a deal with you. We don't have to be on opposite sides here. You clearly have the advantage. I concede there is no getting away this time. Why don't we have a more adult discussion?"

Scofield was now sitting on a small sofa against a nearby wall. He was eating an apple, as if the scene playing out at the table didn't involve him in the least. "I'm listening," he said before taking another large bite.

"I assume you have my..." he almost said 'girlfriend' but decided not to give them even more leverage... "colleague, Doctor Cassidy. I would like to see that she is unharmed."

Scofield let out a breathy chuckle, "Colleague...right."

Palio had told them everything, Pike concluded, or the whole base had been bugged. "Yes, she was not in the jungle prison, so I assume you brought her to the states. I'd like to see her." He glanced up at the TV, her face frozen on the video. "I'd like to see her in person."

"And you think she is here?"

Pike was very sure she was, but let the man play it however he wished. "I don't care where she is, Agent. If you want me to talk, make sure Kate is in the same room with us."

"Professor Shepherd, you aren't in any position to be making demands," Scofield said, his voice rising. "Other than your little stunt overseas, have you seen what is going on out there? Riots in almost every major city, entire police forces laying down their badges and walking off the job. Mass shootings in multiple states. Rumor is, Pakistan is threatening India with a tactical nuke. Nuclear war, Shepard, and you want your goddamn girlfriend to come and hold your hand while you answer a few questions?"

"We like together time, what can I say?"

Pike enjoyed the enraged look once more. Something the other side had taught him was that they only appreciated force and power. Extraordinary little to laugh at in that dimension, and the Alex here was clearly unaccustomed to sarcasm or disrespect.

"Pike, I am still unable to enter this man's mind. He is clearly from the Terra dimension."

Subada's voice inside his head was calming, but the information was not a surprise.

Pike answered subvocally, "That's okay. There are two guards behind me in the shadows. I haven't seen them, but I know they're there. Can you slip into either of them?"

Moments later, Subada came back and said, "No. Neither of them."

"Great. See what you can do to ratchet down some of the tensions with the superpowers, okay? I'll be fine." Subada's presence seemed to reluctantly fade from his mind.

"Give me something, Pike. Something I can take to my bosses so they can see if they could locate the good doctor," Scofield said.

So now he was going to play the good cop. It was tired-assed trope from every crime show Pike had ever seen. He considered the man's words. He was from Terra and apparently had no clue of the existence of New Earth. Pike couldn't give that piece of intel up, though, not yet. He considered what they already knew from listening to his morning briefing at the lab. "Our others from the other Earth are able to SideSlip into our subconscious brain and influence us. Influence us to do terrible things. They have the same tech as we do," he said. While technically, that was not entirely true, it was or should be new information and close enough that it might win him some points.

"How much influence?" Scofield demanded.

Pike smiled but kept his mouth shut. After a full minute, Scofield gave a single head nod, rose, and went to the door banging hard to be let out.

* * *

"Shep?"

Subada's mental voice pierced through the growing fear in Pike's brain. He knew the situation he was in was dire, and worst of all, he'd put himself here. He had hand delivered the GTR exactly what they wanted. "Yeah, I'm here." He closed his eyes and mentally shifted gears to converse with his friend in the mental construct. Once again, he found himself on the balcony overlooking the valley of that very alien version of Earth.

"You okay?"

Pike smiled. "Dude, you can sense everything going on with me right now. You know more about my mental and physical condition than I probably do."

Subada nodded. "Honestly, your heightened emotional state is all I can sense from you right now. You need to see Kate, I get that."

"What about the agent?" Pike asked. "Are you able to SideSlip into him yet and get us the hell out of here?"

"Sorry, no, friend. This is not his world. His other is firmly in control of the Alex from our side."

That had been the assumption, but having it confirmed again did little to ease Pike's worry. "So, he is the one from Terra?"

Subada shrugged, "That would be my guess, but no simple way of knowing."

"What about Kate? Is she okay, can you make sure she's..." Pike found he couldn't finish the sentence.

"Can I make sure she is 'your' Kate? Yes, Shep, I've done that already, and she is. She is also one very pissed off human, so be prepared." Subada turned and looked out over the nearly perfect view of Xylos. "I assume you have a plan."

It was a question, but not one Pike could answer. He had, at best, the vague components of one but offering himself up at the house had been rash, an impulse move at best. He knew Subada could probe his conscious mind and see nothing as well-formed as a plan was present. "Working on it. Dewey okay? And Gohr?" Pike was surprised at the growing level of fondness he had for the diminutive assassin.

"We are fine, all together. They only wanted you. Palio was taken away as well, but he seemed to go willingly, which I guess is not a surprise. They also did a number on your house. Sorry, man."

"Do you know how they got to him? Palio, I mean," Pike asked. The condition of his home was way down his list of priorities today.

Subada didn't answer at once. Finally, he turned and said, "They first tried to use his sexuality against him. It would have brought shame to his family. They have very old traditions and biases, but Palio was defiant. Then, well, they took his little sister."

Palio is gay? Pike had never considered it, not that it mattered. He'd also never mentioned a sister, or family.

Subada managed to share some of Palio's thoughts on what the GTR was doing. Pike understood better the emotional and mental stress they had put his assistant through. What's worse, Subada had done his own investigation revealing the little girl had died or, more likely, been killed shortly after being taken. Palio did not know that. He thought what he was doing, betraying his friends, his research, was what was keeping her alive.

Shit! Pike nearly said out loud. He heard the voices outside the holding cell. *These are supposed to be the good guys. I am an American citizen, so is Kate.*

"He is coming back," Subada said. "If it is any consolation, it doesn't seem like his superiors know what Scofield is doing. Normally, they would not allow this within the confines of your country, although I still don't understand why that is any better or worse. With so many developments happening, they just have their hands full. Crisis management, I believe you call it."

Pike heard the latch on the door begin to open.

"Let me know when we need to act," Subada said before ending the virtual conversation.

Two guards entered the room with a very uncooperative figure struggling between them. Pike saw the leg restraints and the chained wrist cuffs identical to his own. But it was her hair he recognized first. The beautiful red hair now matted and tangled. Then his heart skipped a beat as their eyes met. "Kate!"

76

Pike couldn't take his eyes off her. This woman whom he had known only a few months consumed him fully. She appeared mostly unhurt, tired, bruised and unkempt, but he could see the intensity burning within her at once. She hated her captor with every fiber of her being, yet seeing Pike, her expression suddenly radiated pure joy. Joy that Pike felt just as strongly and had just as much trouble hiding as she.

Agent Scofield nodded to the two guards, who moved back into their standby positions in the shadows. He moved Kate to the chair across from Pike. Her feet shuffled because of the chains, and it broke his heart to see her like this. Her face was unsmiling, but Pike could see the happiness in her eyes. Once seated, she stretched out her hands to him. He tried to take them in his, but his own shackles prevented that. He struggled briefly, attempting to move closer, and eventually lowered his left hand below his seat, allowing him to extend the other hand just far enough to touch hers with a single finger.

"Hey, you," she said in a tone that nearly broke his heart. She knew she was leverage, expendable, and that her love for Pike might very well be his undoing.

Pike nodded, "Love what you've done with the place."

They both grinned as they glanced around the sterile concrete box that held them and then smiled. Pike caught the look in Alex's eyes and was momentarily confused by what he saw. *Was that jealousy?* The agent looked ready to kill them both.

Scofield nodded to the guards. "Get her out. That's all you get for now, Shepard. She's okay. You want to keep her that way, you need to cooperate—fully!"

"No deal. We stay together, or you get nothing from me. I don't trust you people."

Scofield violently jerked Kate up by the wrist chains. "I don't care who you trust."

Kate used the opportunity to deliver a knee into the crotch of the agent just before the guards got to her and pushed her against the wall. Agent Scofield flinched, but then smiled.

"That will cost you."

Pike assumed that the actual Alex back on Terra could likely mute the pain sensors, so a blow that would have most guys writhing on the floor was barely felt. Some of what the Night Gate allowed was beyond his understanding, but this man was having no trouble being in charge. As Scofield closed in on Kate, Pike knew what was going to happen even before it did. Alex backhanded her across the face.

Pike watched on helplessly as spittle and blood spurted from her nose and lips. "You son of a bitch."

"Get her out of here," Alex ordered. "I need a minute." Scofield rubbed at his groin and left the room again. Pike was seething with anger and concerned for Kate. Whatever he was planning had to happen fast. Whatever he was thinking, he knew that fight was not destined to happen here. He needed to work the problem. He repressed his anger, as his analytical brain was already trying to understand the motivation for Scofield. Why was he so focused on his two prisoners? If he was indeed from Terra, what threat did the two of them pose to their plan?

Pike knew Scofield already, knew his 'other's' thoughts in the mirror dimensions. How much of a threat was that knowledge, though? He and Kate were an unknown risk to whatever scheme the other side had, nothing more. Keeping them locked away might make a perverse kind of sense, but still, there was a more visceral hatred coming from the man. It was very much the same feeling his twin on Terra had when he thought of Alex. The look came to him once again. That tiny instant of affection between them. *He's in love with Kate. His Kate, over there. They're obviously more than just collaborators.* The thought felt right but didn't sit with what his Kate had told him about the bond that they shared across the multiverse. *Shit, this is more than I can handle.* He needed sleep, a good meal, and a bourbon. The door opened again, and Alex Scofield strutted back in. Pike would not be getting any of those things anytime soon.

77

Pike lost all track of time; the only real reference point he had was his growing hunger and fatigue. Some of the mental conditioning Subada had helped him develop was helping, but there were limits to what the human body could endure. To be honest, it wasn't the physical stress as much as the emotional that was wearing him down. He also had to admit that the GTR agent was quite effective in his role. The guy was a hardass, but at just the right moments he would suddenly soften and be sympathetic. The effect was to keep his prisoner off balance and vulnerable. More than once it had worked.

"We are about done with this session, Pike," Scofield said as he pulled a tan envelope from his notebook. "There is just one more thing I want you to see."

It took Pike a moment to understand what he was looking at. Scofield had fanned out an array of vivid color photos across the table. Dead, mutilated bodies lay sprawled randomly across a scene of perfectly manicured landscapes of palm trees and tropical flowers. Crime scene photos, Pike realized.

"Miami Beach, eight months ago. Lowes Hotel, you might have heard about it. I believe that was not long before you first met Doctor Cassidy."

"Mass shooting, yeah." Pike forced himself to sound unconcerned, but the images were horrifying. One woman lay next to a man in a business suit. He could only tell it was a woman by the body and bloody dress. Her entire head was missing. Nothing but a smear of red across the lush green grass.

Alex focused on the same photo. "That was the former first lady of Florida. She was one of the first, just after her husband."

"What has this got to do with me?"

"Colonel Thaddeus Lewis," Alex said. "Active duty served his country for decades. A model soldier, in fact. Now he holds the honor of being the deadliest mass shooter in American history."

"Again, what does this have to..."

Scofield cut him off, "You know what good old Thad had to say when they arrested him?"

Pike shrugged, clearly thrown by this new line of questioning.

"He had no memory at all of doing any of it for days. I've seen videos of the interviews. He couldn't accept the fact he had done any of it, especially killing his beloved wife."

Scofield began gathering up the photos but left one. A black-and-white image of a blank-faced man sitting at a table much like Pike was right now. The older black man had puffy red eyes, and a haunted look.

Pike recognized that look, he'd seen it before. Colonel Thaddeus Lewis was suffering from the gap.

"He was one of hers, Pike." Agent Scofield nodded toward the door. "You don't know your girlfriend as well as you think. And the shit you guys were doing is causing all this mayhem in the world. Whatever you are bringing back from the other side wants to kill us."

Pike was left there for another half-hour, just him and the image of the poor man. He knew Colonel Lewis' finger may have pulled the trigger, but it was not him in control.

* * *

Pike was returned to his room; the restraints removed. A tray of food that looked exactly what used to come out of the Marine barracks kitchen sat on the small table with a bottled water. As hungry as he was, the brownish chunks of unidentifiable meat swimming in a sea of greasy liquid turned his stomach. Or maybe it was the photos. He made himself eat and greedily attacked the water. He wanted to talk to Subada but needed time to work the problem alone. Subada was a good friend and a great warrior, but as far as Pike could tell, not mentally superior. He had a more complete repository of knowledge, much of it very helpful, but Pike needed to find his own answers.

Scofield showing him the images had been a deliberate move to separate him emotionally from Kate. Sow the seeds of doubt, a little mistrust, put some cracks into the bond that held them close. Pike took it differently, though. He knew there were parts of the program Kate had not disclosed, including Carpaz's stepfather being one of the main financial backers. Pike was aware of a government connection, the EAS flight, and the agent Winfield in Portugal, but Kate had never offered much more. She may have been ashamed or, more likely, forbidden from discussing the military's roles in her project.

Pike fought to keep the wretched meal down. His stomach was already sour from hunger and was now offering up multiple protests at the meager offering. He lay back on the thin mattress. His eyes searched overhead briefly, then located the small, green light in the corner of the ceiling. Of course, they were watching. *Let 'em*. He closed his eyes and entered the mental construct, his first time here alone. He could invite Subada easily, but now he just wanted freedom to think.

The key was Kate on Terra. A woman he'd never met but who was running the project to attack our world. Maybe he had met her. Why would she not be here alongside her partner? They didn't need to hold his Kate prisoner, simply have Terra's Kate possess her. That was another thing their gate allowed them to do. Total control when they came here, but he was nearly helpless over there? One other fact he'd learned from Adam's memory was they had no prior knowledge of the multiverse. None had ever ventured onto any of the more alien worlds.

They simply knew of this one, their mirror. *Do they know about New Earth?*

Pike Shepard's avatar eased into a seat at the ledge. A storm was brewing down the rift valley. A smell of rain was already in the air. *They know about it now, thanks to me. They also know of the multiverse after spying on Kate for so long. They must think we are further along than they are with SideSlipping. That could be a threat to them. What factors contributed to a timeline being saved versus deleted?* He and Subada had spoken on this more than once, but the answer was still unclear.

He recalled Subada saying, "The likelihood of a species thriving either through sustained population or intelligence growth seems to be the main factor that keeps a dimension on top."

The memory of Subada saying those words was as clear to him as if he were standing there doing it now. So, New Earth, despite seeming to be a better version of this world, might not be the clear winner. Likewise, Terra, just because of the brutality and hatred, might not be the loser. Alex and his people clearly thought this world was the one that had to go. *If I were over there running The Project, what would I be doing to make that happen?* Pike wondered. As his conscious mind drifted off to sleep, completely wrung out from the day's events, the answer slowly came to him.

78

Gohr placed a tender hand on his friend, Julian. Subada remained in the background of the little man's mind. They deserved this moment of privacy. Despite that, whatever knowledge might be locked in Julian's own head was desperately important. Subada had tried many times to slip into the man, only to find nothing but blackness. The gap the man was experiencing was pervasive, as was the addiction. An addiction so profound it extended across the multiverse. The symbiote beings, the Coticas, provided a vision of other worlds' futures, but at what price?

Valerius entered the grand saloon where his stepson's bed had been placed. The medical team had released him from round-the-clock care. Physically, Julian was on the road to recovery. Val knew that was only a part of the battle raging within the boy, an exceedingly small part, he feared.

Now he learned that Kate was indeed also here in the U.S., and her friend Pike had been imprisoned as well. Despite all his wealth, in the end he'd been powerless to protect any of them. The damn GTR had destroyed the very thing that might save them.

"Consigliore Albergoni."

Valerius looked up from where he had sat down, deep in his own thought. Gohr was speaking to him. "Yes, yes, my friend."

"Julian will be okay. As will your Kate, and the one you call Pike Shepard."

"How can you know that Gohr?" Despite the bodyguard's loyalty and unequaled brilliance in battle, he was a simple mind. Rarely had he spoken so many words in one outing.

"They battle enemies I cannot see, but I can feel. It is not a war where my skills are helpful. For that, I am profoundly sorry. I do know they are on their mission, though...I know it is vital that they succeed. Whatever small part I might play, you know I will."

Subada silently watched the exchange. He did help his host get some of the words out, but the thoughts were purely Gohr's own. Likewise, Subada was also feeling helpless, feeling like he was letting his friend down. Nianda had allowed him this quest almost as a fool's errand. The Fade was inevitable the old man had said. But not even Nianda had realized a third timeline was in play. One that, so far, only Shepard had been able to SideSlip to.

Subada left Gohr and Valerius and slipped once more into the poisoned darkness of Julian Carapaz's unconscious mind. He was determined to find an answer, something that might help Pike Shepard save this world. Even as he did so, he could feel The Fade pressing ever closer. The end was coming.

79

Pike slept soundly for several hours, then lay unmoving in the darkness. He attempted to contact Subada with an urgent question, but didn't receive a response. In his sleep, he'd dwelled on the thought experiment. Again, he considered game theory. He was well aware that Adam had slipped into his mind at multiple points in the past. The false memories of Emma, but also other things, bits of knowledge, barely concealed jealousies he'd glimpsed when he returned the favor and slipped into Adam's world. That version of him had not done so in quite some time. Not since being banished from The Project and presumably being arrested.

That version required machinery to SideSlip; Pike knew that he did not. The fact it had been so long also meant the dark Pike was unaware of Subada or Xylos. That was important. That was an advantage he couldn't reveal to anyone.

He didn't want to risk slipping into the other world. If Alex came to get him, he might figure out that Pike had mastered the ability to jump using only his mind. Still, if his crazy, bullshit idea of a plan had any chance of working, he had to try.

* * *

The air was dark and heavy. Terra had a permanent smell, Pike realized. Since everything here was normal to his other, he'd never really given it much thought, but lying here on this bed in the old wooden cabin, it was obvious. A feint smell of rot or decay. It seemed to permeate everything.

"I feel you."

His own voice came back at him through the crisp night air. In the other room, Risson Mack was snoring heavily. A sound eerily familiar to the night sounds his version of Risse had once made.

"I know you can." Pike pushed that thought out. He'd failed utterly in communicating, much less controlling Adam. In fact, he was the one who felt like a prisoner in this world. How many times had his other invaded his mind, paraded through his dreams? Made love to Kate, or even Emily, years earlier.

Adam apparently still could not hear him. That was a problem, as Pike needed this man's help. Nianda had given him some additional ways to communicate. It was time to try them out.

"You and Kate and Alex are pushing your hate into my world in an attempt to destroy it. You have to stop."

"Kate?" Adam asked.

Only a single word of those thoughts had gotten through, Pike realized in frustration.

"Kate is... Kate is unstoppable."

Pike wasn't sure if his twin was just whispering to the night or countering his plea.

He was able to monitor the flow of his other's thoughts. There, when he thought of Kate, what was that?

"The Porta Noctis," Pike said in a hushed, mental voice.

Adam smiled. "The 'Night Gate.'" Then, the man's full understanding of his Kate's project flooded into Pike's thoughts.

They've recruited a SideSlipping army of mercenaries to do battle on our side. Alex Scofield is just the sharp end of the spear.

"They are already there. I am sorry for all the carnage, but it was the only way," Adam said.

"Where is the Porta Noctis? Just on Parris Island?" Pike asked.

Adam didn't answer, but Pike saw it. Mental flashes. Locations all over the country, hell, all over the world. Thousands of individuals, some of whom were well known in our world and others that were nameless entities. What these people were over here was nothing compared to who they might be on the other side.

"Where is Kate? Where is Alex?" He was sure he already knew but wanted Adam to fixate on it.

The man yawned and rolled over. "You have to stop this, Pike. Your world is over, my friend. You are in The Fade, just like us. All we are doing is borrowing a few of your years."

"What is driving your Kate to do this?" Pike mentally pushed so hard he felt the man gasp. "You have to stop her."

Parris Island and Beaufort, South Carolina, looked very different in this world, but some things remained the same. Adam's mind had presented a mental slideshow of the Night Gate facility; Pike could see the night sky beginning to brighten outside the filthy windows of the cabin. He sent one more thought, more of a nudge, but the strongest he'd been able to manage. "You need to go to her, you have to stop this." Then he added, "Tell Risse."

The man began to snore. Pike slipped back to his even darker bedroom in a cell less than a thousand feet and one universe away from where another version of Kate Cassidy was apparently attempting to destroy them.

* * *

The ridiculous next session of questioning went for nine hours. Pike increasingly sought refuge inside the mental construct. Dangerous, but necessary to protect his sanity. Scofield was only present via an intercom a few times, and they had not resorted to torture, not yet at least. A dark-haired woman had done most of the interrogation.

Pike had demanded to see Kate but had been ignored or emphatically refused each time. All he could think of was an evil version of Kate working away diligently in a place almost like this one. Over there, she was prepping soldiers to mentally SideSlip into this world with the sole mission of taking lives, creating havoc. He thought back to some of the names and images he had seen from his doppelgänger. "Fred Granger, a popular TV evangelist. An attractive country music star, several powerful politicians including Jonston Kresse, the senior senator from Maine, who was currently the minority whip. Most likely, they recruited people on that side who had not achieved what their doubles here had. Who knew how many more Colonel Lewises were out there right now plotting the next step in bringing this world to its knees?

That wasn't even the scary part. All they really needed to possess were a couple of world leaders and then start throwing nukes at each other, and The Fade wouldn't even have to finish the job. We would have done it for them.

Finally, the nameless woman going through the same list of questions left the room, and Alex Scofield walked in. Unlike Pike, this man looked fresh and energetic and smelled like he might have just stepped out of the shower.

"Good afternoon, Professor. Sorry, I was otherwise engaged. Your Kate is a delightfully interesting woman. I am sure you know that already."

The man's parlor tricks of manipulation were so obvious as to be laughable, but despite that, it had the desired effect. Rage flashed across Pike's face before he could get it under control.

Scofield leaned in close. Pike could feel the hatred emanating from this man. "Tell me about New Earth."

Fear stabbed Pike right in the gut. Damn him, he had hoped that bit of intel hadn't made it here. That was obviously a fool's wish. He couldn't let them go after that timeline. No way that reality had figured it out, conquered war, disease, pollution...even space travel.

"Fuck you."

Alex smiled, "Elegant, to the point. Clear and concise, as always, Professor." He turned and nodded to the camera mounted in the corner. "Shepard, I need you to understand the stakes are higher. Multiple countries are now at war. ICBMs have launched on several key targets. I should not tell you this, but we are on a military base.

They are on high alert, troops being deployed, aircraft being readied. Within 24-hours, the United States will be involved in a limited nuclear exchange. We just aren't sure against whom yet. Now, tell me what you know about New Earth."

Pike started to give the same response as one of the nameless guards opened the metal door and half pushed and half dragged a rumpled version of a man in. The face was a bloody pulp, but the dark hair and small size could only be one person. Palio.

Scofield moved his foot out of the chair and had the guard pick up Palio and place him at the table. "Pike, now listen, this is very important." Pike was only focused on his friend. Yes, the man had worked with the GTR, supplied them with critical information, but Pike didn't believe he'd done any of it willingly. Palio had been brutally beaten, deep gouges across his face and arms. One eye was closed shut and leaking a milky red fluid. It broke Pike's heart. The kid's beautiful, brilliant mind being abused for the simple reason of leverage.

Pike saw the fingers snapping in front of his face. "Focus, Shepard. Now, as I was saying, you are going to tell me everything I need to know, or your friend here will leave this Earth because of you. Do I make myself clear?"

Alex pulled an item from behind his back. A long square tube with a boxy handle that didn't belong in this world. Pike knew fully what it was, and its very existence horrified him.

"I know this device probably doesn't mean much to you. A little something I had our R&D guys working on. We just sold the patent to H&K for a large sum of money. Heckler and Koch, the weapons manufacturer. You see, this is a gun that fires a round of compressed gas. Dry nitrogen in this case. We call them air rounds. Almost 6000PSI. When the round contacts the skull, it simply passes through the bone then expands exponentially, literally exploding the contents from the inside. Your little friend here is going to get to demonstrate for you if you are not giving me the answers about New Earth. Once he is gone, I will be moving on to Kate Cassidy."

Pike knew Palio's fate was sealed. He was no longer of any value to the GTR and knew too much to be turned loose. Nothing Pike said would change the outcome. This was simply Alex Scofield's macabre sense of theatre, using the boy to make a dramatic point. Still, when Palio's one good eye met his, his heart broke even more. He wanted Subada to slip into his friend and end Scofield's life. He wanted the malevolent entity possessing the agent to be removed. Palio offered a silent pleading look. Pike knew the boy was sorry for betraying his friends.

"Does he know?" Pike asked, turning to Scofield. He was simply buying time and offering the boy a measure of peace, but maybe that was enough.

"About what?" Scofield asked. His grin was predatory and anxious. He smelled blood and was already in anticipation of the coming kill.

"That you killed his little sister. What was her name...Iyana? She was dead, what? Within a week after her kidnapping, yet you forced this brilliant boy to work for you for how long?"

This was clearly information that Pike Shepard should not have, but Scofield remained nonplussed. "I told you, Shepard, the world has changed, the rules have changed. Things are going to shit out there. Do you think anybody gives a damn what happens to this little cunt?" He rolled his wrist and checked his watch. "Twenty seconds, Shepard. Tell me about New Earth. Specifically, I want the quantum frequency you used to access it."

Pike ignored the agent and focused on Palio. "Kate and I both know they forced you to do what you did, Palio. Do you understand me?" Pike hated knowing what was about to happen. He hoped Subada might rush in, the Marines would break down the door, something... anything. Still, he knew it was inevitable. All he could hope was to give this kid peace if he could.

"Ten seconds." Scofield was tapping his watch now.

Pike shook his head subtly. Palio's one good eye dropped in disappointed understanding. "Please take my body back home to my mother."

The nearly imperceptible sound of the gun discharging cut off his request as Palio's head exploded like a ripe watermelon being dropped from a tall building. Pieces of skull, brains and skin covered Pike,

Scofield and much of the room. Pike watched on, horrified, as the kid's lifeless body sagged forward.

"Well, shit," Scofield said, wiping something beige and sticky from his chin. "You see what you did? Now I have to get another shower." He turned to leave. "Hope you're more cooperative tomorrow, Shepard. For Kate's sake, I do."

Pike just stared at the headless corpse, thinking sadly about how little blood there was. A cleaning crew came in the door just before they ushered Pike out. He wanted a shower as well. He had bits of Palio embedded in his skin, his hair, and covering his clothes and body. He was not offered any way of getting clean. Scofield wanted him to live with the consequences of his silence. It took all his control to keep the rage at bay. *Jesus, Pike, you need to focus on the plan.*

80

"Damn, dude, what the hell happened to you? Oh...never mind, sorry." Subada had slipped into Pike's mind and immediately saw the memories of the recent event.

"Where the hell have you been?" Pike demanded.

Subada's measured, resonant voice in his head did little this time to calm Pike from the emotions he was experiencing. Palio dead, the world in crisis, and Kate somewhere close, but going through what?

"Julian is struggling to regain consciousness. I was attempting to guide him back."

"Did you learn anything?" Pike asked silently.

"Only fragments. His broken memory is still trying to catch up to the timeline here. Hold on, Shep, let me go check on your Kate."

Subada's presence leaving was like a cold wind, and almost as suddenly, he was back. "She's sleeping. Physically seems okay, just an emotional wreck. They showed her a video stream of Palio's death."

Ok," Pike said. "Thanks." Pike thought back through what all he had wanted from Subada. How much was still relevant?

"I want to know about Julian but first probe my memories from Terra. See if you can identify more of these people in their Night Gate Project. Scofield said a nuclear exchange somewhere was already underway, and the U.S. would be following within the next day. See if you can identify any of the people who might be initiating this."

There was so much more Pike needed to know, but the rest had to wait. If the United States launched part of its nuclear missile stockpile, then whatever happened after was meaningless. The Fade would be inevitable or possibly, unnecessary. Pike mentally sent the list of other items he needed to know realizing Subada could answer them at the same time.

"You got a lot," Subada said, "but it is going to take me some time to track even just the ones you recognized. The others I can figure out if we have time. You know SideSlipping into any of these people is not something I can do if they are already host for their Terran counterpart."

"But you can get close to them, find a superior, someone who can get in their way or shit, just kill them," Pike said.

He felt the mental anguish from Subada. "They are drones, Pike, they are not doing this by their own free will. I am prohibited from acting against innocents. Nianda will intervene, possibly restrict all of my efforts here."

"They aren't innocents if they're bringing about the destruction of this world! They are the gateway to The Fade"

"I'll do what I can," Subada agreed. "As for the other unspoken questions, I still can't jump into Scofield, same reasons. He apparently never leaves the host body on this side. I don't think you have to worry about your twin slipping back into you, as he needs the equipment at the lab over there to do so. I can provide some mental blocks that might slow him down if he tried. And no, I am still unable to SideSlip into that reality's time stream. I believe Nianda's theory is correct, Terra is already cut off from the network."

"Why? How can they control us, but I can barely even communicate with my other over there?"

"The quantum entanglement that binds your worlds is tenuous," Subada answered. "It may just be the Night Gate. That is a tool I have never encountered personally. While the effects should be equal, I think your world is experiencing decoherence at a faster rate."

Pike had already considered decoherence as a possibility. In the quantum state, they described it as a loss of information, but he tended to think of it more as a loss of connection. It might be a precursor of one world dropping out of the local multiverse network.

"I am sorry, friend, but it seems much of this will be on you," Subada offered with an unusual edge of weariness.

"And we're running out of time, aren't we?" Pike asked.

Subada could tell his friend was thinking mainly about the pending execution of Kate. That was Pike's personal viewpoint. But he'd also accepted that the fate of all humanity was at stake. Subada had also learned something else about Kate Cassidy but elected not to share that with his friend. He felt it would just cloud Pike's mind even more than it already was.

"Pike, we are all the sum of our parts. Our better angels and our darker selves are simply mirrors of who we are. The Pike, Kate, Risse, and even Scofield over there are not as different from the ones here as you might like to believe. We are all heroes in our own stories, you must remember that. They feel justified in doing whatever it takes to save their world."

Pike nodded in the dark cell. The creeping desperation eating away at him with every passing second. "What can I do? They have an army."

"You know what to do, Shep."

81

"Fool, you done lost yo damn mind."

The Terra version of Pike downshifted the old GMC pickup, rolling through a stop sign and then accelerating away. Black smoke billowed from the exhaust. His friend was right. He had lost his mind...probably. Had the Pike from the other world visited him last night? It certainly felt that way, but even he admitted it could have been a dream. Whatever happened, it had motivated him even more to at least check it out.

"You know if we get stopped, they going to put you down. You have a black notice out on you."

"That's from New Mexico, We're in Georgia now." They had crossed the state line coming in from Alabama before sunrise.

"What I is trying to get through your thick ass skull is you are a wanted man, and I am black. Now, I don't care all dat much about you, but I prefer to be alive at the end of this day. Hanging around you could be hazardous to my health. God almighty, Shep, you should come with a government warning label or something."

"Okay then, Risse, why did you come?"

"It's my truck, fool. You think I'm just going to let you steal it?" Risson Mack sat back into the frayed vinyl seat, smiling despite his words. "So, what makes you think that woman will even see you? She could just tell da guards to hold yo ass til the cops come."

The dark world Pike had to admit, his friend had a point. Still, he had to try. "I don't know, Risse. We had a child together. That has to mean something. We loved each other once."

Risson Mack didn't understand any of the science Pike and Kate were into. His friend since childhood was his hero. Pike had saved him from drowning when they were just kids, and Risson had vowed to never leave his side. That got a lot harder as the years passed, especially when Emma got sick. He watched the barren fields stream past as he thought about that child. She had been the bright light in all of their lives, and then she was gone. He had no idea about the Night Gate, but knew it was born of that darkness. "How long to South Carolina, I have to pee."

Pike looked at his watch and did a quick calculation. "Three hours or so. Roads get a little tricky near the coast, so may take a bit more. I'll pull off now if you think this old beater will start again afterward."

"This truck's a classic man, just like me. Leaks a little, though."

"Right...just like you," Terra Pike said, pulling to a dirt lot underneath a massive oak tree. "GMC stopped making trucks, what, forty years ago?"

"Wasn't all that long, I don't think it was. 'Sides, it's a great one. I mean, it got some dings and shit, but who doesn't at our age?"

"You aren't that old, Risse," Pike said as the man unfolded himself from the seat and began unzipping.

"It's not the years that age a man, Shep. It's the miles."

The two friends did their business, then rode on, the silence at times becoming tangible. Risse gave in and turned the radio on and thumbed to find an all-news station. Not that he was desperate for current events, but the foreshadowing of doom seemed to be following them closely on this journey.

"Donald Trump announced an exploratory committee in preparation for the next presidential election," the news anchor said with a hint of sarcasm.

"Just when you thought it couldn't get worse. Lord help us, does that guy ever give up?" Risson asked. "What is this, like the fourth time he says he's going to run?"

"Must be. At least," Terra Pike agreed. "Let's just hope he drops out after the first couple of primaries like he usually does."

"Why would he do it? What drives a man with that much money to even want the job, anyway?"

The dark world's Pike shrugged, "Power, fame, credibility...who knows?" He sat silently for a few minutes. "Would you believe me if I told you there was a version of Earth where he did win?"

"What is this, like your false memory stuff? What did Kate call it, the Mandela Effect?" Risson asked.

"Similar, but no, the Mandela Effect is where some people think Mandela got out of prison and went on to become an influential leader in South Africa. The truth was, he died in prison around 1980. Many world theories suggest that all outcomes of events are possible via branching timelines."

Risse thought about that. He and Pike had discussed some of this many times, but science gave him a headache. "I still don't understand how something happening in another dimension could have any effect here. That's what you're+ saying, isn't it? That's what the Night Gate project is all about, right?"

Terra Pike nodded uncomfortably. He knew his friend felt meddling in stuff like this was bad on a karmic level. "There is some overlap or anchor points between the different dimensions. Our double in the mirror world and we are linked. In certain conditions we can see or feel what they feel and vice versa."

"That was where you hoped to find, Em. I know, Shep." Risse turned the radio back down and just let the road noise fill the silence for a few minutes. "She wouldn't have been your Emma. She wouldn't have been of this world."

"I know that!" Terra Pike snapped. He looked out the window, fighting back the tears welling behind his eyes. "It just hurt so bad to lose her. Everything started falling apart. I...Kate and I wanted to see a version of her that had continued. That was all. We just wanted to know she lived somewhere other than our memories."

* * *

It was mid-afternoon when they reached the lab. Luckily, the Marine Defense Force base, MDF Parris Island, had not yet annexed the industrial structure. That didn't mean there wouldn't be security. This piece of land had to be crawling with agents, and undoubtedly, convicted felon Pike Shepard would be on all their watch lists.

He slipped out of the truck and watched as Risse slid over, dragging his right leg awkwardly from one side to the other. On the way up, he'd come up with the basics of a plan, but it was a fool's errand. He had little hope of getting anywhere close to the control room for the Night Gate. "You know what to do?"

"Yes, Shep, I got it. You only went through it every five minutes for the last two hours."

Terra world Pike nodded and patted his friend. "Thanks, Risse, I owe you."

"You damn right you do. Stupid ass white boy. The brainless shit y'all do just baffles me. Baffles me, I say." He dropped the idling truck back into gear.

"If she won't see me, tell her I'm sorry, and..."

"And you love her. I know, I got that part, too." Risson smiled and pulled away without looking back.

Terra's Pike moved into the shadows of a moss-draped tree to wait. *This is stupid. What would I even say to her if she did agree to meet?* It wasn't like he'd had a major change of heart. His protest about the direction The Project was headed was what drove them apart and, eventually, Alex having him jailed.

82

Pike lay in his cell, exhausted. He had been on Terra periodically through the night, pushing his twin to go to Kate, seek her out and put a stop to these attacks. The mental pushback from his host was relentless. While their goals now seemed more aligned, the other version of Pike Shepard was no mental lightweight. He clearly understood the cost of giving up. Pike still didn't understand all that was happening in that world, but the decay had begun decades earlier. Pollution, political corruption, civil unrest, an almost permanent state of martial law. It was a world out of balance, and attacking this reality was a Hail Mary play at best.

Scofield's guards, whom Pike had started silently referring to as Sleepy and Dopey, came for him before dawn. What little sleep he got had been worrisome and restless. Alex Scofield was sitting at the table eating breakfast. His plate was piled high with bacon, eggs, grits, biscuits, and what looked like sausage gravy. He sipped from a white ceramic mug of coffee. Pike was relieved to see all signs of the execution were gone.

"Join me! Well, not join me," the man said. "I'm not going to share or anything. Just thought we could get an early start today. You know, since we have so much to cover." He pointed the fork at Pike to emphasize his words, then stabbed down for a bite of eggs. "This is delicious. I have to give props. Southern breakfasts are magnificent, truly a thing of beauty." He broke a piece of biscuit and spooned some of the gravy on it before popping it into his mouth.

Pike knew this was another bit of pre-planned melodrama. One more instance of Alex asserting his power. Letting him know fully who was in control. All Pike could think of was how much Palio loved breakfast, his pastries, and expensive morning muffins. He didn't deserve what this shitbag did to him. If only Subada could get into that head, he could end this in seconds. He had also considered having Subada jump into one of the guards and have him attack Alex. That play wasn't viable according to the alien. They apparently were also inhabited by their own dark travelers. That meant they could not be manipulated. No, he was going to have to deal with Alex Scofield straight up.

Pike silently watched the man eat for several minutes. Alex pushed the plate away and motioned with his head toward Sleepy. The guard removed the food and came back several minutes later with Kate. She sat heavily and looked at Pike sadly as Sleepy refastened her restraints to the steel loop mounted on the table.

Pike understood that look. She knew about Palio. Her face was gaunt and pale. She looked sick. He had to get her away from here. This must end today.

He caught her sad eyes and made a motion with his finger on the surface of the table. Kate knew his shorthand well enough to understand the curvy character for 'I love you.' She offered a barely perceptible nod and just a hint of a sad smile.

"Wow, she looks rough. Loving you just drains the essence out of women, doesn't it?" Subada voiced inside Pike's head.

Subada's mental barbs were not what the moment needed, and it took all of Pike's effort not to at least chuckle. Alex had begun his normal parroting of what he needed from them both. Pike had already tuned him out. "How's it going out there?" he asked Subada.

"Well, thanks to the courageous actions of one member of the Joint Chiefs, the country has stepped back from the brink of war with

China. They are instituting a twenty-four-hour stand down with diplomatic talks scheduled for tomorrow on neutral ground. Of course, not everyone is happy."

"That's a relief," Pike said. "How did you manage that?"

"Hmmm, tragic accidents of two of the main saber rattlers on both sides. Before you ask, only one was my doing. Seemed like others in China's chain of command didn't like where this was heading."

"Nianda okay with this?" Pike asked.

"He is very much not happy with my interference. I am not certain how much longer I'll be allowed to continue here."

The thought of doing what came next without his friend was impossible to consider. No way could he manage any of it alone. He noticed Kate was looking at him strangely, as if she knew his mind was literally elsewhere.

Alex slammed a palm down on the metal table.

"He's an excitable dolt, isn't he?" Subada asked, unimpressed.

"Very," Pike answered. "Do you know if Kate is okay? She really looks bad."

Subada's internal voice remained silent long enough for Pike to become concerned. "For a woman facing imminent death, she is doing quite well," Subada finally answered.

Pike heard a large silent 'but' in there. "But?"

"This is something she should tell you herself."

Pike's alarm increased sharply. Alex's hand once again held the weapon he'd killed Palio with. Pike could see specks of brownish-red blood on the polished metal. He pointed it at her head and grinned wickedly at Kate. "Time's up, Pike, you have to start talking."

Unlike the prior day, Agent Scofield kept his distance from Kate. No way was he going to let her get in another strike. Her eyes followed him. Hatred burned like hot coals in that glare.

"What is it, Subada?" Pike asked.

"Bite me, asshole," Kate yelled as she spit on her captor.

"She's expecting, Pike. You are going to be a..."

The blow landed across her cheek and sent Kate sprawling away from the table until her restraints sharply checked her fall. Her unconscious body hung there limply.

Pike jerked toward Kate and was just able to touch her arm before the guards pulled him back. "Check her. Is she okay?" he yelled. He then attempted to stand, staring at Scofield. "I will kill you."

Sleepy and Dopey unhooked Kate and lowered her to the floor. Alex just looked on with disinterest.

"What did you just say?" Pike mentally asked Subada in disbelief.

"She's pregnant, Pike. She's guessing five or six weeks."

And everything inside of Pike suddenly changed. The world shifted, and nothing he thought was important seemed to matter. All that mattered was getting her out of here. They were having a baby together, getting married, growing old, being happy.

"When your girlfriend wakes up, Pike, I am going to kill her," Scofield said flatly. "You have until then to decide if you are ready to help save this world."

"This world or your world?" Pike said in hatred. He hadn't meant to reveal that, but now it was out there.

Alex just smiled and nodded, "Clock's ticking."

"Subada, I have to go," Pike said. "Handle my questioning, please. If he makes a move on Kate do whatever you have to do to stop it."

"I've got it, Shep. Just go."

83

Pike was surprised to find the version of himself on Terra standing in nearly the same spot, just feet from another version of Kate Cassidy. This Kate was not the same, though. She was hard, her eyes cut like razors. Dark hair with just a hint of red but it was cut short and professional.

"We've been through this before, Pike. It's the only way to save us," Kate said, the bitterness clear in her tone.

"Why did you agree to see me then?"

"Well, Risson asked, and despite everything...you know, I still care deeply for him. And you're my husband...were my husband."

Pike wasn't sure how his double, Adam, had gotten into the building, but assumed he'd sent Risse to the lab with the request.

"The divorce isn't final. We are still married," Adam said sadly. "Where's Alex?"

Kate got a disappointed look on her face. "He's in the Gate Room. He's been on the other side constantly for over a week now."

"Wow, so sorry, that must be...must be tough for you both." He didn't mean for that to sound as petty as it did, but he couldn't stop the jealousy.

Pike tried his best to exert control or just communicate with his other. Subada told him he should be able to, he just had to master it. Watching the two former lovers in banal chatter was getting them nowhere.

Risson Mack sat at an empty desk, watching the two of them. He started going through drawers, looking for something to steal or probably eat. They had driven straight through. Not even a sandwich to eat. "Just like old times, ain't it? Fighting just like the good old days," he yelled out as he scored a half full jar of peanut butter from a bottom drawer, "Jiffy, my favorite!"

"Stop Alex. Pull him out of my world and cut control to the others." Pike yelled inside the man's head.

"We have to stop him," Adam said.

"Who? Risse?" Kate asked, confused.

"No, we have to stop Alex. You are destroying that other Earth," Adam said, with Pike pushing more and more into the man's conscious thought.

Kate shot back, "It's not like that, Pike. The mirror world is just an aberration, anomalies that the Universe is always seeking to correct. Each half of the mirror would have to remain in perfect balance with its twin to remain viable otherwise. They will be reintegrated, or one will be deleted. This stasis is the only path forward for long-term survival. They are a threat to our world. Why could you never see that?"

Deep inside his host's mind, Pike saw the parade of images all focusing on their daughter.

"I was looking for Em. That's all, Kate."

Her expression softened by millimeters. She gently touched his arm. "I know you were, but you stopped looking at me. I was right here, and I was hurting just as much as you."

Adam's head dropped. That point was true. He could not challenge his wife on how badly he'd dealt with the grief. Even now he was unsure how the idea of his mind traveling to other worlds came to him, but it had. Thanks to his wife and her wealthy friends, the Night Gate eventually came to pass. Once he understood his daughter did not exist on the other world, he lost interest. Kate and the others did not. That falling out eventually doomed his marriage and ended his freedom.

Inside his doppelgänger, Pike not only saw, but he also felt the loss all over again. He grieved over a daughter that wasn't even his. Two ideas came to him, but he had to make sure Adam heard him. So far, that only seemed to work with emotionally charged thoughts. Well, this one would be exactly that. Pike focused on his own memory. One that was fresh and full of promise. *Will it work, though?*

84

In the interrogation room, Subada dialed back the emotional response and pain receptors in Pike's brain. Despite all the time together, Subada had only actually been in control of the man's body once before. That had been when he was escaping the GTR in a stolen air force jet. He had to admit that time was a lot more fun. Scofield struck Pike again. Subada registered the blow, monitored the pain and damage, then gave an appropriate response. "Pussy, that all you got? I can see why you normally only hit women."

He heard a muffled snort of laughter from one of the guards. Another blow came, this one higher on his head and making even Subada see stars. He lay his head to one side and feigned unconsciousness for a minute. Whatever Pike was doing on the other side, he needed to make it fast. Subada quickly did a mental jump to Kate. She was okay, listening, and like him, feigning unconsciousness, but she was in considerable pain. Subada then tried SideSlipping into either of the guards without success. Both men were still firmly inhabited by combatants from the other side.

The situation was quickly going from challenging to impossible. Subada had one more option to try. Allowing Pike's body to slump farther to one side, he slipped into Julian Carapaz, who was in the twilight realm of consciousness. Subada was instantly overrun with wave after wave of imagery from the man's drug-hazed journeys, most of which he could not fathom. "Julian, we need your help."

Carapaz stirred. His eyes remained closed, but they moved quickly back and forth beneath the lids. Leah watched him, concerned for what he was going through. It was her job, but as she took his thin hand in her own, anyone could see there was more to it than that. "Are you in there, my love?" she whispered softly.

Subada was wondering something similar. He could feel Carapaz's consciousness swimming somewhere below in the depths of his mental abyss. He needed answers; he needed to be back with Pike, protecting Kate from the psycho GTR agent, and he needed to monitor what the various military leaders around the world were doing. This man, though, potentially knew everything that was about to happen and possibly how to stop it. They had gone to great lengths to save a man who very much seemed not to care. Subada would take this chance to help fish Julian Carapaz up from the depths in hopes that it might offer some hope, hope that might make a difference.

Julian, for his part, was adrift in a sea of conflicting timelines, probabilities, and outcomes. He'd already seen a version of Earth that was annihilated by a nuclear war. That was fading from his mind as something more took its place. The invading horde he'd warned Pike about was but one of the potential futures he'd witnessed on Mizar. At first, he had been supremely sure he was right, and everyone else was wrong. That had proven to be foolish. The future was not a straight line to be seen once and locked into place. It was a serpent slithering through darkened recesses, only to emerge somewhere you wouldn't have guessed.

Carapaz felt a presence, someone new, someone inhuman. The feeling was not unfamiliar, the last two years he'd spent more times with inhuman's than his own kind. Until something about this entity felt different.

"Julian Carapaz, can you hear me?" Subada again got no response. He could sense the tension building back in the interrogation room. He knew he could only spare a few more minutes with this man.

Nianda had told him everything would be decided today. Whatever direction Earth was going to fall would not be settled on a remote battlefield, but inside that small interrogation cell. "Julian, what was the future you saw for your planet?"

Subada saw hordes of invaders, countless thousands migrating over from a world Pike had been calling Terra. The scale of their Night Gate project was overwhelming. He'd been busy for days just trying to prolong the actions of a handful of well-placed operatives. Julian had seen many, many more coming. "Can they be stopped?"

A fractured vision surfaced of an empty desk at the White House. A military man with blood splattered across his chest and face sat on one of the two sofas, keying something into a laptop. That was the nuclear code, the presidential football, Subada knew. The level of destruction about to be unleashed in this world would rival the assault his own people had tried in an attempt to stop The Fade.

Julian's barely conscious mind offered up one more image. A lifeless body lying in a pool of blood. An arm with a small tattoo that he knew well. *Kate!* Subada hadn't spent much time with her, but felt she was a good person, a strong-willed, intelligent woman. More importantly, she carried Pike's child, and her love for him was genuine.

Subada was not a master of space or time. Nianda's people had such experts that could supposedly discern false timelines from real. Subada didn't have the luxury of putting in a request for them. Whatever the future, he had to assume it could be changed. If he lost Kate, he would lose Pike, too. He knew that without question.

85

The memory on New Earth of Emma eating with her family got through to Pike's host loud and clear.

"She's alive!"

"What do you mean, Pike?" Kate said, as she scanned a tablet of incoming messages. "By the way, someone from the state police is at the gate asking to see me."

"Emma."

Adam staggered back as his mind flooded with more images of his daughter.

"She's older, college maybe. I...I think the Pike from the mirror world wants me to see this."

"Emma never existed over there, remember?"

"I know, Kate, I don't understand it, but these are his memories. He's in my head right now."

"You are seeing this now? Right now?" Kate asked incredulously. "So that Pike is in control of you?"

Adam nodded, then said no. "Maybe, I don't know, but I know this vision is real."

"Not possible. I know for a fact that Pike is nowhere near a Gate Room. Or launch chair... whatever they call it. "

"What do you mean?" Adam asked.

"He's being held prisoner. He is being questioned. Both he and that Kate are." She looked away quickly, she hadn't meant to reveal that much to her already overwrought husband.

Pike showed his twin more of New Earth, enough for him to realize Emma was really alive in yet another dimension. This was dangerous, but he had to make the call. Alex already knew about New Earth, so the others here would soon enough. He hoped Nianda was right, and they could not reach that dimension. Still, the knowledge that there was at least one other mirror dimension, one in which things had worked out better for the Shepard family, might help.

"She's alive, honey. Not over there, but in a different dimension where the other Pike has traveled. He's seen her."

Kate struggled to maintain her composure. Some part of her need for what he was saying to be true leaked through that hard exterior. She wanted to see what he was seeing. She wanted to know that some part of herself...her baby lived on. *No!* She could not let herself fall into that pit, not ever again. She had been through hell because of their mutual obsession. It had been a fool's quest, and it nearly cost her everything. "It doesn't matter."

"What do you mean, Kate? Of course, it matters," Adam said firmly. "Risse, tell her."

"Cops are coming, Shep. You need an exit strategy or, well...you know. Your ass and mine both is gonna be ventilated."

Adam didn't seem concerned with his own fate. "Why are they prisoners, Kate? Who is behind that?" He had no affection for their opposites in that realm, but that didn't mean he wanted them harmed. They had done nothing wrong. His twin on that version of Earth drank too much, stayed sad and blamed too much shit on childhood medical issues, but despite that, he wasn't a bad sort. "Who is doing it?"

She looked away. "Who do you think?"

"Alex. That bastard," Adam growled.

Deep in the man's brain, the conscious part of Pike Shepard showed one more image. Alex threatening to kill Kate, striking her and then a final bit of knowledge. The understanding that she was also pregnant. His ability to communicate with his other was growing by the second.

Adam's face drained of color. "Risson, we have to stop him. She's..." He struggled to get the words out. "She's pregnant!" He'd already started for the Gate Room, but the last line he directed back toward Kate, who stood frozen with indecision. "She's pregnant and your Alex is going to kill her."

"Pregnant," she whispered softly, as if that was an impossibility. That would explain why she'd been unable to link with her for the last few weeks. The Night Gate system had some shortcomings. Targeted connections could fail for a variety of reasons, but pregnancy had been one of the first they discovered. Something about the maternal bonds seemed to reach down even on a quantum level to prevent external interference.

When Adam, Kate, and Risse entered the Gate Room, Pike was momentarily awestruck. The scale was massive, unlike the small launch room on Diego Garcia with a dozen launch chairs. This room was at least ten times larger. He saw at once the launch chairs were vastly different. These were pod-like creations. Much like an enclosed version of the lay-flat airline seats some airlines provide. In one of the few that was unoccupied, he could see several monitors. Ports for IV hookups, something that had to be waste disposals. The entire headrest was an array of sensors and electrical hookups. These travelers were not going for quick trips. He instinctually knew they did not return when the subject went to sleep.

"No, we only slip in during the sleep cycle," his dark twin said, obviously hearing Pike's thoughts more clearly now. "That's why we call it the Night Gate...or Porta Noctis. We found by slipping in while the conscious brain was at rest, we could exert a higher level of control even after they awoke. The subconscious mind is really the one in charge, after all."

Well, shit, Pike thought. *That seems so obvious. Why had we not even considered it?*

"Where is he?" Adam yelled. "Risse, look for one labeled Scofield."

"Kate, where is his gate station?" She was just entering the room. In the distance, Pike saw two police officers being escorted in by a tall black man in a military uniform. "Hurry, Risson, we have to find him."

He began running through the countless rows of occupied chairs. Risson hobbled along, trying to scan the names displayed above each of the closed pods. "Dammit, Shep, I'm too old for this shit."

Adam was running nearly flat out as he got to the end. Knowing this was just one of several gate facilities boggled the mind. He had to admit Kate and Alex had been productive.

"Pike, they want to talk to you." Adam heard the fear in his wife's voice echoing across the cavernous space. The tone left no doubt that it had been more than just a request.

Risse was just ending with his section and shaking his head. Panic overtook Adam. Maybe he'd overlooked it in his rush. He scanned the room. *What have I missed?* He had ducked down, hoping the officers wouldn't spot him over the building canopy of the travel pods. He caught Kate looking his way and subtly lifting her chin in a direction behind him. Turning around, he caught a glimpse through a secondary door on the back wall. Motioning to Risson, the two men crouched low and made a mad dash through it, then eased the door closed. They turned around and found they were in a small cubicle. Some sort of monitoring room by the looks of the equipment. Unfortunately, they were also trapped. Pike could see no other way out. Kate hadn't been helping.

86

"Doctor."

The slap came suddenly. While Kate had been feigning unconsciousness, the pain in her side and abdomen were nearly impossible to ignore. Now the bone rattling blow from the agent made her cry out, something she'd been determined not to do. She couldn't help it; she was about to die and something inside of her already felt broken. If she was pregnant, and she was nearly certain now, this man seemed determined to make her lose it.

One of her swollen eyes opened just a sliver. She saw Pike slumped in the chair like a marionette with the strings cut. Her heart ached for him. He too was going to die, and it was all her fault. She felt the guards lifting her off the cool concrete floor, then felt the hard chair beneath her again. Her focus swam in and out. Dark spots blanketed the space when she opened her eyes again. The effects of the last blow would fade, though. Right now, she needed to think...no—she needed to push Scofield even farther over the edge. She'd managed to do it before. Could she do it again?

The agent walked over to her, grinning deliriously. She laboriously lifted her head to look toward him, then vomited all over the man's shirt and trousers. Scofield shouted an obscenity before moving back and raking a hand across his shirt. His face was a mask of disgust as he looked at a red stain across the white shirt.

"Raspberries...I think," said Kate with as much amusement as she could manage. Once again, she saw the rage flare in the man's expression.

"Clean that up. I'll be back in a minute. Can't believe I have to get another shower because of this bitch. Wake the other one up, too. He needs to watch this." Scofield slammed the door as he left, already unbuttoning the soiled shirt.

Kate used the time to determine what was wrong with her and to look at the man she loved. He was unconscious but appeared to be in good shape. Why was he here, though? He had gotten away. Then she realized he would have done it on purpose. He must have let himself be captured. That was the only reason he would have done it, and the realization made her cry. She wiped her eyes, unwilling for any of her jailers to feel like they were the cause. Pike Shepard loved her, she knew he would, they always did wherever they were, but somehow this meant more than she could understand. It seemed they had spent so little time together, but in other ways, also lifetimes together. Some part of each of them had always yearned for the other.

A half hour later the door opened, and Scofield returned in fresh clothes He stayed well clear of her this time. "Shepard?" he barked questioningly at the shorter of the two guards.

"Seems to be coming around, sir," the man said with a thick Brooklyn accent. He was holding an ammonia capsule under Pike's nose to help rouse him from unconsciousness.

"Doctor Cassidy, would you care to know what is going on out in the world? I mean, before I end you and your boyfriend, that is?"

She shrugged. "They didn't deliver my morning paper today, so sure, knock yourself out."

Scofield smiled. Her defiance and flippant responses reminded him of her other back on his own world. Killing this Kate would be bittersweet, but also quite satisfying.

87

Pike's dark-world host looked at his friend in frustration. "We're pretty well screwed..."

"Come on, Shep, figure it out. Work the goddamn problem. Ain't that what you always say?" Risse said, looking nervously back at the Gate Room they had just been in.

Pike had no desire to die in this place, nor have his lifelong friend go to prison...or worse, but he saw nothing that might help. The space they were in was much smaller than the Gate Room. By the looks of the equipment and storage racks, it was a medical prep area for long duration jumps. Several medical couches were affixed to the floor, and cabinets and racks lined the walls. Portable monitoring stations were pushed into a line in a narrow corridor along the far wall. He knew the purpose, he'd been in rooms just like it, but the medical needs of the jumpers had never been his concern. So, everything in here was alien. Still, there had to be a way. His wife wouldn't have purposefully trapped them *...would she?*. "There must be another way out, Risse, look for it." He began moving racks and heard Risse doing the same.

"Shepard!"

The voice echoed through the space with confident authority. The sound sent shivers up Adam's spine. He knew that voice. It belonged to a man he was very familiar with. "Shit!" he said, staring into the brick wall. "Why him?"

"I may have something," Risse said from the far corner. He was struggling to move the line of monitors out of their storage area. Pike rushed over to him. Then the voice called out again.

"Security is surrounding the building, Shepard. This is my facility now."

They gave the mass-murdering asshole a goddam promotion, Adam thought bitterly. *They sent me to jail and gave him Night Gate.*

"Is that Alex?" asked Risson as he pulled the last of the monitors free from the narrow slot built into the wall.

"No, it's the military commander of The Project. Colonel Thaddeus Lewis."

Risse stopped what he was doing and looked up. "Wait, what?" He pushed the cart away and began wedging himself into the narrow space. "Isn't that..."

"Yeah, it's the same man I was sent to prison for trying to kill," answered Adam. The mission Lewis had been sent on was necessary to the Night Gate Project. That was according to the directors, but Adam had just found it inordinately cruel. He'd lost many allies in his protest over the assignment. Alex Scofield had championed it as driving a stake into the heart of the other reality, but Adam had found it all repulsive. His attempt to stop it was unplanned and rash and obviously didn't work. In fact, they made him watch the entire debrief of the assignment when the colonel returned. Then Pike's host had faced a quick military tribunal before being whisked off to federal lockup.

Pike saw the small entrance past Risse's head. It was designed so the med techs could simply deposit the mobile stations from the next room. It was tight for Risse and would be nearly impossible for himself, but they were quickly running out of options. He pushed sideways into the darkness behind his friend. Adam continued to hear the muffled sound of Colonel Lewis, and soon it was joined by an even more familiar voice, Kate. She was calling on him to come out as well. He struggled in the tight space; it was so cramped he could not even expand his chest to take a full breath. Still, he pushed on.

"You know..." Risse started, his voice labored to get the words out. "I might be wrong."

"How so?" Adam managed to say after several failed attempts.

"She may not love you anymore."

Adam laughed and immediately found himself stuck. "Stop it," he muttered as he forced the air out of his lungs and sipped in a small breath. The light at the far end was getting brighter. Another room ahead.

Pike watched helplessly as his host navigated the small space. He felt the conflicted emotions about his wife. This Kate seemed so different from the one he loved, but how would she have been in this world? He realized Subada was correct. He was very different from his other but also very much the same. At the core, the character was nearly identical. It was simply circumstances that had shaped each of them in different ways. He needed to get back to his world, check on his Kate, but if he failed here...what was the point? *Please, Subada, take care of my world,* he prayed silently.

The sound of Colonel Lewis accompanying Kate was closer now. Pike wondered briefly about how tough of a man, a black man, Thad Lewis was to have risen up through the ranks in a world as segregated and full of hate as this one. His host could no longer turn his head sideways to see where he was going, but he heard Risse give a sigh as he apparently emerged into the next Gate Room.

Adam was not a fan of confined spaces, and this one had been worse than he imagined. The end had to be close, and finally, his left hand that was on the wall ahead felt empty space. He moved like a kid at Christmas, the last couple of feet to freedom. The hand holding the rifle pointed at his head abruptly flushed that joy away. Two uniformed guards were positioned between him and Risson Mack, who stood defeated, with his arms raised high overhead.

"Pike Shepard. You have forfeited your right to more merciful punishment. Prepare for execution."

88

"Jenkins, hold her head."

One of the guards stepped from the shadows and cautiously placed hands on both sides of Kate's head. She struggled, and the man's vice-like grip ratcheted up even more.

"My dear Doctor, I am afraid our time is quickly coming to a close." Alex began slowly withdrawing an evil-looking weapon from a shoulder holster. He spoke to the guard. "I want her eyes on me. I need to see her when she realizes that we are done here."

Kate wasn't sure if the speech was for her benefit or for Pike's, who sat glassy-eyed staring across the room. She was terrified, but not so much for herself. During the last several hours, a strange sense of detachment had come over her, and she finally thought she knew why. *I am definitely pregnant.* She moved her eyes past Scofield to look at Pike. *We're going to have a baby.* The words were unspoken, but she still wanted him to know, even if it wasn't going to come true.

She saw intensity flair in Pike's gaze and somehow felt confident that he already knew. Where there had been vacancy, now there was fire in those eyes, one she had grown to know all too well. "Scofield," she said, glancing back into the agents cold dark eyes. "You must be a pitiful lover. All dick and no balls, right?" She braced herself for another blow. She just prayed it would not be to her stomach.

Instead, the man just smiled. "We are just one reality within a multitude of universes, Kate. Isn't that what you believe? That is what your research seems to have proven."

Kate wasn't sure where this was going, but Scofield kept talking, not waiting for a response. The menacing weapon in his hand never wavering far from her direction.

"It stands to reason in other worlds we may be having this same conversation. Maybe you are the one holding me prisoner in a few. On others, the two of us may have been partners." He leaned in, his mouth only inches away from her own. "Maybe even more."

She could smell the coffee on his breath. And something deeper, a rot bubbling up from the depths of the man's soul. "No one could ever love you."

Agent Scofield leaned back and did something to the weapon. She heard a fast hiss of air. "I am going to put this in your mouth and blow the back of your skull off. And ... just so you know, I am not from your world, neither are my men. We are here to set this reality on a path to destruction. Does it all begin to make sense to you now? You were only important to us for your research. My dimension has not been able to reach the other worlds in the multiverse. Most of my team doesn't even believe what you are doing. The truth is, you made far less headway than your boyfriend. He discovered something none of us expected."

Kate glanced at Pike, who was showing no emotion but was focusing intently on the wrist restraints and loop of chain linked to the table. She'd never seen a look with more intensity on anyone. She wanted to tell him she loved him; she wanted him to know about the baby; she wanted to tell him goodbye, but clearly, he was not giving up...not yet. Pike twisted one wrist beneath the other on the tabletop. The effect was awkward unless he was using it as a pivot...Her thoughts were interrupted as Agent Scofield raised the gun toward her mouth.

In near silence, with the warrior Subada piloting, Pike's body launched up and over the table in a somersault, trailing the heavy metal chair he was strapped to. The movement was so graceful it was elegant. Packed within that inertia was a man intent on doing damage.

Subada then snapped Pike's leg down, connecting with Scofield's wrist in a vicious crack. The gun fell to the floor, releasing a violent puff of air. The chair, still fastened to Pike, reached the zenith of its arc. It came down on top of Scofield, burying the man in a violent interaction of inertia and mass. Pike's arms were now stretched out behind him, still anchored firmly to the hook on the table. Still, he had Alex's head between his legs and was desperately trying to squeeze the life out of his body. Subada knew how to kill, and even restrained, he wasn't going to be deterred. Just then, a sound of snapping electricity and a surge of pain shot through Pike's body so powerfully that even Subada's near superhuman skills couldn't overcome. The legs relaxed slightly, and Alex slipped down to the floor, gasping for air.

89

Despite what his body was going through back in its reality, Pike Shepherd's conscious mind had no sensation other than the massive dose of fear his host, Adam, was experiencing. Realizing he was about to be executed, it was not an inappropriate sensation. A quick look around the room had shown him that the space was significantly smaller than the previous Gate Room. It was also better equipped, probably for the VIP travelers. He'd also noticed a single door along the westernmost wall. The two guards were speaking into their radios. The man on the other end was Colonel Lewis.

"Shepard," Pike voiced to Adam. "I am going to need to take over for a few minutes." If his other heard the mental whisper, he gave no indication. Now it was time to see if what Nianda and Subada had trained him on would actually work. His mind was already in battle mode, mentally racing through the position of the guards, the approaching colonel, Kate, and his friend Risse. He drew from his twin's partial knowledge of weapons and tactics. In milliseconds, he had formulated multiple attack vectors, ruled them all out and started over. Then, without warning, Risson Mack moaned loudly and collapsed.

Both guards turned, and Pike took the opportunity to go on the offense. He hated using lethal tactics, but Subada's training didn't include much in the way of non-deadly force. In the alien's mind, a wounded combatant was still a combatant. He leg-whipped the closest guard, then pivoted and drove an elbow into the face of the second. Blood sprayed as he felt the cartilage give way beneath his blow. The first guard was bringing up a handgun. It looked like a modern Glock 22, but bulkier, and an extended magazine. Pike gripped the man's forearm and twisted back violently at the elbow, bringing the man's own body weight to bear against the relatively weak joint.

The laws of physics were similar enough to his own world when it came to mass and inertia. The joint failed with a muted snap. The guard was going down as Pike pulled the trigger, ending his suffering. It was only then he realized the weapons were internally sound suppressed. The other guard was rising, one hand to his broken nose and his other was holding the deadly weapon Pike had seen Alex use back on his world when he'd ended Palio's life.

The guard fired, but Pike's enhanced reflexes anticipated just enough that the compressed air round grazed his host's temple. It burned like hell, but nothing permanent. Pike dropped and fired in one fluid move. The guard fell backward; the life leaving the man's body even before it knew it was dead.

"Damn, Shep, when you learn how to fight?" Risson asked.

"Later, man. You okay?" Pike asked his friend.

"Yeah, I was faking. You looked like you was cooking up something."

He patted Risse on the back. "I was, but thanks for the distraction." Pike saw a row of about a dozen launch stations positioned in parallel lines. One of these had to be Alex. "Help me look for Scofield. We only have a few minutes."

They ran down the line, the display above each chair clearly showing the name and photo ID of the agent inside. Pike got to the end of his without seeing the man. "Anything?" he yelled to his friend.

Risson just shook his head. Then, that one door to the side burst open. Colonel Lewis marched inside, gun in hand.

"Hope you gots another plan there, brother," Risse whispered while taking cover behind one of the units.

Looking down at the launch pod he was standing beside, Pike realized he did have a plan.

90

Subada fought off most of the effects of the taser, but it still left the nerves in Pike's body scrambled and unable to put up a fight. Agent Scofield was down with a broken wrist, but Subada using Pike's body that way had likely done nothing more than buy them a few more minutes. One guard, the one Pike had nicknamed Dopey, untangled him from the tabletop and pushed him violently back toward the floor. His legs dropped to the concrete with a thud as his wrist restraints kept his arms attached to the loop on the table. The pain would have been unbearable had Pike been conscious, but Subada had turned all pain receptors down to minimum levels. He needed to focus. Harming his friend was inevitable at this point. He just needed to make sure it counted for something.

"Kill him," a voice growled from the other side of the table. A bloody hand was all that was visible as Agent Scofield attempted to pull himself up with his one good arm.

Subada focused on Kate and saw her eyes go wide as he heard the guard moving up behind him. The barrel pushed against the back of Pike's head. Even Subada had to admit he was out of ideas. He heard the man's breathing slow and felt the pressure on his head increase as the man tensed to fire.

"Wait," Scofield ordered. "We still need him. Do her instead."

Subada felt the weapon move from his head, then saw the barrel aimed at Kate. The woman he had sworn to protect.

"What are you waiting for — do it!" Alex bellowed, spittle flying across the table.

The guard steadied his aim squarely at her head and began squeezing the trigger. Subada was expecting a loud report but saw the gun's aim begin to drift, then the hand released it completely. The guard dropped to the tabletop, alive and apparently uninjured but babbling.

Subada knew what had happened; he had SideSlipped away or worse.

91

"Goodbye, Dopey," Pike said, raising the gun back up. He glanced at the pod display and read the man's name. "Jenkins." He'd recognized the face as one of the guards back in his reality. Maybe that would slow things down, but he still had to find Alex. Unfortunately, several more armed men had joined Colonel Lewis. These men looked like regular Marines. They had the stubby, urban assault rifles, and they were all pointed toward him. Pike looked past the colonel to Kate, she gave a tiny nod. He pulled the trigger.

"You just shot that man while he slept," Lewis bellowed in disbelief. "And the guards."

"Where's Alex Scofield?" Pike gave as a response.

"Director Scofield has a private launch pod," the colonel said as his men approached. "One you won't be getting near."

"I'm sorry, Risse," Adam whispered at his friend, who was still taking cover several yards away.

"Did we do some good?" Risson asked.

Adam wasn't sure, he definitely hoped so. "Yes, Risse, we did good, we did very good."

Internally, the darker version of Pike's voice said, "Life is tough when you must die to save yourself. Love our wife, Pike, and our daughter."

At the sound of the colonel's gun firing, Pike saw Risson Mack on the move, then he decided to slip back into his own body. He said goodbye to Terra.

* * *

Pike reopened his eyes to a scene of complete chaos and unbelievable pain. "What the fu..." he bit the comment off seeing Kate's look of terror and then registering the armed guard beside him. He wanted to see which one it was but couldn't see past the weapon.

"It's okay, Shep, it's me." Then the guard he'd called Dopey spun and shot Sleepy in the chest. Blood blossomed across the man's uniform. Scofield, whom Pike hadn't even noticed, suddenly was up and firing the angry little ventilator weapon, striking Jenkins, AKA Dopey, in the right shoulder. From a distance, the air rounds were much less effective, but they still did a tremendous amount of damage to flesh and bone. The guard's shooting arm hung limply, the pistol still in the man's hand.

Pike quickly guessed much of what must have gone on and correctly assumed Subada had taken over Jenkins' body as soon as Pike's bullet severed the brain stem in his body back on Terra. Kate was looking at him, confused. "Relax, Kate, please try to stay calm."

She had no intention of relaxing, though. She'd been through enough. Alex moved to use her as a shield, but Subada calmly took the guard's weapon in his left hand and expertly fired past Kates's ear. The shot clipped the agent in the neck. Blood spurted briefly, but it wasn't the arterial spray Subada had been hoping for.

Scofield used one hand to try to staunch the flow as he fired another air round at Jenkins. Subada felt the impact in his gut and knew it had done real damage. He couldn't lose the only advantage he had in this fight. He pushed off the wall and headed for a better shooting vector on Scofield. He felt his vision narrowing and the strength rapidly sinking in the man's body. *Just a little longer.*

Scofield sensed what was going on as well and moved to keep Kate between him and his new opponent.

Kate hated this man with everything in her being and locked eyes with Pike as she made a decision. Alex Scofield had moved in as close as he could get to her, so most of his body was shielded. He moved the weapon past her to get one more shot. Kate used the opportunity to seize the barrel, which he immediately jerked back on. Her arms were restrained like Pike's but gave her just enough freedom to push the weapon under the agent's chin just as Alex finally fired. The round did exactly what he'd promised them it would do. The hypersonic super-cavitating ball of compressed dry nitrogen shattered the skull into a cloud of microscopic debris. The decapitated body of Agent Alex Scofield bounced off the rear wall before tumbling to the floor.

Subada managed to unlock Kate's restraints before the body he was inhabiting succumbed to his wounds. She, in turn, unlocked Pike's restraints, then wiped the blood from her mouth and kissed him. "I think being a killer turns you on, dear," he quipped.

She smiled. "First time in days I haven't needed to throw up, go figure."

Pike felt Subada re-enter his mind. "Can you get us out?"

"I can. Apparently, the agent and the two guards were the only ones who knew all of what was going on. Our friends are at the gate."

Pike followed his sub-vocal instructions and led Kate down a darkened corridor to an unmarked door. Minutes later, they strolled past a guard positioned at the gate. Subada had slipped into the guard briefly, and the man just smiled and waved as they passed. Kate looked at Pike questioningly but said nothing. Despite the joyous news that she wanted to share with this man, they had both been through too much today.

* * *

The unlikely pair of Dewey and Gohr met Pike and Kate just outside the entrance to the base. Dewey threw his arms around Pike, then turned and did the same to Kate. He eyed the blood-soaked clothes in disbelief. "Is it over?"

"For now," Pike answered, the exhaustion evident. One arm badly needed medical attention, but he was overjoyed to have made it back out and to see his friend. Gohr then came over and stuck out a hand. Pike shook it, with his only good arm.

Gohr reached out and hugged Kate. Pike had never thought about the two of them knowing each other, but it was obvious now. "It is good to see you again, Professor Shepard," Gohr stated simply before revealing the barest hint of a smile.

Pike was not sure he'd ever heard the man say that many words at one time. At least not when it was actually Gohr and not Subada. "Thanks, Gohr."

Pike took Kate's hand in his and turned to Dewey as they walked toward a waiting SUV. "I think we need a doctor...then can we go home."

"Your friend, Val, has his medical suite at your disposal. Going home may take a little longer cuz.." Dewey opened the car door for his friend... "the fire kind of got out of hand after they captured you."

The cabin is gone? Subada had warned him. Somehow, that stung nearly as much as all the other atrocities the GTR agents had committed. "Well, shit." He and Kate slid in, she took his hand once more, and leaned her head on his shoulder. He noticed her other hand softly resting on her stomach as she began to softly hum a tune that he instantly recognized. It had been playing on his record player the morning they had first met in this world.

EPILOGUE

The sailboat moved gracefully around the bend, well beyond Fort Remorse, the Beaufort Marina, and the Woods Memorial Bridge. Pike looked down at his own fresh tattoo inside the arm handling the tiller. It matched Kate's $i\gamma \cdot \partial\psi = m\psi$. The equation of Dirac describing two particles that at some points are entwined, which will remain connected forever, even if they are light-years apart. He now knew the full truth of that formula.

As they entered the shallows near Blackwater, the familiar shoreline came into view. Kate gasped when she saw the site of the old fish-camp. "It's incredible, Pike." Her gaze was centered around the point of land jutting out into the bay. The place his cabin had once occupied.

Minutes later, they bumped to a gentle stop as the boat kissed up next to the familiar dock. From what she could see, the dock was the only original thing still here. Everything else was new. Pike helped her up and out. The magnificent house that stood where the cabin had been took her breath away. It was somehow both classic and modern. It seemed perfectly suited for the land.

"Still upset with me for not letting you see it until now?"

Kate shook her head. This had been Valerius' surprise gift to them for bringing Julian back to him. Pike had the plans, but Val insisted on footing much of the bill for his new business partner. "I love it!" she squealed. Pike and Dewey had worked hard on the house. Pike seemed to have the entire design memorized from the beginning. He'd only taken one break a few months earlier. That was to accompany Palio's body back to his village along with his sister's ashes. Subada had to come back several times to help make that happen. First, to locate the bodies, then to direct the right people to do what was needed. For Kate and Pike both it was difficult, but it was the right thing to do. Palio had betrayed them, but for all the right reasons.

Kate waved at their friends gathered on a patio beside the beautiful new home, her home now. "Oh, my, I know that smell." They were gathered around what had to be a steamer pot of traditional Lowcountry seafood boil. Pike's classic music was streaming from hidden speakers outside. He was still a man out of sync with time, but it no longer seemed to matter.

As they neared the group that had gathered, Pike noticed Julian Carapaz resting on a chaise. Despite the happy occasion, his face looked pinched and drawn. He was the one man here who might know more, but so far, he'd not revealed a thing to anyone.

The house was perfect, but Pike had seen it before on a world not so far removed from this one. He turned Kate to face him. "I love you." He looked down at her swollen belly. "I love you both."

Kate's smile lit up her face as she leaned in for a kiss. "Emma will be the happiest child in South Carolina."

His eyes watered...he'd not suggested the name to her. That had all been her decision. It was one filled with joy and fear for him. Would this Emma have the future he'd glimpsed on New Earth, or would it be more tragic, like the fate of Terra? It would be neither, he decided. It would be her own life, her own future. Subada had told him before he left him that it wasn't over, it was simply delayed for the moment. Humanity in this reality still had to face the likelihood of fading away, but until then, they could grow, love, and maybe even thrive. "Enjoy your life, Shep," he'd said. "None of us know absolutely what the future holds. I'll be seeing ya, Dude."

Sweet dreams that leave all worries behind you. But in your dreams, whatever they be, dream a little dream of me.

-End-

MESSAGE FROM THE AUTHOR

Thank you for reading my novel *The Night Gate.* I hope you enjoyed it. If you would be so kind as to take a moment and leave a review, I would be very grateful. As an independent author, reviews and referrals are essential, and really the only way to compete with the major publishers and big-name writers.

What parts of *The Night Gate* are real?

Thank you for reading my novel *The Night Gate.* I hope you enjoyed it. I'm often asked what in my books is real and what is simply made-up. I think the best science fiction are those works with a strong foundation in hard science.

Even though my stories are fiction, I try to tell the most compelling stories I possibly can. Much of that comes about by including science and technology that is just a few steps beyond where we are currently. I strive for accuracy and to introduce ideas that I hope will prove entertaining, fascinating, thought provoking, and possibly even unbelievable. This book started off as a fairly straight-forward romp across the multiverse. Little did I know how many areas of scientific discovery I would touch on by the end. I do a considerable amount of research for all my novels, but I will admit *The Night Gate* has far more speculative science than many of my other works. Still, I thought it might be fun to briefly venture into this book's content and help separate the facts from the fiction.

What makes Humans Special? — Or, said another way, what makes us human? Sure, let's start with the easy question first. Ha! In the story I touch on this point several times and the truth is—we simply don't know. Maybe nothing. Perhaps any creature could in time reach a similar level of

'being.' Humans and apes share over 90% of the same DNA. Of course, both apes and humans also share about 50% of the same DNA with the bananas we both eat.

Some of us would point to the possibility of a soul that separates us, others the ability to think, our intellect, or specifically the ability to think in the abstract. Some have proposed that it is our very brain that is the key. If you do enough research, you will find that the answer to the question is nearly always subjective and most often geared to the particular field of study the research is coming from. In studying ideas like this, I began to develop the concept of separating the 'mind from the meat' mentioned in Chapter 19. Despite biological advantages, we are simply not that far away (biologically) from other forms of life on planet Earth. So, what else is involved in sentience or consciousness?

One angle I did find compelling was this: what if a portion of our brain actually extends into other dimensions? A team of researchers in the Swiss research initiative, Blue Brain Project, published a paper in 2018 entitled "The Human Brain Can Create Structures in Up to 11 Dimensions." While it sounds impressive, that in itself probably is not what makes us special. After all, as you see below, other life taps into the quantum realm to exist, so why shouldn't we?

I will tell you in the end I came away with a big "No one knows" to this question. The answers seem to range from language to God, but something is clearly different with us. We have exceeded a natural mandate to simply survive and reproduce. This should have been the extent of our evolution, but it wasn't — why? I'll keep exploring, and I hope you will, too.

Quantum Biology — The idea that many (maybe all) living things use quantum effects to their advantage is still somewhat controversial but is increasingly becoming more accepted. For a good layman's starting point in considering if consciousness, photosynthesis, and avian navigation are quantum effects, I would direct you to the following article:

The Scientist (2019) "Quantum Biology May Help Solve Some of Life's Greatest Mysteries."

After my own research, I am convinced that evolution is dependent on quantum mechanics; indeed, it may be essential for life itself to exist. Our sun wouldn't shine without the amazing properties of the quantum realm. At the atomic level, protons can pass through a seemingly impassable energy barrier. How? By existing in many places at once. DNA itself is affected similarly when random variations occur in a fixed strand all because of quantum mechanics.

European robins' and other animals' migration habits are based on quantum level sensitivity to the earth's magnetic field. This sensitivity is in their eyes, *Nature* (2021) "Birds Have a Mysterious 'Quantum Sense.' For the First Time, Scientists Saw It in Action."

Photosynthesis, how plants convert sunlight into sugars and energy, is now thought to be a quantum level process. Many of these are a result of the uncertainty principle where you can never be precisely sure where a particle is. It is in no fixed location until you observe it. You also have to think of things like photons and protons as waves, not particles, to fully understand this.

Scientists can mostly understand the hard-wired mechanisms of the brain, the computing parts that enable us to drive a car, walk upright or eat an apple. They can't explain the abstractions such as recalling eating that apple or driving that car or visualizing the most perfect sunset.

Microtubules were discovered by accident in the 1960s. Over the coming decades, they proved to be among the most versatile biological structures in nature. Tubulin, a flexible protein, assembles into a long chain to create microtubules. These 25-nanometer-wide tubes—thousands of times smaller than a red blood cell—are found in every cell in plants and animals. I will go ahead and admit that following this research is a daunting task with many twists and turns. It even touches on God and religion at times.

While many of the findings are controversial, my very broad takeaway is that these sub-atomic actions on the quantum level will likely be found to be not just essential but the very foundation of life itself and a large part of what it means to be human.

Quantum Entanglement — I have tackled the bizarre phenomena of entangled quantum particles in several novels already. Since it is a process that we utterly fail to understand, I normally just take a practical approach on how we might use it. To go back, I am talking about two sub-atomic particles that become 'entangled,' or paired, and thereafter mirror each other's behavior even at great distance. Einstein famously called it 'spooky behavior at a distance.' In *The Night Gate,* I simply take it to another conclusion that it is what connects us to our counterparts out in the multiverse. This, of course, is my own invention but played well with many of the existing theories.

Many scientists do now believe that consciousness is a quantum phenomenon. A quick search will reveal numerous books on the subject. Everything written in the novel about the quantum realm is based on widely accepted, accurate science of the time except, of course, the ability to journey to other worlds with one's mind. This isn't possible—that I know of :)

Microtubules — As described in the story, microtubules are real. They are incredibly small, cylindrical shaped components of neurons deep inside our brains. The discovery of quantum vibrations in microtubules inside brain neurons corroborates an older theory that suggests consciousness itself is crested in this process. The idea is also called the Orch Theory. The idea that more is going on at the quantum levels was examined in *Nature* magazines' "Bundles of Brain Microtubules Generate Electrical Oscillation." An excellent scientific journal is available at *The Royal Society,* "Quantum computation in brain microtubules?" After absorbing as much of the often baffling science involved here, I couldn't help exploring the most extreme possibilities of this potential connection we all have to the quantum world.

Space Elevators, Fusion Energy, Autonomous Cars and Video Walls — As in many of my novels, I include copious amounts of what could be viable 'near-future' tech in this one. Self-driving cars are already here, and smart roads are coming. These are roads that help with traffic management, pedestrian safety, and potentially even help power your vehicles.

When the idea for this book first occurred to me, I thought self-driving cars would be decades away. Which just goes to show that even those who follow science and technology as closely as I do can be easily surprised by the pace and ingenuity of human invention.

Gauging by the rapid increase in the typical HD television, having an entire wall made of them might also not be far away. While 4K screens have grown to truly monstrous sizes, OLED—which seems to be the most lifelike of the current technologies—is still under a hundred inches maximum size as I write this. But that barrier will likely be broken in months. According to some experts the acuity of the human eye is based on an angle. Its limit for 20/20 vision at what would be normal viewing distance is 2k HD, or 1920x1080 pixels. So, the reality is 4K and above is actually better than the real world. The ability for cinematographers to oversaturate colors allows them to create more vivid scenes than would exist naturally. Of course, Pike's (Rembert's) smart home on New Earth had numerous integrated technologies based around that video wall, all of which I can easily see becoming commonplace in just the next decade.

'Space elevators might take a bit more time, *but* maybe not as much as you think. If you've never heard of them, the idea has been around for quite a while. I first ran across the idea back in the 60s reading something by Arthur C. Clarke. It essentially is a tethered weight placed in orbit along the equator of the earth. The rotation of the planet keeps the counterweight stable high above, and your freight elevator can lift cargo up to low orbit much more safely and efficiently than a rocket burning millions of pounds of chemical propellants trying to escape the gravity well of our planet.

The technology is relatively straightforward. The challenge, as I understand it, has been one of materials. The cable, in particular, would need to extend up about 35,000 kilometers. The sheer weight of that tether alone would be massive on the anchoring point, and any weak point would quickly become a single point failure. Something all engineers cringe at. Exotic materials, like carbon nanotubes, might point us the way forward as these diamond-like tough strands of material could be wound into an ultra-light but very durable cable that could reach out into space.

We tend to think of nuclear energy as involving splitting atoms apart. This is nuclear fission. Nuclear fusion is fusing atoms together in a controlled way, much like what happens inside the sun. This releases nearly four million times more energy than a chemical reaction such as the burning of coal, oil, or gas and four times as much as nuclear fission reactions (at equal mass). The other main advantage is that fusion does not produce radioactive, toxic waste products like fission does.

A type of reactor called a tokamak overcomes the need to have a star handy to make the reaction occur. These reactors use confining magnetic fields to control the flow of plasma used to generate the electricity. There are challenges to these technologies from finding the raw ingredients needed to initiate breeding, like tritium, to scaling up the power to usable levels. The running joke in this industry is, "We are always thirty years away from a workable fusion powerplant." With the rapidly skyrocketing demand for abundant electricity and the dwindling supplies of fossil fuels, fusion may indeed be the way forward for the next generation.

The Texas Clocktower Massacre — Sadly, yes, this is a real thing and is accurate as portrayed in the book. On July 31, 1966, former Eagle Scout and Marine, Charles Whitman, wrote a note about his violent impulses saying, "After my death, I wish an autopsy on me be performed to see if there's any mental disorders." The note described his lack of understanding at the urges he was feeling. That night, Whitman went to his mother's home where he stabbed and shot her. Upon returning to his own home, he then stabbed his wife to death.

The following morning, Whitman headed for the 307-foot tower at the University of Texas in Austin with several pistols and a rifle after stopping off at a gun store to buy boxes of ammunition and a carbine. Packing food and other supplies, he proceeded to the observation platform, killing the receptionist and two tourists before unpacking his rifle and telescope and hunting the people below. Before he was gunned down, Whitman had killed 16 people and wounded more than 30 others.

I did not include the excerpt in the book to offer an excuse for this man's actions. Like many, though, his behavior was so out of character, so random as to be perplexing. They did an autopsy on Whitman to try to understand his motives and actions. The initial autopsy discovered an astrocytoma tumor in his brain but concluded that it had not influenced his behavior during the shooting.

False Memory Syndrome, a.k.a The Mandela Effect— Would you trust a memory that felt as real as all your other memories, and if other people confirmed that they remembered it, too? What if the memory turned out to be false? This scenario was named the 'Mandela Effect' by the self-described 'paranormal consultant' Fiona Broome. She had discovered that other people shared her (false) memory of the South African civil rights leader Nelson Mandela dying in prison in the 1980s.

Is a shared false memory really due to a so-called 'glitch in the matrix,' or is there some other explanation for what's happening? Broome attributes the disparity to the many-worlds or 'multiverse' interpretation of quantum mechanics.

Of course, there are also more likely reasons, such as the example of Hamilton—the man, not the musical. At some point in their education, most Americans learn that Alexander Hamilton was a Founding Father but not a U.S. president. However, when a study on false memory investigated whom most Americans identify as U.S. presidents, the subjects were more likely to incorrectly select Hamilton but not several actual former presidents. This is likely to be because neurons encoding information about Hamilton were frequently activated at the same time as neurons encoding information about former presidents.

If you Google 'False Memory' or 'the Mandela Effect' you will find numerous examples online, many of which I hid inside *The Night Gate* as Easter eggs for top readers looking closely. This is a real phenomenon, and while it has been linked as potential evidence of the many-worlds theory, I just like the added complexity it added to the storyline.

Hemispherectomy (corpus calloscotomy) — This medical procedure is accurate as described in the story. It involves separating the left half and right half of the brain surgically, normally an extreme last-step treatment. It is a rare surgical procedure done for epilepsy which is not responsive to medications. It is typically done in children and very rarely successful in adults.

I was surprised to learn that this procedure is not typically fatal, and, in fact, patients may live nearly normal lives, but there are some possible side-effects such as the ability to see and draw two objects at the same time. I included this dramatic condition on our protagonist because I wanted him to think differently than other humans. Some of this is driven by a brilliant book, *Incognito: The Secret Lives of the Brain* by David Eagleman. The author dives into many topics of cognitive function, consciousness, and neuroscience but perhaps none more so than his 'rival' brain theory.

To paraphrase the concept, your brain does not make decisions based on intellect, or not intellect alone. We are not biological computers; our brain is far more complex. Instead, we should think of the brain as a committee of subagents, or rivals, who compete with each other to offer up the winning answer. As Eagleman states, our brains are hard-wired to run on conflict as this is the most efficient way of producing the best outcomes. As I journeyed down this path, I took an imaginative leap to the Hive Brain Theory and what if some of those 'subagents' were not just taking up residence in our own heads but in someone else's.

Is Reality Just a Simulation? — This is a challenging subject for most of us to even consider, but approaching it rationally, scientifically, it is incredibly difficult to guarantee we aren't living a matrix-style dream reality. A virtual environment in which we may be nothing more than bits of code running on a master programmer's supercomputer. I will admit I was amused the first time I heard this; the second time I was curious as to why it was still being discussed, especially by those I consider to be very smart people.

"If we are living in a simulation, then the cosmos that we are observing is just a tiny piece of the totality of physical existence," Oxford philosopher Nick Bostrom said in a 2003 paper that jump-started the conversation about what has come to be known as the Simulation Hypothesis. "While the world we see is in some sense 'real,' it is not located at the fundamental level of reality."

Scientific American in October of 2020 published an article entitled

"Do We Live in a Simulation? Chances Are about 50–50." Then, in April the following year, it offered a related piece called "Confirmed! We Live in a Simulation." Both are excellent reads but do little to settle the question.

The discussion in many ways mirrors much of the same ground as religion and ultimately seems just as difficult to prove or disprove scientifically speaking. There has been much thought given to experiments that might help answer the question mainly by looking at our universe on the very smallest scale to see if the 'illusion' of reality holds up. When you consider the behavior of really small things, such as the entangled quantum particles I describe in this book that behave a certain way only when an observer is present or mirroring the behavior over long distance, it does make you wonder if there is something to all of it.

Pocket Universes, Mirror Worlds and the Multiverse — As a kid, I remember one of the big questions I always pondered on was this: If you could go to the very edge of the universe...the absolute end...and then took one more step, where would you be? (Yes, I was a weird kid). Still, that question haunted me the entire time I was writing *The Night Gate*.

Like nearly everything else in this book, this is a complex subject with many competing theories. I'll shamelessly admit to picking and choosing the ones that fit my story the best, but I do attempt to be fair and accurate with the science. When I began, I was simply going to write about the other realities, worlds that were very different than our own. To be honest, the idea of parallel worlds, or mirror universes, troubles me on a very basic level. The more I investigated it, though, I kept coming back to the thought of 'what if.' It could potentially explain a lot of things we don't fully understand. It also gave me the perfect antagonist, another version of ourselves, fighting hard to preserve their world.

I invite readers who are interested to check out a very good synopsis on Space.com by Robert Lawrence Kuhn called "Confronting the Multiverse: What 'Infinite Universes' Would Mean." Another excellent book I reference in *The Night Gate* is *The Hidden Reality* by noted theoretical physicist Brian Green. The analogy I use of multiverse form, quantum tunneling, and pocket universes were all heavily influenced by the ideas in his excellent books.

ABOUT THE AUTHOR

JK Franks is the popular author of numerous post-apocalyptic and near-future techno-thriller novels. He is an admitted tech geek, science nerd, cyclist, and storyteller. JK Franks' world was formed by a childhood growing up during the Space Age when he developed a love for books. He became an avid student of history and science and a regular reader of everything from reference books to dusty, old biographies. Once he discovered science fiction, he never looked back.

His work is mostly near-future thrillers, characterized by meticulous research, hard science, and a gritty, seldom-matched realism. "I hate stupid characters," states Franks. "Or even worse, smart characters, acting stupid." All of his work combines his passion for hard science fiction, well-crafted characters, and superb storytelling.

No matter where he is or what's going on, Franks tries his best to set aside time every day to answer emails and messages from readers. You can visit him on the web at www.jkfranks.com. Please subscribe to his newsletter for updates, promotions, and giveaways. You can also find the author on Facebook or email him directly at media@jkfranks.com.

OTHER BOOKS BY JK FRANKS

OTHER BOOKS BY JK FRANKS:

The Catalyst Series

Book 1: Downward Cycle

Life in a remote, oceanfront town spirals downward after a massive solar flare causes a global blackout. But the loss of electrical power is just the first of the problems facing the survivors in the chaos that follows. Is this how the world ends?

Book 2: Kingdoms of Sorrow

With civilization in ruins, individuals band together to survive and build a new society. The threats are both grave and numerous—surely too many for a small group to weather. This is a harrowing story of survival following the collapse of the planet's electrical grids.

Book 3: American Exodus

This companion story to the Catalyst series follows one man's struggle to get back home after the collapse. No supplies, no idea of the hardships to come; how can he possibly survive the journey? Even if he survives, can he adapt to this new reality?

Book 4: Ghost Country

Since the solar superstorm and CME almost two years before, the Gulf Coast town of Harris Springs, Mississippi, has suffered from gang attacks, famine, and hurricanes and has battled a crusading army of religious zealots. Now, they face their greatest challenge: outsmarting a tyrannical president and escaping an approaching pandemic.

Cade Rearden Thrillers

Book 1: State of Chaos

He's exhausted and brutally traumatized. Now, Spec-Ops Captain Cade Rearden must finally listen to the voices in his head...or everyone on Earth may die. If you like near-future technology, complex heroes, and high-octane action, then you'll love JK Franks' explosive high-tech adventure.

Book 2: Midnight Zone

Nightmares are real in the cold, dark waters of the deep. National Security Agent Cade Rearden is used to secrets. Assigned to protect the ultra-dark-ops organization known as The Cove Project, he grapples with his role of defending a country still in crisis after a deadly super AI has devastated much of thc U.S.

But when part of his team mysteriously disappears beneath the idyllic waters of the Caribbean, Cade finds himself thrust into a web of lies and mystery, at the heart of which lies an eons-old secret that somebody will kill to protect. Grappling with his inner demons and struggling to locate his friends, Cade stumbles upon a government cover-up...and terrifying creatures, hidden miles beneath the surface of the ocean.

The Fade Novels

The Night Gate

Since losing his daughter seven years ago, Pike Shepard has struggled to maintain a normal life for himself in the coastal community of Blackwater. It's a quiet life, until a beautiful scientist shows up on his doorstep with a desperate plea for help. Dr. Kate Cassidy has uncovered a new aspect to quantum entanglement: the ability to not just see the multiverse but a way to travel through it. Her device allows them to SideSlip between parallel dimensions that are at once familiar and quite bizarre, wondrous, and terrifying. Pike learns they aren't the only ones with this ability, and the others want them gone.

Connect with the Author Online:

** For a sneak peek at new novels, free stories, and more, join the email list at jkfranksbooks.com or jkfdanks.com.

Facebook: facebook.com/groups/JKFranks/

Amazon Author Page: amazon.com/-/e/B01HIZIYH0

Goodreads: goodreads.com/author/show/15395251.J_K_Franks

Other Sellers https://books2read.com/catalyst1

Websites: JKFranks.com or JKFranksbooks.coim

Twitter: @jkfranks

Instagram: @jkfranks1

www.ingramcontent.com/pod-product-compliance
Lightning Source LLC
Chambersburg PA
CBHW020259030826
48979CB00026B/1522/J

* 9 7 8 1 7 3 6 2 1 5 3 3 3 *